"All that you can see before you is Vigrið, the Battle-Plain. The land of shattered realms. Each steppe of land between the sea and those mountains, and a hundred leagues beyond them: that is where the gods fought, and died, and Snaka was the father of them all; some say the greatest of them."

Thorkel grunted. "Snaka was of course the biggest. He was the oldest, the father of the gods; Eldest, they called him, and he had grown monstrous huge, which you would, too, if you had eaten your fill each day since the world was born. But his children were not to be sniffed at, either. Eagle, Bear, Wolf, Dragon, a host of others. Kin fought kin, and Snaka was slain by his children, and he fell. In his death the world was shattered, whole realms crushed, heaved into the air, the seas rushing in. Those mountains are all that is left of him, his bones now covered with the earth that he ruptured."

Breca whistled through his teeth and shook his head. "It must have been a sight to see."

"Heya, lad, it must have been. When gods go to war, it is no small thing. The world was broken in their ruin."

"Heya," Orka agreed. "And in Snaka's fall the vaesen pit was opened, and all those creatures of tooth and claw and power that dwelled in the world below were released into our land of sky and sea." From their vantage point the world looked pure and unspoiled, a beautiful, untamed tapestry spread across the landscape in gold and green and blue.

But Orka knew the truth was a blood-soaked saga.

She looked to her right and saw on the ground the droplets of blood from the injured wolf. In her mind she saw those droplets spreading, growing into pools, more blood spraying, ghostly bodies falling, hacked and broken, voices screaming...

This is a world of blood. Of tooth and claw and sharp iron. Of short lives and painful deaths.

By John Gwynne

THE FAITHFUL AND THE FALLEN

Malice
Valor
Ruin
Wrath

OF BLOOD AND BONE

A Time of Dread
A Time of Blood
A Time of Courage

THE BLOODSWORN TRILOGY

The Shadow of the Gods

THE SHADOW OF THE GODS

BOOK ONE OF
THE BLOODSWORN TRILOGY

JOHN
GWYNNE

orbitbooks.net

This book is a work of fiction. Names, characters, places, and incidents are the product of the author's imagination or are used fictitiously. Any resemblance to actual events, locales, or persons, living or dead, is coincidental.

Cover design by Bekki Guyatt
Cover illustration by Marcus Whinney
Map by Tim Paul
Author photograph by Caroline Gwynne

Orbit
Hachette Book Group
1290 Avenue of the Americas
New York, NY 10104
orbitbooks.net

First Edition: May 2021
Simultaneously published in Great Britain by Orbit

Orbit is an imprint of Hachette Book Group.
The Orbit name and logo are trademarks of Little, Brown Book Group Limited.

Epigraph quotation from "Seeress's Prophecy", *The Poetic Edda* translated by Carolyne Eddington (OUP)

Library of Congress Control Number: 2020947123

ISBNs: 978-0-316-53988-3 (trade paperback), 978-0-316-53987-6 (ebook)

Printed in the United States of America

LSC-C

Printing 12, 2024

For Caroline,
My love,
My heart,
My everything.
Always

VIGRIÐ
THE BATTLE-PLAIN
OSKUTREÐ
ELDRAFELL
THE VAESEN PIT
THE VAESEN PIT
ISKALT
LAKE HORNDAL
THE BONEBACK MOUNTAINS
THE GRIMHOLT
SNAKAVIK
RIVER SLAGEN
SVELGARTH
DARL

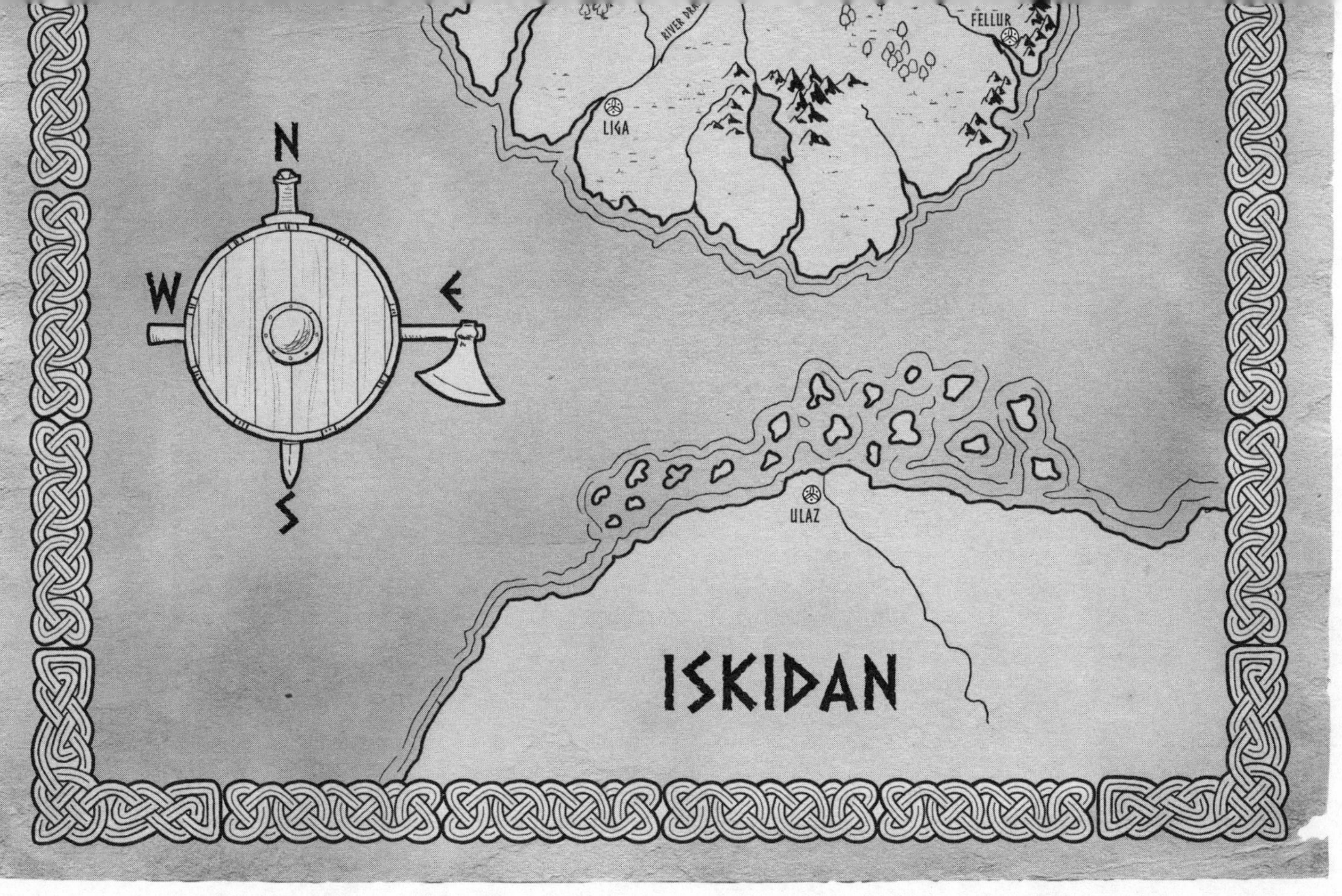
FELLUR
LIGA
N
W
E
S
ULAZ
ISKIDAN

There comes the shadow-dark dragon flying,
The gleaming serpent, up from Dark-of-Moon Hills;
He flies over the plain, and in his pinions
he carries corpses.

The Voluspa

CHAPTER ONE

ORKA

The year 297 of Friðaröld, The Age of Peace

"Death is a part of life," Orka whispered into her son's ear.

Even though Breca's arm was drawn back, the ash-spear gripped tight in his small, white-knuckled fist and the spearhead aimed at the reindeer in front of them, she could see the hesitation in his eyes, in the set of his jaw.

He is too gentle for this world of pain, Orka thought. She opened her mouth to scold him, but a hand touched her arm, a huge hand where Breca's was small, rough-skinned where Breca's was smooth.

"Wait," Thorkel breathed through his braided beard, a cold-misting of breath. He stood to her left, solid and huge as a boulder.

Muscles bunched in Orka's jaw, hard words already in her throat.

Hard words are needed for this hard world.

But she held her tongue.

Spring sunlight dappled the ground through soft-swaying branches, reflecting brightly from patches of rimed snow, winter's last hoar-frost kiss on this high mountain woodland. A dozen reindeer stood grazing in a glade, a thick-antlered bull watching over the herd of cows and calves as they chewed and scratched moss and lichen from trunks and boulders.

A shift in Breca's eyes, an indrawn breath that he held, followed by a burst of explosive movement; his hips twisting, his arm moving.

The spear left his fist: a hiss as sharp iron sliced through air. A flush of pride in Orka's chest. It was well thrown. As soon as the spear had left Breca's grip she knew it would hit its mark.

In the same heartbeat that Breca loosed his spear, the reindeer he had chosen looked up from the trunk it had been scraping lichen from. Its ears twitched and it leaped forwards, the herd around it breaking into motion, bounding and swerving around trees. Breca's spear slammed into the trunk, the shaft quivering. A moment later there was a crashing from the east, the sound of branches cracking, and a form burst from the undergrowth, huge, slate-furred and long-clawed, exploding into the glade. The reindeer fled in all directions as the beast loped among them, oblivious to all around it. Blood pulsed from a swarm of wounds across its body, long teeth slick, its red tongue lolling, and then it was gone, disappearing into the forest gloom.

"What . . . was that?" Breca hissed, looking up at his mother and father, wide eyes shifting from Orka to Thorkel.

"A fell-wolf," Thorkel grunted as he broke into motion, the stealth of the hunt forgotten. He pushed through undergrowth into the glade, a thick-shafted spear in one fist, branches snapping, Orka and Breca following. Thorkel dropped to one knee, tugged a glove off with his teeth and touched his fingertips to droplets of the wolf's blood, brushing them across the tip of his tongue. He spat, rose and followed the trail of wolf-blood to the edge of the glade, then stood there peering into the murk.

Breca walked up to his spear, the blade half-sunk into a pine tree, and tried to pull it free. His body strained, but the spear didn't move. He looked up at Orka, grey-green eyes in a pale, muddied face, a straight nose and strong jaw framed with crow-black hair, so much like his father, and the opposite of her. Apart from his eyes. He had Orka's eyes.

"I missed," he said, his shoulders slumping.

Orka gripped the shaft in her gloved hand and tugged the spear free.

"Yes," she said as she handed Breca his spear, half-an-arm shorter than hers and Thorkel's.

"It was not your fault," Thorkel said from the glade's edge. He was still staring into the gloom, a thick braid of black, grey-streaked hair poking from beneath his woollen nålbinding cap, his nose twitching. "The fell-wolf startled them."

"Why didn't it kill any of those reindeer?" Breca asked as he took his short spear back from Orka.

Thorkel lifted his hand, showing bloodied fingertips. "It was wounded, not thinking about its supper."

"What did that to a fell-wolf?" Breca asked.

A silence.

Orka strode to the opposite end of the glade, her spear ready as she regarded the dark hole in the undergrowth from where the wolf had emerged. She paused, cocked her head. A faint sound, drifting through the woodland like mist.

Screams.

Breca joined her. He gripped his spear with both hands and pointed into the darkness.

"Thorkel," Orka grunted, twisting to look over her shoulder at her husband. He was still staring after the wounded wolf. With a last, lingering look and shake of his fur-draped shoulders he turned and strode towards her.

More screams, faint and distant.

Orka shared a look with Thorkel.

"Asgrim's steading lies that way," she said.

"Harek," Breca said, referring to Asgrim's son. Breca had played with him on the beach at Fellur, on the occasions when Orka and Thorkel had visited the village to trade for provisions.

Another scream, faint and ethereal through the trees.

"Best we take a look," Thorkel muttered.

"Heya," Orka grunted her agreement.

Their breath misted about them in clouds as they worked their way through the pinewoods, the ground thick and soft with needles. It was spring, signs of new life in the world below, but winter still clung to these wooded hills like a hunched old warrior refusing to let go of his past. They walked in file, Orka leading, her eyes constantly shifting between the wolf-carved path they were following and the deep shadows around them. Old, ice-crusted snow crunched underfoot as trees opened up and they stepped on to a ridge, steep cliffs falling away sharply to the west, ragged strips of cloud drifting across the open sky below them. Orka glanced down and saw reed-thin columns of hearth fire smoke rising from Fellur, far below. The fishing village sat nestled on the eastern edge of a deep, blue-black fjord, the calm waters shimmering in the pale sun. Gulls swirled and called.

"Orka," Thorkel said and she stopped, turned.

Thorkel was unstoppering a leather water bottle and handing it to Breca, who despite the chill was flushed and sweating.

"His legs aren't as long as yours," Thorkel smiled through his beard, the scar from cheek to jaw giving his mouth a twist.

Orka looked back up the trail they were following and listened. She had heard no more screams for a while now, so she nodded to Thorkel and reached for her own water bottle.

They sat on a boulder for a few moments, looking out over the land of green and blue, like gods upon the crest of the world. To the south the fjord beyond Fellur spilled into the sea, a ragged coastline curling west and then south, ribbed and scarred with deep fjords and inlets. Iron-grey clouds bunched over the sea, glowing with the threat of snow. Far to the north a green-sloped, snow-topped mountain range coiled across the land, filling the horizon from east to west. Here and there a towering cliff face gleamed, the old-bone roots of the mountain from this distance just a flash of grey.

"Tell me of the serpent Snaka again," Breca said as they all stared at the mountains.

Orka said nothing, eyes fixed on the undulating peaks.

"If I were to tell that saga-tale, little one, your nose and fingers would freeze, and when you stood to walk away your toes would snap like ice," Thorkel said.

Breca looked at him with his grey-green eyes.

"Ach, you know I cannot say no to that look," Thorkel huffed, breath misting. "All right, then, the short telling." He tugged off the nålbinding cap on his head and scratched his scalp. "All that you can see before you is Vigrið, the Battle-Plain. The land of shattered realms. Each steppe of land between the sea and those mountains, and a hundred leagues beyond them: that is where the gods fought, and died, and Snaka was the father of them all; some say the greatest of them."

"Certainly the biggest," Breca said, voice and eyes round and earnest.

"Am I telling this tale, or you?" Thorkel said, a dark eyebrow rising.

"You, Father," Breca said, dipping his head.

Thorkel grunted. "Snaka was of course the biggest. He was the oldest, the father of the gods; Eldest, they called him, and he had grown monstrous huge, which you would, too, if you had eaten your fill each day since the world was born. But his children were not to be sniffed at, either. Eagle, Bear, Wolf, Dragon, a host of others. Kin fought kin, and Snaka was slain by his children, and he fell. In his death the world was shattered, whole realms crushed, heaved into the air, the seas rushing in. Those mountains are all that is left of him, his bones now covered with the earth that he ruptured."

Breca whistled through his teeth and shook his head. "It must have been a sight to see."

"Heya, lad, it must have been. When gods go to war, it is no small thing. The world was broken in their ruin."

"Heya," Orka agreed. "And in Snaka's fall the vaesen pit was opened, and all those creatures of tooth and claw and power that dwelled in the world below were released into our land of sky and sea." From their vantage point the world looked pure and unspoiled, a beautiful, untamed tapestry spread across the landscape in gold and green and blue.

But Orka knew the truth was a blood-soaked saga.

She looked to her right and saw on the ground the droplets of blood from the injured wolf. In her mind she saw those droplets spreading, growing into pools, more blood spraying, ghostly bodies falling, hacked and broken, voices screaming . . .

This is a world of blood. Of tooth and claw and sharp iron. Of short lives and painful deaths.

A hand on her shoulder, Thorkel reaching over Breca's head to touch her. A sharp-drawn breath. She blinked and blew out a long, ragged sigh, pushing the images away.

"It was a good throw," Thorkel said, tapping Breca's spear with his water bottle, though his eyes were still on Orka.

"I missed, though," Breca muttered.

"I missed the first throw on my first hunt, too," Thorkel said. "And I was eleven summers, where you are only ten. And your throw was better than mine. The wolf robbed you. Eh, Orka?" He ruffled Breca's hair with a big hand.

"It was well cast," Orka said, eyeing the clouds to the west, closer now. A west wind was blowing them, and she could taste snow on that wind, a sharp cold that crackled like frost in her chest. Stoppering her water bottle, she stood and walked away.

"Tell me more of Snaka," Breca called after her.

Orka paused. "Are you so quick to forget your friend Harek?" she said with a frown.

Breca dropped his eyes, downcast, then stood and followed her.

Orka led them on, back into the pinewoods where sound was eerily muted, the world shrinking around them, shadows shifting, and they climbed higher into the hills. As they rose the world turned grey around them, clouds veiling the sun, and a cold wind hissed through the branches.

Orka used her spear for a staff as the ground steepened and she climbed slick stone that ascended like steps alongside a white-foaming stream. Ice-cold water splashed and seeped into her leg-bindings and boots. A strand of her blonde hair fell loose of her braid and she pushed it behind one ear. She slowed her pace, remembering Breca's short legs, even though there was a tingling in her blood that set her muscles thrumming. Danger had always had that effect on her.

"Be ready," Thorkel said behind her, and then Orka smelled it, too.

The iron tang of blood, the stench of voided bowels.

Death's reek.

The ground levelled on to a plateaued ridge, trees felled and cleared. A large, grass-roofed cabin appeared, alongside a handful of outbuildings, all nestled into a cliff face. A stockade wall ringed the cabin and outbuildings, taller than Orka.

Asgrim's steading.

On the eastern side of the steading a track curled down the hills, eventually leading towards the village of Fellur and the fjord.

Orka took a few steps forwards, then stopped, spear levelled as Breca and Thorkel climbed on to the plateau.

The stockade's wide gates were thrown open, a body upon the ground between them, limbs twisted, unnaturally still. One gate creaked on the wind. Orka heard Breca's breath hiss through his lips.

Orka knew it was Asgrim, broad shouldered and with iron-grey hair. One hairy arm poked from the torn sleeve of his tunic.

A snowflake drifted down, a tingled kiss upon Orka's cheek.

"Breca, stay behind me," she said, padding forwards. Crows rose squawking from Asgrim's corpse, complaining as they flapped away, settling among the treetops, one sitting upon a gatepost, watching them.

Snow began to fall, the wind swirling it around the plateau.

Orka looked down on Asgrim. He was clothed in wool and breeches, a good fur cloak, a dull ring of silver around one arm. His hair was grey, body lean, sinewed muscles showing through his torn tunic. One of his boots had fallen off. A shattered spear lay close to him, and a blooded hand-axe on the ground. There was a hole in his chest, his woollen tunic dark with crusted blood.

Orka kneeled, picked up the axe and placed it in Asgrim's palm, wrapping the stiffening fingers around it.

"Travel the soul road with a blade in your fist," she whispered.

Breca's breath came in a ragged gasp behind her. It was the first person he had seen dead. Plenty of animals; he had helped in slaughtering many a meal for their supper, the gutting and skinning, the soaking of sinew for stitching and binding, the tanning of leather for the boots they wore, their belts and scabbards for their seaxes. But to see another man dead, his life torn from him, that was something else.

At least, for the first time.

And this was a man that Breca had known. He had seen life's spark in him.

Orka gave her son a moment as he stood and stared wide-eyed at the corpse, a flutter in his chest, his breath quick.

The ground around Asgrim was churned, grass flattened. A scuffed boot print. A few paces away there was a pool of blood soaked into the grass. Tracks in the ground led away; it looked like someone had been dragged.

Asgrim put someone down, then.

"Was he the one screaming?" Breca asked, still staring at Asgrim's corpse.

"No," Orka said, looking at the wound in Asgrim's chest. A stab to the heart: death would have come quickly. And a good thing, too, as his body had already been picked at by scavengers. His eyes and lips were red wounds where the crows had been at him. Orka put a hand to Asgrim's face and lifted what was left of his lip to look inside his mouth. Gums and empty, blood-ragged sockets. She scowled.

"Where are his teeth?" Breca hissed.

"Tennúr have been at him," Orka grunted. "They love a man's teeth more than a squirrel loves nuts." She looked around, searching the treeline and ridged cliff for any sign of the small, two-legged creatures. On their own, they could be a nuisance; in a pack, they could be deadly, with their sharp-boned fingers and razor teeth.

Thorkel stepped around Orka and padded into the enclosure, spear-point sweeping in a wide arc as he searched.

He stopped, stared up at the creaking gate.

Orka stepped over Asgrim into the steading and stopped beside Thorkel.

A body was nailed to the gate, arms wide, head lolling.

Idrun, wife to Asgrim.

She had not died so quickly as her husband.

Her belly had been opened, intestines spilling to a pile on the ground, twisted like vines around an old oak. Heat still rose from them, steaming as snow settled upon glistening coils. Her face was misshapen in a rictus of pain.

It was she who did the screaming.

"What did this?" Thorkel muttered.

"Vaesen?" Orka said.

Thorkel pointed to thick-carved runes on the gate, all sharp angles and straight lines. "A warding rune."

Orka shook her head. Runes would hold back all but the most powerful of vaesen. She glanced back at Asgrim and the wound in his chest. Rarely did vaesen use weapons, nature already equipping them with the tools of death and slaughter. There were dark patches on the grass: congealed blood.

Blood on Asgrim's axe. Others were wounded, but if they fell, they were carried from here.

"Did men do this?" Thorkel muttered.

Orka shrugged, a puff of misted breath as she thought on it.

"All is lies," she murmured. "They call this the age of peace, because the ancient war is over and the gods are dead, but if this is peace . . ." She looked to the skies, clouds low and heavy, snow falling in sheets now, and back at the blood-soaked corpses. "This is the age of storm and murder . . ."

"Where's Harek?" Breca asked.

CHAPTER TWO

VARG

Varg twisted to look back over his shoulder as he ran, stumbled, almost fell and carried on running. The rocky banks were giving way to black sand and shingle as the river widened, the dense trees and cliffs that had hemmed him in thinning and retreating as he drew closer to the fjord. Already he could smell the market town of Liga, a host of scents and sounds assaulting his senses.

Another look back over his shoulder: no signs of pursuit, but he knew they were there. He increased his pace.

How long have I been running? Nine days, ten?

He touched a hand to the leather pouch at his belt, sucked in the salt-tinged air and ran on.

His legs burned, lungs heaved and sweat trickled in a constant stream into his eyes, but he kept his pace, deep breaths, long strides.

I could run for ever, if only there were ground before me for my feet to tread. But the cliffs have steered me to the sea, and it is close. Where will I go? What should I do?

Panic fluttered through his veins.

They must not catch me.

He ran on, shingle crunching beneath his tattered turn-shoes.

The river spilled into a fjord, widening like a serpent's jaws about its prey and Liga came into view, a market town and port built upon the fjord's south-eastern banks. Varg slowed to a stop, put his hands on his knees and stared at the town: a bustling, stinking mass of buildings strewn along a wide, black-sanded beach and rolling back as far as the slopes of the fjord would allow. A stockade wall ringed the town, protecting the buildings and humanity crammed within. The town climbed the flank of a slope, a grass-turfed long-hall with carved, curling wooden beams built on the high ground, like a jarl in the high seat of a mead hall, looking out over his people. The sky above was thick with hearth smoke, the stink of grease and fat heavy in the air. Jetties and piers jutted out over the blue-black water of the fjord, a myriad ships rocking gently at harbour. One ship stood out among the others, a prow-necked, sleek-sided *drakkar*, a dragon-ship, looking like a wolf of the sea among a flock of sheep. All around it crowded slender *byrdings* and a host of *knarrs*, their bellies fat with merchant wares from places Varg had no doubt never heard of. He did not even know how old he was, but in his remembered life he had counted thirty hard winters and back-breaking summers that he had spent shackled to Kolskegg's farm, only twenty leagues north-east along the river, and in all of those years his master had never taken him to Liga on one of his many trading trips.

Not that he wanted to go. The smells repulsed him, though the blending scents of fat and cooking meat were making his belly rumble, and the thought of being so close to so many people was incomprehensible to him. He took a few unconscious steps away, back towards the river-gully he had been running through.

But I cannot go back. They will catch me. I have to go forwards. I need a Galdurman, or a Seiðr-witch.

He rubbed his stubbled head and reached inside his cloak, pulling out a thick iron collar. Another search inside his cloak pocket and he drew out a key, unlocked the collar and with a shiver set the cold iron around his neck, snapping it shut. He locked it and put the key back in his cloak. For a few moments he stood and twisted his neck, grimaced. A shuddered breath. Then he stood straight, brushed down his mud-stained tunic and pulled his woollen cloak-hood up over his head. And walked on.

A wide, rune-carved gate stood open, two mail-coated guards

leaning against one post. One grey-beard, who sat upon a stump, and a younger woman, dark hair braided tight, a seax hanging from the front of her belt, a spear in one fist. She eyed Varg as he approached, then stepped forward, barring his way.

"Your business in Liga?" she said.

"Finding rooms for my master," Varg said, his eyes downcast. "I have been ordered on ahead." He gestured vaguely behind him, into the river valley.

The guard looked him up and down, then over his shoulder, at the empty mouth of the river valley.

"How do I know that? Who's your master? Pull your hood down."

Varg thought about the answers he could give, and where they would lead, and what they would give away. Slowly he pushed his hood back, revealing his stubbled hair, his mud- and sweat-stained face. He opened his mouth. A cart rolled up behind him, pulled by two oxen; a fine-dressed merchant sat upon the driving bench, a handful of freedmen with spears and clubs in their fists.

"Let the man through, Slyda," the grey-beard grunted from his stump.

"My master is Snepil," Varg said, saying the first name that came into his head. Snepil was a man that he knew would not be following him soon, as the last time Varg had seen him Snepil's eyes had been bulging and his last breath had hissed and rattled from his throat as Varg throttled the life from him. He couldn't remember how he came to have his hands around the man's throat, only remembered blinking as Snepil's rattling death filtered through some red mist in Varg's head.

She eyed him one more time, then stepped out of his way and waved him through.

Varg pulled his hood back up and slipped into Liga like lice into a beard, the scents and sounds hitting him as if he had dived into water. Timber-sided buildings lined wide, mud-slick streets, and traders were everywhere, clamouring, their trestle-benches edging the streets and laid out with all manner of goods. Bolts of dyed cloth, bone needles and combs, axe heads, knives, fine-tooled scabbards, bronze cloak pins and amulets, wooden bowls, bundles of linen and wool, tied bales of wolf and bear skins, reindeer hides, pine marten and fox pelts. Varg's eyes widened at the sight of walrus tusks and ivory. Others were selling horns of mead and ale, bubbling pots of rabbit and beef stew steaming over pit fires, turnips and carrots bobbing, fat glistening. Quartered steaks of whale meat, smoked herring and cod hanging. He even saw a trader selling vaesen body parts: Faunir's dried blood; a troll's tooth, big as a fist; a bowl full of skraeling eyeballs; and a necklace made from the needled hair of a Froa-spirit. It was endless, and overwhelming.

A spasm in his belly reminded him that a long time had passed since he'd last eaten. He was not sure exactly how long, but it was at least three days ago, or was it four, when he had been lucky enough to snatch a salmon from the river. He strode over to a trader who was standing behind a big stew-pot and using a cleaver to quarter a boar's leg joint. The trader was a broad-bellied and wispy-bearded man wearing fur-trimmed boots and a fine green woollen tunic, though the tablet weaving around the neck and cuffs was dull and frayed.

Varg stared into the pot of stew, saliva flooding his mouth, the churning and twisting in his gut abruptly painful.

"Something to warm your belly?" the trader said, putting the cleaver down and lifting a bowl.

"Aye, that'd be good," Varg said.

"A half-bronze," the trader said. Then paused and stared at Varg. He put the bowl down and pushed Varg's hood back, looked at his short, stubbled hair. His eyes narrowed.

"Away with you, you dirty thrall," the trader scowled.

"I can pay," Varg said.

A raised eyebrow.

"I'll see your coin, first," the trader said.

Varg reached inside his cloak, pulled out a pouch, loosened the leather-draw and fished out a bronze coin. He dropped it on the trader's table, the coin rolling and falling, revealing the stamped profile of a woman's head. A sharp-nosed profile, hair pulled severely tight and braided at the neck.

"A Helka," the trader said, his beard twitching.

"Queen Helka," Varg said, though he had never seen her, only heard snatched talk of her: of her hubris, thinking she could rule and control half of Vigrið, and of her ruthlessness against her enemies.

"Only calls herself queen so she can tax us down to our stones," the trader grunted.

"No good to you, then?" Varg said, reaching for the coin.

"I didn't say that," the trader said, holding a hand out.

Faster than it took to blink, Varg snatched up the cleaver the trader had put down and chopped at the coin, hacking it in two. He lifted one half up between finger and thumb, left the other hack-bronze on the table.

"Where'd a dirty thrall come by a pouch of Helka-coin, anyway? And where's your master?" the trader grunted, eyeing him.

Varg looked at him, then slowly put a hand out towards the coin again.

The trader shrugged and scooped a ladle of stew into the bowl, handed it to Varg.

"Some of that bread too," Varg said, and the trader cut a chunk from a black-crusted loaf.

Varg dipped the bread in the stew and sucked it, fat dripping down his chin, into his newly grown beard. The stew was watery and too hot, but it tasted like pure joy to Varg. He closed his eyes, dipped, sucked, slurped until the bread was gone, then upended what was left of the stew into his mouth.

He put the bowl down and belched.

"I've seen hungry men before," the trader said, "but you . . ." He whistled, gave a half-smile.

"Is there a Galdurman, or Seiðr-witch in Liga?" Varg asked, cuffing stew from his chin.

The trader signed a rune across his chest and frowned. "No, and what do you want with the likes of them?"

"That's my business," Varg said, then paused. "That's my master's business. Do you know where I can find one?"

The trader began to turn away.

Varg put the other half-bronze back on the table.

The trader looked at him appraisingly. "The Bloodsworn docked yesterday. They have a Seiðr-witch thrall."

The Bloodsworn!

The Bloodsworn were famed throughout the whole of Vigrið, and most likely beyond. A band of mercenary warriors who hired themselves out to the highest bidder, they hunted down vaesen-monsters, searched out god-relics for wealthy jarls, fought in border disputes, guarded the wealthy and powerful. Tales were sung about them by skálds around hearth fires.

"Where are they?" Varg said.

"You'll find them in Liga's longhouse, guests of Jarl Logur."

"My thanks," Varg said. Then he dipped his hand back in his pouch and threw another hack-bronze on the table.

"What's that for?" the trader said.

"Your silence. You never saw me."

"Saw who?" said the trader, looking around, a smile twitching his thin beard, even as his hand snaked out and scooped up the coins.

Varg's hand darted out, faster than the trader's, and gripped the man's wrist. He stared into the trader's eyes, held his gaze a long moment, then let go; in the same movement he swept the cleaver from the table and hefted it.

"How much?" he said.

"You can have that," the trader shrugged.

Varg nodded and slipped the cleaver inside his cloak, pulled his hood back up and walked into the crowd.

He made his way through the streets of Liga, past a quayside that heaved with activity, men and women unloading a newly docked merchant *knarr*. Its belly was wide and deep, sitting low in the water. Varg thought he heard the muted neighing of horses from deep in its hull and two more similar-looking ships were rowing into the docks. A group of strange-looking men and women were disembarking from the moored *knarr*. They wore caps of felt and fur and silver-buckled kaftans, with their breeches striped in blues and oranges, baggy above the knee, wrapped tight with *winnigas* leg-bindings from knee to ankle. Their skin was dark as weathered leather and they were escorted by a handful of warriors who wore long coats of lamellar plate that shimmered like scales as they moved. They had curved swords hanging at their hips, the men with long drooping moustaches, and their heads were completely shaven, apart from a long, solitary braid of hair. Varg paused and stared at them as they turned and shouted at sailors on the ship, gangplanks slamming down on to the jetty, pier-cranes swinging to hover over the ship's belly.

"Where are they from?" Varg asked a dock worker who was hurrying past with a thick coil of rope slung over her shoulder.

"Iskidan," she grunted, not slowing.

"Iskidan," Varg whistled. The land beyond the sea, far, far to the south. Varg had heard tales of Iskidan, of its wide rivers and grass plains, of its beating sun and of Gravka, the Great City. Part of him had thought it just a tale, a place to escape in the mind during the cold, harsh months of winter.

Varg took one last look at the strangers and then walked on, turning into another street that steepened, climbing a slope towards the cliffs that brooded over the town, Jarl Logur's mead hall nestled at their foot. The reek of fish lessened as he climbed, replaced by urine and excrement. Steps were carved into the street that led to a wide-arched gate, beyond it the thick-timbered beams of the mead hall visible. A press of men and women were shoulder to shoulder on the steps. Varg paused a moment, looking for a way through, and then slipped between a man and a woman, trying to thread his way up the steps.

A hand grabbed his shoulder.

"Wait your turn, like everyone else," a woman said. She was dark-haired, her face hard and sharp, her eyes cold. A woollen tunic and fur-edged cloak were draped about her shoulders, a weapons belt around her waist with scabbarded seax and hand-axe hanging from it.

"I need to see the Bloodsworn," Varg said.

"Ha, don't we all?" the woman said. "What makes *you* so special?"

Varg looked at her, then at the crowd around him.

"All these, they are here for the Bloodsworn?" Varg said.

"Aye," the woman grunted, "what else?"

"Why?" Varg asked.

"There's an empty sea-chest and a spare oar on their *drakkar*," the woman said.

"Empty sea-chest?" Varg frowned.

"Are you touched in the head?" the woman said, prodding his temple through his cloak-hood with a hard finger. Varg didn't much like it. "One of the Bloodsworn has been slain, and they are holding a weapons trial to fill his place."

"Ah," Varg nodded, understanding blossoming.

"So, wait your turn," she said, then looked him up and down. "Or are you in a rush to have your arse dumped in the dirt?"

Laughter rippled through those around them.

Varg just looked at the ground and waited.

The crowd shuffled up the steps. As Varg drew closer to the mead hall the sounds of shouting drifted down to him, punctuated with cries of pain. A slow, steady stream of bloodied faces filtered back down the steps, some groaning and supported by others. Others were carried unconscious.

Varg reached the top step and looked over the shoulders of those in front of him. An arched gateway led into an open space before Jarl Logur's mead hall, a huge building of scrolled timber sitting upon thick stone footings. In the space before the hall the ground was trampled and muddied, dark patches glistening here and there. Warriors ringed the area, fifty or sixty of them, hard-looking men and women, some wearing *brynja* coats of riveted mail with swords at their hips. Varg had only seen a sword once before, when the local *drengr* had visited Kolskegg's farm to collect the tax due to Queen Helka. Varg had suspected that sword was worth more than all the goods loaded upon a wagon and the chest of coin that Kolskegg had given the man. Varg's eyes were drawn to a bald-headed, thick-muscled warrior, more grey than black in his braided beard. He wore a plain-scabbarded sword at his hip, a fine *brynja* of riveted mail over his broad frame and rings of gold and silver wrapped around his arms and neck. The sword and *brynja* alone were probably worth as much as Kolskegg's farm. There was wealth to be had in death-dealing. The bald man was talking to a raven-haired woman, a pattern of blue tattoos across her lower jaw and throat. The Seiðr-witch. Varg blinked in surprise at the iron collar around her neck, and instinctively put a hand to his own throat. The old warrior was leaning upon a long-axe as he spoke, the butt stuck in the ground, the single iron blade hooked and cruel-looking. Varg was accustomed to axes, the callouses on his hand testament to long years of use, but this was not an axe made for chopping timber. This was made for killing. Varg looked away, the sight of it setting some uneasy feeling trickling through his veins. All of the warriors in the square bristled with a mass of assorted weapons hanging from weapons belts. Big round shields were slung across their backs, some propped against the wall and steps of the mead hall. A few were painted pale blue as a winter's sky with a red sail upon it, Varg recognising that as the sigil of Jarl Logur, but most of the shields around the square were painted crow-black, each one with a splattering of red across the pitch-paint, as if someone had cast droplets of blood across each shield.

In the centre of the square two men were fighting. Or more accurately to Varg, a man and a tree were fighting. The shorter one was light on his feet, a round shield in one hand, dancing around the bigger man, who was stripped to the waist, woollen breeches tied with rope, with a red braided beard that dangled to his waist. He was thick bodied and limbed, muscles knotted and bunching like the roots of an old oak. As Varg watched the smaller man feinted right and then darted left, stepping in and slamming the iron boss of the shield into red-beard's ribs. A hook from his right hand into the stomach. A grunt from red-beard was the only acknowledgement, one arm swinging, catching the smaller man across the back of the head as he tried to duck and leap away. He staggered, stumbled back a dozen steps, his legs abruptly loose. Red-beard stomped after him.

"Name," a voice said. Varg blinked, tearing his eyes away from the spectacle.

"Name," the man said again, leaning against the gatepost with his arms folded. He was roughly the same height as Varg and slim-built, red hair neatly braided and a trimmed beard oiled and gleaming. He was clothed in a well-cared-for *brynja* of riveted mail, fine scrollwork knotted along the scabbard of his seax.

"Varg," Varg said. His natural response to a command was to obey unthinkingly. On Kolskegg's farm anything other resulted in a thump or the lash.

"Varg what?"

Varg blinked.

The slim man sighed.

"This is the way it works," he said. "I say *name*, you give me your full name. For example, I am Svik Hrulfsson, or Tangle-Hair, on account of my hair never being tangled. So, let's start again. Name?"

"I don't know," Varg shrugged. "I never knew my father or mother."

Svik looked him up and down.

"You are sure you want to do this?" he said.

"Do what?"

"Fight Einar Half-Troll."

"I don't want to fight anyone," Varg said, "and especially not someone with a name like Half-Troll." He took a deep breath. "I want to hire your Seiðr-witch."

Svik blinked.

"Vol is not for hire," he said, glancing at the tattooed woman talking to the bald man.

"I must speak to her," Varg said. "It is . . . important."

"Aye, to you, maybe. But to us," Svik shrugged, "not so much."

"I must speak with her," Varg said, feeling panic begin to bubble in his belly.

"What is so important? You need a love potion? Want to hump some fine-looking thrall on your farm?"

"No!" Varg exclaimed. "I don't want a love potion." He shook his head. "It is more important than that."

"More important than a hump?" Svik said, raising an eyebrow. "I did not know that could be true."

Chuckles from the crowd behind Varg.

"I need your Seiðr-witch to perform an *akáll*."

Svik frowned. "An invocation. That is a serious business."

"It is a serious matter," Varg said, fingertips brushing the pouch at his belt.

"The answer still is no," Svik said. "Vol uses her talents for the Bloodsworn. No one else. She is not for hire. Even if Queen Helka herself marched up those steps and asked for it, the answer would be the same."

Varg felt his hope draining away, a coldness settling in the pit of his belly.

A crunch from the square. Varg looked to see the huge warrior – Einar Half-Troll – punch the other warrior's shield. The wood cracked, shattering and spraying in splinters.

"Why does Einar not have a shield?" Varg asked.

"To give the others a chance." Svik shrugged. He leaned forward. "It's not really much of a chance," he whispered.

Einar grabbed his opponent by throat and crotch, lifted him squeaking into the air, then hurled him to the ground. There was a dull thud, the squeaks cut short, the man on the ground abruptly still. Men and women ran in and carried the unconscious warrior out of the square.

Varg looked at Einar, thick and solid and menacing, a few red marks on his body the only evidence that he'd already fought at least a score of fights. He looked back at Svik.

"I'll fight him," Varg said.

CHAPTER THREE

ORKA

Orka walked alongside the wagon, the bodies of Asgrim and his wife Idrun laid out upon the wagon's flatbed. They were covered with a coarse woollen blanket, blood seeping in patches. Orka sniffed and looked around. The trees were thinning about them, the ground levelling as they took the winding path to Fellur, the fishing village on the banks of the fjord.

Breca was leading the wagon, one hand on the lead-rein of a shaggy pony they had found in Asgrim's stable, his short spear in his other fist, Breca using it like a staff. Orka had given him the task of leading the wagon, something to focus his mind on after the sights at Asgrim's steading, and she wanted to watch the treeline either side of the path.

There are killers abroad in these hills.

They had searched Asgrim's steading and found no sign of Harek. Thorkel had found tracks upon the path that wound down the hillside, the ground churned, but the tracks had left the path soon after, heading back into dense woodland. After a heated discussion they had agreed that Thorkel would follow the tracks while Orka and Breca took the bodies down to Fellur. Orka wanted to be the one to take the dangerous path, to track Asgrim's killers, but they both knew that Thorkel was the better tracker. In the end Thorkel had given her a smile and loped off into the trees, quiet as smoke, for all his bulk. Orka had scowled at his back, her worry manifested as anger. Then she snorted her disapproval and stomped down the path, ordering Breca to lead the pony.

"Will Papa find Harek?" Breca asked, keeping his eyes on the ground in front of them. They had left the snow behind them in the high places, the path turning to puddles and mud where it had been snow and ice.

"Maybe," Orka grunted. She looked back, up at the cloud-wreathed hills. Thorkel had sworn to her that if he found the boy and Asgrim's killers he would return to her, not take them on single-handed.

But he is a liar. And it will tear at him to leave the boy in danger. If he still lives.

She was eager to hand the corpses of Asgrim and Idrun over to Fellur's jarl and go in search of her husband, before he got himself into trouble.

Fellur appeared through the trees, the village a few dozen reed-thatched, wattle-and-daub buildings huddled close, a larger longhouse at its centre. A small stockade surrounded the village, though the timbered wall was rotten in places, and ended a long way short of the dark-sanded beach.

But they are safe enough down here. The vaesen prefer the quiet, dark places, where they can remain hidden.

Orka could see fishing nets hanging on the beach, drying out and waiting for repair. A handful of timber piers that jutted out on to the fjord were mostly empty, only a few fishing boats and *byrding* coasters moored there.

Goats bleated as the wagon rolled passed them, Orka lengthening the stride of her long legs to draw level with Breca.

A guard stood leaning against one of the gateposts, a man Orka had seen before, though she did not know his name. He nodded to Orka, not bothering to look inside her wagon. Whenever she and Thorkel came to the village it was with a wagon loaded with pelts for trade, so why would this time be any different? Orka nodded to the guard and passed through the gate, feeling a building pressure in her head and chest. She looked up at the gate's crossbar that ran above her and saw the gleam of bone sunk deep into the timber: the knuckle-bone of a dead god, still beating with a remnant of its power, helping to keep the vaesen out of the village. The pressure in Orka's head lessened as she moved into a muddy street, away from the gates. Though there were no guards on the gate the village was busy enough, people milling, moving in a stream towards the village's longhouse. That was where Orka was headed, for that was where she expected to find Sigrún, Jarl of Fellur.

She led Breca past mud-churned pigpens, past the orange glow and hammer-thud of a forge, then past the tavern, the reek of ale, barley and urine thick in the air.

"What is this?" a man said as he emerged from the tavern, blinking at the daylight. Orka knew him: Virk, a fisherman she and Thorkel had traded with many times. He was a big man, broad-faced and straight-talking. He had injured his arm when his fisher boat had been caught out at sea during a storm, and so was letting his two sons ply the seas while he healed. He was blurry-eyed, red veins in his cheeks. Orka took a sniff and curled her lip. By the reek of him he was better off at sea.

"Asgrim and Idrun." Orka nodded into the wagon.

Virk stared at the bloody stains on the wool blanket covering the two bodies.

"And Harek's gone," Breca piped.

"How?" Virk said, others gathering around the cart.

"Not of old age," Orka muttered and walked on.

Virk followed them, others with him, word spreading.

The wagon rolled into a courtyard before the longhouse, where forty or fifty people were gathered, at least half of the population of the village, others still arriving.

A young man stepped out of the longhouse: Guðvarr, nephew of Jarl Sigrún and one of her *drengrs*, another three warriors behind him. Guðvarr walked with a swagger and stopped between two wooden pillars at the top of wide steps that led down to the courtyard. A sword was hanging at his hip, his red woollen tunic embroidered with swirling tablet-weave at the neck, cuffs and rim. A silver arm ring wrapped around one arm. His black hair was oiled and pulled back, tied at his neck with leather and a silver wire, the wisps of a first beard on his chin. A ball of moisture glistened at the end of his pointed nose. Orka glanced down at her son. By the light in Breca's eyes, any man with a sword was enough to impress his saga-filled head.

"What is going on here?" Orka asked Virk, who had come to stand at her shoulder. He was a tall man, but he still had to look up to meet her eyes.

"Guðvarr came down the river on a *snekke* this morning. Word is that Jarl Sigrún has sent him ahead of her return."

"Jarl Sigrún isn't here?"

Virk looked at Orka like she was touched.

"Jarl Sigrún was summoned . . . " He coughed. "I mean *invited*, to Queen Helka's court in Darl. She has been gone more than two months."

Orka raised an eyebrow and nodded.

"I have news," Guðvarr called out, the crowd quieting.

He let the silence grow, clearly enjoying his moment before the crowd.

"I am to tell you that Jarl Sigrún will be back with us within a nine-day. She bid me tell you that Queen Helka is just, and good and wise, and that we could do worse than swear our oaths to her. To be under her care would be a benefit to our village."

"Care!" Virk muttered. "Not so long ago we were all freedmen and women in Fellur, and queens and kings were arseling-jarls who had grown too big for their boots."

Orka did not disagree with him.

"You mean RULE, not CARE," Virk shouted, others in the crowd adding their voices.

"Times are changing," Guðvarr answered, glowering at Virk and the crowd. "Jarl Störr threatens in the west, the vaesen are growing ever bolder, murdering and stealing. We are better off uniting with the strong, and Queen Helka is the strongest."

More muttering.

"When Jarl Sigrún returns, there will be an Althing, held on the Oath Rock, where all can have their say about these important matters," Guðvarr called out, gesturing to a rocky island that stood in the fjord, green with moss and dense with bracken and wind-blasted trees.

Voices called out, protesting, asking questions.

"Save your moaning for my aunt and the Althing," he growled. "That is all."

Orka took the lead-rein from Breca and clicked the pony on, pulling the wagon through the crowd. People parted for her.

"*Drengr* Guðvarr," Orka called out, her voice loud, cutting through the crowd.

Guðvarr paused and turned, looked down at Orka, Breca and the wagon. He wiped the drop of snot growing at the end of his nose.

A silence fell around her as she led the wagon to the steps of the longhouse, wheels creaking as the pony came to a stand.

"What is this?" Guðvarr said as he stepped down the first two steps and stood staring at the bloodstained blanket in the wagon. The three warriors with him, two women and a man, all came to stand behind him. They carried spears, axes and seaxes hanging at their weapons belts.

"Asgrim and Idrun," Orka said. "I was with my husband and son, hunting in the hills. We heard screaming, went to look and found Asgrim and Idrun murdered in their steading." She pulled back the blanket.

Gasps rippled around the square.

"You see," Guðvarr cried out. "Vaesen doing murder in our own hills. We need the strength of Queen Helka."

"Vaesen did not do this," Orka said.

"Oh ho, and how do you know that?" Guðvarr said, looking suspiciously at Orka. The ball of snot was starting to grow at the end of his nose again. "Are you a Seiðr-witch to see the past?" He looked at Orka with a sneer on his face, as if he had won some great contest of wits.

"I don't need to be a Seiðr-witch to know a sword wound to the heart when I see one," Orka said. "Vaesen hunt with tooth and claw, not swords of iron." She paused, looking at the sneer that twisted Guðvarr's lips. "I would have thought Guðvarr the fierce *drengr* would have known that at a glance." She regretted the words even as they were leaving her mouth, knew that they would only bring her trouble. But she didn't like the twist of his smug, arrogant face.

A few sniggers around the courtyard and Guðvarr flushed red.

He scowled at Orka. "Loners, living in the wild, they were asking for trouble."

"Asgrim and Idrun did not ask for this," Orka said.

"And Harek, their son, has been taken," Breca squeaked in his high voice.

"Children taken," Virk said. He had followed Orka through the crowd. "That is not the first time I have heard this."

Orka frowned at him.

Guðvarr walked down the longhouse steps and stood before Orka. She was taller and wider than him, but he had the hubris of the powerful in his eyes: that belief that one is better, faster. She felt a tingle in her blood, a sharpening of her senses. The herald of violence.

"If I say they were asking for trouble, then they were asking for trouble," Guðvarr said, his voice a hiss, like a sword leaving a scabbard. "As are you."

The three warriors on the stairs took a step closer, hands moving to rest close to weapons.

Orka stared at Guðvarr, felt muscles in her jaw twitch. Felt her blood pounding through her veins. Heard distant voices in her head, screaming, an image in her mind, an axe carving into a skull . . .

"You are shaking," Guðvarr said. "Do you fear me? You would be wise, if you did."

Orka blinked, saw there was a tremor in her arm, her fist, passing into her spear. She looked at Breca, who was looking from her to Guðvarr with worried eyes.

Orka took a deep breath.

"I brought them here because I thought Jarl Sigrún would wish to know there are killers and child-stealers in her hills," Orka said, choosing her words slowly. Her heart was thumping, blood shivering through her veins. She chose to control it. *Tried* to control it. "And to see if Asgrim and Idrun had kin here. They should have a barrow raised over them, as is proper."

A silence. Guðvarr stared up at Orka. She returned his stare, flatly. Felt the hot flush of emotion leaving her, replaced by a coldness filling her veins. Some deep part of her knew that was a bad sign.

"Mama," a voice said, filtering through the ice-fog in her head.

"Mama, Papa is coming," the voice said, something tugging her sleeve.

"Orka." Thorkel's voice.

Orka blinked, tore her eyes away from Guðvarr and saw Thorkel approaching, pushing through the crowd, spear in his hand, his nålbinding woollen cap damp with sweat.

"Is all well?" Thorkel asked, his eyes flickering from Orka to Guðvarr and the other *drengr* warriors on the steps. His black brows knotted, a thundercloud, his mouth becoming a hard line. He seemed to swell in size as Orka saw the anger fill him, the light in his eyes shifting from concern to some flat, dead-eyed stare.

"We were talking about raising a barrow over Asgrim and Idrun," Orka said, blowing out a long, slow breath. She forced a smile of greeting on to her face and Thorkel's cold, hard lines softened a little.

Guðvarr looked from Orka to Thorkel. She saw him looking at Thorkel's spear, at his size.

"My husband has been tracking Asgrim's killers. They took his son, Harek."

"Did you find them?" Guðvarr asked Thorkel.

"No," Thorkel said.

Guðvarr's lip curled back into what Orka thought to be his permanent sneer.

"I followed their tracks to a river," Thorkel continued, "one of the many that feed out of the hills into the River Skarpain. There were signs of three boats pulled up on to the bank. Whoever slew Asgrim and Idrun took to the river and disappeared."

Guðvarr nodded. "We will look into it."

Orka thought about pressing Guðvarr, of asking him how many

spears he would take with him; would he use hounds; would he send people and boats up the River Skarpain.

Instead she looked from Thorkel to Breca.

This is not our fight. Not our problem.

“Home,” she said to them, then turned and walked away.

CHAPTER FOUR

VARG

Varg walked into the square before the mead hall. He stepped over a pool of congealing blood and stopped.

His own blood was rushing in his ears, muting sound, though he could see smiling faces and mouths moving among the crowd lining the square, coin being exchanged. One woman with two wolfhounds at her feet watched him as she bit into an apple. She was lean-muscled with silver-grey hair knotted like rope, a white scar running through one ruined eye. She was clothed in a *brynja*, a spear in her fist, axe and seax suspended from her belt. She looked too old to be a warrior, with deep lines around her eyes and mouth. As Varg's eyes met hers she smiled at him, but Varg saw no comfort in it. It was the kind of smile one gives a fool when they believe they can fly and leap from a cliff.

She dropped her apple and fished out a coin from a pouch at her belt, gave it to a man standing close to her.

They are betting on how quickly I lose, he realised.

Einar was bending to mutter something to the grey-bearded bald man and the tattooed woman. As he did so he wiped blood from his knuckles with a rag and passed it over to another warrior, a tall, blonde-haired woman, another of the Bloodsworn, going by her black shield and *brynja*. She took the rag and stuffed it in her weapons belt, then picked up a wooden shield that was leaning against the mead hall steps. Her eyes met Varg's and she strode to him, offered him the shield.

Varg looked at it. Strips of limewood glued and bound with a rim of rawhide, an iron boss at its centre, a wooden handle riveted across the back.

"More useful if you hold it, rather than look at it," the woman said to him. Her nose and chin were long and thin, sharp as a *drakkar*'s prow.

Varg shook his head. "Don't want it," he said.

"Don't be an idiot. How long are you going to last against Half-Troll without it?"

Varg shook his head again. The truth was, he'd never held a shield before, let alone used one in a fight.

"It's your life," the woman shrugged.

"But look after this for me," Varg said, taking his cloak off and folding it, holding it out to her.

The woman took it, curled her lip and dropped it on the ground.

"I'm no one's thrall to be ordered," she said. "What's your name?"

"Varg," he said.

"He has no name," Svik called out to them.

"And no shield," she answered Svik. She looked back at Varg. "And no sense." Then she turned away.

"VARG NO-SENSE TO CHALLENGE EINAR HALF-TROLL FOR A PLACE IN THE BLOODSWORN'S OAR-BENCH AND SHIELD WALL," she bellowed as she walked back to the bald man and Einar. A roar went up from the crowd as Einar stepped into the square. His brows knotted as he saw Varg had no shield, but he walked on.

Close up Einar was bigger than he'd first appeared. His face was all slabs of bone and red hair, his fists the size of anvils.

Varg touched the pouch at his belt, glanced at Vol the Seiðr-witch, who was watching with dark eyes, then he looked back at Einar.

For you, Frøya. I do this for you.

He drew in a deep breath and shook out his arms and hands, bounced on the balls of his feet.

Einar loomed over him, blotting out the sun.

"When you go down, stay down," the big man grunted at him, and swung a right hook.

Varg ducked the hook, whistling over his head, and darted close, releasing a flurry of punches to Einar's gut, the slap of meat. It was like punching a tree. Einar gave no visible sign that he had felt anything. Varg ducked and stepped right, avoided another hook that swept over his head, stepped in and kicked at Einar's knee. The big man grunted, beard shifting as his mouth twisted.

You felt that, didn't you, big man.

A huge hammer-fist came hurtling down at Varg, who swayed and stepped right, air hissing past his face, and threw his own punch at Einar's groin.

Varg had fought before, many times on the farm. The first time had been before he could grow hair on his chin, fighting among the farm's thralls for an extra bowl of broth for Frøya, who had been shivering with a fever. Then more frequently as he found it a sure way to secure a few secret coins or extra meals. And finally, for Kolskegg, once his master had heard about his fast fists, putting Varg to work in bouts against the champions of other landed men. He had earned Kolskegg a chest of silver, and in the process fought many men and women bigger and stronger than him, but he'd not fought any man that could stand after a blow to their stones, no matter how big or strong they were.

Varg's blow was perfectly timed, a straight right, his legs well set, the power from his legs and hips channelled into his twisting arm, wrist snapping just before impact.

Pain exploded in Varg's fist, shot through his wrist, up his arm and he staggered back a step. There had been no soft, squashing connection; instead Varg's fist crunched into something hard as iron.

"Ha," Einar grinned. "Little men have tried that before. Jökul the smith has made me some protection." And then he swung a meat-hammer fist at Varg's face.

Despite the pain exploding in Varg's hand he managed to move, Einar's fist connecting with Varg's shoulder instead of his chin. The blow lifted him from his feet and sent him twisting through the air, crunching to the ground and rolling in the mud.

Einar strode after him.

Varg scrambled on to hand and knees, his injured fist clutched to his side. Waves of nausea pulsed from his gut. Then Einar's boot connected with his ribs and he was lifted from the ground, weightless again, spinning.

The ground rose up to greet him, his head slamming into the mud. Stars exploded, his vision blurring, pain in his ribs screaming. He forced himself to roll, climbed to one knee, saw Einar closing on him again.

"I told you to stay *down*," Einar growled.

A bloom of anger in Varg's belly. The pugil-ring was the only place where he could not be told what to do. Where he had been free. Where the rage he always felt was unchained. It flooded through his veins now, white-hot.

Varg bunched his legs and leaped at Einar, snarling, rolled between the man's feet and came up standing behind him. He punched once with his good hand to Einar's kidney, then kicked into the back of the big man's leg, sending him stumbling to one knee.

A silence from the crowd, as if everyone were holding their breath, then a huge roar.

Einar backhanded Varg, catching him on the side of his chin. It was a weaker blow, past its snapping point, but it still sent Varg to the ground. Einar climbed to his feet, face mottled with anger and raised a boot to stamp on Varg's head.

Varg rolled, wrapped his arms around Einar's ankle as his boot slammed into the mud, and pulled himself tight to the man.

"Get off, you little shite," Einar grunted as he shook his leg, but Varg held tight. Pain was flaring everywhere now, Varg moving to a place beyond it. He opened his jaws and bit into Einar's leg, through woollen leg wraps and breeches into the flesh of Einar's calf.

Einar bellowed.

Varg tasted a spurt of blood, bit down harder.

The scream shifted higher in pitch.

Einar was abruptly still and through one eye Varg glimpsed a fist hurtling towards his face. He bit down harder, grinding his teeth.

White light exploded in his head.

★

Pain. Like hammers in his head. Knives in his side. Deep-stabbing needles in his hand. He tried to open his eyes but found he couldn't.

Am I dead? Is this Vergelmir, Lik-Rifa's chamber? Or have my eyes been stitched shut by a mischievous fetch?

More pain, all over, but spiking in his head, his ribs, his hand. A sound, the murmur of water. He groaned, got a mouthful of grit for the effort and rolled on to his back, lifted his good hand to his eyes and felt something crusted and sticky. Dried blood. He rubbed and managed to open his eyes a crack.

The moon and stars above, a ghostly blur in a death-black sky.

I am alive, then.

For a moment he was memoryless: he had no idea where he was or what had happened to him.

He licked his teeth and scabbed lips, tasted salt and iron, spat blood on to the sand.

Not just my blood.

A fluttering sound recalled, a man bellowing in pain.

An image in his mind, a huge fist speeding towards him.

Then memory crashed in like a dam breaking.

Einar Half-Troll, the Bloodsworn . . .

He pushed himself upright, saw that he was sitting on a black-sanded bank, behind him wind sighing through the branches of trees. A thousand lights glimmered from Liga, a glow leaking into the sky above it like light from a dying fire, all locked tight within the town's stockade walls. Ships creaked and swayed on their moorings on the fjord, the moon and stars turning the dark waters to molten silver.

He put a hand to those parts that hurt the most. His ribs, a hand over his woollen tunic. No broken skin, just painful to the touch. Probably a broken rib or two. He looked at his injured hand, the knuckles purple-black in the night, and swollen. He tried to make a fist, but the pain and swelling stopped him. Then he put his good hand to his face. A gash over his eye, blood crusted upon it, the whole side of his face swollen, his jaw throbbing. One tooth loose.

His fingertips brushed the iron collar around his neck.

Panic.

The key. My cloak.

He staggered to his feet, ignoring the pain, checking himself over, a surge of relief that his pouch still hung at his belt. He fumbled at the leather draw, blew out a long breath when he saw the contents were still there.

But my thrall-collar . . .

And then he saw it, a darker shadow on the black sand: his woollen cloak, neatly folded. He bent, lifted it, checking the hidden pockets. Something heavy and cold: the cleaver he had taken from the trader; in the same pocket the bag of coin, by its weight untouched, and then he found the key.

A long, frozen moment, relief flooding him, and he put the key to the lock, fumbling with one hand, finally a *click* as the key bit. The collar creaked open on sweat-rusted hinges and he put it back in the cloak pocket, along with the key.

He walked unsteadily to the fjord's edge, kneeled and cupped his hands, sipped the cold water. It was like slivers of ice in his throat and belly, painfully sharp and refreshing. He splashed his face and spent a while trying to wash the blood away, then shook his head, droplets spraying. Filled a water bottle from his belt. When he was done, he stood, shivering, and clumsily threw his cloak around his shoulders, pinned it and walked wearily towards the treeline.

Stepping among the trees he threaded his way up a gentle slope through the pine, maybe thirty or forty paces, until he could no longer see the shimmer of the fjord behind him. Moonlight filtered down from above, silver dappling the ground as branches swayed. Dropping to his knees he scraped the woodland litter away until he had cleared a circle of hard-packed earth, then set about finding something that would burn. He returned with an armful of dead timber and set it down on the cleared space, reached for his kindling pouch, pulling out a stone and striking-iron, and a handful of dried kindling, and then set to sparking a fire. Soon he was blowing gently on the first sparks, fanning the flames into life.

Keeping busy was good, because a wave of despair was building within him.

He had failed.

Sitting back, he held his hands out to the fire, trying to chase the ice from his bones, and stared into the flames.

Frøya, I am sorry.

He felt the grief welling, that he had kept shut tight somewhere deep in his mind, in his heart, walled in tight. Despair like ice clawed and cracked at those walls. He put his head in his hands, a sob building in his chest, writhing up into his throat, unstoppable. Tears rolled down his cheeks and memories of Frøya filled his mind. His sister. His only friend.

He had no memory of his father or mother, only what he had been told by Kolskegg, who had bought him and Frøya when they were bairns. Kolskegg had told him that Varg's parents had sold him and Frøya for a loaf of bread and a dozen duck eggs when Varg was five winters old, Frøya four. All their lives spent as thralls, each other their only solace, their only comfort. He rested his hand on the pouch at his belt.

And now she is dead, and I don't know how to avenge her.

After a while Varg looked up, rubbed his eyes, winced at the pain.

This is not the end, he told himself. *I have come too far to just give up now. There must be a Galdurman or Seiðr-witch somewhere in all of Vigrið that will help me, for coin. I will find them, wherever they are. And if I cannot find them in Vigrið then I shall travel the whale-road sea to Iskidan, and search all of the Shattered Realms until I have found someone to help me.*

I will go on.

He sucked in a long, ragged breath, pushing his memories back, somewhere deep and dark.

A twig cracked in the woods.

Without thinking he scrambled to his feet, kicked at the fire, sparks exploding. Stood there, listening, staring into the shadow-black.

A low, rumbled growl.

A figure burst from the undergrowth, a man dragged by a hound on a leash, more shapes behind him. The hound leaped at him.

Varg stepped to the side, snapped his left arm out, shoving the leaping hound away. The force of his blow sent him stumbling into a tree, and sent the hound crashing on to the fire. More sparks erupted, the hound yelping, fur igniting.

"Thought you could run from us for ever," a voice snarled, coming from a woman that stepped around the houndsman, a spear levelled at Varg's chest.

Varg pushed off the tree, reaching inside his cloak, the spear stabbing into bark. He fumbled the cleaver out and chopped at the spear shaft, splintering it, ducked as the woman still clutching the haft used it like a club attempting to cave Varg's skull in. A slice of the cleaver as Varg stumbled away; a scream; the woman clutching her ribs and dropping to her knees.

The hound was rolling, yelping and whining, flames in its fur, the houndsman tearing his cloak off and wrapping it around the animal, trying to put the flames out. Other men appeared from the gloom: three, four more at least, it was hard to tell in the murk, but Varg saw all had spears in their fists. He looked wildly around and ran for a gap in the trees. A crack to the back of his legs and he stumbled, tried to right his balance but tripped over a root, fell to one knee, put a hand out to save himself and yelled, pain shooting through his injured hand.

Another blow across his shoulders, sending him face first to the ground; a mouth full of pine needles and dirt. He rolled, lashed out with the cleaver, felt it bite into someone's leg, heard another scream. A man dropped to the ground beside him, tearing the cleaver from Varg's grip.

A foot kicked Varg in the chest as he tried to rise, another man stamping on his wrist, pinning him. Varg snarled, tried to roll and a spear butt clubbed him across the forehead, sent him crashing back to the forest litter. Blood in his eyes. A spear hovered over his throat, another man standing on his other wrist, pinning him wide.

Varg stared up, breathing hard, blood pounding in his head.

"You thought I wouldn't find you," the man looming over him said. His face was lit by the stuttering fire, shadow and flame. A broad man, black-bearded, a scar running through his lip that twisted his mouth into a permanent sneer.

"Leif," Varg spat, "you should not have followed me."

"Ha," Leif grunted. "You'd have to run faster and further to hide from me, after what you did to my father. Butchered like an animal. I only knew him by his chain."

Varg did not remember. It had been a red-tinged haze, only coming back to his senses as he choked the life from Snepil. He had sat back, then, dazed, blood and carnage all about him.

"You've lost your collar, Varg the thrall," Leif said.

"I am *no* thrall," Varg grunted. He pulled in a breath through his pain. "Your father cheated me. I earned my freedom and your father broke his oath. I am a freedman, no different from you." One of the men pinning Varg kicked him in the face. He spat blood.

Leif laughed.

"You are Varg the thrall, and you are *my* thrall, now. My property. You belong to me. Leif Kolskeggson; son of the man you murdered." Leif glanced at one of the men beside him. "Put a collar and chain on this dog." He touched his spear tip to Varg's chest, traced it over his torso, then slowly slid the blade's edge across Varg's ribs, a line of blood welling. "I am going to bleed you, but death would be too much of a kindness to you," Leif said. He stabbed his spear into the ground and squatted down beside Varg, checking him over for weapons. There was a chink of metal as Leif reached inside Varg's cloak and pulled out the bag of coin.

"Stolen from my father, no doubt," Leif said and spat in Varg's face. "I am going to chain you to my horse and drag you all the way back to my farm-steading," he said slowly, taking care over his words, anger putting a tremor into them. "Once there you will have the lash, until you can no longer stand. Until I have seen your bones. And then I shall put you back to work. For me. Making me coin for the rest of your stinking, miserable life."

Varg twisted and writhed, heaved one hand free. Booted kicks rained in, curling him up. He lay their gasping.

"My leg," a voice whimpered close by, the man Varg had struck with his cleaver. The blade was still embedded in his leg.

"Bastard thrall's cut me, broken my ribs," another voice wheezed: the woman, sitting propped against a tree, one hand pressed to a black glistening wound in her side. Leif stood, walked over to the man and leaned down, grabbed the cleaver's wooden handle and wrenched it free of the injured warrior's leg, eliciting a high-pitched scream. "Orl, tend to their wounds," Leif ordered the man still sitting close to the fire, patting his hound down. The flames were out, patches of fur blackened, the hound whining. Orl stood and moved to the injured man and woman, giving Varg a dismayed look. He was old, his grey hair thin and lank, and he wore an iron collar around his throat.

"You hurt my old girl," he muttered at Varg as he pulled a knife and kneeled beside the wounded woman, began cutting at her tunic and cleaning her wound. The hound limped after him.

Leif hefted the cleaver.

"Murdered my father," Leif said, and slashed the cleaver through the air. "Slew three other freedmen." Two more slashes of the cleaver, air whistling. "Now you injure two of my *hird*." He pointed the cleaver at Varg. "I'll give you part of your punishment now, I'm thinking. One for you to think over on the journey back to my steading." He looked at the two men standing over Varg. "Pull his arm out; hold him tight."

Varg stared at Leif, then at the two men as one gripped his hand, the other twisting his other arm up behind his back.

He's going to cut my hand off.

Varg hurled himself against the men, straining and thrashing, but the man behind him held him tight, a white-hot pain lancing into his shoulder, his arm close to breaking. He collapsed, gasping.

"Don't worry. When we get home, I'll have Orl carve you a hand of wood, so you can still work on the farm," Leif said, his lips twisting.

A sound behind Leif, of branches snapping. Leif paused, all of them staring into the darkness.

A man stepped out of the woodland, tall and broad, with a bald head and grey beard. A coat of mail shimmered in the moonlight. He held a bearded long-axe in both hands. Like a staff. There were shadows behind him, patches of deeper darkness. The silver-haired woman appeared, two wolfhounds at her side. They were snarling, hackles raised.

"Let him go," the grey-beard said.

Leif raised the cleaver high.

The grey-beard moved, faster than Varg could track, and then Leif was doubled over, the cleaver falling to the ground. The men holding Varg burst into motion, reaching for their spears, stabbing at the grey-beard as Leif coughed and retched on his knees.

The wolfhounds leaped forwards, jaws latching on to the arm and leg of one man, dragging him to the ground.

A cracking sound and trees ruptured apart, Einar Half-Troll emerging, a punch sending one of Leif's men hurtling through branches, disappearing into the darkness. Another figure darted past the grey-beard: Svik, the slim, red-haired man who had first spoken to Varg. His face was twisted in a snarl, his seax in his fist, cold iron gleaming. He swayed around a stabbing spear, stepped in close and ran the seax-blade along the spear shaft, slicing. A scream and severed fingers fell to the ground. The spear dropped and the slim man grabbed the screaming warrior by his woollen tunic, dragged him forward and headbutted him. He fell with a gurgle.

Silence in the clearing: just heavy breathing, the wind in the trees, Leif groaning. Varg stared at the fallen men, too stunned to move. Leif was still on his hands and knees, one hand cupping his groin. Saliva dribbled from his mouth. Orl sat against the tree, eyes wide. His hound growled at the newcomers.

Svik strode towards Orl and growled at the hound, a deep, animal sound, and the hound tucked his tail between his legs, whined, and pressed tightly into Orl.

Svik laughed as he wiped blood from his forehead and braided hair.

The grey-beard stepped past Leif and stood over Varg.

"He's . . . mine," Leif spluttered. "My thrall, and mine by right of weregild. He must answer for . . . murder."

"No," the grey-beard said, his voice like gravel. "He's one of the Bloodsworn now."

CHAPTER FIVE

ELVAR

"ROW, you *niðing* bunch of gutless troll-turds!" Sighvat bellowed as he beat time on a barrel with a knotted lump of rope.

Elvar gritted her teeth and dragged on her oar, the muscles in her back and shoulders screaming. A swell lifted their *drakkar* high, her dragon-prow pointing at the slate-grey sky and Elvar's oar breached the water. She felt a weightlessness in the pit of her stomach as she lost her balance and almost slipped from her sea-chest, then the prow was surging down, cutting into the ice-flecked waves. An explosion of sea spray crashed over the bows, the wind whipping it across Elvar's back like hailstones. She cuffed sleet and a strand of her blonde hair from her face, corrected her oar, found her rhythm and bent back to the rowing, losing herself in the motion, muscles contracting, extending, a burning deep in every fibre. In front of her Grend's broad back filled her vision, the grey streaks in his hair made dark with sweat and salt-spray. Beyond him, glimpsed through the rhythm of Grend's lean and pull, was fat-bellied Sighvat beating time, and behind him in the stern stood Agnar, her chief. He was laughing like it was his name-day with a belly full of mead, his blond braid of hair whipped by the wind. His hands gripped around the tiller, wrestling the steering oar as he fought to guide the *Wave-Jarl* between the arms of two curving promontories, the open sea and glowering clouds behind him.

"ROW!" Sighvat yelled again and fifty oars dipped into the white-frothed sea, backs bending, straining as the *Wave-Jarl* carved her way through the waves.

"BEACH!" a voice cried from the *drakkar*'s bow, and Elvar felt a burst of new strength at that cry, a hope that the toil and muscle-burning would end. They had found Iskalt Island easily enough, marked by the red veins of fire that glowed within the mountain that dominated the island, but finding a beach to land upon had been harder going. She bent and pulled, bent and pulled.

Somewhere behind her torn fragments of Kráka's chanting drifted back to her, the Tainted thrall singing her dark magic to keep the serpents and other sea vaesen from their *drakkar*'s hull.

A black-granite spur of rock appeared to her left, seals and puffins upon it regarding the dragon-prowed ship as it slipped past them. Elvar felt the sea calm about the *Wave-Jarl*, as if obeying some rune-cast spell. The rowing became easier as they swept into a natural harbour, waves gentling, a white-flecked wake rippling wide behind them. Agnar barked a command at Sighvat.

"HALF-TIME!" Sighvat bellowed and decreased the rhythm of his barrel-thumping.

Elvar slowed her strokes and felt excitement bubbling, melting her exhaustion.

We are here.

Another shouted word from Agnar.

"OARS IN!" Sighvat yelled. He ceased his beating on the barrel and strode along the deck, passing Elvar and heading to the prow. Elvar dragged her oar back through the hole, hearing the clatter of wood as oars were laid in their racks, and swivelled the oar-hole plug into place. There was the crunch of timber as the *Wave-Jarl* ground along a wooden pier and then Agnar was tying the tiller and striding along the deck, yelling orders.

Elvar stood, stretched, hearing bones click in her neck and back, then threw open her sea-chest. She unrolled a strip of sheepskin, pulled out her *brynja*, the riveted mail glistening with oils from the sheepskin that protected her precious mail from rust. With long-practised ease she lifted the coat of mail, threaded her arms through it, then heaved it up over her head. A wriggle and shake and it slipped over her shoulders and down her torso. A thin belt buckled tight to take the weight of mail from her shoulders, and then she was reaching for her weapons belt, sword, seax and axe suspended from it. She drew her sword a handspan to check it hadn't snared, then let it drop back down: a habit she had learned from Grend since the first day she had laid her hands around the hilt of a sword. Last of all she reached into her chest for a nålbinding cap of coarse wool, pulled it over her head and then lifted her helm, polished plates of banded iron, a curtain of riveted mail to protect her neck, adjusted it so that her vision was good through the spectacled eye-holes, then buckled it tight. She flashed a grin at Grend as he went through the same process, the warrior rolling his shoulders to settle his *brynja*. He gave her a flat stare, his face creased and dour, which only helped to broaden her own smile, then she was reaching for her shield that stood wedged into a rack along the top-rail, tugging it free and slipping her hand around the wooden grip, fist settling into the boss. She moved to a rack of spears, took hers and waited for Agnar's orders, eager to disembark.

Agnar was calling out names, ten or twelve, those ordered to stay with the ship and guard it, then he was shouting for the rest to disembark and they leaped from the top-rail on to the wooden pier Sighvat had moored them to, Elvar and Grend among them.

Flecks of snow drifted on the wind among the sleet, the clouds above swollen and bloated. Elvar looked around and saw that the pier led on to a shingle beach. Nets were hanging upon poles, drying or ready for repair, crab-catching willow-baskets piled together, sat before a cluster of smokehouses. An old, rotted hull lay abandoned, terns and herring gulls perched upon it, eyeing these newcomers. The beach rose sharply, shingle shifting to earth and, upon a ridge overlooking the beach, a few dozen buildings huddled close together, lines of thin smoke rising, disappearing into the snow-laden sky. Beyond the buildings there was a treeline of aspen and birch, more buildings squatting beneath boughs. The land rose into foothills, turning quickly into towering, granite-faced cliffs as sharp as jagged teeth that rose towards the peak of the island's mountain of flame. Thin, red tendrils dissected the cliffs, glowing within the dark rock like forge-fire.

There was movement in the village, fur-draped people emerging from doors, staring. Some running, others clutching spears and hunting bows.

I hate bows, Elvar thought and spat on the pier, curling her lip. *A coward's weapon. How can a warrior earn their battle-fame killing at a distance?*

She hefted her shield, painted red with a sword, axe and spear crossed upon it, the weapons lined in swirling knotwork.

"By the dead gods, but it's cold," Biórr muttered. He smiled at her as he said it, shield slung across his back, stamping his feet and blowing a cloud of misted breath into his palms.

Elvar just looked at him, saw the interest in his eyes and looked away.

"It's a fine day," she said. In truth she was feeling the corpse-cold seeping into her, now her muscles were cooling, silent as death. Beside them the *Wave-Jarl* creaked, rising and falling on the swell, the blue-black sea glistening and sluggish with ice. Spring was just a distant word, this far north.

"Elvar, Grend, with me!" Agnar shouted and warriors parted to let her through. Elvar held her head high, knowing the honour Agnar was showing her, youngest of his warband.

Youngest, and fiercest, she thought, and that was no easy claim, looking at the grim-eyed warriors she passed, all of them battle-scarred and heavy with sharp iron. She glanced over at the deck of the *Wave-Jarl*, saw the warriors left to guard it staring at her, and Kráka slumped across the prow, her sweat and sea-drenched black hair plastered to her head, like the collapsed wings of a crow. She shifted as Elvar passed her, turning to look at the young warrior, her thrall-collar and chain rattling. One of the ship-guards gave her a kick and she flinched, raising her hands. Elvar looked away.

Agnar stood waiting. A black bearskin cloak was cast over his mail, silver torc around his neck and rings thick upon his arms, shield in one fist, his other hand resting upon a sword at his hip.

At his belt hung a tattered, blood-crusted strip of wool. A thick band of his blond hair ran down the middle of his head, tied into a warrior-braid, the rest of his head shaved to stubble. He pulled on and buckled his helm as Elvar approached him.

Sighvat glowered at Agnar's shoulder, mail stretched tight across his bulk, a bearded axe hanging at his belt. He held a hemp sack flung over one shoulder, and in his other fist he gripped a chain. At the chain's end a man squatted, shivering and cowering, hair long and lank, eyes sunken to black pits, a tattered sealskin cloak wrapped around him.

"With me," Agnar said to Elvar as she reached him, then he turned and strode along the pier, Sighvat dragging the chained thrall, Elvar and Grend striding behind them. The pier shook as the rest of the warband thumped along after them.

Agnar lifted a horn to his lips and blew, the sound dragged by the wind, ringing mournfully across the beach.

Shingle crunched beneath Elvar's boots as they stepped from the pier and strode up the beach, a crowd forming before them.

"We are the Battle-Grim," Sighvat bellowed in his deep-bellied voice. "We are the slayers of the vaesen, hunters of the Tainted, the reapers of souls. If you have not heard of our battle-fame, then we will gladly teach it to you."

Grunts and laughter among the warriors at Elvar's back.

The crowd before them milled, muttered among themselves, maybe sixty or seventy villagers wrapped in sealskin and fur, some children clinging to legs, others peering from doorways. Among the crowd spears were held ready, some levelled. Elvar saw arrows nocked. She could see the question in their eyes. Saw them hovering on that knife's edge of violence. They outnumbered the Battle-Grim and were lean and hard-looking. Elvar knew only the strong could survive this far north, where the world seemed to unite against the living and the vaesen were bolder. But as tough as these villagers were, they were not the Battle-Grim, steeped and honed in war and blood, and among those facing them Elvar could only see a handful holding shields, and none wore mail.

"Watch them with your hawk eyes," Agnar muttered to Elvar as he halted on the beach, Elvar, Grend and Sighvat behind him, the rest of the warband spreading wide.

"SHIELDS!" Agnar called out and behind her Elvar heard the crunch of linden-wood slamming together, the shuffle and grate of boots on shingle as the line tightened.

"There is a man among you," Agnar shouted. "Berak is his name. Tall, wide as a barn. Scars down one side of his face. A woman and child are with him. He would have arrived here maybe two or three days gone. Give him over to us, and your blood will not stain this beach."

Elvar watched faces, saw fear in some, saw pride, animosity, anger in others.

Agnar pulled the tattered strip of wool from his belt and lifted it high.

"I will find him with or without your help. My *Hundur*-thrall has his scent. He will not escape me." Agnar dropped the blood-crusted rag to the man at the end of Sighvat's chain, who looked at the rag as if it were a poison.

Sighvat yanked on the chain around the thrall's throat.

"*Hlýða*," Agnar growled and a ripple of red veins tremored through the thrall's collar.

The thrall whimpered, then picked up the rag and buried his face in it, snuffling and snorting.

"Your choice is to help or hinder," Agnar continued. He looked at them all, pulled a pouch heavy with coin from his belt and cast it on the beach in front of him.

"Your choice is to prosper or die." Agnar shrugged, as if he cared not which of those choices they made.

A tall man stepped forwards, wrapped in fur and sealskin, a spear in his fist, a long knife at his belt, the hilt carved from walrus ivory. His beard was braided many times and bound with bone rings.

"I am Hrut, Jarl of Iskalt," the man said.

Jarl! Elvar thought, looking him up and down. *Where is your gold or silver? Where is your sword, your mail? You would not be allowed in a jarl's outhouse on the mainland.*

"And I know of no Berak living upon my island," Hrut said.

"You do know him," Agnar said. "But you may not know that he is TAINTED!" He bellowed that last word, spittle flying. "He is gods-touched and will bring only blood and slaughter upon you. Do not protect such as he."

Elvar saw movement towards the back of the crowd. A tall man with a spear and a cloak of stitched white-fox pelts draped across his shoulders was stooping to speak to a young girl at his side, surely little more than seven or eight winters. She nodded and scurried away across the beach, threading between the huts.

"There," Elvar said to Agnar, pointing with her spear at the speeding child.

Agnar strode forwards, stepping around Hrut, but the jarl took a step to his right, placing himself in front of Agnar.

Agnar stopped, looking over his shoulder at Elvar.

"Follow the girl," he said, then drew his sword and there was blood in the air. It was a move Elvar practised every day, turning the draw into a diagonal strike, from left to right. Agnar disguised the manoeuvre behind his shield, realisation dawning in Hrut's eyes only as he saw the glint of steel. He had a moment to move his spear and stumble away, but Agnar's sword sheared through the spear haft and on, the sword tip cutting into Hrut's beard, slicing through his chin and lower lip. Blood sprayed, teeth flying.

Hrut bellowed with pain and rage and Agnar stepped in, his shield raised, sword stabbing.

The crowd behind Hrut yelled their outrage, many of them lowering spears and leaping forwards. Arrows hissed and whistled through the air.

Elvar burst into motion, bounding around Agnar and Hrut even as the Battle-Grim behind her yelled a war cry and advanced, weapons thumping on shields. There was a crunch of gravel behind, booted feet following her, and Elvar didn't need to look to know it was Grend. She sprinted around the fringe of the crowd, all of them focused on Agnar and Hrut, rushing to defend their jarl. A man with a nocked bow curled around the flank of his kinsmen, drew and loosed at the Battle-Grim. A scream from the beach. Elvar swerved, the villager seeing her only a fraction before she slammed into him. Her shield boss crunched into the side of his head and he dropped like a cut sail.

Elvar stood over him, searched for the girl, saw where she had disappeared among the huts on the beach. She ran on.

There was a movement to her right and instinctively she ducked and swayed, twisting to bring her shield around.

A spear blade grated across her *brynja*, a spark of steel, then Elvar's shield rim was slamming into the spear shaft, sending the woman wielding it stumbling away. Elvar chopped with her sword, cut deep across her attacker's shoulder and back, slicing through fur and leather. Blood spurted and the woman yelled, staggering forwards, dropping to one knee. She swung her spear, the intent to hamstring Elvar, and then her head exploded, Grend's axe crunching into it. The spear dropped with a clatter to the shingle. Grend snarled, ripped his blade free, blood and brains spattering his face. A shared look, then Elvar was running on. She glimpsed Sighvat and the thrall following behind Grend, and also Biórr.

Then Elvar was among the buildings, searching for any sign of the girl who had run from the beach. She stopped, holding her breath to listen. Screams drifted on the wind from behind her, the clang of iron. She shut it out, heard whispered voices, one deep, almost a growl, and she ran on. Twisting through a snarl of buildings, swerving around fishing nets hanging for repairs, she came to a door swinging on a hinge. A timber-framed hut to the rear of the village, the walls caked with clay and wattle and daub. It looked like it was only big enough for one room. Elvar slowed, hefted her shield, peered through the open door into shadowed darkness, glimpsed the soft glow of a fire. Grend skidded up next to her and Elvar gestured for him to circle around the back of the hut. A silent nod and then she was moving, kicking the door hard, to slam into anyone standing behind it as she burst into the room, shield raised, spear high, twisting to defend against any lurking attacker.

The hut was empty.

A fire pit had been scraped into hard earth in the centre of the hut, flames flickering. A pot hung over it, suspended from an iron chain. Fish stew bubbled. A table, three chairs, two straw beds. Elvar stabbed into the straw, then saw light leaking into the hut. A hole, low in the back wall, wide enough for a large man to crawl through.

Grend's booted feet and grey-wool leg-wraps appeared.

Elvar kicked the wall, wattle and daub crumbling loose. Kicked again, more hard-packed clay falling, revealing the hazel rod wattle core. Grend's axe swung and a section of the wall crumbled.

They stood there, staring at one another.

She heard heavy breathing and the clank of chains behind her. Sighvat and the thrall appeared, Sighvat pushing through the doorway, his bulk blocking out the light. The thrall dropped into a crawling squat, nose to the ground, snorting.

Biórr appeared, face flushed with battle and the sprint up the beach.

"Is it him?" Sighvat grunted at the thrall. The man on the end of the chain crawled over to the cot and buried his face in the straw, sniffing deeply. He looked up at Sighvat and nodded.

Footsteps. Agnar appeared in the doorway, his sword red to the hilt, warriors thick as smoke behind him.

He looked from Sighvat to the thrall.

"Where is he?" Agnar grunted.

Elvar pointed through the hole in the wall. Grend was searching the ground for tracks.

"That way," the dour warrior said, straightening and pointing with his bloodied axe, towards the treeline and shadowed woods, Iskalt's mountain of fire dark and brooding.

"After them," Agnar said.

CHAPTER SIX

ORKA

Orka woke with a gasp. For a moment she did not know where she was, could only see a vivid picture in her mind, of blood and battle, bodies falling around her, the roar of the sea, the sounds of violence. The battle cries and death screams were sharp and as clear as if she were standing in the middle of the bloody conflict, rather than lying upon a sweat-soaked mattress of straw in her own steading. She stared at the timber beams above and took a long, ragged breath as recognition seeped into her. As the tension eased, she loosened her white-knuckled fist around a clump of her mattress.

The grey of dawn crept through shutters. Thorkel slept beside her, his hairy back to her, one foot out of the woollen blanket. His chest rose and fell in slow, gentle rhythm, a rumbling snore deep in his throat. Orka reached out to touch him, fingertips hovering over his skin.

Let him sleep. Why burden him with my weakness.

She withdrew her arm and swung her feet over the side of the bed. Sat there a while, head in hands, allowing her body to settle and the sweat to dry. She wished there was a jug of mead or ale at the bedside, felt the need for it in her bones. To dull the memories, the pain. She felt a flash of resentment towards Thorkel, as he had asked her to drink less. Then she pulled on a pair of woollen breeches, leather boots and a linen tunic, and padded across the room, opening the door slowly so as not to wake Thorkel. Her thought was to start a hearth fire and then wake Thorkel and Breca with some porridge, honey and cream, but as she walked into the hall of their cabin, which took up most of the building, apart from hers and Thorkel's bedchamber, she knew something was wrong, like a tingling in her blood.

Where's Breca?

She looked to his cot, close to the burned-out hearth fire, where he liked to go to sleep with the blurred glow and crackle of embers in his eyes and ears.

It was empty, the woollen blanket thrown off.

A trickle of ice in her veins; worry fluttering like wings in her chest.

"Breca," she called as she searched the hall, quickly looking behind tables, piled blankets, in cupboards. There was a sound behind her as Thorkel emerged from their chamber, barefoot, with breeches on and a blanket wrapped around his shoulders. He was blinking, the muscles in his face not yet caught up with the fact that he was awake.

"You're making enough noise to wake the dead gods," he muttered.

"Breca's not here," Orka snapped, a coil of dread in her gut putting some bite in her words.

"Outside?" Thorkel suggested. "Fetching water, firewood?"

"*I* do that in the morning. He sleeps until I wake him," Orka said.

"You do? He does?" said Thorkel, frowning.

Orka scowled at him. "This, from the man who usually sleeps like a bear in his winter's cave until the smell of porridge wakes him."

"Fair enough," Thorkel shrugged. "Still, he might be outside. Something might have woken him, like his bladder."

"He's not an old man, like you. He can hold his piss."

Thorkel opened his mouth, clearly thought better of it and disappeared back into the bedchamber. He re-emerged, boots on and tugging on a woollen tunic as Orka was reaching for her spear in a rack, throwing open the doors and striding out into daylight.

She stood on the first step that led down into their courtyard, scanning the steading. The woodshed, forge, charcoal kiln were all clearly empty and undisturbed.

"Breca," she cried as she hurried down the steps, mud soft under her boots. Past the herb and vegetable patch and beehive. She peered into the barn as she passed it, where their shaggy pony stood with his head over the stable door, regarding a hay bale with a two-pronged fork stuck in it, just as Orka had left it last night. Striding on, Orka stopped at the stream that flowed fast and clear through the steading, crouched beside a moss-slick rock. She stuck the butt-end of her spear into the icy water, jabbing it beneath an alcove under the rock.

"Spert, wake up," Orka grunted.

A dark shape appeared, as long as Orka's arm and wide as one of Thorkel's tree-stump legs, uncoiling from beneath the rock and spreading into the stream. Its chitinous, segmented body straightened, tapering to an oily sting, sharp as a needle that curved over its back. A multitude of long legs clawed into the stream's bank and it crawled towards Orka, its head breaking the water.

"*Food*," the Spertus croaked, its voice like scratching dry skin. It looked up at Orka with a too-human face, bulbous eyes under grey sagging skin, and a mouth full of too many sharp-spiked teeth.

"Have you seen Breca?" Orka asked the creature.

"*Spert sleep until food*," the creature muttered. It looked around, searching for Breca, who usually brought it a bowl of porridge mixed with blood and spit each morning. "*Hungry*," it complained.

"I should kill you, you useless creature," Orka grunted as she stood.

"*Ungrateful*," the creature grated, a hiss of scraping skin. "*Spert work hard. Spert protect you from vaesen*."

"If you protect us, then where is Breca?" Orka snarled.

The Spertus blinked.

"*Can't watch everything, everyone, all the time*," it grumbled. "*Have to sleep sometime*."

"Orka," Thorkel called from behind her.

She stood and turned, and there was a splash and ripple of water as Spert submerged and returned to his chamber beneath the rock.

Thorkel was kneeling by the single gate that was built into the larger gates that were only ever opened when taking their pony and cart to Fellur with goods to trade. Otherwise they came and went by this single door. It opened with an iron latch-bolt. Orka ran to Thorkel, fear pounding in her head like a drum.

"He was here," Thorkel said, pointing at a clear boot print in the mud, half the size of hers. "And he has used this gate." The iron bolt was drawn, the gate just pulled to. Thorkel pushed it open, looking out on the glade beyond their steading, bordered by woodland. There were more boot prints in the mud.

Panic, like a viper's venom, flushed through her veins.

Virk's words from Fellur village whispered in her head.

Children are being taken.

"Others?" Orka asked. She was too full of anger and anxiety to read the ground. Her eyes searched the glade beyond their walls, tried to pierce the shadows beneath the woodland. "Has he been taken, like Asgrim's boy, Harek?"

"No signs of anyone else," Thorkel said, rising. He passed through the rune-marked gates and turned left, Orka following. Thorkel had buckled on his weapons belt, seax and hand-axe hanging from it, and Orka had her spear.

Enough to look after ourselves, if it comes to blood.

They padded across an open glade, a few patches of snow left among the grass that was wet with dew starting to steam as the rising sun washed the glade. Then they were passing beneath high boughs, moving north-east from their home, into a twilight world. Orka followed her husband, knew Thorkel was the better tracker. He loped along, every few heartbeats his eyes scanning the ground then flitting up ahead of them. Their path curled to follow the stream that flowed through their steading, moving steadily upstream, climbing a gentle slope. Orka looked above and to their flanks, searching for the telltale movements of vaesen or other predators, but saw nothing. The woods were silent and still, as if holding their breath.

Where is he? If someone or something has hurt him, I will . . .

An image in her mind of an axe falling, blood spraying.

She sucked in a deep breath, feeling the rage building, the ice in her veins tingling, with an act of will pushing it back down. Her son needed her, and all that mattered was finding him. A white-blinding anger would not help that.

The ground levelled and they crested a ridge and saw a pool spreading before them, its cold waters black and still. The stream that fed into their steading ran from here.

"Breca," Thorkel cried. A shadowed form crouched at the pool's edge.

"Papa," Breca said, looking up at them, his small voice loud in the stillness.

Orka sped up, passing Thorkel and running to her son, a flush of relief and joy melting the icicles of fear in her chest. Breca was crouched by the poolside. White lilies floated, pale as winter. Orka dropped to the ground and skidded up to Breca upon her knees, wrapped her arms around him, crushed him so tight in an embrace that he grunted and gasped.

She kissed his cheek, blinked tears from her eyes, stroked his unruly black hair.

"Come away from the water's edge," Thorkel said as he reached them, eyeing the water suspiciously. He sniffed. "Smells like Näcken to me." He drew his seax and stabbed it into the soft loam. "Move away," he repeated.

"Why are you out here?" Orka breathed as she pulled Breca away from the water's edge.

The thought that a Näcken should not be this far from its mountain river entered her thought-cage, but it was pushed aside by her worry and relief at finding Breca.

"I heard a sound," Breca said as Orka released him. He looked down at his cloak, which was folded in his lap, and pulled it open.

Orka gasped, fell back on to her backside.

A creature lay curled in Breca's lap, maybe half the length of one of Orka's legs, if it stood upright. It had arms and legs with thick, pointed claws where fingers and toes should be, and fragile, parchment-thin wings wrapped about its torso. Blood leaked from beneath one wing, staining the skin. With a sharp nose and chin, it was hairless with large, black eyes and ink-dark veins threading pink, hairless skin, like a newborn rat. It turned its head, looked up at Orka and opened its mouth, which was very wide, revealing two rows of teeth, the outer one sharp, the inner row flat, like grindstones. A thin line of blood trickled from a cut on its lip.

"A tennúr," Thorkel said from somewhere above and behind Orka.

Orka slipped to one knee and backhanded Breca across the cheek, throwing him flat on his back.

"You left our steading, left safety, for *this*," she snarled, rising to her feet. "Vaesen lurk out here, and there are murderers and child-stealers." Wordless sounds escaped her throat. "You witless fool, you could have been taken, eaten, *killed*." The fear of that filled her and she lifted her arm for another slap.

The tennúr still in Breca's lap spread its wings with a snap, shielding Breca, and it bared its teeth and hissed at Orka. Though it looked too weak to stand.

Thorkel caught her wrist, wrapped it in one of his huge hands. "You've made your point."

She could have fought him, would have won, but long years had taught her to trust her husband's judgement, even when her blood was high and she didn't agree with him. Especially when her blood was high and she did not agree with him.

Breca was looking up at her, the skin on his cheek already swollen and bruising. His eyes flickered to his father.

"It was a foolish thing, leaving the steading," Thorkel said, his voice and eyes hard. "We are fortunate to have a son who still draws breath and who still has all of his blood in his veins."

Breca's bottom lip trembled.

Thorkel sucked in a long breath. "How did you find it?"

"I heard it scream," Breca said, looking at the tennúr, which had collapsed back into his lap again, wings once more wrapped tight about it. "It's in pain."

You could have been in pain. Or dead.

Orka opened her mouth to scold him some more.

"It's quiet enough now," Thorkel said.

"That's because I gave it one of my teeth," Breca said and smiled, a gap in his gums proving the truth of his words.

"What!" Orka hissed.

"You told me, tennúr love teeth. One of my first teeth is loose, so I pulled it out and gave it to her." He shrugged, putting a fingertip to the red hole in his gum. "Another is growing through."

"Her!" Orka said.

"Aye. Her name is Vesli. She told me."

Orka shook her head. Thorkel whistled.

"Can we keep her?" Breca asked, looking at them both with pleading eyes.

The sound of Thorkel's laughter echoed through the trees.

CHAPTER SEVEN

ELVAR

Elvar blinked sweat from her eyes, her vision blurring for a moment as she searched the gloom.

"Halt," Agnar called out, about a dozen strides ahead.

Warriors about her stuttered to a halt.

Elvar blew out a misted breath and wiped the sweat from her eyes, shrugged the shield from her back and set it down against a tree, then squatted beside a fast-flowing stream. Grend stood over her, then took a few steps into the gloom, eyes always searching.

They were high into the hills, snow falling heavily now, flakes drifting down through the canopy, thicker around the stream, its edge crackling with ice. Elvar tugged off a glove with her teeth and unstoppered her water bottle, drained it in one long draught, then leaned out and dipped the leather bottle into the stream's centre, where it was not frozen, refilling it. Water bubbled, so cold it felt like it was burning Elvar's fingers like fire. She took another long sip. The water was sharp as ice in her throat, and clear, the stones on the bottom of the stream shimmering with veins of colour.

It had been a long, hard climb since the fishing village. Through a break in the trees Elvar could see the village far below her, the *Wave-Jarl* moored in the bay, all of it blurred by the snow. A fence-line stood in a half-circle between the village and the trees. Wooden stakes, rune-marked to protect against vaesen. From this height she could still glimpse faint smudges on the beach, bodies and blood on the shingle marking the site of the battle.

Not much of a battle, it was over almost as soon as it began.

Agnar had slain the jarl, Hrut, and a dozen others had fallen against the Battle-Grim's shield wall. That had been enough to convince the rest of the villagers to throw down their weapons. The only casualty among the Battle-Grim had been an arrow in Thrud's calf. Elvar thought she could still hear his cursing drifting up to her on the wind and snow, his fury that he had been left behind. Agnar had left another dozen warriors with Thrud to watch over the prisoners, leaving twenty-six of them to follow their chief into the wooded and snow-shrouded hills.

"On your feet," Sighvat bellowed as Agnar took a few steps into the trees.

"*Hundur*, lead us on," Agnar said to the thrall, who squatted to sniff the ground, nose sifting through a light covering of snow, then bounded on, the chain fastened to its collar pulling tight as Sighvat lumbered after it. Elvar stoppered her bottle and hung it from her belt, pulled her glove back on, stood and slipped on a snow- and ice-covered rock. A hand grabbed her arm, steadying her, and she looked into Biórr's face. Without thinking she returned his easy smile. His grip lingered and she shook her arm free and slung her shield across her back. Grend stepped between Elvar and Biórr, glowering down at him.

Biórr smiled and stepped away.

"Just helping," he said. He looked at Elvar. "I don't think your father likes me."

He is not my father, she thought. Then they were moving out, into the shadows.

The path was narrow, following the stream on their left, but on the right the boughs were high, and the trunks spaced wide. Elvar picked up her pace and stepped from the path, padding across a thin covering of snow, made spongy with forest litter beneath, and moving up the line so she was closer to Agnar, Sighvat and the thrall. Grend followed, a few paces behind her.

There were more footsteps behind her and she glanced back and saw Biórr leave the path and head into the woods as well, his feet tracing her and Grend's boot prints.

A dark mound appeared in the path ahead and the thrall slowed, stopped before it, sniffing. The mound was steaming, snowflakes drifting upon it and melting. Lumps protruded from it.

Elvar moved closer, a foul stench hitting her, clawing up her nose.

"Troll dung," the thrall said. It reached out, grabbed a lump jutting from the pile and pulled at it. A sticky slap sounded as it came free and the thrall held up a large bone, a leg or arm: Elvar could not tell for the excrement and slime that dripped from it. A fresh wave of stench hit, snatching her breath away, burning her throat, and she lifted her arm to her nose, fighting the urge to retch.

Agnar stared into the woods, a scowl on his face. His head swept left to right, and then he saw Elvar wide on his flank.

"Elvar, Grend, Biórr, as you are so keen to lead, you can be the boar's snout and scout ahead." He said it with a grunt, but Elvar knew the honour Agnar was giving her. "Stay within sight," he added.

Elvar nodded, felt a flush of pride and fear. Pride to be picked, fear that she might run into a full-grown bull-troll. Trolls were not to be sniffed at. The Battle-Grim had hunted them before, for a price, but not when they were at half strength, and running blind through a forest. Trolls were fiercely territorial, a male usually solitary unless there was a female in season close by, in which case males would compete for her affections, fight, mate and remain with her for the duration of her gestation and a month or two after his brood had been born. After that he would return to his territory.

So, there could be one, two or more, if the cow-troll has given birth. And newborn trolls were not much smaller than Elvar, strong and nimble when they were born, voraciously hungry. And notoriously fond of human flesh.

"Let's pick up the pace. I don't want my prize ending up in a troll's belly," Agnar said.

Elvar set off, veering back on to the path and breaking into a slow jog, Grend staying in the woods level with her, Biórr moving to her left, and then running parallel to the stream, his boots crunching in snow. Elvar felt her heart beating time as she loped ahead, eyes scanning the path and woodland. The path steepened and twisted, veering around rocks that were becoming more frequent. Something caught her eye, a silver line glistening in diffuse patches of daylight that filtered through the trees.

A strand of cobweb, thick as Elvar's finger, ran from the rotted, hollowed trunk of a pine tree up into higher boughs. Elvar tracked it upwards, saw the cobweb spiral, spreading wide among the branches, dark husks hanging. Rats. A crow. A pine marten, big as a cat.

Frost-spiders.

Elvar shrugged her shield from her back and into her fist as she ran, whistled, drawing Grend's and Biórr's eyes, and pointed with her spear.

There are too many of us, Elvar thought, but her eyes searched the boughs, just in case. She'd seen what a frost-spider's venom could do, freezing blood in veins and stopping the heart.

Snowflakes as big as leaves drifted down about her, muting the sounds of the forest. Grend was a dark shadow flitting on her right, Biórr slower, navigating the snow and rocks of the stream's bank, which was becoming deeper and wilder, foam-flecked. Snow fell thicker about Biórr, the canopy thinner above the stream, which made his route slicker and harder to navigate.

That will teach him for following me. He has some stones, though, risking Grend's ire.

Elvar glanced back, glimpsed the thrall on the path, moving in a stooping run, Sighvat puffing like a bellows behind him.

A sound filtered through the forest, a distant, constant hissing, like an angry cat. It grew louder. *A waterfall?* Whatever it was, Elvar was running towards it, her lungs and legs starting to burn, then a new sound pierced the forest. A huge, roaring bellow cutting through all else, for a few moments drowning out the roar of the waterfall.

"Troll," she said, an attempt at warning Grend and Biórr, but the word came out of her mouth a rasp rather than a warning shout. It wasn't needed, though; Grend and Biórr both heard it, judging by the way they slowed, their eyes flitting from the path ahead to Elvar.

She couldn't see anything but held her spear up as a warning to Sighvat behind, then she ran on, though more cautiously than before.

The path steepened, then levelled out and Elvar spilled out on to a snow-covered plateau, blinking as trees thinned about her. A torrent of molten fire plummeted down a granite cliff, like a waterfall, roaring and hissing, cascading into a molten pool that bubbled and churned. Snow fell upon it, melting and hissing, sending a permanent mist swirling into the air.

On the fire pool's eastern edge two figures stood, a woman and child, as close to the pool as they could bear, waves of heat rolling off the molten rock. And between Elvar and the woman and child were two others, one taller than the other.

A troll and a man.

They were fighting.

The man was broad and thick-bearded, wrapped in fur, his head roughly in line with the troll's belly. He held a spear two-handed, was jabbing and ducking as the troll swung a club of knotted wood, spiked with iron nails as long as Elvar's forearm. An explosion of turf as the club tore into the ground, the man leaping away, falling, rolling, staggering back to his feet, stabbing with his spear at the troll's leg.

"MINE!" the troll roared, deafening, even over the din of the molten waterfall and fire pool.

Grend stepped close to Elvar, Biórr just standing and staring.

The thrall loped up to Elvar's side, and there was a clink of chain as Sighvat huffed up the slope and into the open glade, sweating, cheeks red. He dumped the sack he'd been carrying on to the snow with a rattle of iron.

Agnar and more warriors emerged from the trees, spreading wide around Elvar.

The troll was naked, a young bull, judging by the sharp, stubby antlers curling from its thick, moss-covered skull and its swollen testicles, swinging like two rocks in a sack. Tusks jutted from its lower jaws, legs thick as pine saplings, its scaled skin scabbed and patched with moss and lichen.

"MINE," it roared again.

"No, that man's mine," Agnar growled, though Elvar knew the troll was referring to the land. To its territory.

"MINE!" the troll bellowed, spittle flying, eyes and veins bulging with rage, and it swung its club, the man stumbling away, the weapon crunching into a tree, a ripping sound as roots tore and the tree swayed, toppled. The iron nails stuck in timber, dragging the troll off balance, and the man stepped in and lunged with his spear, scouring a red line along the troll's ribs.

With a bellow of pain the troll ripped its club free in a spray of splinters as it spun to face the man.

"Best be putting that troll down. I need that man," Agnar shouted. "In pairs, no shield wall; it will only give the beast a better target."

Sighvat reached into the sack at his feet and pulled out a hammer and a thick iron pin, lifted the thrall's chain and dragged him to the nearest tree, then threaded the pin through the chain and hammered it into the trunk. He returned to the sack and pulled out a new collar and more chain.

Elvar stepped forwards, then paused as movement from the mother and child caught her eye. The mother took something from within her cloak, shaped like a wax tablet or parchment book, though Elvar had only seen a handful of those in her life, and all had been in the courts of wealthy jarls. The woman pulled her arm back and threw the item through the air, spinning high and arcing down into the pool of fire. Flames were erupting from it before it even touched the molten rock. A hiss and it was gone. The woman yelled something to the man fighting the troll, who bellowed back at her, and then the woman was tugging the child away, both of them breaking into a run and climbing a steep slope of scree, studded with pine, a twisting path among them. Elvar touched Agnar's shoulder and pointed at them.

"Good." He barked commands and four warriors ran for the slope and path.

Elvar hefted her spear and hurled it, but saw it skitter off the troll's scaled shoulder. With a hiss she drew her sword as Grend stepped close to her. Together they strode towards the troll and man, lifted their shields, locking tight, Elvar's sword raised high, pointing out over her shield's rim. The snow turned to sludge underfoot as they drew closer to the molten pool, waves of heat rippling across them. Other warriors moved forward in twos, scattered wide, approaching in a loose half-circle.

Someone hurled a spear, the blade slamming into the troll's back. It was well thrown and pierced the thick troll hide, but not deeply. Blood seeped in a line down its back, ran in the folds of muscle.

The troll roared its pain, reached around for the spear in its back, ripped it out and spun away from the man it was trying to crush, its slabbed brows knotting in confusion. It looked at the spear in its fist, then it saw these new warriors approaching it. Its face twisted and bunched, muscles bulging, veins and tendons in its neck standing rigid.

"MINE, MINE, MINE!" the troll screamed, loud enough to make the world shake, and it broke into motion, thick nails on its huge three-toed feet sending up gouts of snow and earth. The sight of these new intruders in its domain must have sent it into a greater level of apoplexy, because it forgot it held a club and just lowered its head and charged with its antlers and tusks, as it would against a rival bull competing for mating rights.

Warriors leaped away, but despite its bulk the troll was fast, and it clipped the shield of one warrior. His shield exploded like so much kindling and antlers and tusk punched through mail and skewered the warrior's torso. The woman he had been partnered with flew through the air and crashed into the molten pool. A scream cut short as she was incinerated with a hiss of sizzling flesh and then a few flakes of ash floated on the heat thermals.

The troll skidded to a halt, raised its head, the warrior impaled upon him screaming even as he chopped feebly at the troll's head with his axe. The troll grabbed the warrior's arm and shook his head, blood pouring like rain. A savage wrench, the warrior's screaming rising in pitch as flesh, tendon and muscle ripped, bone cracked, and then the warrior's arm was dangling in the troll's fist.

It shook its head, muscles in its back and neck rippling, and the dying, whimpering warrior fell from its antlers, crashing into two more warriors.

More spears were hurled, one punching into the troll's shoulder, another lodging between its ribs. Blood oozed like ichor. The troll screamed, lashed out with its club, smashing another shield, breaking the arm of the woman holding it. She stumbled away, the troll following, club rising.

Elvar darted in, Grend following her. She moved in from the side, running as the troll's club whistled through the air and crunched down on to the woman with the broken arm. A wet slap, punctuated with the crunch of bones breaking, and she was gone, unrecognisable, just a pile of shattered bones in a sack of skin. Blood hung in the air like mist.

Agnar ran at the troll's back, dropped his shield and leaped, stabbed two-handed with his sword into the troll's back, high. Elvar heard the grate of iron on ribs, Agnar's blade sinking deep.

The troll let out a scream that set snow tumbling from pine boughs, arched its back, arms flailing, Agnar trying to cling on to his sword hilt, failing and flying through the air.

Elvar ducked under pendulous testicles as the troll twisted and turned, trying to reach the pain in its back. She stabbed her sword into the troll's thigh, high, hoping that its body worked like hers.

A fountain of blood jetted around her hilt as her sword found an artery and smacked her in the face, sending her sprawling, her sword still lodged. She stumbled away, Grend catching her, swinging his axe at testicles that slammed into them like a hammer, and they both fell to the ground.

Dark blood pulsed with the troll's heartbeat: three, four pumping spurts and the troll was swaying, sinking to one knee. It stared at Elvar lying on the blood-slushed snow.

"Mine," it said, like a confused child, and then crashed to its side in an eruption of snow, sighed, and was still.

A victory cry rang out in the glade, the Battle-Grim shaking shields and spears in the air.

"Are you hurt?" Grend asked, rising and offering her his hand.

"I . . . no," Elvar said, climbing to one knee and taking his wrist, pulling herself upright. She was covered in thick, steaming blood, but it was not hers. She strode to the troll and gripped her sword hilt, put a boot on its leg and heaved. With a sucking squelch the blade pulled free.

Shouts, another scream drew her attention and she whirled to see the man who had been fighting the troll stabbing one of the Battle-Grim with his spear. The blade had scored a deep wound across a man's shoulder. As Elvar watched his shield arm dropped, and the spear stabbed into his throat, a burst of bright blood as he fell gurgling. Six or seven warriors pressed in about the fur-clad man, all with shields raised, a half-circle closing tighter. Sighvat was behind them, swinging a chain around his head.

Now that the fur-clad man was stood close to other men and women rather than the troll, Elvar realised that he was huge, tall and broad, swathed in furs, his beard hanging almost to his belt. He swung his spear in vicious swipes, backing away from the shields closing about him.

He moved closer to the molten pool, heat battering at his back, the pool and waterfall hissing and deafening. Sparks flickered along his fur cloak, his hair sizzling as he took another step backwards. He stopped, face twisting, realising he was trapped. A shift in his eyes as he looked at the Battle-Grim closing about him. A deep breath, muscles tensing for a charge, and then Sighvat's chain crunched into his head, hurling him to the ground, his spear falling away. He pushed himself on to all fours, blood welling, pouring down one cheek. He rose to one knee, hand grasping for his spear. Sighvat pushed through the Battle-Grim and punched the fallen man on the chin, his head snapping back, and he fell again, rolled on to his side, spitting blood. Began to rise.

How is he still conscious? Elvar thought. She had seen Sighvat in the pugil-ring. When he punched someone, they usually didn't get back up.

Agnar appeared, striding over, his sword retrieved from the troll's back and dripping with gore. Elvar and Grend followed.

Sighvat was booming orders, warriors holding spears at the fallen man's throat while others pinned iron collars and chains around his wrists. A thrall-collar appeared in Sighvat's big fists as the prisoner was dragged to his knees, arms bound. Sighvat moved to place the collar around the man's neck, but his eyes bulged at the sight of the iron collar and he dragged two warriors holding his chains off their feet, started to rise.

Agnar stepped forwards, his sword levelled at the man's throat.

"I would stay still, Berak, if I were you," Agnar said.

The big man froze, looked at the sword point at his throat, then up at Agnar.

"You have the wrong man," he said.

"No, you are Berak Bjornasson. I have tracked you a long way."

The man shook his head.

"Take the chains; it is your best choice. Struggle again and I shall have Sighvat beat you bloody with the collar that you will be wearing. There is no escaping us. You must know this."

The man looked from Agnar to the warriors behind him, eyes flickering across Elvar and Grend. Over twenty warriors, all pointing sharp iron at him.

He lowered his head.

"I am not who you think I am."

"My *Hundur*-thrall says that you are." Agnar pointed his sword at the thrall still pinned to the tree. He looked over at them, his face creased with misery.

Sighvat slipped the collar around the man's throat and tapped the pin in with the pommel of his seax.

"He is mistaken," the fur-clad man said, his shoulders slumping.

"Are you sure about him?" Elvar whispered to Agnar.

Agnar looked at her, frowned.

"Yes," he said.

"It is only, he is big, yes, strong, yes, but I have seen . . . " Elvar paused, choosing her words carefully, as there were more ears than Agnar's around her. "I have heard tales of the *Berserkir*. I expected . . . more."

Agnar shrugged. "Watch," he said, then looked away towards the slope, where warriors were returning with two captives, a woman and child. "Bring them to me," Agnar said.

The woman and child were pushed stumbling to Agnar, their wrists bound with rope. Agnar grabbed a fistful of the child's unkempt black hair. He took his sword and touched its edge to the child's throat.

"No," the woman cried and Sighvat clubbed her across the shoulders, knocking her to the ground.

"Show yourself," Agnar said to the man, who returned his gaze.

Agnar drew the sword back a half-inch, a red line trickling down the boy's neck.

"Don't," the man said. A shift in his voice, deeper, more a growl than a word.

Agnar smiled. "I will bleed him here, now; watch as his life spills on to the snow and you can see him flop and die like a gutted fish."

Elvar looked away. Killing children was not her way of earning her battle-fame.

"Watch him," Agnar snapped at Elvar, and she focused on the prisoner on his knees.

The man closed his eyes, seemed to take in an impossibly long breath.

Agnar jerked the boy's hair, a yelp breaking from his lips.

The man's eyes snapped open. They were flecked with amber, now, inhuman. As Elvar stared at him he seemed to swell, to grow, the furs about his shoulders and chest straining.

"Let him go," he snarled, and his mouth looked different, the tips of his teeth sharp.

"No," Agnar said, and twisted the boy's hair again. Another yelp.

The man lurched to his feet, roaring, and surged at Agnar, arms reaching, dragging six men and Sighvat along with him, as if they were puppies holding on to a wolf.

Or a bear.

"*HALDA!*" Agnar bellowed, taking an involuntary step backwards.

There was a flash of red fire in the iron collar about the fur-clad man's neck and he stumbled another step, took another as if wading through water, then stopped. Froze. He glared at Agnar, every muscle in his body quivering as if he fought against some invisible restraint. His eyes were threaded with red veins, foam and blood on his lips where he was snarling and gnashing his teeth, his hands grasping. Elvar noted his nails had grown, become more like claws.

"On your knees," Agnar said.

The man glowered at him, a mad rage in his eyes.

"*Á HNÉN!*" Agnar yelled and the fur-clad man dropped to the ground, panting.

The boy and woman were sobbing.

Agnar looked at Elvar.

"You still have your doubts?" he asked, a smile twitching his lips.

Elvar shook her head.

Agnar looked back at the man at his feet.

"You are Berak Bjornasson, and the blood of the dead god Berser flows in your veins. You are Tainted, you are *Berserkir*, and you are wanted by three jarls for murder, blood-debt and weregild. And now you are mine," Agnar said, and smiled. "You will fetch a fine price."

He looked around him, at the dead troll, at his warriors, both standing and fallen.

"Gather our dead. Butcher the troll. Bring all that is of value."

CHAPTER EIGHT

ORKA

Orka sat on the steps of the hall at their steading, running a whetstone along the blade of her seax. She kept one eye on Breca, who was collecting eggs from the chicken roost. The lad was constantly looking from his task to a small handcart. It had a bandaged tennúr sitting in the back, propped up on blankets.

The steps creaked and Thorkel sat down beside her.

"That's a hard-thinking look you have upon your face," Thorkel said, leaning close to look into her eyes. He stroked a strand of blonde hair out of her face, streaked with iron. "And I would like to know what is going on in that thought-cage of yours?"

Orka took her eyes from Breca and looked at him.

"I am thinking that you cannot say no to our son," she said flatly, looking pointedly back at the tennúr in Breca's cart.

A twist of Thorkel's lips, a shrug of his shoulders. "Aye, I may be guilty of that, but then, he has your eyes, and I'm not remembering the last time I said no to you, either. You two have a strange power over me."

"You wouldn't dare say no to me," Orka said, not able to keep the hint of a smile from softening the hard line of her mouth.

"Ha, true enough," Thorkel grinned. He leaned closer and brushed her cheek with his lips, his beard tickling her.

"But you are too soft on him," she said.

"Or maybe it is that you are too *hard* on him," Thorkel breathed.

Orka snapped a glare at him. "It is a hard world, and we will not always be here to protect him from it. We are not just his parents; we are his teachers, too."

"Aye, we are," Thorkel agreed. "But he is ten winters old, and he has learned much already. Let him be a boy. Plenty of time yet before he steps out into that dark world."

"And what if that tennúr decides to cut our throats in our sleep, or we catch a fever and die? How will all your softness help Breca then?"

Another shrug from the big man. "The tennúr will not harm him, or us. We have seen enough of life's sharp edge. At his age I wore a thrall's collar and my back had been opened by a lash." He looked at Orka. "Remember what we have seen and suffered. I would shelter him from that, while I can."

Orka nodded and stopped sharpening her seax. The blade's edge gleamed, sharp as a razor. "Aye, I feel that too. But I worry. We will not always be here to protect him . . ."

Thorkel wrapped an arm around her shoulder and squeezed her so hard she felt her bones grind.

"Ach, woman, you worry too much," he said, a finger tracing the sharp line of her cheek and jaw. "Look around you. We live free; we are the masters of our own steading, no oaths or bonds to tie us. The air is clean and pure up here. Spring is upon us, the sun is shining, and we have a fine son to raise." He gave Orka a smile, and a look she knew well. "I have been thinking, perhaps Breca would like a little brother or sister, to help him with his chores."

"Ha," Orka sniffed, "it is dangerous when you think. Besides, we are too old."

"Old!" Thorkel said, grinning now and stretching his arms wide. "I feel like a young colt with green meadows before me. I will always be here, with you and Breca." He stamped a foot on the stair and snorted like a stallion. "These are the days we dreamed of. Now that they are here, are real, let us enjoy them."

Orka shook her head. "You are like rune-magic to me, Thorkel Ulfsson. How is it that we have faced the same horrors, fought the same battles? The terrible things we have done. And yet . . . " She sighed. "I do not feel like a young horse before green meadows. How are you so strong, where I am so weak?"

"Weak? Are you moon-touched, woman? I would not challenge you to an arm-wrestle, let alone a *holmganga* duel."

"I do not mean physical strength, or skill with a blade. I mean strong *here*." She prodded her own head, hard, felt a ripple of anger flickering through her. Why could she not just rest, cut the ropes that moored the ghosts of the past to her?

Thorkel sighed, and she could see the care in him leaking from his eyes.

"I make a choice, each and every day," he said, his smile gone now. "I think on what I have. On what is before me. You. Breca. And they make my heart swell and my head giddy. There is no room left for any dwelling on the past."

She looked at him then, his nose twisted from being broken too many times, his eyes dark and kind, deep lines around them. Leaning forward she put a hand behind his neck and pulled him close, kissed him hard.

When she let him go Thorkel was grinning again.

"Ah, but I love you," he breathed. "And I love my son." He looked over at Breca, a bruise purpling on his cheek where Orka had cuffed him. "He has learned his lesson today."

"Has he?" Orka asked, looking at Breca. He was pulling the handcart by a rope towards the stream, lifting out a bowl and squatting beside Spert's rock. The creature's grey-skinned head breached the water and regarded him.

"*You're late. Spert dying of hunger,*" the creature grumbled.

"Here you go, then," Breca said, placing the bowl down on a rock beside the stream. "Best eat before you collapse and die." The many-legged creature crawled out of the water, its segmented body glistening. Spert paused, lifted its head and sniffed, its spiked antennae twitching.

"*Vaesen,*" it hissed, and abruptly its mouth seemed to grow, skin peeling back, the bones of its jaws protruding, opening wide, its teeth sharp and slick. It hissed, a black vapour issuing from its throat, becoming a cloud in the air.

"NO," Breca said, holding up a hand. "It's only Vesli." He pointed at the wounded tennúr in the cart, who was staring at Spert, her lips drawn back in a blend of fear and threat, like a cornered fox.

The black smoke pouring from Spert's mouth stopped bubbling, hung in the air.

"She is injured, has been outcast by her pack. She is alone, just like you were."

"*Don't trust vaesen*," Spert muttered.

Breca laughed.

"*You're* vaesen," he said.

"*Huh*," Spert grunted. "*Tennúr are sly, not to be trusted. They will steal your teeth*." One of Spert's many legs rose and stroked his bristling fangs. "*Spert like his teeth*."

The tennúr shifted in the cart, the blanket around her falling away to reveal the bandages Breca had wrapped around her wounds.

"*Vesli be* true," she said in a voice like the rustle and scrape of wind through leaves. "*Vesli swear oath to Spertus and Maður-boy*." She looked from Spert to Breca. "*Vesli swear to be a friend to Spertus and Maður-boy. And friends don't steal teeth*."

Spert stared at Vesli, his too-small, old-man face creased and thoughtful. "*Swear it with blood, then. Blood is binding*."

Vesli looked from Spert to Breca. With a shrug and ripple of her wings she placed a taloned finger against her palm and drew it slowly across her skin, blood welling. She bunched her fist, blood dripping.

"*Vesli swear to be faithful and true, to the Maður-boy Breca, and to his guardian Spertus. Vesli swears it on her life-blood*."

Spert regarded her, then his body also rippled, like a shrug, and he took a deep breath, sucking back in the black mist that was hanging in the air. His head dropped into the bowl and he began to eat his porridge mixed with Orka's blood and spit, for it was she who had caught him and bound him to her, all those years ago. There was much slurping and sucking.

"It looks like he has a new pet to play with. As if Spert wasn't enough," Orka said, frowning.

"That evil little bastard is no pet," Thorkel said. "But Spert does his job well enough. We all sleep safer for him. And that tennúr, it will be bonded to Breca now. It owes him a blood-debt, if it survives. I think he is safe enough. And besides, vaesen live a long time and friends are good. Does it ease your mind that Breca will have a tennúr watching over him when we are food for worms?" He smiled at her, prodded her shoulder.

"You won't be smiling so much when you wake up to find the little shite has stolen all the teeth from your gums."

Thorkel blinked at that and put a hand to his mouth.

"Do you think she would?"

Orka sheathed her seax in its scabbard and stood.

"That thing you said earlier, about making a brother or sister for Breca . . . " She held out her hand and Thorkel smiled up at her.

"We'd best be quick about it. Your smile won't charm me the same once it's just red gums and your teeth are in Vesli's belly."

Thorkel took her hand, pulled himself upright and they walked into their hall.

A sound drifted through the steading. A horse's whinny, the jangle of harness and the steady rhythm of hooves.

"Breca, take your new friend inside," Orka called out as she stepped inside the hall and reached for her spear. She stood at the top of the steps, listening, as Thorkel disappeared into their hall. He reappeared with a long-hafted axe in his fists, the haft as tall as him, the blade bearded and sharp. Orka stared at it, in her head heard an ear-splitting scream and saw a warrior silhouetted by flames swinging a long-axe, gore dripping. She felt her skin prickle with sweat, then looked at Thorkel, saw that he had that flat, dead-eyed look, like a shark when it strikes.

Thorkel looked back at her.

"There are child-stealers in this land. They'll not be taking my son from me."

A curt nod from Orka. She shook her head and gave a shudder of muscle through her whole body, as if shaking off memories like a horse does flies.

Together they strode to the gates as Breca swept the tennúr into his arms and ran up the steps into the hall.

The horses' hooves grew louder, more than one, and Orka strode to their gate, Thorkel at her shoulder. A thumping on timber sounded, like a spear butt or sword pommel.

"Thorkel, Orka, open your gates," a voice called out.

Orka reached them first. She pulled back a bolt and looked through a spyhole, then nodded at Thorkel. Together they shouldered the oak beam that barred the gates and dropped it. With a creak of hinges they swung the gates open.

Three riders sat looking down at them: a young man and two women, all warriors, the man with a sword at his hip, belted over a fine *brynja*, a glistening bead of snot clinging to the end of his long nose. The other two wore boiled leather and wool, felt and fur caps on their heads. Spears rested in the crooks of their arms.

"Guðvarr," Thorkel said with a nod to the man. Orka saw the light return to his eyes. They both knew these three were not the child-stealers. They would not have been capable of putting Asgrim and Idrun in the ground.

"And what brings three *drengr* warriors to our gates?" Orka asked. "You are a long way from Fellur."

Guðvarr stared down at Orka, looking like he'd eaten something that had left a sour taste in his mouth. Orka wished he would wipe the snot from his nose.

"Jarl Sigrún is returned to us," Guðvarr said. "She has called the Althing. Six days from now, on the Oath Rock in the fjord."

"You have come all this way to tell us that?" Orka said.

"Aye. Serious matters are to be discussed. Jarl Sigrún wants all who live within her domain to be present, to hear what she has to say."

"And if we do not want to hear what she has to say?" Orka growled.

Guðvarr blinked, as if that thought were an impossibility.

"Then you should find somewhere else to live," one of the other *drengrs* said, a tall, wiry woman with brown braided hair and a face of sharp ridges and angles. "If you choose to dwell within Jarl Sigrún's realm, under her protection, then you will be at the Althing."

"Well said, Arild," Guðvarr grunted.

"Our thanks," Thorkel said. "You are welcome to some food and drink, and to rest your horses. It must have been a long, hard ride." He waved a hand, gesturing at the courtyard and hall.

"No," Guðvarr said with a shake of his head. "We have three more steadings to visit, and then we are riding back for Fellur." As he tugged on his reins and his mount turned away, Guðvarr looked back over his shoulder.

"Six days, at the Oath Rock," he said, and then they were riding away across the glade, following a narrow path into the trees.

Thorkel and Orka closed the gates and barred them.

"I do not want to go to this Althing," Orka said. "With Sigrún talking of Queen Helka, of jarls and queens and their petty squabbles."

"I do not want to go either," Thorkel said. He was tugging his beard, a distant look in his eyes. "But we do not want to attract attention, either, by staying away. It will be noted, if by no one else then by Guðvarr."

"He is an arseling," Orka growled.

"Aye, that he is," Thorkel agreed. "An arseling who will flap his lips about us. I say we go to this Althing, keep our heads down and our lips stitched shut, and then leave quietly." He shrugged. "A voice in my thought-cage is telling me we need to hear what Sigrún has to say. If Helka has her eyes on Fellur and these hills . . ."

They shared a look as Breca stuck his head out of the hall, the tennúr cradled in his arms.

"We'll go to Sigrún's Althing, then," Orka said, blowing out a long breath and nodding her head, though she felt a wyrm of fear slithering in her belly. She had seen that look in Thorkel's eyes before, and it had never meant anything good.

CHAPTER NINE

ELVAR

Elvar woke shivering, muted light glimmering in her eyes. Her back ached, stones from the beach felt through her cloak and mail. The rhythmic ebb and flow of wave over shingle was the first sound she heard. Above her an awning rigged with spear-shaft posts was heavy with last night's snowfall, a spare sail used to provide some kind of protection against the weather. She rolled and crawled out from under it.

The sun was rising behind her, molten bronze gilding the hills and mountain that dominated this island, and to the west, over the sea beyond the rise and creak of the moored *Wave-Jarl*, the sky was a pale, cold blue, the wind off the bay feeling like shards of ice scraping across her skin. The sea moved sluggishly, patches of ice that the spring thaw had broken free from the Frost-Isles further north floating thick and churning on its surface. In the distance she saw the silhouettes of other islands, like the humped backs of submerged giants. White-flecked waves lapped the shore.

I hate the north. She stood and stretched, the sealskin cloak she had used as a blanket falling open as she rolled her shoulders, adjusting the weight of her *brynja*. They were still on the beach at Iskalt, and though the villagers were subdued and kept under guard until they left, she felt safer in her coat of mail.

Other shapes still slept beneath the awning. She saw Biórr's long boots poking out, that others laughed at. Higher up the beach she saw Grend was crouched beside a fire, ladling porridge from an iron pot into wooden bowls. He saw her and strode over, shingle crunching beneath his boots.

"Snow's passed," he said, handing Elvar the porridge. She wrapped her hands around the bowl, heat seeping through her nålbinding mittens.

"You were supposed to wake me for last watch," she said with a scowl. Her body was grateful for Grend's kindness, after the fight with the troll and hard climb into and out of the hills, but she had not risen to her position in the Battle-Grim through avoiding duties. She was the one who always did *more*, and now she had earned her place in the front row of the shield wall.

Kindness makes you soft, her father's words whispered.

She blew on her porridge and spooned some into her mouth, enjoying the warmth.

"I couldn't sleep," he shrugged. The black circles around his eyes betrayed him for a liar. He was no young warrior any more, the winters laying heavy upon his back, though he could most likely still put any one of the Battle-Grim on their arse, even Sighvat. Elvar had seen him do it, when the mead was flowing around a hearth fire and the warriors were bragging, hurling their challenges like spears. Grend never bragged. He did not need to. Just looking into his eyes was enough.

There was a rumble, like distant thunder, but Elvar felt it rise up through her boots, a tremor in her bones, stones on the beach shifting like sand through fingers. In the distance the slopes of the fire mountain heaved, trees rippling, banks of snow falling and the red veins of molten fire flared bright. Elvar felt a rush of fear, the world seeming to pause as all on the beach stopped what they were doing and stared at the mountain.

And then the world returned to normal, the rumble fading like a distant storm.

"Lik-Rifa chafes at her chains," Grend muttered.

"The dragon-god is long dead, if she ever lived," Elvar replied.

Grend looked at her as if she were moon-touched. "All know she did not die on the day of *Guðfalla* with the other gods," Grend grunted. "She was trapped by deep-cunning in a chamber beneath Oskutreð, the Ash Tree, and so could not stand beside her father, Snaka."

Elvar shrugged. "And what would a dragon find to eat for nearly three hundred years in a chamber of stone and root and soil?" Elvar snorted. "If she ever lived, she is surely dead of starvation."

"She tears at the souls of warriors as they pass through her chamber on the soul road," Grend said, "all know this. This is why we must die with a weapon in our fists, to fight her as we pass through Vergelmir, her dark chamber. It is the warriors' last test."

"A faery tale to make children behave," Elvar said, remembering the stories her father had told her and her brothers of Lik-Rifa, and how she would eat children who strayed from their homes at night.

"Then how do you explain that?" Grend said, nodding at the red-veined mountain. "Did you not feel the earth move?"

"Because I do not know the reason for a thing, does not mean that a dragon-god did it," Elvar said.

"This is why you have no friends," Grend huffed and shook his head.

"Huh," Elvar grunted and went back to her porridge.

As she ate, she searched the beach and saw warriors from the Battle-Grim emerging from village huts, many rolling barrels of pickled fish and brine-salted shark meat down to the pier and the *Wave-Jarl*. Two men carried a rope-tied bundle of walrus ivory. Others hefted rolled furs on their shoulders, pelts of bear and reindeer and arctic fox. Two warriors herded a half-dozen bleating goats down the beach to the pier. Agnar appeared in his black bearskin cloak, Sighvat behind him, leading the *Hundur*-thrall and the new captive, Berak, by chains, a dozen Battle-Grim warriors following them. Other warriors appeared, escorting Berak's wife and child on to the beach.

Agnar saw Elvar and changed his course, striding towards her as Sighvat put a horn to his lips and blew, the sound loud and melancholy, echoing along the beach. All who were still clinging to sleep beneath the *Wave-Jarl*'s spare sail were awake now, crawling out on to the shingle and grumbling at the cold. Spear shafts were taken down and the sail rolled. Elvar saw Biórr rise to his feet, bleary-eyed, black hair a tangle. He saw her and dipped his head, gave her a smile.

"I don't like him," Grend growled.

"You don't like anyone who likes me," Elvar replied.

Grend shrugged, not disputing that fact.

Agnar stopped before Elvar and Grend. He reached inside his cloak and pulled something out, opened his palm. It was one of the troll's tusks, long as a knife, a hole bored in one end with a leather thong threaded through it. He lifted it over Elvar's head and placed it about her neck.

"You did well," Agnar said, then walked on. Sighvat followed, the *Hundur*-thrall walking with head bowed and shoulders slumped. Berak, the new prisoner, had his eyes fixed on his wife and child, who were being led towards the pier. The iron collars around his neck and wrists had rubbed his skin raw.

Elvar grinned at Grend, feeling her chest swell with pride as she lifted the tusk and looked at it. A troll's tusk was worth more than its weight in gold, but Elvar did not care about that. It was the honour Agnar gave her, the battle-fame she had earned that set a fire in her chest. All around her the Battle-Grim were looking and nodding. They all wore some kind of trophy from a kill, a bone or tooth, a tusk, a nail, all gifted to them by Agnar when he thought they had earned it.

Little more than three years I have sailed with the Battle-Grim, and climbed high as any in that time.

"You struck the killing blow," Grend said, a smile even touching the corners of his mouth, the glint of teeth within his grey-streaked beard. "It is only just."

Elvar gave Grend her empty bowl and walked to the makeshift tent where the sail had already been rolled, retrieving her shield and spear. Grend strode past her, squatted in the foam and washed the bowls out. At the end of the pier warriors were boarding the *Wave-Jarl*, loading barrels and pelts. Elvar saw the captive woman and child sitting and waiting at the pier's edge, the boy dangling his legs over the shingle and foam.

Biórr approached them with two bowls of steaming porridge and offered them to the woman and child. Cautiously the woman took a bowl and said something to her son. Biórr crouched and gave him his porridge.

Then Agnar was bellowing orders and everything became a whirl of activity, warriors boarding the *Wave-Jarl*, stepping from the pier's boards over the top-rail and on to the ship's decks. Elvar strode from the beach to the pier, past a rack where the butchered troll's skin had been scraped of fat. Beside the rack sat a sack piled with the troll's skeleton, its flesh boiled from its bones. There were barrels packed with the valued parts of the creature, its skin rolled, teeth in a clay jar, the testicles in brine, heart and liver in a barrel hard packed with ice. Toenails for grinding into powder. All of it would fetch a good price.

Elvar stepped lightly from the pier on to the ship's deck, shuffled around the goats that were being herded to the rear of the ship and penned beneath an awning of spare sail. She stacked her spear in the racks amidships, exchanging them for her oar, and then made for her chest. In the curve of the bow, beneath the *drakkar*'s prow, Kráka the Tainted thrall was curled in sleep.

Elvar reached her chest and wedged her shield into the rack pinned along the top-rail's rim, tugged off her mittens, unbuckled her weapons belt, wrapped it around her sword, axe and seax, then opened her chest and lay them inside. She took off her other belt, which held her pouch of kindling and medicine pouch and also helped to take the weight of her mail, and placed that in the chest too. Bending over she wriggled out of her *brynja* like a snake shedding its skin and wrapped the mail coat in sheepskin. Then she was closing the lid, pinning her sealskin cloak about her with an iron brooch and tugging her mittens back on.

All those around her were going through the same process, warriors stacking and storing provisions, loading their chests, storing their weapons and mail. Sighvat was at the rear of the deck, securing the two collared thralls with iron rings and pins hammered into the top-rail. The woman and child were pushed under the awning to sit with the goats.

Something drew Elvar's eye, in the water off the starboard side of the *drakkar*. Lumps of ice moved there, and one lifted against the swell of the outgoing tide. A splash, a ripple and a wake of white foam.

"WARE THE WATER!" Elvar yelled.

A moment's silence passed as heads turned to her, even as she was leaping from her sea-chest and running for her spear. Then there was an explosion of ice and sea spray as a shape burst from the water, a serpentine body, its scaled head as big as one of the huts on the beach, mouth gaping with rows of razored teeth, soft flesh inside its mouth a deep, blood-flushed red.

"*SJÁVARORM!*" Agnar bellowed as the sea serpent's head struck at the awning where the goats were bleating. Blood and screams as the jaws clamped tight, the head rearing with a mouthful of bloodstained sail and half a shredded goat dangling. The other goats leaped away, the captive woman and boy hurled in different directions.

Spears flew at the serpent, some piercing its sinuous, grey-green hide, dark blood oozing. Its head reared high, jaws opening as it swallowed the half-goat into its throat, then its head and part of its body crashed down on the deck, the top-rail splintering, ship pitching wildly, voices screaming. Sighvat stomped forwards and swung a hand-axe that crunched into the serpent's body, just below the base of the skull. The serpent thrashed, slamming into Sighvat and sending him flying from his feet, then slithered the other way and connected with the captive boy, who was trying to reach his mother. He was hurled into the air and flew over the ship's side into the sea.

Berak the *Berserkir* roared and leaped after his son, the chains around his neck and wrist yanking him back. He thrashed and screamed, but the chains held tight.

Without thinking Elvar found herself leaping on to the top-rail, searching for any sign of the child. A shadow beneath the waves, sinking, then she was dropping her spear, sucking in a deep breath and leaping into the sea.

She heard Grend's voice, shouting her name.

Ice water, so cold it felt like a vice, crushed her chest. She saw the child, looking up, eyes bulging, arms reaching, and she kicked her feet, clawing her way towards him. Fingertips touched, then with another kick of her feet she had his wrist; she turned in the water and swam for the surface. The body of the serpent was close by, thick as a tree, descending into watery murk. Then she was breaking water, gasping cold air into her lungs as the serpent reared back from the *Wave-Jarl*'s deck and crashed back into the water, a wave that sent her and the child surging away from the ship.

A figure leaped from the ship's deck; there was a splash as Grend hit the water, taking powerful strokes as he swam towards her.

The boy had his head above water, was shouting, calling for his mother or father, Elvar thought, and thrashing in the water like a speared seal.

The serpent heard, its head snapping round, black eyes focusing on them. With an undulating ripple through its body it was speeding towards them, its muzzle cutting through water like a *drakkar*'s prow, a wake lifting Grend high. He bellowed, swam harder, but Elvar knew he was not going to reach her before the serpent. He changed course, veered in towards the sea creature, crashed into its body and dragged a knife from his belt, stabbing frantically. The sea frothed red, but the serpent took no notice.

Elvar reached for a weapon, found nothing, then remembered she'd packed her weapon's belt into her sea-chest.

I'm going to die.

Fear swept through her, the serpent's jaws opening, water dripping from rowed fangs.

She gritted her teeth, cursed the serpent as it sped at her, sucked in a breath as she prepared to dive beneath the waves with a foolish hope of evading the serpent's jaws.

A ripple ran through the creature's body, and a new sound filtered over the waves, a high-pitched, keening song. The serpent's head turned, rising from the water, its body slowing as it looked back at the ship.

A figure stood on the top-rail, a woman, and she was singing.

The serpent's head hovered above the water, its body coming to a standstill, just floating on the sea swell. Then it let out a stuttering hiss and dived beneath the sea, the bulk of its body rising and then sinking, a spray of water from its tail, and in heartbeats the sea was calm, as if the serpent had never been.

Grend reached her, wrapped an arm around her and dragged them towards the ship. A rope was thrown down for them, arms reaching, pulling them up on to the deck, where Elvar flopped like a fish, gasping and shivering.

The boy's mother ceased her singing and ran to her son, prising him from Elvar's arms, hugging him tight, the boy sobbing.

"Fool," Grend muttered as he fell over the top-rail and lay beside Elvar, then he sat and looked at her. "Are you hurt?"

"No," she said, "though I can't feel my toes."

"I hope the fish have chewed them off and taught you a lesson. Fool."

"You followed me. What does that make you?" Elvar said, grinning.

"An even greater fool," Grend muttered.

A hand touched Elvar's cheek: the boy's mother.

"Thank you," the woman breathed.

Elvar nodded, looking into the woman's eyes. Pale, grey-blue like the sea on a wind-calm day. Her hair was fair, face pale; a glimpse of blue tattoos spiralled beneath the tunic and cloak pulled tight around her neck.

"What did you throw into the molten pool?" Elvar asked her, her voice quiet and low.

The woman blinked, her lips hardening, and she stared back at her.

Agnar appeared over them, looking at the boy's mother.

"So, you are a Seiðr-witch, with Snaka's blood in your veins," he said, a smile splitting his face. "If the gods were not all dead, I would think they were smiling on me."

The woman said nothing.

Agnar's eyes narrowed. "Use your powers on my crew and there will be nothing left of your son to feed a serpent," he said.

The woman held his gaze and gave a curt nod.

Agnar smiled.

"Dry clothes for them," he called out, then he turned and strode along the deck, past pools of blood and water as warriors set about clearing pieces of goat from the deck and checking the hull's strakes where the serpent had crashed into the ship. Agnar approached the *Wave-Jarl*'s prow, a rune-carved dragon glaring out at the sea, where Kráka the thrall sat, staring up at Agnar.

He pulled an arm back and slapped her face.

"Your task is to protect my ship and crew from sea vaesen," he growled.

"I am sorry, lord," Kráka said, blood leaking from her lip. "I was not prepared, was asleep." She shook her head. "I have sung a protection all the long way here." Her face was grey as an ash tree, with deep-sunken lines as if her face was melted wax.

The Seiðr-song takes its toll.

Agnar lifted his hand to strike Kráka again, but paused and lowered his arm.

"Perhaps I have asked too much of you." He dropped one of the troll's antlers into her lap, her long, bony hands stroking the soft, velvet-covered prongs.

"Some power for you," he said. "For the journey home."

"Thank you, lord," she breathed.

"See us through these waters," Agnar said, touching his fingers to the iron chain that bound her, "and keep the serpents from our hull."

She looked up at him.

"*Hlýða og fá verðlaun*," he grated in the Galdur-tongue, veins of red tracing the cold iron, a map of fire around Kráka's throat.

"Yes, lord," she said, nodding.

Agnar turned and strode back to the tiller, the ship cleared now, the surviving goats penned, and men and women sat at their sea-chests, waiting.

Elvar stripped out of her wet clothes and pulled on wool breeches and tunic, then made her way back to her sea-chest, sat and drew in a deep breath. Her blood was still speeding through her veins, the thrill of standing in death's shadow, the elation at cheating death, a flood of her senses, the joy of *being alive*. Grend sat in front of her and gave her one final dark look.

"OARS!" Sighvat cried and Elvar swivelled the oar-plug that covered the oar-hole, threaded her oar through it and sat on her chest, holding the oar hovering above the swell and slap of the waves.

The mooring rope was loosed, and spears pushed them away from the pier, the outgoing tide tugging them into deeper water.

"OARS!" Sighvat bellowed and fifty oars bit into the cold sea.

"PULL!" and Elvar was moving, back and shoulders put to the heave and roll as Sighvat found a knotted line of rope and beat time on an old shield. The *drakkar* moved sluggishly at first, pulling out into the bay, then picking up speed, cutting a white wound through the green-black waters, an ice-wind from the north carving tears from Elvar's eyes, though her body was warm in fifty heart-beats, and soon after sweat was steaming on her brow.

They passed through the curling arms of black-granite rock that formed the bay, the seals and puffins still there. And then they were pulling out into open sea, the wind slamming into the starboard, waves abruptly higher. Elvar spied movement in the water, the swell and slither of things beneath the waves as Agnar wrestled the tiller, then the prow turned southwards and Kráka began her serpent-song. It cut through the hiss of the wind and roar of the sea, spreading like a net, and the hint of things beneath the waves faded.

"MAST!" Sighvat yelled, and a dozen warriors shipped their oars and jumped to the deck, slotting the mast into its hole amidships, wedges hammered into place to hold it steady, while others tugged on the halyard rope and raised the yardarm, the *Wave-Jarl*'s white sail unfurled, hanging limp like an empty mead skin for a few heartbeats as the rigging was tied off, then catching the north-westerly that was ripping through this channel among the islands, and the *drakkar* leaped southwards like a sea stallion.

"OARS!" Sighvat bellowed, and Elvar lifted her oar from the water, pulling it back in, water dripping, and set it amidships. She sat on her bench and sucked in deep breaths, feeling the burn in her back and shoulders slowly fade.

A figure sat next to her and she looked up to see Agnar. He was grinning, as he always was when they were at sea. Sighvat stood by the tiller and rudder, steering them southwards.

"You are either very brave, or very crazy, maybe even moon-touched," he said, shaking his head, "leaping into a serpent-infested sea."

Elvar shrugged, not sure which one it was. Courage or madness.

Maybe madness. I do not take the time to think about it. Can that still be courage?

Agnar took a gold ring from his arm and slipped it around Elvar's upper arm, squeezing it tight.

"My thanks, lord," she breathed.

"Courage and madness in the face of vaesen-serpents are both admirable qualities, and deserve rewarding," Agnar said.

His smile faded.

"You should know, I am planning on taking our prize to Snakavik. Jarl Störr is famed for his *Berserkir* thrall-guard, and I am thinking he will give us the best price."

Elvar stared at Agnar. She felt like a stone had just been dropped into the pit of her stomach, dousing the joy she had felt at Agnar's ring-giving.

Agnar shrugged. "Best you know now. Will this be a problem to you?"

"No," Elvar said when she found her tongue, though the churning in her belly told her different.

"Good," Agnar said, standing. "You have climbed high in the Battle-Grim," he said. "Think of this as another battle, but one you fight with your wits and cunning, not the edge of your blade."

Elvar nodded and Agnar walked away.

Grend turned on his sea-chest and just stared at her.

"We are going home then," she said.

CHAPTER TEN

ORKA

Orka climbed the winding path that led to the Oath Rock. A westerly wind hissed across the island in the fjord and whipped the waters around it, sending white-tipped waves on to the beach before the village of Fellur. Orka paused, and looking back saw a host of boats rowing across to the Oath Rock island, mostly fishing boats and light *snekkes*, though Orka saw a *drakkar* pull away from the village's pier. Thirty oars made for a small *drakkar*, though its hull and strakes were sleek and wolfish, the prow tall and proud. Seeing it stirred Orka's blood.

Jarl Sigrún and her *drengrs*.

"Come on, Mama," Breca said, pulling at her sleeve. He was excited at his first Althing, and Thorkel was striding ahead of them, disappearing around a curve of moss-covered rock. Orka grunted and walked on, following a path that twisted up through bracken and wind-blasted trees until it levelled out and spilled into a clearing. The remnants of a huge, rune-carved stone stood there. It had stood taller, once, but now it was smashed to little more than a stump, the faint angles of runes barely visible in the jagged shards of its base.

Breca gasped as he saw the rock, then frowned.

"What's wrong?" Thorkel said as he leaned against the trunk of a twisted hawthorn tree. He wore his grey nålbinding cap and a wolfskin cloak over his woollen tunic, a seax and hand-axe hanging at his belt.

"It's smaller than I thought," Breca said.

"Well, it was bigger once. Maybe as tall as a mead hall," Thorkel said. "It has been smashed with hammers."

"That is a shame," Breca said.

Thorkel raised an eyebrow.

"Why destroy something that someone cared enough to build?" Breca said.

"Ha, that is some deep-thinking, there," Thorkel smiled. "Hmm, some take pleasure in destruction. But this is different. This was an oath stone, where humankind swore their blood oaths to the gods, pledged their allegiances, worshipped them. And worshipping the dead gods is forbidden, now, punishable by death."

An image flashed through Orka's mind, of a woman hanging in an iron cage, ravens picking at her eyes and tongue.

"That doesn't seem fair," Breca said. "What harm can it do?"

"What harm?" Thorkel laughed. "The dead gods caused a *lot* of harm, most would say. They broke the world. That is why they are hated, why when the few survivors of the *Guðfalla* emerged from the ruin of Snaka's fall they hated and hunted the offspring of the gods, those whose blood was tainted with the gods' bloodlines."

Breca chewed his lip as he thought about that.

"Then why do they hold the Althing here?"

"Another good, deep-thinking question," Thorkel shrugged. "Perhaps because the past runs deep in our blood and bones," he muttered. "A rope we cannot see, binding us to it, whether we like it or not."

Orka could see by the frown on his face that Breca didn't much like that answer. She stood by her husband, letting the hawthorn tree and Thorkel's bulk shelter her from the worst of the wind's bite. She nodded a thanks to Virk, the fisherman who had invited them on to his boat, along with his two sons Mord and Lif, and rowed them over to the Oath Rock.

The clearing was filling with people, come from many leagues around for this Althing. Tents filled the meadows around Fellur, as the Althing could go on for a number of days and all who lived within the boundaries of Jarl Sigrún's land were supposed to attend, or at least a representative from every family. Orka saw fisherfolk and farmers, tanners and blacksmiths, shipwrights and leatherworkers, all manner of people who dwelled within the boundaries of Jarl Sigrún's domain, and that had been growing each year, along with the fair-fame of her name.

Orka caught Virk's eye and she beckoned him over.

"Our thanks," she said, "for rowing us over." She offered him a nugget of hacked bronze.

"Keep it," Virk said, "and think kindly of me when you next bring your pelts to the village."

Orka nodded. "That we can do, as long as we have a seat on your boat back to shore when this is done."

"That would depend on how kind you will be with your pelts," he smiled.

"Tell me," she said, leaning closer and whispering, "is there any word of Asgrim's boy, Harek?"

Virk's smile withered and he shook his head.

"Guðvarr sent some scouts to the river, where your husband followed the tracks. But no more than that. No boats sent down the rivers, no hounds." He shook his head. "He did not care. Asgrim and Idrun were freedmen, had as much right to justice as any, but . . ."

Orka knew. She remembered Guðvarr's words.

They were asking for trouble, Guðvarr had said. Orka felt her lip curl in anger at the memory of it. *Asking for trouble, as if living a life apart from the village makes us less.*

"And other children?" she asked Virk. "You said Harek is not the first child to be taken."

Virk shrugged. "The Haraldursons from Howbyr, they had two daughters and a son taken, their cots empty in the morning, just gone. And a family in Kergarth, I forget their names. Found dead, like Asgrim and Idrun, and their sons missing." He looked at her. "That does not sound like a coincidence to me."

Orka nodded. Howbyr was ten or twelve leagues north, and Kergarth was six leagues east along the coast.

"There are other rumours, of more children taken, but I do not know for sure."

"It must be *niðing*, lawless men," Orka said, "stealing children and selling them on as thralls." An image came to her mind of Breca being snatched in the night, dragged away. An iron collar snapped around his throat. Wings of fear fluttered in her chest, followed by a shiver of anger. She rested a hand on Breca's shoulder.

"I agree," Virk said. "Maybe *we* should try hunting them, see if we can do better than Guðvarr. That shouldn't be hard: he is a pup playing at being a jarl."

"Catching thieves and killers is different from catching fish," Orka said.

"I have not always been a fisherman," Virk said with a shrug, dropping a hand to rest on the axe head that hung at his belt. "And I do not think you and your husband have always been trappers."

"We live in Vigrið, the Battle-Plain," Orka said with a shrug. "Only fools do not learn how to protect themselves."

Virk held his hands up at Orka's flat stare. "Your past is your business. But I'd rather have you or Thorkel at my shoulder in a scrap than that snivelling weasel." He nodded towards Guðvarr. "And these *niðings* . . . " His face twisted. "Murderers and child-stealers, they do not deserve to breathe our air."

Orka nodded. She had known there was more to Virk than fishing, had seen men like him before, their emotions always bubbling below the surface like serpents beneathe the fjord's still waters, violence only a short explosion away. She knew well enough that the braggarts like Guðvarr were not the real warriors. It was the ones who never *threatened* violence . . .

The murmur of many conversations faded and Orka looked up to see warriors enter the clearing: a dozen *drengrs*, Guðvarr among them, swaggering in his *brynja* and sword at his hip, the permanent drop of moisture still hanging from the end of his nose. The women who had accompanied him to Orka's steading were there, Orka remembering Arild, the one with a face like a butcher's cleaver. They were all gleaming in mail, polished leather and arm rings of silver or bronze, spreading in a half-circle before the shattered remnants of the oath stone, allowing Jarl Sigrún to step out into the clearing, another dozen *drengrs* behind her.

She was tall, though not as tall or wide as Orka, but there was a strength and grace in her walk that spoke of a warrior. She wore a coat of riveted mail and had a silver torc around her neck, more rings of silver upon her arms. She had not become a jarl by kind words and good deeds; she was a warrior who had carved a piece of land for herself and fought all who challenged her. Men and women had stood with her, drawn by her strength and promises of land and status, and so her power had grown. It was a story Orka had seen a hundred times over. Where once this land had been free, it was now being swallowed piece by piece by petty jarls, men and women who hungered for wealth and power. Some were more successful than others, their battle-fame spreading, their wealth growing, warriors flocking to them. Jarl Sigrún was not the most powerful, but she was still a force to be watched. The fact that she had ruled here for eight years and was still breathing said much.

A pace behind her like a faithful hound another warrior strode: a woman, her face lean and scarred, the sides of her head shaved and pale, swirling with tattoos, a thick strip of grey-black braided hair running across the top of her head. She wore plain breeches and a tunic of wool, and had two seaxes hanging at her belt, one across the front, one suspended behind her back.

And she wore a thrall's collar.

But it was to her eyes that Orka was drawn. Flat and merciless, they scanned the crowd, as if weighing up their prey.

Jarl Sigrún had many thralls, to clean and cook and work her farms, but Orka had never seen her with a warrior-thrall before. And this one had a look that Orka had seen before.

A hopelessness that leaked from her.

The sight of her set Orka's skin crawling, as if spider-legs scuttled down her spine.

"Welcome, all," Jarl Sigrún said as she came to stand before the shattered oath stone, her *drengrs* arrayed about her like a curling hand, the warrior-thrall prowling behind her. Sigrún's voice was strong and confident, rising above the hiss of the wind and reaching across the crowd of hundreds. "I am not one for the flapping of lips and tongue, so I will say this straight and simple. I have sworn my oath to Queen Helka." She pulled up the woollen sleeve of her tunic and showed a fresh-scabbed cut on her forearm. "And sealed it with my blood."

A ripple of murmurs sounded around the clearing.

"You have come to tell us the good news of higher taxes, then," Virk called out beside Orka. Other voices shouted their agreement, and their anger.

Jarl Sigrún turned her eyes on Virk and held his gaze a long moment. Virk returned it. Orka could smell the anger seeping from him.

"No, I have come to tell you that the world is changing, and we must change with it," Sigrún said. "I became jarl of Fellur eight years ago and swore on my blood and life to protect the village, and those who lived within it. That is what I have done, and I have spread that protection, making life safer for you all on the plains and hills as far as your eyes can see."

"On a cloudy day, perhaps," one of Virk's sons whispered to the other.

"But I *cannot* protect you from what is to come," Sigrún said.

"Life is good here as it is," Virk answered, his sons adding their voices. "We do not need change, or Helka."

"Aye, life has been good, here at Fellur, but life runs in seasons, and seasons do not last for ever. Jarls are rising throughout all Vigrið, powerful jarls that I can no longer protect you from. Jarl Störr in the north-west has spread his borders ever south and east, and he has his eyes on this land. This fjord. Jarl Orlyg sitting in Svelgarth to the east has raided our lands. And Queen Helka, she too is . . . ambitious."

Ambitious jarls, I have seen the price of that. And Helka calls herself a queen. She would lift her head above the pack and rule them. It is as Thorkel feared. Worse.

Orka shared a look with Thorkel, whose brows were knotted in a thundercloud.

"She wants our land, and the fruits of our labour," Virk cried. "She would make of us tenants who pay tribute for land we've hunted and tamed and farmed with our own hands, no help from her."

The warrior-thrall stopped pacing and turned her flat eyes upon Virk. She stood unnaturally still.

One of Virk's sons touched his arm, but he shook it off.

Many shouts from the crowd agreed with Virk.

A man stepped forwards, a fine red felt hat upon his head, trimmed with fur, a pale beard hanging with gold rings across the breast of his red-wool tunic. Orka and Thorkel had traded with him before: Fálki Torilsson, once a farmer, now made wealthy by deposits of tin found beneath his pastureland.

"Virk speaks what many of us are thinking, Jarl Sigrún," Fálki said with a respectful bow. "And I am also thinking that we will be taxed for the honour of Helka's protection?" he added.

Jarl Sigrún shrugged. "Most likely, Fálki," she said. "It is the way of the world. Look at Iskidan in the south, a vast realm ruled over by one city, Gravka, and by one lord, the emperor Kirill. That is the way that Vigrið is going. It will happen soon. In our lifetime. The season is changing, autumn to winter, maybe, but there will be a spring beyond that, for those that survive the cold."

"Aye, Helka would make herself an emperor, like Kirill of Gravka," Virk spat. "But don't forget that his throne is built upon a mountain of corpses, that there are more thralls than freedmen in Iskidan, and that they sacrifice children."

Jarl Sigrún laughed. "I thought you above a child's saga-tale, Virk."

"It is true, I have sailed the whale road and *seen* it," Virk said.

"And you have drained many a mead horn, too, and perhaps dreamed of these things," Sigrún said, her *drengrs* laughing, Guðvarr loudest of all. "If these things were truth, I would do all in my power to not let that happen here." Jarl Sigrún frowned. "But I will not lie to you, Helka will want our coin, and our oaths. And I will tell you a harder truth; if I said *no* to her, she would still come and take this land for herself. We have not the strength to stop her. She would come, kill me and our strongest and put one of her own in the mead hall as jarl." She shook her head.

Orka nodded and thought well of Sigrún for admitting this hard truth. But her mind was running ahead, seeing in vivid colours the path Helka would take, the fields of blood and corpses she would tread in her quest to rule all Vigrið.

"But there will be benefits too," Jarl Sigrún said.

"Benefits!" Virk snorted, though others such as Fálki listened attentively.

"Aye, such as being on the winning side. It is only a matter of time before Störr and Helka face one another, and the winner will take all Vigrið. That could go well for us."

"And what if Helka loses?" another voice called out.

"She will not lose," Sigrún said. "I have seen her *drakkars*, and her warband. The bones of the dead god Orna rear over her fortress at Darl. I have seen the wings." She looked slowly across the crowd. "She will not lose." Her gaze fixed on Virk. "And taxes are a part of life, they are the road to safety and long-life. Queen Helka will protect us from the greater battles of Vigrið, and I will continue to protect you all, as best I can."

A thought was growing in Orka's mind, memories of battle and blood circling in her head like sea serpents smelling blood in the water.

"She will ask for a *hird*-offering from here," Orka said, for a moment not realising that she had uttered the words out loud.

Thorkel grunted and shifted against his tree, those close to Orka turning and staring at her.

She remembered Thorkel's words.

We will go to the Althing, keep our heads down and our lips stitched shut . . .

"Is that not so, Jarl Sigrún?" Orka asked her.

"She may," Jarl Sigrún said grudgingly.

"She will," Orka said. "She will take all with a strong arm that own a spear or axe to fight her war for her, the people of Fellur swelling her warband's ranks." Orka looked around at the crowd, seeing that realisation dawning in their eyes. The thought of putting down their tools and sharpening their spears and axes, of seeing their sons and daughters carried off on the wave of war.

"That is a long way from now, and much can happen," Sigrún said. "But it would be better than sitting in our fields and fisher boats when Jarl Störr's warband sweeps over the horizon or rows into the fjord. He will not offer us protection. He will offer us iron and blood and the thrall's collar. This is the only path I can see to protect us all."

"Protect us?" Virk said. "When you cannot even protect us against murderers and child-stealers?"

Jarl Sigrún's eyes flittered to Guðvarr.

"My nephew has told me of this, of Asgrim and Idrun."

"And Harek," Breca said, his voice high and shrill.

Orka felt a swell of pride for her son, having the stones to speak up for his friend in a gathering like this.

"Aye," Virk said, stepping out of the crowd. "A child stolen and two murdered, all living within your borders, under *your* protection." He looked at the gathering. "What protection is that?" he spat.

"You should step back, and close those flapping lips," Guðvarr said.

"And you should learn how to conduct a search, and fulfil your duties in your jarl's absence," Virk grunted. A few laughs rippled through the crowd, along with nodding heads and a murmur of agreement.

Guðvarr's lips twisted and his neck flushed red. He took a step towards Virk.

"My nephew has told me of this crime," Jarl Sigrún said, her voice loud and harsh, stopping Guðvarr. "He did all that could be done."

"That is a lie," Virk snapped.

Jarl Sigrún stared at him.

"You should not speak to your jarl so," the warrior-thrall at Sigrún's shoulder said, something in her voice silencing the whole clearing.

"You will ask my aunt's forgiveness for your insult," Guðvarr said.

Virk looked from Guðvarr to Jarl Sigrún, eyes flickering to the warrior-thrall at her shoulder.

"Forgive me, I meant no insult to you, Jarl Sigrún," Virk said, "I do not think you a liar." He paused, looking from her to Guðvarr. "The blame of it lies at your nephew's feet."

"I did all I could to find them," Guðvarr snapped, his voice rising.

"You squeak like a wire-trapped ferret," Virk said, "and as you cannot even find your nose to wipe it, how are you capable of finding stolen children, murderers and thieves?"

There were snorts of laughter at that.

Guðvarr's eyes bulged, his mouth moving, strangled sounds escaping his throat. He cuffed the end of his dripping nose.

"*Holmganga*," he snarled. "I challenge you, here, now." His hand moved to his sword.

"Guðvarr, stop this now," Jarl Sigrún snapped.

"It is too late," Guðvarr spat. "The challenge is out, before my jarl, before the people of Fellur, and before the oath stone. There is no going back."

Jarl Sigrún shook her head.

She knows as well as any that Guðvarr cannot take his challenge back, Orka thought. *And Virk cannot decline, not if he would walk away from here with any honour.*

Virk took a step deeper into the clearing, eyes locked with Guðvarr's.

"I accept your challenge," he said.

Jarl Sigrún sucked in an angry breath.

"Very well," she snapped. "Each of you, choose a second, and make your preparations. We will break until you are both ready and the hazel rods have been laid."

Virk turned and walked back to his sons.

"What are you doing?" one of them said. "He's a *drengr*!"

"He's a pup grown mighty in his own head because his kin is a jarl," Virk said, calm now. He looked at Orka.

Thorkel must have known what was coming, because he opened his mouth and started to raise his hand, but the words were already leaving Virk's mouth.

"Will you be my second?" Virk asked Orka.

Orka looked into Virk's eyes.

"One of your sons, Mord or Lif, should do that. You have kin at your back."

"No. If I lose and they are my seconds they will try to fight Guðvarr." He leaned close to her. "And they have some weapons craft, but they are no match for a *drengr*," he whispered. "All I ask of you is, if I lose, to remind them of the rule of *holmganga*, and to put my axe in my fist, so that I would not walk the soul road weaponless."

Orka sucked in a breath and looked at Thorkel. He was frowning and shook his head, but he knew already what her answer would be.

Orka nodded. "Aye, then," she said. "I will do it."

CHAPTER ELEVEN

VARG

Varg opened his eyes, looking up at blurred shapes and shadows. He blinked, his vision slowly focusing, images coalescing into timbered beams and a vaulted roof. Pigeons were cooing in the rafters, and a raven, black and hunched, seemed to be staring at him. Sunlight filtered through smoke holes and shuttered windows.

Varg tried to roll, something poking and scratching into his back, but the effort seemed too much for him, so he flopped back. There was a smell of stale mead, of cold fat and grease and woodsmoke. Of sweat and urine. A murmur of voices passed close by, and further away he heard the thud of wood hitting wood, a few shouted curses. He became aware of a dull pain in his side, sharper in his ribs when he tried to move.

"Aha, so Varg No-Sense is awake," a voice said. Footsteps and a face appeared over him. A handsome face, a red beard cut neatly and gleaming with oil.

"Svik," Varg said, the sound croaking through the dry pit of his throat, stumbling over his lips. He tried to roll on to his side again, but it seemed like a task too difficult for his body to complete.

"Here, give me your hand, you flopping fish," Svik said, all smiles. He gripped Varg's wrist and pulled him up so that he was sitting propped with his back against a timbered wall. He was in a large hall, a makeshift bed of rushes bunched close to the wall and behind a thick wooden pillar, a swirling pattern of elaborate knotwork carved into it. Two long tables and benches ran the length of the hall, hearth fires between them, the tables ending at the foot of a large dais. Upon the dais another long table stood, at a right angle to the other two, so that whatever lord or lady sat there they could look out at their people. The ground was covered in dried rushes, which were the culprit of the scratching in his back, and there were wet patches here and there, of spilled ale or urine from a night's feasting, he imagined. He saw that his cloak had been folded beneath him, used as a pillow, and he reached out and touched it, felt something solid wrapped within it. His thrall-collar, and his cleaver.

He felt weak as a newborn lamb, his limbs like lead, his head too heavy for his neck. His throat was dry, a foul taste in his mouth. He ran his tongue over his teeth and grimaced.

"What have you done to me?" Varg said and looked accusingly at Svik, who was staring at him, clothed in a fine tunic of green herringboned wool, silver rings coiled thick on his arms, and another of twisted silver wrapped around his neck, two serpent heads at each end.

"Saved your miserable life," Svik said, still smiling. "You had a fever, from the spear wound in your side that your friend Leif Kolskeggson gave you."

Leif!

Varg looked down and lifted his tunic, bloodstained and torn where Leif had cut him with his spear. He saw a long red wound, neatly stitched with cords of boiled gut or tendon. The wound had been cauterised, the flesh around it red and raw. Memories fluttered in Varg's head like moth's wings, a bald man offering him a strip of leather to bite on.

"Ah, you remember now, then," Svik said. It wasn't a question.

"Aye," Varg grunted, rubbing his face with the palms of his hands. Leif's attack came back with too-vivid clarity, a host of memories tumbling over themselves, like water over rapids in a river. He hissed. A hand snapped down to his belt and he found his pouch.

"Nothing of yours has been touched. We are not thieves," Svik said. Then his mouth twisted. "Well, not unless you have something worth stealing, which you don't."

Varg undid the clasp on the pouch and reached inside, blowing out a sigh.

"You see?" Svik said. "Would you like some cheese?" He opened a pouch at his belt, took out a slab of hard cheese and cut off a thin slice.

Varg's belly growled as he took the cheese and swallowed it almost whole. He frowned and lifted his right hand in front of his eyes. Made a fist. It wasn't hurting. Well, it ached, but there was no stabbing pain like he had felt before. He checked his body over, fingertips searching. He remembered waking by the fjord feeling like he had been beaten by a troll, his ribs cracked, face swollen, one eye almost shut. Now there was a faint echo of that pain, but it was dull and distant.

"How long?" he asked Svik.

"Six days," Svik said. "I thought you might die, but I kept the rats from gnawing on your toes, just in case. Here, drink this." He offered Varg a drinking horn.

Varg sniffed it.

"Not very trusting, are you?" Svik said, his pleasant smile never leaving his face, as if he were amused at some joke that Varg did not understand. "It's just watered ale."

Varg sipped; it was cold, like liquid joy in his mouth. He tried to stop himself gulping it all down in one long draught.

"Why did you help me?" he asked. "I lost against Einar."

"*Everyone* lost against Einar," Svik said. "That was never a question. It was how you lost, though." Svik whistled and shook his head. "Einar is still limping. You *bit* Half-Troll. I have never seen such a thing, though it may take Einar a while to forgive you. Here." Svik took the empty horn from Varg and replaced it with a wooden bowl and spoon, porridge steaming, a dollop of honey in it.

"Slowly," Svik said, as Varg burned his mouth.

"This is . . . delicious," Varg breathed. The porridge was creamy and hot, the honey sweet. Varg closed his eyes, the pleasure of food and ale consuming him. He forgot about Svik and Einar, about Kolskegg and the Bloodsworn, and just ate.

The sound of chuckling brought him back to himself and he opened his eyes.

Svik was laughing.

"You are a man who enjoys the simple things in life."

"I have not eaten properly in . . . " he paused. "A long time."

"I can tell. You look like a half-starved wolf caught in a wire-trap."

Varg ate some more porridge, forcing his eyes to stay open.

"My thanks," he mumbled through a full mouth.

Svik dipped his head.

There was a scrape of feet on rushes and Varg looked past Svik. A tall warrior was striding towards them with a black shield in her fist: the blonde woman who had offered Varg a shield before his bout with Einar. She was not wearing a *brynja* coat of mail now, just a plain woollen tunic belted with a strip of tablet-woven wool, but something about her, the way she walked, the way her eyes fixed on him like a predatory hawk: she looked . . . dangerous.

She came to stand over Varg, staring down at him, ignoring Svik.

"Get up," she said.

Varg blinked.

"Nice to see you, too, Røkia," Svik said.

"Shut up, you strutting peacock," Røkia said, her eyes still fixed on Varg.

"What's a peacock?" Varg asked through a mouthful of porridge.

"A vain, arrogant, self-loving oaf," Røkia said.

"She's showing off," Svik said. "Peacocks are birds: large, impressive, beautiful birds. They can only be found in southern Iskidan, beyond the great city of Gravka."

"Get up," Røkia said again, ignoring Svik as if he did not exist. "And take this." She waved the black shield at him.

"I told you, I don't fight with a shield."

"You called him No-Shield, and No-Sense, remember?" Svik said.

"Exactly," Røkia said. "Fighting without a shield makes no sense. You cannot be part of the Bloodsworn and not know your way around a shield. Glornir's orders, not mine. I don't care if you get chopped into a thousand pieces in your first shield wall, but Glornir is my chief, so, get up. Take it."

First shield wall!

Varg gulped and looked at Svik. He felt like his body had been wrung through a mangle, and the porridge was heavy in his stomach. The thought of fighting in a shield wall was not a pleasant one.

"She has a point," Svik said with a grin. "You wanted to be one of the Bloodsworn." He shrugged, still smiling. "And if Glornir has said do it, then best be getting on with it."

"Glornir?" Varg said.

"The one who saved your life," Svik said.

"Our chief. Glornir Shield-Breaker," Røkia said.

"He has a lot of names," Svik said with a shrug. "My favourite is Glornir Gold-Giver."

Røkia curled her lip in distaste at Svik.

Varg remembered him, the bald warrior stepping into the woodland glade as Leif was about to chop his hand off. He owed this man. But he also remembered why he had come here, why he had fought Einar Half-Troll.

Vol, the Seiðr-witch.

Carefully Varg put the empty porridge bowl down on the ground and stood. The room moved a little and he swayed. Røkia shoved the shield at him and he gripped the rim, bound in rawhide. Røkia turned on her heel and strode across the hall, Varg seeing she had a shield of her own slung across her back.

Varg looked at Svik.

"I suggest you follow her," Svik said. "Unless you want a tongue-lashing to go with the beating I suspect she is about to give you."

Varg sucked in a deep breath, turned the shield and gripped its wooden handle, his left fist slipping into the curve of the iron boss, and followed Røkia. Now that thirst and hunger were not screaming at him, questions were starting to gather in his head, circling like a murder of crows.

He stepped out through open-flung doors into bright spring sunshine, two wooden pillars framing wide steps that led down into the courtyard where he had fought Einar Half-Troll. Judging by the sun it was a little past midday. The courtyard was full of warriors sparring, the Bloodsworn's black shields spattered with red, and a few of Jarl Logur's blue shields with red sails bright upon them. He saw Einar Half-Troll instantly, the big man standing head and shoulders over the tallest men and women there. He was sparring against two of Logur's warriors at the same time, Einar gripping a shield as big as a table in one meaty fist, an axe in the other.

Varg searched for Vol, the tattooed Seiðr-witch, but he could not see her. Elsewhere in the courtyard he saw the silver-haired woman sparring with a man, her two hounds lying stretched in the sun, watching her. Close by he saw the bald man with the grey beard who had saved him in the woods beyond Liga.

Glornir.

He was sparring against a warrior who stood out from the rest of the Bloodsworn. A slim warrior of average height, but his head was shaved, apart from a long, thick coil of braided hair, black and gleaming as polished jet. His skin was dark where all the others in the courtyard were fair, and he wore a grey Kaftan of wool, buckled down the centre, with baggy breeches, wrapped tight with *winnigas* from ankle to knee. The man was holding a black, red-spattered shield and a curved, single-edged sword. There was something about him that looked familiar.

"Stop staring like a virgin in a brothel and get down here," Røkia yelled up at Varg. Warriors' heads turned towards him, smiles and laughter. Varg coloured and hurried down the steps, feeling the stitches in his side pulling.

Røkia was stood at the bottom of the steps beside a stack of spears in a barrel.

"I need to speak to your Seiðr-witch," Varg said, feeling the death of his sister like a heavy weight upon his heart. He had a task to complete, the responsibility of it a consuming fire.

"Have you used a spear before, No-Sense?" Røkia asked him, ignoring what he'd said.

"Aye," he nodded. "A boar hunt." In truth, he'd been given a rust-bladed spear riveted into a warped shaft of ash. He had been one of many beaters, flushing boar out of dense woodland on to the bright-bladed, straight-shafted spears of Kolskegg and his freedmen. Varg had only seen the boar's arse as it ran away from him.

"Good, have this pig-sticker, then," Røkia said as she threw him a spear.

Varg caught it clumsily in his right hand, then tried to grip it two-handed, but his shield rim *clunked* into the spear shaft. He'd forgotten he held a shield in his other fist.

"No, that is not a two-handed spear. You are not *good* enough for that," Røkia said as she marched to him.

"Shield work, first," she said, shaking her head, leaning her spear against the wall of the mead hall and gesturing for Varg to do the same.

"I have questions. I need to speak to your Seiðr-witch," Varg said.

"Your questions can wait. Glornir told me to start your training, so that is what will happen. And Vol isn't here."

"Where is she?" Varg asked.

"So," Røkia said, ignoring him again. "Two types of fighting. One on one, or in the shield wall. We'll start with one on one. Hold your shield ready."

Varg looked at her, saw the set of her jaw and knew he wasn't going to get anywhere by arguing.

And I owe these people a debt. They saved me from Leif, saved my hand.

He raised the shield so that it covered him from chest to thighs, his arm held tight to his body.

"No," Røkia said as she straight-kicked his shield, sending him stumbling back into the mead hall steps, where he fell back on to his arse. A spike of pain jolted through his wound. He heard a chuckle behind him and looked to see Svik leaning against one of the mead hall pillars, arms folded and a smile on his face. He gestured for Varg to get back up.

"Like this," Røkia said, hauling him upright before he had a chance to stand. "First, set your feet." She looked down at him, mouth twisted as if about to berate him, then paused and nodded.

"Huh," she said, raising one brow. His feet were set shoulder-width apart, left foot leading, a bend in his knees.

"So, you know never to stand square-on." She looked at him suspiciously. "Why?"

"Because if you get hit like that you fall," Varg said.

Varg had never used a shield before, but he'd fought a hundred bouts with his fists, and he knew balance was everything.

"Huh," Røkia said with a curt nod. "Now raise your shield."

He hefted it, pulled it tight to his body.

A twitch of Røkia's lips. "I will tell you once only how to do something. Like this." She gripped Varg's shield rim and pulled the shield away from his body, opening up a gap between his arm and torso. "This way, if something stabs your shield and punches through the wood – spear, sword, arrow, axe – then it will not also hit your body, and so, you will not die straight away." She looked him in the eye. "Most warriors think this is a good thing, no? To live a little longer."

He nodded.

"A shield is not only for protection," Røkia continued. "It is a weapon, too. A shield rim to the mouth can relieve you of many teeth, and the boss can fracture your skull." She grinned, a fierce glee in her eyes that Varg found unsettling. "But first, we will think of defence. So, protect your body by having some space between it and the shield. But your arm must brace it, tight to the shield from wrist to elbow, or the weakest of blows will rock your shield and open you up for something sharp and painful. Understand?"

Varg nodded. He had always been quick to learn, whatever task he had been given on Kolskegg's farm. It was as if he saw a picture in his mind of what Røkia was describing.

Røkia stepped away, grabbed her spear, twirled it into an overhand grip and stabbed at him.

Varg took the blow on his shield, then another, and another, all at different points, high, low, on the boss, at the rim, all testing his grip and balance, each one sending a jolt through his hand and arm, rippling up into his shoulder. The force of Røkia's blows increased, wood splintering. Eventually Røkia nodded and lowered her spear blade.

"Huh," she grunted, which Varg thought must be Røkia's way of saying *good*.

Varg reached for his spear, leaning against the wall.

"What are you doing?" Røkia snapped.

"Spear work now?"

"Ha," Røkia scowled. "You are a shield master already, then?"

"No," Varg said, "but what else is there to learn? It's just a shield."

A cold smile spread across Røkia's face. "Leave the spear where it is. Most fights do not take place with one combatant standing still, no?"

"No," Varg agreed.

"So, perhaps you should learn how to *move* with a shield, and how to defend against a foe who *moves* around you." She stepped close to him, eyes level with his. "Raise your shield," she said. Varg set his feet, hefted the shield as she'd taught him. And then Røkia was moving, feinting left and darting right, her spear jabbing: a pain in Varg's shoulder; a gasp of surprise and shock as he realised she'd just cut him. Not deep, but enough for blood to bloom on his tunic. Then she was behind him and he was jumping away before he got a spear in the back, turning, raising his shield. She was smiling as she stepped in, her spearhead lunging low.

"Never lose sight of me by hiding behind your shield," she hissed as she moved. "That way lies a quick death."

Varg thrust with his shield to deflect Røkia's stabbing spear, but somehow she shifted her weight and swayed back, fluid and smooth as mist. The spear spun in her hand, reversing her grip, and then the blade was at his throat.

Varg froze, breathing heavily, and felt a bead of blood trickle down his neck.

"Ready to learn?" she asked him as she pulled her blade away.

"Yes," Varg said.

CHAPTER TWELVE

ORKA

Orka stood beside Virk. She held a shield loosely in her fist, given over at Sigrún's order by one of the Jarl's *drengrs*. Two more shields were leaning in the grass against a tree. Virk stood patiently, his hand resting upon the axe in a loop on his belt. They watched silently as men and women laid and pegged hazel rods to the ground, marking the square that Virk and Guðvarr would fight in. Guðvarr stood on the far side of the square, glowering at Virk, the *drengr* woman who had accompanied him to Orka's steading leaning close, whispering in his ear.

"Arild is telling him how to kill me," Virk said. It seemed to amuse him. Much of his rage and tension had evaporated, now that he was set on this course. Orka had seen that in old warriors, before. He smiled at her. "You are my second; should you not be giving me advice on how to win?"

"Put your axe in his skull," Orka said.

Jarl Sigrún walked to Guðvarr and leaned close to him, her mouth moving.

"Everyone is telling him how to kill you," Orka commented.

Virk barked a laugh.

Guðvarr stepped away from Sigrún, a scowl on his face.

A hand tugged at Orka's sleeve and she looked down to see Breca.

"What are they doing, Mama?" he asked, looking at the warriors laying out the cut-down hazel rods.

Orka squatted beside Breca.

"This is a *holmganga*," she said. "A ritual duel used to settle disputes. It is done this way, so that it is fair, and so that the kin of the losing party cannot claim weregild or blood feud."

Breca nodded slowly at that. "Why the hazel rods?"

"They fight within the square. If one of them puts a foot over a hazel rod then he has yielded, two feet over and he has fled. *Holmganga* is the old tongue for *going to the island*. It was thought that a fight on an island was better, if you could find one, because there is no running away. That means the matter is more likely to be dealt with quickly. If someone runs, then the other must hunt. As we are already on an island, Guðvarr's challenge can take place here."

Breca nodded, taking it all in. "And why has Virk been given three shields?"

"It is part of the rules," Orka said. "If a shield is destroyed, there will be a pause while it is replaced. Three shields broken, well . . ." she shrugged. "You deserve to lose."

"Ready," a voice called out, Jarl Sigrún stepping into the hazel square, her warrior-thrall at her shoulder. She beckoned for Virk and Guðvarr to join her.

"Fight well. Don't die." Breca said to Virk as he stepped into the square.

"Stay close to your father," Orka said to Breca as she followed Virk.

"The rules of *holmganga* abide here," Sigrún said as they reached her. "You must agree: first wound, submission, or death." She gave Guðvarr a hard look. He glared back at her, then looked away.

"Submission," he mumbled.

Ah, that is what Jarl Sigrún was whispering in his ear, then, Orka thought.

"A wise choice," Sigrún said. "I would rather the people of Fellur fight our enemies, not each other."

Sigrún looked at Virk.

"Agreed," he said, though he looked disappointed.

"Good," Sigrún nodded. "Then fight."

Jarl Sigrún and her thrall stepped out from the square as Orka handed Virk the shield in her fist. He took it, hefted it first, checking its weight.

"How is it?" Orka asked him, knowing that this was the injured arm that had kept him on land and out of his fishing boat.

"Fine," Virk grunted, though he was quick to drop his arm, holding the shield loosely at his side. He slipped his axe from his belt and gave it a lazy circle with his wrist. A farmer's axe, made for fence-building and woodwork, but its blade was sharp and it looked well balanced.

It will cleave a skull as well as a timber post.

Orka leaned close to him.

"Cut him quick. He doesn't have the stones to see his own blood leaking from his skin," she whispered to Virk and then she was walking away, stepping over the hazel rods and standing beside Virk's sons. Thorkel and Breca were close, the crowd packed tight, excitement a tremor in the air. Virk just nodded at Orka's words, his eyes fixed on Guðvarr now, who was taking his shield from his second, Arild. Then she was stepping from the hazel square and Guðvarr was drawing his sword. A fine blade, Orka noted, its pommel three-lobed, hilt bound with leather and silver wire.

"Do you know how to use that, weasel-turd?" Virk said.

Guðvarr's face twisted and he ran at Virk, who stood waiting. A heavy, overhand swing from Guðvarr and Virk raised his shield and stepped back, taking the power from Guðvarr's blow. Guðvarr followed Virk with a flurry of wild swings, Virk stepping away from each one, taking the blows on his shield, the rawhide rim sliced, slivers of wood spraying.

Looking at the two warriors it was easy to think that Guðvarr would soon have Virk on his knees. Virk wore no mail or leather, just a woollen tunic and under-kirtle, had an injured arm and was a fisherman by trade, whereas Guðvarr was young, dressed in a fine *brynja* and held a sword in his fist. And he was a *drengr*, a position held by proven warriors who were battle-trained.

But Guðvarr had seen little battle, or none, Orka thought. *Though he does have some sword craft.*

Orka noted how he maintained his balance, even when swinging such heavy blows with his sword, and he held his shield well.

He has spent long hours in the weapons court. But fighting well in training is different from putting steel into another man's flesh. And his anger is ruling his head.

Another sword blow hacked into Virk's shield and the fisherman retreated another step, close to the hazel-rod boundary now. Orka saw his face pinch with pain, his shield arm falter.

Guðvarr smiled and took another overhand swing at Virk's head.

Virk took the blow on his shield and twisted his arm, guiding Guðvarr's sword wide and down, chopping into turf. A side-shuffle to the right from Virk as Guðvarr stumbled forwards, off balance, and Virk chopped with his axe into Guðvarr's shoulder. There was a crunch of iron as *brynja* rings sprayed, and a spurt of blood and yelp of pain from Guðvarr as he fell forwards, dropping his sword and crashing to his knees, tangled in his shield and falling on to his face.

Shouts sounded from the crowd, Virk's sons yelling their voices hoarse.

Guðvarr squirmed on the ground, ripped his arm free of his shield and twisted on to his back as Virk stood over him, the fisherman's face twitching with elation and the battle-joy. He raised his axe and Guðvarr lifted an arm over his face, squealing.

"To submission," Guðvarr squeaked.

Virk's arm hovered, lowered.

"You have fled, weasel-turd," Virk snarled at Guðvarr, nodding at where the *drengr* lay sprawled the wrong side of the hazel rods.

Guðvarr's face twisted with shame and pain as he tried to reach for his sword; he whimpered as his arm flopped, the axe wound in his shoulder having severed muscle.

Virk kicked Guðvarr's sword away. "You are nothing but a *niðing* weasel-turd," Virk shouted loud. "Now, say it: you submit to me, weasel-turd."

Guðvarr glared up at him.

"Say it," Virk snarled.

"You are the *niðing*," Guðvarr spat up at him. "Win or lose, this changes nothing. You will always be a worm beneath my feet."

Virk stood there a moment, Guðvarr's words sinking deep. A ripple of twitches flickered across Virk's face, then he snarled as he bared his teeth and raised his axe high.

Guðvarr screamed as the axe slashed down at his head.

Jarl Sigrún screamed.

Orka bunched her legs, leaping to knock Virk away from Guðvarr.

A glimpse of something in Orka's peripheral vision, then a body crashed into Virk before Orka could reach him, hurling Virk to the ground. Orka stumbled through the space where he had just been standing. She staggered on a few paces, then righted her footing and turned, staring at the ground.

Virk was thrashing, fighting something that lay on top of him.

Guðvarr was dragging himself away with his uninjured arm.

Orka blinked and squinted at Virk, trying to understand. Then a body snapped into focus, laying entwined with Virk.

It was the warrior-thrall, her two seaxes in her fists, stabbing a savage flurry of blows into Virk's torso. He screamed, blood spraying.

The thrall spat and snarled in Virk's face, her seaxes carving into him, blood drenching the ground, all around staring. Breca was close, open-mouthed and wide-eyed.

Virk's axe fell from his fingers and his arms flopped, head lolling, screams fading to a hiss.

The thrall stopped stabbing, white froth edging her lips, her eyes amber-hued. Her jaws opened wide revealing teeth that were abruptly sharp, and she let out a bestial snarling sound and lunged forwards, her mouth clamping on to Virk's face, tearing, rending.

Orka burst into motion, feet slipping as she threw herself at the thrall, a voice in her head screaming at her to stop, saying that Virk was already dead, that there was nothing to do.

No, Orka snarled back at herself as she moved. *I am his second and he fought well. He won; he does not deserve this dishonour. To be mauled.*

A few paces separated her and the thrall, and then another figure stepped forwards, tall and broad, and kicked the thrall in the ribs.

There was a tearing sound of flesh as the kick lifted the thrall into the air, ripping her jaws free of Virk's face. She flew through the air a half-dozen paces, rolled, then came out of it in a half-crouch, amber eyes blazing, searching for her assailant.

It was Thorkel.

He stepped over Virk's body and set his feet.

The thrall bared her teeth at him, blood dripping.

"The man is dead; your task is done, Ulfrir-kin," Thorkel said.

The thrall leaped at him, her seaxes still in her fists.

"NO," a voice yelled, sounding like Jarl Sigrún to Orka, who was still moving, level with Virk's body now.

Thorkel side-stepped the leaping thrall and threw a punch into her head as she passed him, sending her careening to the ground. At the same time he grunted as one of the thrall's seaxes slashed at his body, a red line appearing through his torn tunic.

White rage exploded in Orka's head and she threw herself at the thrall.

"*NIðUR, Á JÖRðU, HLÝDDU MÉR*," a voice bellowed. A flash of red burst through the thrall's collar and she screamed and collapsed to the ground, limbs twitching.

Something grabbed Orka, hands pulling her, and she turned and thrashed, snarling, to fight the arms wrapping around her.

"It's me, it's me," a voice said in her ear, over and over: Thorkel's voice, melting the cold-fire in her head.

"Mama, Mama," Breca was crying.

Deep, ragged breaths and Orka felt the rage drain; saw Thorkel's face pressed tight to her.

"All right," she exhaled and Thorkel stepped back, nodded at her.

Orka looked around and saw Virk's sons, Mord and Lif, crouched beside their father, the crowd in the clearing all staring. She put a hand to Thorkel's side; her fingers came away red.

"You are cut," she said.

"A scratch," he growled, his eyes shifting from Orka to the thrall.

Jarl Sigrún stood over the thrall, her mouth a tight line. *Drengrs* had filled the hazel square, weapons drawn.

"I told you to stop him, not kill him," Jarl Sigrún said, her voice cold and hard as iron.

The thrall glared up at her, her eyes still amber, her teeth sharp and red.

"You are my thrall, you *will* obey me," Sigrún said, but the thrall's eyes glared their amber-hued defiance, her lips curling back in a snarl.

"*Brenna, sársauki*," Sigrún said: another flash of red veins through the thrall-collar and the thrall whined. The amber faded from her eyes, and there was a ripple through her jaw and lips, her teeth losing their edge.

"*Brenna, sársauki*," Sigrún repeated, louder, harder: red fire glowed in the heart of the iron collar and the thrall thrashed and yelped, like a hound tied to a stake and beaten.

"Mercy, lord," the thrall hissed. "I serve you," she groaned, and crawled towards Jarl Sigrún, touching her forehead to the jarl's boots.

Jarl Sigrún nodded, then looked up from the thrall to Virk's body. His sons were kneeling beside him, weeping.

"Give us justice," the older one, Mord, said to Jarl Sigrún.

"Your father broke the *holmganga*," she said. "All at this Althing heard: Virk and Guðvarr agreed to fight to submission. Guðvarr submitted, and yet Virk lifted his blade for a death-wound."

"He was goaded by that . . . *niðing*," Lif, the younger son said, pointing at Guðvarr.

"Be careful, child," Guðvarr said, back on his feet now, Arild binding his shoulder, "else I shall challenge you to *holmganga*, too."

"Silence," Jarl Sigrún snapped at Guðvarr, who looked sulkily away.

"Virk broke the *holmganga*, so justice has been done," Sigrún said to Lif and Mord. "Though . . . " she glanced at the thrall and shook her head. "Wrap your father's body and take him from here." She looked up at the gathered crowd. "The Althing will break awhile, to allow Virk's kin to do what is proper."

"Help me get them out of here, before they get themselves killed," Thorkel said quietly to Orka as he strode over to Virk's two sons.

"Here," Thorkel said, unfastening the pin of his brooch and laying his cloak across Virk.

Orka grabbed Breca's hand and pulled him with her, and together they helped Mord and Lif to wrap Virk's body.

When they were done, the four of them lifted Virk's body on to their shoulders and carried him from the clearing, Mord and Lif weeping quietly. As they turned a bend in the path Orka looked back. The crowd were raising the hazel rods and filling the square, heated conversations spiralling, a space left around the dark patch of Virk's blood. Sigrún was talking to Guðvarr, and the thrall was sitting at Sigrún's feet. She was watching Orka and the others, and at the same time she raised one of her seaxes to her mouth and licked the blood from it.

CHAPTER THIRTEEN

VARG

Varg walked into the mead hall. He was exhausted, sweat stinging his eyes, his filthy tunic clinging to him, every limb aching as if they were filled with lead. Røkia had kept him working in the courtyard long after everyone else had finished their sparring and filtered away. The only thing that had stopped her maniacally training him through nightfall and on until dawn was a shouted order from some disembodied voice that Varg suspected was Glornir. He seemed to be the only person that Røkia would take an order from.

It was dark now, and torches were lit in the mead hall, flames flickering, shadows dancing and smoke hanging thick in the rafters. Thralls were preparing the mead benches for supper.

Varg saw his cloak was still folded as a pillow behind a column, so he picked it up.

"Sit there," Røkia said from behind him, where she walked with Svik, the two of them whispering some muted conversation. Varg swayed, put a hand on the bench to steady himself and looked where Røkia was pointing. There was a space on the end of one long bench, the furthest point from the high table. Varg sat without thinking. Røkia and Svik strode past him and Røkia paused, turning to look down at him.

"You have fought before," she said to him.

"Yes," Varg admitted, "but only with my fists."

"Huh," Røkia grunted.

"And with your teeth," Svik added, his smile twitching his red beard. "As is evidenced by the teeth marks in Einar Half-Troll's leg, and his limp."

Varg shrugged.

Svik laughed.

Røkia walked away.

"You did well," Svik said before he followed her.

"I fear I may die," Varg muttered, finding it hard to even control the movements of his jaw.

"We are all born to die," Svik called back over his shoulder.

The hall began to fill, men and women entering, all setting their shields and spears around the halls' outskirts and taking their places on the mead benches as thralls were filling the long tables with food and drink: bowls of creamy skyr yoghurt and curds, pots of honey. Boards were full of dried and smoked sliced mutton, trenchers of rabbit and beef, slabs of whale meat and barrels of horsemeat floating in whey. Fresh-baked bread, still hot from the ovens. Dried cod, pungent and salty. Herring fermented in brine, blood pudding, cauldrons of stew glistening with fat and bobbing with carrots, parsnips and onion, and horns of warm mead spiced with juniper to wash it all down. Varg had never seen so much food and drink in all his life, the scents almost overwhelming. His stomach growled like a bear waking in his cave.

Jarl Logur sat at the high seat, barrel-chested with a belly that strained his fine-embroidered tunic. His grey hair was long and braided, gold-wire running through it. Gold hung from his neck and arms and, to Varg's eyes, he looked like a man who laughed a lot. He was certainly laughing now, leaning to whisper into a woman's ear, seated on his right. She was tall and elegant with an open, honest face. Her hair was plaited and piled on her head, more grey than blonde, and she wore a wool dress of deep blue, an embroidered *hangerock* apron over it. A tablet-weave belt jangling with keys was tied about her waist. She laughed as she pushed Logur's shoulder away. Glornir, the bald chief of the Bloodsworn, sat on Logur's other side. And beside him sat Vol, the tattooed Seiðr-witch, a thrall-collar tight about her tattooed neck.

Røkia and Svik strode along the mead benches, Svik swaggering as if he owned the hall, taking a seat at the long table on the opposite end from Varg, as close to Logur and Glornir on their high table as a warrior could sit. Varg saw Einar Half-Troll there, too, and the strange-looking man he had seen sparring with Glornir with the shaved head and long braid of hair.

A young man sat down with a thump next to Varg, looking to be half Varg's age. He had a shock of black unruly hair on his head, straggly twists on his chin, and sharp blue eyes. He wore a tunic blackened with singe-spots, his hands and wrists thick.

"So, you're the murderer," he said.

"Murderer!" Varg scowled. "I am no murderer."

"I heard you were being hunted for murder," the young man said.

"It was not murder," Varg said with a growl. "It was a fair fight, if you call four against one fair."

"Makes no difference to me," the young man shrugged. "You're one of us, now." He grinned. "Name's Torvik," he said, offering Varg his arm.

Varg looked at it a moment, then took it.

"Varg," he said.

"I know your name," Torvik said. "You're Varg No-Sense, the madman who bit Half-Troll."

"I don't know why everyone keeps talking about that," Varg muttered.

Torvik laughed, as if Varg had made a fine jest.

"Eat," Torvik said, tearing a chunk of bread from a loaf in front of him and dipping it into a bowl of stew. "You must be ravenous as a winter-starved wolf, after being whacked and worked by Røkia all day."

Varg didn't need telling twice. He started with a thick slab of bread and butter, curds of cheese and salted cod. Each mouthful tasted like gold. The mead was warm and sweet, the sound of talk and laughter filling the room. Soon the pains of his body were dimming.

"Are you Bloodsworn, or one of Jarl Logur's *drengrs*?" Varg asked Torvik through a mouthful of flaking fish.

"I am Bloodsworn," Torvik said, sitting up straighter. "Well, I will be. I am a scout for the Bloodsworn under Edel."

"Edel?" Varg asked.

"She is the scoutmaster," Torvik said, pointing to the silver-haired woman who sat close to the high table, her hounds tearing at joints of mutton she was feeding them.

Varg nodded.

"And I am also apprenticed to Jökul Hammer-Hand," Torvik said, pointing elsewhere in the mead hall, along the table to a broad, thick-waisted man who sat close to Svik and Røkia.

"A blacksmith?" Varg asked, looking from the man to Torvik and the scattered burns on his tunic and arms.

"Not *just* a blacksmith, though he is the best smith in all Vigrið," Torvik said.

"The fastest, at least," Varg said, "to keep the Bloodsworn's kit maintained."

"Aye, he is fast, as well, but look." Torvik held out his arm and pulled the sleeve of his tunic up, revealing a twisted arm ring of silver, threaded with bronze, two hounds' heads at the terminals. Varg sucked in a breath, it was beautifully crafted, and probably worth more coin than Varg had earned in the pugil-ring.

"What do you mean, you *will* be Bloodsworn?"

"I have not yet taken the oath, but I will. Glornir says all who would be Bloodsworn must prove themselves first, with some act of courage or loyalty."

Varg nodded.

"So, we two are on the same journey," Torvik said, smiling at Varg. "We will be like brothers," he pronounced.

"I have no brothers," Varg said. "Only a sister."

"We will be *like* brothers," Torvik said through a mouthful of stew. "You have a sister?" he asked.

"She is dead," Varg said and filled his mouth with food, ending the conversation.

The mead flowed as the meal progressed, the voices of Bloodsworn and *drengrs* rising as sagas were told and great deeds were bragged about. A noise drew Varg's eyes, Einar arm-wrestling three of Logur's *drengrs* at the same time. Half-Troll laughed as he slammed their arms into a trencher of vegetables, and other warriors roared their approval.

Thralls flitted among the tables, clearing empty trenchers, refilling jugs and horns and bowls, Varg looking at them with an uncomfortable feeling in his gut. It was not so long ago that he had been one of them. Varg knew that where he was sitting now was the least honoured position in the hall, furthest away from the jarl, but just to be *sitting* at the table was almost incomprehensible to him, an honour he had never expected or thought possible. Saved by the Bloodsworn, training with them in the weapons court, eating and drinking at a jarl's table because he was one of them. It was more intoxicating than the mead in his drinking horn and belly. He felt laughter bubbling in his throat at the absurdity of it all, but he also felt a seed of pride swell his chest.

Frøya would be amazed to see this, and proud.

Another feeling swelled in his chest, something that was almost as incomprehensible to him as his freedom. He felt a glimmer of joy.

And with that came a flush of guilt, to be enjoying himself when Frøya lay cold in the ground.

There was something else. Something that Torvik had said squirmed through his thought-cage like a maggot in rotting meat.

All must prove themselves first.

He sucked in a deep breath, frowning.

A banging: Jarl Logur was thumping on a table.

"A fine feast," he said, as silence settled, "and *skál* to you all." He raised his drinking horn to them and drank deeply.

"*SKÁL*," voices cried, echoing from the rafters, as all reached for mead horns, Varg raising his own horn and drinking.

"But what is a feast without a saga-tale to stir our blood, eh?" Logur said, to more shouting and table-thumping. Logur grinned, mead dripping from his beard, and gestured to a figure standing in the shadows of a pillar. A man stepped out, holding a seven-stringed lyre crooked in one arm. Dark-haired and handsome, he wore a green tunic of wool, knotwork embroidered around the neck and hem, and silver arm rings glowing red in the torchlight.

A deep silence settled as he stepped up on to the dais.

"Galinn, the Skáld of Liga," Jarl Logur said, "finest skáld in all the world."

"My thanks, Jarl Logur, most generous of lords beneath the sun and moon," Galinn said.

"Who am I to argue with famed Galinn?" Logur said with a smile, warriors chuckling. "And it is true, with half a loaf and a tilted bowl I have made me many a friend," he added as he sat back down.

Galinn stood and looked out over the tables, then put his fingers to his lyre. Its music was sweet and melancholy, bringing to Varg's mind the sound of water flowing, of wings beating, and then Galinn began to speak.

The Vackna rang loud,
Waking-horn bold and blaring,
In the hills ringing as red sun was rising,
Filling all Vigrið,
This Battle-Plain,
This land of ash,
This land of ruin.
Gods stirred from slumber deep,
Fell Snaka, the slitherer shed his skin, that slayer of souls.
Wolf-waking, hard-howling Ulfrir, the breaker of chains ran roaring,
Racing to the Guðfalla,
The gods-fall.
Orna, eagle-winged came shrieking,
wings beating,
talons rending,
beak biting, flesh tearing.
Deep-cunning dragon,
Lik-Rifa,
Corpse-tearer from Dark-of-Moon Hills, tail lashing as she swept low.
Berser raging, jaws frothing, claws ripping.
Gods in their war glory, Brave Svin, mischievous Tosk, deceitful Rotta,

Gods and kin, their warriors willing,
Blood-tainted offspring, waging their war,
all came to the Battle-Plain.
Death was dealt,
Red ran the rivers,
Land laden with slaughter's reek.
There they fought,
There they fell,
Berser pierced, Orna torn, Ulfrir slain.
Cunning Lik-Rifa laid low, chained in chamber deep,
Beneath boughs of Oskutreð, the great Ash Tree.
And Snaka fell, serpent ruin, venom burning, land-tearing, mountain breaking,
cracked the slopes of Mount Eldrafell.
Frost and fire,
Flame and snow,
Vaesen clambered from the pit,
And the world ended . . .
And was born anew . . .

A silence settled, all staring at the skáld, though, if they were like Varg, all were lost on the Battle-Plain, seeing the war-hosts rage and Snaka's fall as if they were standing there in its midst.

There was a booming on the mead hall doors: for a moment Varg thinking he was still deep in the tale, hearing the echo of drums beating, warriors screaming. Then the mead hall's doors creaked open and a gust of cold wind swept in, setting torches flaring and crackling, its icy fingers dragging Varg from the skáld's saga-song.

Figures stood in the open doorway: two of Jarl Logur's warriors, clothed in mail with spears in their fists, and between them four others. One man was dressed in a fine wool kaftan and fur-trimmed cap, his breeches baggy and striped, wrapped tight with *winnigas* from ankle to knee. The other three, two women and a man, were clothed in coats of lamellar plate, glistening like fish-scales in the torchlight. They all wore iron helms with horsehair plumes and curtains of riveted mail to protect their necks, and carried a quiver and bowcase hanging from their belts, as well as curved swords and small bladed, long hafted axes. The man's helm was edged with gold, and gold wire wrapped the leather hilt of his sword. They all had long, single braids coiling from beneath their helms, like the man Varg had seen sparring with Glornir.

A hawk sat upon the man's forearm, its wings glossy and with a sharp hooked beak.

Varg remembered seeing others that resembled these people, disembarking from a ship on the docks when he had first entered Liga. A ship from far-off Iskidan, a dockworker had told him.

The noise of feasting faded, all eyes on the newcomers.

The two *drengr* guards escorted the visitors, until they came to a halt before the dais where the high table sat, Jarl Logur looking down upon them. The skáld Galinn had disappeared.

"Sergei Yanasson of Ulaz calls upon the hospitality of Jarl Logur," one of the *drengr* guards proclaimed, and the man with the fur-trimmed hat stepped forwards and gave an elaborate bow.

"Greetings, Jarl Logur," Sergei said. "It is an honour to stand in your mead hall. Your wealth, battle-fame and hospitality are known across the whale road, in faraway Iskidan and all the realms of the Great Khagan, Kirill the Magnificent."

"Welcome, Sergei," Logur said with a wave of the hand. "And dispense with the horseshite, you old fox; we have known each other too long." Logur stood and stepped down from the dais, wrapping Sergei in his arms and squeezing him tight. When they parted Logur held Sergei at arm's length, smiling and looking into his face.

"Why are you speaking as if we are only meeting for the first time, my friend?"

Sergei dropped his head. "You do me much honour, a humble merchant from the southlands," he said. Then he shrugged. "I bring great and important guests from my homeland, and I wanted to make a grand entrance."

"Ha, now *that* is better," Logur said, smiling, his eyes moving to the man and women behind Sergei. "And who are these great and important people that you have brought to my hall?"

"This is Prince Jaromir, son of the Great Khagan," Sergei said, stepping aside, "escorted by two of his *druzhina*, as is his right."

"That is not such a great honour," Torvik whispered to Varg. "It is said that the Great Khagan has two hundred concubines and a thousand children, and wherever the Khagan goes he is attended by two *hundred druzhina*."

"Prince Jaromir, welcome to my hall," Jarl Logur said, with a dip of his head and a gesture of his hand.

Jaromir unbuckled his helm and one of his guards stepped forwards and lifted it free. His head was shaved, a blond braid curling over his shoulder. He regarded Logur with piercing blue eyes, his face angular and handsome with a short, neatly cropped beard. He dipped his head to Jarl Logur.

"Forgive my arrival, unannounced," Jaromir said. "I would have sent messengers ahead, so that you could prepare a reception worthy of me, but I have travelled with speed, and I did not want word of my arrival to precede me." He glanced around the hall, then back at Jarl Logur.

The silence in the hall deepened; only the crackle of torches could be heard, punctuated by the hawk snapping its wings out and screeching. It made Varg jump.

"Welcome to the Battle-Plain, where the war of gods was fought and felt hardest," Jarl Logur said. "You are welcome to my hearth fire, to my food and drink, and a seat at my table." His smile broadened, teeth flashing. "As a humble Jarl, that is the best I can do, even for a prince of Iskidan."

"My thanks." Jaromir dipped his head again, a short, sharp movement reminiscent of the hawk upon his arm. "But I have not ridden across Iskidan and sailed the whale road to sit at your table and eat your food. Much as it looks . . . delightful. I have come—"

"You cannot have him," a voice said behind Jarl Logur.

All turned to look at Glornir.

He was still seated, leaning back in his chair.

"What?" Logur said.

"Sulich," Glornir said, nodding his head towards the shaven-haired warrior who sat among the Bloodsworn. "Prince Jaromir cannot have him."

Jaromir stared at Glornir, then turned his head much like the hawk on his arm to regard Sulich, sitting in between Einar Half-Troll and Svik. Sulich did not return his gaze; instead he slowly reached out and speared a slice of smoked mutton. He put it in his mouth and chewed with apparent relish.

"Who are *you*, to say no to Jaromir, a son of Kirill the Magnificent, a prince of Gravka and all Iskidan?" Jaromir said to Glornir.

"Who am I?" Glornir said. "No great lord or jarl, or prince, like you. But I am chief of the Bloodsworn, and with that comes responsibility to my crew. Gold-Giver, they call me. I am sworn to provide for them, and protect them."

"And Shield-Breaker," Røkia said.

"Soul-Stealer," Svik added.

"Slicer, hacker, crusher," Einar Half-Troll said, brows knotted in a thunderous glower.

Glornir shrugged. "I have many names," he said. "But the heart of this is that they have sworn an oath to me, and I to them. To stand together. To fight together. To live or die together. Sulich has sworn that oath, sealed it with his blood. So, you see . . . " He stood slowly, cracked his neck one way, then the other. "You cannot take him."

"He has committed crimes. Great crimes that he must answer for," Jaromir said.

"I fear you are not understanding me," Glornir said.

One of the women behind Jaromir stepped forwards, her fist wrapping around the hilt of her sabre. "I shall take his head for his insolence, Great Prince," she hissed.

Chairs and tables scraped as over sixty warriors stood in the hall, all of the Bloodsworn rising. Beside Varg, Torvik stood, and before he realised what he was doing, Varg found himself on his feet too.

"Hold," Sergei cried, spreading his arms and jumping between the *druzhina* warrior and Glornir. "This is not the way, my prince," he pleaded, bobbing his head. "Their ways are not our ways; we must excuse their barbarian manners."

Jaromir looked from Sergei to Glornir.

"Hold, Ilia," Jaromir said. "We shall take our esteemed friend Sergei's advice." He looked to Jarl Logur.

"My apologies," he said to the jarl. "I do not mean to bring bloodshed to your hall. But this is a serious matter and I will see it resolved." He looked around the mead hall. "Liga is a trading port, and it has given you all that you have, but there are finer latrine-pits in Gravka than this hall. I could be *good* for this town; I could be good for you, bring in a river of wealth you have never imagined, if we were to come to an agreement."

Logur looked at him.

"I wish no bad blood between us," the jarl said, "but the lore of our land does not support your claim. You cannot march into a jarl's hall and make these demands. Where is your proof? Your evidence? The witness of reliable, honoured freedmen? This is a matter for the Althing." He shrugged. "And Glornir is my friend," he answered.

"I have evidence, and witnesses," Jaromir said. "Think on what I have said. I shall return on the morrow with all that you ask, and I shall ask you for justice. Again. I will not ask a third time." He turned on his heel and strode from the hall, his hawk letting out another shriek.

The doors closed with a thud and silence settled over the room.

"What an arseling," Svik said.

CHAPTER FOURTEEN

ELVAR

Elvar lifted her oar and dragged it clear of the oar-hole as the *Wave-Jarl* glided through the foaming surf and grated on a shingle beach. Agnar was unstrapping the steering oar and raising it so that it would not snare on the ground below the shallow water. Sighvat leaped overboard and splashed through the surf on to a narrow beach, a handful of the Battle-Grim following him. Gulls circled and screeched above them, launching from their sea-cliff nests.

They were two days south from Iskalt, roughly half the distance to Snakavik already covered with the help of a strong north-westerly that had filled the *Wave-Jarl*'s sail and sent them speeding south. The wind had changed, now, hissing cold and sharp from the east and slowing their progress. Agnar had chosen this island to camp upon, the most southerly tip of the Frost-Isles, as he had seen the glimmer of a beach which offered safe landing, and the bunching of storm clouds on the horizon that encouraged them to seek shelter. The sun was a pale cloud-wreathed glow dipping behind steep, grassy slopes as the Battle-Grim disembarked and shored the *Wave-Jarl* with ropes tied to rocks. The beach was too narrow for them all to camp, so, while most of them had been dragging their *drakkar* above the tideline on the beach, Biórr and a few others had been sent to scout for a decent site to camp. As Elvar was leaning and breathing hard from tugging on a rope, the young warrior returned, telling them he had found a spot at the top of a nearby slope that would keep the *Wave-Jarl* in sight. Agnar left five men with the *drakkar*, Thrud among them because of his arrow wound, and the rest of them followed Biórr as he led them up a winding path, Thrud's complaints echoing louder than the gulls' screeching. Sighvat led the new prisoners, Berak and his wife and child, and the Seiðr-witch Kráka and the *Hundur*-thrall followed close behind. The path twisted through grass and heather and finally spilled on to a level plateau. An open space of goat-cropped grass ran up to a slab of moss and lichen-covered granite as tall as a mead hall, and as wide as one. Alders clustered along the plateau's eastern fringe, protecting them from the searing wind.

"A good spot," Agnar pronounced, looking back down the steep slope to see the *Wave-Jarl* on the beach below them. The Battle-Grim proceeded to make camp, scraping a pit in the ground, searching for dead wood for a fire and a stream to fill water bottles. As darkness settled, flames were crackling and a pot of stew hanging from an iron frame was bubbling away, the smell of mutton and fat making Elvar's belly growl. Sighvat was ladling out bowls for the Battle-Grim, filling Elvar's and then Grend's behind her. Elvar turned to see Kráka, the Seiðr-witch, standing and staring up at the slab of moss-covered granite they were camped against. She reached out a hand, her fingertips brushing the rock face.

"What are you doing?" Agnar asked Kráka. He had been sitting with his back to the rock.

"This is an oath stone," Kráka said.

"It's a small mountain, is what it is," Sighvat said, looking the granite up and down, a few of the Battle-Grim laughing.

"All of the oath stones have been destroyed," Grend said beside Elvar, which she knew.

Agnar stood, frowning. "*Hundur*," he called, and the *Hundur*-thrall loped over, head bowed, and took some deep, snorting breaths.

"I can smell nothing, lord," the thrall said to Agnar.

"Here," Kráka said, her fingers tracing lines through the moss. The thrall scraped the moss away and pressed his face to the granite, sniffing again.

"Yes," he breathed. "It is there: blood spilled, oaths sworn, faint as a memory."

He began to scrape more moss away.

"There is an easier way," a voice said: the captured woman, rising from where she had been sitting with her husband and son.

"Uspa, no," the prisoner, Berak, said. He moved to grip her hand, his chains clinking.

"Leave her," Agnar snapped at Berak. "Easier way to what?" he asked Uspa.

"To see the oath stone," Uspa said.

"I can see it already," Sighvat said, frowning. "It's so big it's hard to see anything else."

"I mean, to see what is inscribed upon it," Uspa said.

Agnar looked from Uspa to the rock.

"Show me," he said.

Uspa walked forwards.

"Mama," her son called out after her.

"It's all right, Bjarn," she said, giving him a reassuring smile. As she drew close to the slab of rock and Agnar she held her palm out.

"Cut me," she said.

Agnar drew his seax and touched it to Uspa's palm, a line of blood welling. She let it pool, made a fist, spreading it, then opened her palm and pressed it to the space the *Hundur*-thrall had cleared of moss.

Elvar stared, realised she was holding her breath and forced herself to breathe.

Nothing happened. She saw Uspa's blood trickle down the rock, a black, glistening trail across the granite, finding a path.

Then, a shuddering ripple passed through the granite, as if it were some ancient giant roused from death and taking its first tremulous breath. A cloud of dust drifted from the rock. Elvar heard Sighvat suck in a sharp breath as a glow spread from Uspa's palm like a line of molten metal poured into a cast, spiralling out from the Seiðr-witch's palm, spreading across the granite face, making the moss and lichen glow. More lines of fire appeared, filling the rock, down to its roots, wide and high. The moss and lichen began to blacken, to burn and hiss and peel, falling away to reveal the rock face beneath.

Elvar just stood, open-mouthed and staring, all of the Battle-Grim in silence around her. Grend put his hand to the axe hanging from his belt. Sighvat stood with a forgotten ladle full of stew in his fist.

And then Uspa pulled her hand away, stepping back to stare at the rock face, along with the rest of the Battle-Grim.

Runes traced across the granite face, and images, filling it, like a tapestry emerging from the ground at their feet and rising up to touch the sky, filling Elvar's vision. Images of a pale dragon caged and raging, locked within a chamber among the roots of a great tree. A wolf upon a plain, a thick chain binding him, small figures swarming, stabbing, the wolf's jaws wide as it howled.

"Ulfrir, wolf-god," Kráka breathed.

"It's the *Guðfalla*," Biórr whispered. "The gods-fall."

So many images, Elvar struggled to take it all in: figures hanging from the boughs of trees, many of them, skeletal wings spiking from their backs.

"The Gallows Wood," Elvar said. She remembered that tale, of how the gods Orna and Ulfrir had found their firstborn daughter slain, her wings hacked from her back. Lik-Rifa had done it, the dragon, Orna's sister. As vengeance Orna and Ulfrir had hunted Lik-Rifa's god-touched offspring and slaughtered them. Ripped their backs open and hacked their ribs apart, pulling them out in a parody of wings and hanging the corpses from trees.

The blood-eagle, it was now called.

The first blood feud, Elvar thought.

The images went on and on, telling the tale of the gods at war: Berser the bear, Orna the eagle, Hundur the hound, Rotta the rat, many, many more; and Snaka, father, maker, coiling about them all, glowing venom dripping from his fangs as he entered the blood-fray and consumed his children.

"I thought all of the oath stones had been destroyed," Sighvat said.

"We are on the arse-end of the world," Agnar said. "This one has survived." He was still staring up at the huge slab, eyes following the glowing lines as they traced the images.

"So, that is where your bloodline comes from," Agnar said to Berak in his chains. He pointed to an image of a giant bear, jaws wide, spittle spraying.

Berak said nothing, just glowered at the image.

"They are the fathers and mothers of all us Tainted," Kráka said. "Snaka loved his creations, when he was not feasting on them, and so did his children." She stared at the serpent-coils that spiralled across the granite.

"Why did they fight?" Sighvat muttered. "What started this war, led to the near-destruction of all?"

"Jealousy and murder," Uspa said. "Blood feud. Lik-Rifa the dragon thought her sister was plotting her death, and Rotta the rat fuelled her paranoia. She murdered Orna and Ulfrir's daughter, created the vaesen in secret, would have used them to destroy Orna and all those who supported her. But Orna found out and lured Lik-Rifa into the caverns and chambers deep within the roots of Oskutreð, the great Ash Tree, and with her siblings bound Lik-Rifa there. That is what caused the war."

"Lik-Rifa is a faery tale," Elvar said into the silence.

"How can you say that?" Sighvat spluttered. "Just look at it. Look at her."

"They are stories carved in stone," Elvar said. "Some of it I believe, but only where there is proof that I can see and touch. The Tainted are real, yes, those who have a remnant of a god's blood in their veins. I see Hundur the hound's blood in you . . ." She pointed at the *Hundur*-thrall. "Berser the bear in you . . . " She pointed to Berak. "And Snaka in you both." A wave of her hand at Kráka and Uspa. "I heard your serpent-song, and saw it turn the Sjávarorm away, so there is my proof. And many other Tainted I have seen on my travels with the Battle-Grim – in far off Iskidan we have seen the blood of the Bull in human form, of the Hawk and the Horse. But never, in all my life, have I seen a dragon-born, or heard tell of one from the lips of someone I trust. Think on it: have any of you seen or heard of a dragon-born Tainted?" She looked around the glade, at Battle-Grim and Tainted alike. Saw warriors shaking their heads, muttering that they had not. "You see," Elvar said, "they do not exist. They cannot. Lik-Rifa is a faery tale, made up to entertain, and to scare children into behaving."

A silence stretched, all thinking on Elvar's words.

Uspa hawked and spat, which made Elvar frown.

"If I have learned anything from my travels," Agnar said, "it is that there is much in this world that I do not know or understand. Just because I have not seen a thing does not mean it is not out there. And I hope that the dragon-born *do* exist, because I think they would fetch a good price and line all our chests with gold!" A cheer rippled through the Battle-Grim. Agnar shrugged and smiled, looking at Uspa. "At the very least it is a good tale, and a worthy reminder of why we must hate the gods, and hunt down their offspring. Their greed, their jealousy, their blood feud near destroyed the world, and that is why they can never be allowed to hold power in this world again, even in the form of their Tainted children." His smile withered and he spat on the ground, then looked back up at the glowing oath stone.

"At least we have something to light our meal, and can sleep knowing that nothing will be able to sneak up on us in the dark."

Elvar woke with a gasp, eyes snapping open. Or she tried to gasp. A pressure about her throat, constricting. The ground beneath her shifting. Only one of her eyes opened, a faint glow in the air from the oath stone, but her other eye was dark, as if the eyelid was sealed with congealed blood. Her wrists and ankles were held, and something was slithering across her body. She tried to move, struggled, felt movement: something wet and slimy constricting, squeezing.

"Grend," she managed to wheeze, turned her head a fraction and saw Grend lying close by; for a moment struggled to understand what she was seeing. Something was covering him, pale and translucent, oozing across his body like whale blubber melted in a pot.

Then she saw them.

Night-wyrms. Thin and pale, each one as thick as a thumb, as long as a seax, but there were hundreds of them, no, thousands. Between her and Grend Elvar glimpsed them squirming and wriggling from the ground like a bucket of slime-covered maggots; beyond Grend more of the Battle-Grim were struggling, Kráka and the prisoners, too.

Elvar resisted the urge to scream: knew if she opened her mouth they would be swarming into her throat, choking her. She felt their slimy segmented bodies wriggling across her face, bristles scratching.

Grend wrenched his head to stare at Elvar, a wordless scream behind his wide eyes. One of the night-wyrms was prising its way into his clamped-shut mouth, another one squirming up his nose. One of Grend's hands moved, a snarl of wyrms slithering, their bodies still locked in the earth, pinning him.

With a muffled roar, Berak surged up from the ground, his chain rattling, veins bulging in his neck as he tore himself free of the wyrms, their bodies flung through the air. Berak stood there, rage flexing across his face, shuddering through his body, then he was reaching down and tearing wyrms from his wife and son, dragging them to their feet.

A scream: fat Sighvat bellowing, terror-filled, but Elvar saw him moving, ripping his arms free of the earth, night-wyrms flung through the air and then his huge bulk was rolling, squashing wyrms beneath him. Elvar heard their skins popping, could see hundreds of tiny explosions of fluid, and then Sighvat was on his feet, axe and seax in his fists and he was swiping at the creatures snaring Agnar.

A wyrm touched Elvar's nose, paused in its writhing, then began to squirm up her left nostril. She whimpered, screamed inside; bucked and flailed as she felt the segmented creature pushing into her.

A figure loomed over her: Agnar, stamping and chopping. She heard Grend's voice, shouting, roaring, the sound of iron hissing through air and then her right hand and leg were free. She rolled, ripping at the wyrms that were wrapped around her left wrist, tore them from the ground, segmented bodies stretching, ripping, and then she was on her hands and knees, gasping, Grend dragging her to her feet. She snatched at the wyrm that was burrowing into her nose, caught its tail end and pulled, resisting the urge to wrench it free, knowing that would likely leave half of the creature inside her face. With a sucking sound the wyrm came free, slipping from Elvar's nose and dangling in her fist. It wriggled and twisted and she flung it to the ground and stamped on it. She gagged and vomited bile.

"Are you all right?" Grend asked her, still stamping on the creatures that were wriggling on the ground, trying to wrap around his ankles and drag him back to the ground.

"Fine," Elvar spat, drawing her seax and slashing furiously at wyrms slithering around her boots.

Everywhere the Battle-Grim were on their feet, though Elvar saw one figure half-buried in the shifting ground, dead eyes staring, the warrior's throat shifting with wyrms wriggling inside him.

Biórr had thrust a kindling branch into the embers of the fire and was now burning the night-wyrms away. They hissed and sizzled and popped. Others kindled branches into flame and joined Biórr, and the wyrms wriggled away, squirming back into the ground.

And then they were gone, leaving Elvar and the others standing there, staring, panting. She looked up at the oath stone, saw its glow was fading but still there, pulsing in the dark.

Did the oath stone call to them, somehow? Draw them here? Never have I seen them in such numbers . . .

Agnar coughed and spat, glaring at the dead wyrms strewn about the glade.

"I'm never sleeping again," Sighvat said.

"Back to the *Wave-Jarl*," Agnar ordered.

CHAPTER FIFTEEN

ORKA

Orka shook the black pan sitting on an iron grill over her hearth fire. Flames flared as slices of smoked ham and chopped onions crackled and smoke drifted up to the high beams of their steading, searching for the smoke hole.

Orka saw small fingers reach into the pan and slapped them with her wooden spoon.

"Wait until it's ready," she said.

"But my belly's growling like a new-woken bear, Mama," Breca said.

"And mine," Thorkel muttered, sitting in a chair and sewing a patch in his nålbinding cap.

"*Smells good*," Vesli the tennúr squeaked beside Breca.

Orka frowned at the tennúr, who had followed Breca's every step from the moment he passed through their steading's gates. The vaesen's wounds seemed to be healing well.

"I hope Mord and Lif are all right," Breca said.

"As long as they do nothing stupid, they will survive," Orka said, thinking of how she and Thorkel had restrained Mord from snatching up his father's axe and hurling himself at Guðvarr and Jarl Sigrún's thrall.

They had been home less than half a day, having stayed at Fellur a while to help Virk's sons raise a barrow over their father. Afterwards Mord and Lif had welcomed them to their hearth and fed them well on salted cod and smoked salmon, but the mood had been dour. Mord had muttered oaths of vengeance and Lif had shed constant tears. By the time Orka, Thorkel and Breca left, the two boys had calmed a little, both pale and red-eyed. Thorkel had invited the young men to their steading in the hills, but they had declined. Many boats still bobbed out on the fjord, moored to the Oath Rock as the Althing continued, and Thorkel had advised the two brothers not to return to the gathering.

It was late, now, the darkness thick as oil outside, a wind soughing through the forest, and all of them were tired and hungry, after their climb into the hills and then seeing to the chores of the steading. Spert had complained vehemently that they were conspiring to starve him to death, neglecting to bring him his blood and spit-soaked porridge on time, but Breca had eventually placated the vaesen creature with a bowl twice as large as he was usually given. Spert was asleep in his small underwater cave now, satiated and swollen.

Orka picked up a wooden bowl and gave it to Breca, took some flatbread that had been warming on stones around the hearth fire and spooned some skyr and thyme on to it, then stabbed a slice of ham and placed it on the flatbread, finally pouring fried onions on top of it all.

Breca took his eating knife and skewered the ham, ripped a chunk off and stuffed it in his mouth. He made huffing noises as he tried to chew, the meat too hot.

"Have some patience. You'll scald your belly," Orka said to him.

Thorkel held his plate out and Orka filled it. He stroked the back of her hand as she did so, sending a warm sensation tickling into her belly. She was glad of it, because a wyrm of worry had been squirming in her gut since they had carried Virk's corpse from the Oath Rock. She had thought it would fade once she was back in her home, away from the Althing, but instead the sensation had grown inside her, a creeping dread spreading through her veins like poison.

Orka filled her own plate, then looked down at Vesli, who was staring up at her, pointed nose twitching, a line of drool glistening from mouth to chin. With a grunt Orka nudged some of her ham and onions into a bowl and held them out for the tennúr. Tentatively the creature reached out and took the bowl, then dipped its head. There was a chewing, grinding sound, as Vesli tore through the food.

Orka frowned.

"I hate Guðvarr and Jarl Sigrún," Breca said abruptly, his eyes fierce as he blew on his hot food.

Orka was still watching the tennúr eat, its two rows of teeth slicing and grinding at an alarming rate. The bowl was empty in heartbeats. Vesli smacked her lips and licked her chin, then looked up at Orka.

"*Tasty,*" Vesli said. Orka just scowled, imagining her crunching through human teeth.

"Hate?" Thorkel said, raising an eyebrow, onions stuck in his beard. "Hate does no one any good," he shrugged. "Sometimes killing has to be done, but do not do it with hate in your heart. It will eat at you, like maggots laid beneath the skin."

"But what they did," Breca said. "Virk *won*, and then they killed him. It is not fair."

"No," Thorkel agreed, "it is not. But Vigrið is not fair. All that can make the world fair is this." Thorkel leaned forward in his chair and put a finger to Breca's temple. "Your thought-cage. The choices you make. Choose to treat others fairly: you'll sleep better for it."

"But what about when others don't treat *me* fairly, like they didn't treat poor, dead Virk fair," Breca said, his face screwed up in anger.

"Aye, that's a deep-thought point for one so young," Thorkel said through a mouthful of flatbread and skyr. "If you can walk away from a fight and keep your head and your honour, do so. Virk spoiled for a fight, and he won, you're right. But picking a fight with your jarl's nephew was not a deep-cunning choice. If Virk had held his tongue, or spoke with more respect and less anger, he would most likely still be breathing."

"*Did he have good teeth?*" Vesli squeaked.

They all stared at the little tennúr.

"*The dead do not need their teeth,*" Vesli shrugged, looking at the floor, a ripple in her paper-thin wings.

Thorkel laughed.

"If I were a grown warrior, I would have helped Virk," Breca said quietly. He looked at Thorkel. "I want to learn sword craft."

"I prefer an axe," Thorkel said.

"Axes are for splitting wood," Breca grumbled.

"They are just as good as swords at splitting skulls," Thorkel said, quiet for a long moment, then he shrugged. "Probably better. A weapon is just hard, sharp steel. A tool, nothing more, only as good as the one holding it."

"I want to be good with a sword," Breca said stubbornly.

Thorkel shared a look with Orka and blew out a long breath.

Orka leaned back in her chair, crossing her feet and eating as Thorkel spoke on, talking to Breca about honour, about peaceful living. She knew he had the right of it, though part of her had agreed with Breca when she had been stood back in the hazel square, looking at Virk's lifeless body. He should be avenged, and by rights his sons should do the deed. But they were too young and unskilled in weapons craft, and too fiery to go about it in a way that they may live to look back on and savour the deed.

It is a dark world, and dark deeds rule it, drag us down a white-foamed river we cannot resist. An image of Guðvarr, the honourless weasel lying in the hazel square, eyes blank and staring, an axe in his skull . . .

She blinked and shook her head, realising the road her thoughts were taking her down and not liking it. Thorkel's voice seeped into her, deep and reassuring, calming her, like a fire pushing back the darkness that churned and coiled in her veins. Her eyelids drooped, sleep dragging at them.

A hand touched her foot and Orka jolted awake. She jumped, reaching for her seax at her belt, then saw Thorkel's face smiling at her.

"You were snoring loud as a bear," he said.

"Huh, and you are a fine one to talk about that," she said, sitting up in her chair.

The fire still flickered, Breca and Vesli sitting beneath the table.

Breca was carving at a lump of wood with his knife while he chatted with the tennúr.

"Time to snore in a soft bed, I'm thinking," Thorkel said to her.

"Aye," Orka grunted, rising and stretching.

They all set to their night-time chores. Breca collected the empty plates and cook-pan, and he loaded his small cart and pulled it out of the chamber, taking it to the stream to wash. Vesli fluttered her wings and perched upon the pile of plates and pans, and Orka and Thorkel followed them out into the darkness.

Each of them lit a torch and carried it with them, Breca giving his to Vesli to hold. Thorkel went to the gates, to check the bolts and locks, and then to make his customary patrol of the stockade wall. Orka strode for the barn, placed her torch in an iron sconce riveted to the barn's gate, then proceeded to check on their pony. She spent some time mucking out his stable, filling his hayrack. When she finished, she gave him a handful of oats from a hemp sack and scratched his head while he chewed.

When Orka left, taking the guttering torch from the barn door, she saw the others had all finished their chores. She crossed the open courtyard and stepped into the hall. The fire still flickered in its hearth-ring, burning low, illuminating the room in ripples of amber and shadow. Breca was already in his cot, tucked under a woollen blanket and Vesli was curled on the floor beside him. Orka squatted down beside her son and just watched him a moment: his face pale and still, chest rising and falling in a slow, steady rhythm. Around his neck a wooden pendant hung by a leather thong. A sword, small but well carved with a three-lobed pommel and a curved crossguard. Orka snorted a laugh.

He is stubborn. He wants to learn sword craft, and this will be our reminder, every day. Thorkel must have drilled a hole in it and found some leather.

She reached out and stroked his hair and Breca opened his eyes, large and serious.

"I feel sad for Mord and Lif, Mama," he said sleepily.

"I know you do," Orka said. "And I'm glad that you do. It tells me that you have a big heart."

"How are they going to live without their papa?"

"Well, if they can control their anger and not get themselves killed in a *holmganga*, then they won't starve. Virk has taught them well; they have a fisher boat and a trade. That is what we try to do, as parents. Teach our children how to survive when we are gone."

"I don't *ever* want you or Papa to go," Breca said. He blinked, eyes bright with sudden tears.

It is inevitable. Death comes for us all, Orka thought, though she did not speak her mind. She could already imagine Thorkel giving her his thundercloud frown.

"What were your mama and papa like?" Breca asked her.

"I hardly remember," Orka said. "I have stray images of them, like leaves floating in a pool. My mother's smile, combing her red hair." *Her screams. The back of my father's hand . . .*

"How old were you, when they died?"

"Ten, eleven winters?"

"If you die, *I'll* never forget *you*," Breca said, eyes wide and dark.

"I wanted to forget them," Orka shrugged. "I am glad that you do not feel the same way."

"Mama, were you . . . " Breca faltered, looking away.

"What?" Orka said. "A question is better out than in."

"When we took Asgrim and Idrun's bodies to Fellur, that man, Guðvarr, he said you were shaking, said that you were scared of him . . . "

"Aye, he did," Orka said, remembering the little weasel standing on the steps of Jarl Sigrún's mead hall, snot dripping from his nose. "What of it?"

"Were you . . . scared?" Breca asked her.

Orka remembered the feelings that had swept through her, memories of blood and death, a cold rage spreading through her limbs, making her blood tingle and her muscles twitch. It had been a fear, of sorts. Not of Guðvarr, but of what she might have done to him.

"I was," Orka said.

Breca's mouth dropped.

"Fear is no bad thing," Orka said. "How can you be brave if you do not feel fear?"

"I don't understand," Breca said, frowning.

"Courage is being scared of a task and doing it anyway."

Breca's brow knotted as he thought on that, and then he slowly smiled. His eyes shifted focus and he scowled and sat up in bed, reaching over Orka's shoulder.

"What is it?" Orka said, turning.

Breca stood in his cot, standing on his tiptoes, trying to reach a spiderweb in the crook of the beam. A moth was stuck in it, wings flapping, and a bloated spider had emerged from its lair, standing on a vibrating thread.

"Leave it, Breca. It is nature's way. This is a red world of tooth and claw. The bird eats the mouse, the cat eats the bird, the wolf eats the cat, and so on. You cannot change this."

"Ah, but, Mama, look how frightened that moth is," Breca said, jumping now, but still not able to reach the web. "To see your death approaching with fangs like that, to be poisoned but still alive while your life is sucked from you. Surely that is no good death?"

Orka shrugged. He had a point.

The spider began to scurry along the thread towards the frantic moth.

"And if you were caught in a snare, or I, and someone could help us," Breca said, "but instead turned their backs and walked away, what would you have to say about that?" He jumped higher, managed to touch the web and the scuttling spider froze.

If someone left you to die, I would throttle the life from them. I would stab them and gut them and . . .

Orka shook her head.

"There is too much room in that thought-cage of yours," Orka grunted, but she stood and swiped at the web, knocking the moth free. It fell on to the floor, spun in a circle to shake off the last of the web that clung to it, then it was free and flying away.

Breca smiled at her, as if he had won a battle.

"Go to sleep," Orka said, leaning over and tucking Breca back into his cot, kissing his cheek. He wrapped an arm around her and squeezed her tight, then settled back into his mattress of straw and down. Orka stood and padded to the back of the hall. As she stepped through the door into the chamber beyond, she looked back. Breca was curled in his bed, woollen blanket pulled up tight to his chin. Beside him she saw the glint of Vesli's eyes in the firelight, watching her. She closed the door.

Moonlight threaded through shuttered windows, silvering her bedchamber, the bulk of Thorkel a snoring lump in their bed. Quickly she took off her boots and woollen socks, unbuckled her belt and laid it on a wide chest at the foot of their bed, pulled her wool tunic and linen undertunic over her head, climbed out of her breeches and slipped into bed beside Thorkel. He reached out a big hand and touched her hip.

"Now, do you want to be telling me what's troubling you?" he murmured, his voice thick with sleep.

Orka sucked in a deep breath, felt the wyrm in her belly uncoil. "Sigrún's new thrall," she breathed.

A silence. Thorkel rolled over, facing her. His eyes gleamed in the moonlight.

"Aye. She is *Úlfhéðnar*," he said.

"She tasted your blood. I saw her lick it from her seax." Orka's fingers found the wound, a thin line across his ribs, scabbed now. It had not been deep.

"You do not know that. It could have been Virk's blood. And anyway, she is *Úlfhéðnar*, not a *Hundur*. It would mean nothing to her."

"The Tainted are interbred now, you know that. She could be *both*."

A long sigh from Thorkel.

"We should leave this place," Orka said. "Now, before it is too late. Move far from here, away from petty jarls and their petty squabbles, away from Helka and Störr and their war of greed."

"But this is our home. We have built it with our hands, our blood and sweat."

"No, *this* is my home," Orka said, placing her palm over Thorkel's chest. "You and Breca are my home. Wherever we are together, that is home to me."

They lay in silence awhile, Orka's palm on Thorkel's chest, fingers threaded through his wiry hair, his hand upon her hip.

"Heya, you are right," Thorkel said, breaking the silence.

Orka felt a wash of relief. She had been expecting a hard fight.

"Good," she said. "I'll go to the Ash Tree in the morning, speak to the Froa."

"Aye, in the morning," Thorkel said. "But now . . ." His hand moved from her hip, tracing the dip of her waist, higher.

Orka found his lips in the darkness.

Orka slipped out of the bedchamber and closed the door on Thorkel's sleeping form. She found an empty bowl on the table and spat into it, then pulled her seax from her belt and pricked a red spot on the heel of her hand, letting it drip into the bowl and mixing it with her spit.

That should keep Spert from mutiny, or ending his own life through hunger.

She padded through their hall, glancing at Breca, just a dark shadow curled on his cot. Vesli stirred but did not wake. At the doorway she paused and selected a spear from their rack, thick-shafted ash with a leather cover over the long blade. She glanced up at Thorkel's long-axe that hung over the doorway, then stepped outside. All was darkness, moonglow fading with the coming of dawn.

"Spert," Orka whispered as she strode to the stream and jabbed her spear butt under the creature's rock. A ripple and splash.

"*Mistress?*" Spert mumbled as he emerged from the water.

Orka squatted beside him. "I have a task to complete, but should be back before midday. Watch over the steading until I return."

"*Yes, mistress,*" Spert said. He paused, his antennae twitching. "*Hungry,*" he muttered. "*Midday is a long time. Will you leave Spert to starve and die, like before?*"

"You didn't die," Orka snapped. "More's the pity." She drew in a deep breath. "Breca will warm your porridge as soon as he wakes. He will be out with your breakfast soon enough," she said, then stood and made her way to the gate, threw her spear over the timber wall and then leaped and grabbed its rim, heaved herself up and over and dropped down on to soft earth. She didn't want to leave the steading with the gate unlocked.

Reaching for her spear she set off, heading south-east, crossing the open space around their steading and slipping beneath the trees. It was dark as pitch, but Orka knew the way. A fox's trail wound its way upward through the trees, and she reached a high ridge as the sun clawed its way over the edge of the world, a glow gilding over the treetops of a valley that fell away before her a molten red.

She made her way down the ridge, using her spear butt as a staff, and as the ground began to level the sun had reared over the hills. The murmur of a river grew louder. Usually when she reached this point, she felt a change deep inside her, like the relief that comes with a long-held exhalation, but not now. Instead the tendrils of dread that had faded last night were back, twisting and coiling in her veins.

The trees about her thinned, fractured beams of light breaking through, and then she was stepping out into a meadow, a river running through it. Before the meadow was a gentle hillock, and upon it an ash tree.

Orka stumbled to a stop, just stood and stared, mouth open, her spear hanging limp in her hand.

The Ash Tree had been destroyed. A hacked, blackened stump stood on the hillock, the trunk of the tree lying splintered across the ground.

"No," Orka whispered. She broke into a run, eyes scanning the meadow. "Froa," she called, though she knew it was useless. Froa was the spirit of the Ash Tree, a creature of wood and bark and sap, and her life was bound to the ash tree she was born from and guarded. Then she saw her: a shape on the slope of the hillock, lying beside the fallen trunk. Orka ran to her, skidded to a standstill and looked down at a figure in the grass: a tall woman like a statue carved from wood, taller than Orka, of indeterminable age, hair coiling around her body as long as her waist, thick with leaves and twigs. Her eyes were wide and bulging, arms stretched out towards the fallen trunk, mouth open and fixed in a scream of agony.

The last time Orka had seen her, Froa had laughed and danced and offered Orka a hand of friendship. Orka stared down at the corpse. Froa's body had been chopped and hacked, splintered; here and there were blackened patches where she had been burned.

"Froa, what have they done?" Orka breathed as she dropped to her knees.

Froa, spirit of the Ash Tree, guardian of the forest, born of a seed from Oskutreð, the great tree that had stood at the heart of Vigrið, the Battle-Plain, as the gods-fall had raged. Orka reached out and stroked Froa's face. It was cold and hard.

"I wanted to give our thanks for your protection while we have lived within your forest, and ask your advice, of where we could go; a place where one of your kin still dwell."

Froa's frozen death-scream stared back at her.

Ach, who, or what, has done this? Who would dare? And who has this power?

Froa were powerful vaesen, their spirits bound to their tree of ash. They lived and died with it, so this Froa would have fought savagely to save the tree. Orka stood and walked to the stump of the ash tree. It had been hacked with many axes, and burned, too, bark black and blistered in great patches. Looking at the ground she could see great swathes of earth had been upturned, roots of the tree visible where it had lashed its assailants, and there were dark patches in the grass. Orka crouched, touched one with her fingertips. The blood was dark and congealed, almost black.

She stood, searched the area, found more patches of blood.

Many did this, and some died, or were grievously injured. They took their dead with them.

The dread that had been lurking in her veins surged.

Whoever did this, are they the ones who murdered Asgrim and Idrun, and stole Harek?

A sound on the breeze, faint and ethereal, coming from the west, beyond the ridge Orka had climbed to get here.

Screaming.

CHAPTER SIXTEEN

VARG

Varg woke to pain. His body ached, a throbbing in his muscles that he had never experienced before, and he had worked a farm since before he could remember, and fought in the pugil-rings. He rolled and sat up, groaned.

I hate Røkia.

Various scabs pulled where she had nicked him intentionally with her spear, and his muscles ached as if fire were flowing through his veins, his left arm and shoulder from wielding a shield for a whole day, his back, torso, legs from trying to avoid Røkia stabbing him. And his right hand was blistered from the spear shaft she had eventually allowed him to hold.

But the pain in his body was as nothing to the pain in his head. A constant, rhythmic thumping, that reached fingers down his neck and into his churning belly.

He closed his eyes and put his head in his hands.

I hate mead more than I hate Røkia.

"No lamb for the lazy wolf," a voice said.

"Huh?" Varg grunted, opening one eye.

"You're a late riser, then," Svik said, looming over him.

"Late?" Varg frowned, opening both eyes. The light seeping into the hall was bright, felt like it was burning into his skull. On the farm he had always risen before dawn, so in truth Svik was right, but these were exceptional circumstances. First, he had been beaten close to death by a man called Half-Troll, which didn't happen every day, and then he had been kicked and beaten by a group of freedmen intent on chopping his hand off and dragging him fifty leagues across rocky ground. For six days he had sweated and writhed in a fever, and when he awoke he had been mocked, trained, stabbed, pushed and stabbed again by a lunatic woman with murder and contempt in her eyes. And finally, he had woken with what felt like a miniature Jökul the smith living inside his head, pounding and beating on an anvil inside his skull.

He looked up at Svik.

"What's wrong?" Svik asked him.

"When I woke, I thought I was dead," Varg mumbled. "And when I sat up, I wished that I was. I am *never* drinking mead again."

"Ha," Svik laughed, deep and genuine. "If I had an arm ring for every time I've heard that – or said it myself, for that matter – I would be rich as a jarl."

Thralls had set fires in the hearths and hung black-iron pots over the flames, other warriors already risen from their beds of rushes around the hall's edge, the smell of porridge and honey hanging thick in the chamber. Varg's belly growled.

"You're lucky Røkia is talking with Glornir, otherwise she would likely be prodding you with her spear for more training."

"Stabbing me with it, you mean."

"Aye, true enough," Svik smiled.

He is always smiling, and mostly at my misfortune.

Varg tried to stand, swayed, and Svik offered his hand.

Varg frowned at it and instinctively pulled away.

"Accepting help is not a weakness," Svik said as he grabbed Varg's arm and heaved him upright.

Varg shrugged. "Where I come from, help would not be given, even if I asked for it."

"You are not there any more," Svik said, for a moment his smile gone, his eyes serious.

That will take some getting used to. Varg had never asked for help, or even thought about asking, knowing that none would be given.

He had lived friendless and lonely for so long that it was just the natural state of life for him, his sister Frøya his only friend.

He looked over at Røkia, who was still standing with Glornir. Vol the Seiðr-witch had joined them, and Jarl Logur, along with his wife and a handful of his oathmen. Varg strode towards them, breathing slowly in an attempt to control the churning in his belly.

As he reached the dais he became aware of a new pressure building in his head, as if a weight were pushing down upon him. He looked up, but saw only a thick-beamed rafter, a raven sitting upon it, its black eye twinkling. Then he saw something was embedded into the rafter, something pale and long, like a sliver of bone. One end of it glinted like silver.

"I will not place you in this position." Glornir's voice grated like surf on a shingle beach. "You have been generous beyond thanks, already, putting up with my stinking crew drinking your mead, eating your meat and humping thralls in your rushes."

"You are welcome always, Glornir. The Bloodsworn will always have a place at my hearth fire, whether it be for a day or for a winter."

"We are grateful," Glornir said, "and we will surely return. But today, we will sail with the tide. My crew are restless, anyway. They are not made for idleness."

Logur grunted and embraced Glornir. "I shall see that you leave with full barrels and bellies," he said. "I shall arrange it all." And he walked away, his guards following.

His wife lingered a moment. "He means that he will ask *me* to arrange it all," she said with a smile.

Glornir dipped his head to her.

"My thanks, Sälla," he said, and then she was walking away, too.

Glornir looked up and saw Varg and frowned.

"Eavesdropping is not an admirable quality," he said.

"I was not," Varg said. "I . . . wanted to talk to you."

Glornir gave him a flat look.

"Talk, then."

Varg saw them all staring at him. Glornir, Røkia, Vol. Svik behind him. Edel the scoutmaster with her two hounds. Members of the Bloodsworn.

How did I come to be here? Life is sweeping me on a great wave.

"My thanks, first," Varg said. "You saved me, from Leif Kolskeggson, for which I am grateful."

Glornir dipped his head, an acknowledgement, but he said nothing.

"Huh," Røkia grunted.

"You said *first*," Vol said, her voice soft, a surprise coming from her hard-lined face, accentuated by blue tattoos knotting her neck and lower jaw. Below the tattoos a thrall-collar sat on her neck, though she acted like no thrall Varg had ever known. There was a confidence about her, and a dignity in her gaze. "Which means, you have something else to say?"

"I do," Varg nodded. He closed his eyes, remembered Frøya's face. "I have a request. A task that can only be performed by a Galdurman, or a Seiðr-witch." He opened his eyes and looked only at Vol, now.

"What task?" Vol asked him.

"An *akáll*."

Vol clicked her tongue. "That is no simple task," she said. "To relive the last moments of a life . . . "

"I know, but it is . . . *everything*, to me."

"You need—" Vol began.

"No," Glornir grated, interrupting.

Varg looked from Vol to Glornir.

"I was told that Vol worked her craft for the Bloodsworn. That is what Svik told me. That the only way for her to undertake this task for me was if I became one of the Bloodsworn." Varg looked accusingly at Svik, who shrugged.

"This is a truth," Svik said, his infuriating smile lurking at the corners of his mouth.

"And I am Bloodsworn," Varg continued, looking to Glornir now. "You said the words yourself, to Leif Kolskeggson. Or should *Liar* be added to the many names of Glornir Gold-Giver?"

Hisses, indrawn breath, from Røkia and others in the hall. Dark looks.

"You are not Bloodsworn, yet," Glornir said.

Varg scowled. "Then why did I fight Einar Half-Troll, get myself beaten to a pulp? Get stabbed and abused by her?" He jabbed a finger at Røkia. She smiled back at him, a cold smile that set his blood thrumming, anger rising.

"And why did I save your life, when Leif stood over you with a cleaver and named you murderer?" Glornir said quietly.

"I am no murderer," Varg said slowly, controlling the anger he felt bubbling in his veins.

"So you say," Glornir replied, "and I shall know what you are soon enough. But answer my question. Why did I save your life?"

Varg blinked, emotions swirling, confusion and anger mixing within him.

"I don't know," Varg breathed. "Svik said it was because I bit Einar . . . " He trailed off, realising how ridiculous that sounded.

"I saved you because you have potential," Glornir said. "You have a foot in the mead hall, but you are not yet one of us. To be Bloodsworn is an honour, and one that is not undertaken lightly. We do not allow just any warrior with fast fists to become one of us. You have to have the right . . . *qualities.* Skill in battle. You lack weapons craft, yes, but Røkia tells me you are fast and have balance, and a warrior's spirit. We saw that when you fought Einar. Courage and strength are necessary to be one of us, obviously, but you must have more than that. You must have the right qualities *here.*" He stepped forwards and prodded Varg on the forehead. "And here." A finger poking his chest, over his heart. "Loyalty, devotion unto death. Do you possess those qualities?" Glornir shrugged. "Time will be the judge. Until then, think of yourself as an apprentice. We will teach you, feed you, protect you. In return you will learn, you will obey, you will fight. And then . . . " Glornir smiled, which changed his face. "We will see." He sniffed, wrinkled his nose and looked Varg up and down, at his blood-crusted, sweat-stained tunic, the grime and dirt on his skin.

"Here," Glornir said, reaching inside a belt-pouch and handing him a small bag. It chinked with coin. "Buy yourself some kit. If not we'll most likely be putting you in a barrow after your first scrap, not listening to your oath. And we sail with the tide, so be quick at it."

Varg looked at the bag.

"Don't be a fool," Svik said. "Take it."

Varg did. "My thanks," he muttered, and then Glornir was walking away. Vol looked at him a long moment, then followed Glornir.

"Glad we've got that cleared up," Svik said, rubbing his hands together. "Now, let's go and spend that coin."

CHAPTER SEVENTEEN

ORKA

Orka ran, her chest heaving, lungs burning. She could smell smoke on the air. The vale of the ash tree was far behind her, she had climbed the ridge at a run, crossed it and was plummeting down the far slope through woodland, towards her steading.

The flicker of flames through branches. Sweat stung her eyes, her limbs heavy, branches whipping her skin, but she ran on. The sounds of shouting. A cloud of black smoke rolled through the woodland.

A rhythmic thud, a tremor in the ground and ripple in branches, as if Berser the dead god had awoken and was pounding on a war drum.

She ran on, heard voices mingled with the crackle of flame.

A crash, a battle-cry, a scream, high and terrified.

Breca.

Fear and rage bubbled inside her, merging, feeding her. The clash of iron and steel, more screams.

Vines snagged her feet, sending her stumbling, but she steadied herself with her spear and ran on, swerving around trees, carving a path through ferns and sedge. Her heart pounded in her chest, blood beating loud in her skull. The ground began to level, and she knew she was close to her home. Abruptly she realised that the noises had stopped. She heard only the crackle of flame, thick banks of cloud swirling among the trees.

And then she was bursting into the clearing around her steading.

The gates were open, one hanging on a single hinge. Beyond the gates and stockade the walls and roof of her hall were on fire, flames blazing and reaching into the sky. Gouts of black smoke swirled through the courtyard, obscuring much.

Orka pulled the leather cover from her spear blade, dropping it as she ran for the gates. Passing through them she saw that the timber post where the *galdr-runes* that protected the steading were carved had been burned and obliterated, which only a Galdurman or Seiðr-witch could have done.

The courtyard was churned with boot prints. Chickens and goats lay dead, scattered around, the barn and stable doors open, Snort the pony was nowhere to be seen. A shape draped on the rock by the stream: Spert, unnaturally still, black ichor oozing from a hole in his segmented body. Smaller bodies lay around him, a dozen tennúr vaesen. All appeared dead.

Orka's eyes swept the steading, piecing together what had happened. The doors to her hall were smashed and splintered, bodies lying across the entrance.

The steading was attacked and Thorkel retreated to the hall, barred the gates. They set fire to the hall and smashed the doors in. Thorkel held them there, where it is narrowest, rather than let them in.

She bounded up the steps, glancing at the corpses as she stepped over them. A man and woman dressed in woodland leathers and fur. Both bore savage red wounds, deep as bone. Inside the hall rush-reeds were burning in patches on the floor, fiery lumps dropping from the burning roof and exploding on the ground into eruptions of sparks and flame.

Two more dead in the hall; a trail of the dead leading towards a mound of figures piled on the ground, back by the hearth fire.

She ran through the hall, swerving around patches of flame, through thick smoke until she was standing over the bodies.

Five or six corpses, men and women intertangled, limbs splayed, great wounds gaping. One man with a long-axe still embedded in his head, skull split open from crown to chin. Others looked like they had been torn apart, ripped with tooth and claw.

Thorkel lay at their centre.

The hilts of two seaxes protruded from his torso, one high in his chest, one in his belly. He was covered in blood, from his own wounds as well as those lying dead around him. His chest was still moving, blood speckling his lips with shallow, ragged breaths.

"Breca?" she said to him, but he did not respond.

"BRECA!" Orka bellowed, turning in a circle, frantically scanning the room, but she only heard the crackle of flame, the creak of the hall's timbers. She grabbed bodies, pulled them away from Thorkel, searching for her son. She saw a smaller form beneath a woman, dragged her free and saw Vesli, the tennúr. The vaesen lay still, wings loose, face and head slick with blood.

Thorkel's eyes flickered open and he saw her.

"They took Breca," he grunted, a line of blood trickling from the corner of his mouth.

Orka stooped and slid her arms under his shoulders, hands gripping him, and she pulled, dragging him from the hall. He tried to speak, but his voice was a wheeze that she could not hear over the flames.

Suddenly there was a ripping, tearing sound and a portion of the roof gave way, collapsing inwards, a crash and an explosion of flames, a glimpse of blue sky above. The hall creaked, timbers protesting, flames crackling, smoke billowing, a waterfall of sparks cascading around Orka.

She dragged Thorkel out of the hall, down the steps and lay him on the ground. He was ashen, the blood on his lips bright and stark against alabaster skin. Orka kneeled beside him, held his head, stroked sweat-stuck hair from his face, fear a fist clenching around her heart.

Thorkel's eyes fixed on hers.

"They took him," Thorkel breathed again, fresh blood on his lips. "I could not stop them." A pause, a spasm of pain twisted his lips as he took ragged breaths. "I tried."

"I will get him back," Orka said, fury and fear swirling in her blood. She wanted to run and chase after her son, to find him and hold him, to rip and kill and tear those who had taken him, to stamp on their skulls and claw the throats from those who had done this to her Thorkel. But she could not leave his side.

Thorkel's lips moved, breath hissing, and Orka leaned closer.

"Dragon-born," he grunted through clenched teeth, red-flecked spittle on his lips and chin as his body stiffened with a convulsion of pain.

"Breathe. Keep breathing," Orka said: a command, a plea, to Thorkel's failing body.

"I am . . . sorry," Thorkel said, his voice little more than a sigh. His fingers twitched, reaching for her. And then he was gone.

"No," Orka said, a whisper as she gripped his hand, shook her head. Tears blurred her vision, her jaw and throat tight, constricted. Hard to breathe. "No, no, no, no, NO!" she screamed, lifting her head and howling at the smoke-smeared sky.

Orka lay Thorkel's head on the ground, stroked his lips with her fingertips and then wiped his blood across her face, from forehead to chin in ragged stripes. Slowly she stood, a cold wind searing through her heart. She checked her weapons belt, palms brushing the hilt of her seax and small axe, then looked about for her spear before remembering she had dropped it in the hall to carry Thorkel. With fast, deliberate steps she strode back into the hall, held her breath and plunged through thick smoke, back to the pile of bodies around the hearth fire. She grasped her spear and heard a sound, a hiss, and saw that the tennúr Vesli was moving. Orka swept the tennúr up. The vaesen's eyes were open, though unfocused.

One more thing.

She strode to Thorkel's long-axe, the blade buried in a man's skull, put a boot on the corpse and ripped the axe free, then she ran from the hall, timber pillars cracking, splintering, caving in.

There was an explosion of smoke and flame as Orka leaped from the doorway, down the steps, the hall collapsing behind her. She sucked in a deep lungful of air as a cloud of smoke and ash engulfed her, then waited for it to settle. Once she could breathe air again, she lay Vesli upon the ground beside Thorkel. The vaesen was breathing, limbs twitching. Orka placed the haft of the long-axe in Thorkel's hand, folding his fingers around it. Then she was striding from the courtyard, out through the stockade's gateway and searching for tracks.

They were not hard to find, many boot prints flattening the grass, and one set of horse's hooves, heading east into wooded hills. There was blood, too. Bright droplets of scarlet sprinkled across the ground. She looked back through the gates of the steading, at Thorkel's body, and then she was moving, breaking into a loping run through the clearing and into the trees, following the blood and tracks of those who had murdered her husband and stolen her son.

They had made no attempt at stealth, a wide path trampled through the undergrowth. Orka followed them eastwards, the trail slowly curving north, downhill, Orka guessing where they were headed before she heard the sound of the river.

The same as Asgrim's killers. Thorkel followed their tracks to a river. He said three boats. A crew anywhere between twelve and thirty. Less the ten that Thorkel has sent along the soul road.

She increased her speed, the path clear, the thought of Breca setting a fire in her belly. Thorkel's face hovered in her thought-cage: the blood on his lips, his words a whisper inside her skull. Grief swelled in her chest, melding with a forge-fire rage. Fear, anger, grief all spiralled and surged through her, merging into something new.

The sound of running water, and then, piercing through it, the scream of a horse.

Orka slowed, glanced up, saw it wasn't long past midday. The trees were thinning. She glimpsed a fast-flowing river ahead, the diamond-glitter of icy meltwater from the mountains. Figures: two, three, maybe more. She stepped from the path into the undergrowth, crept in a half-circle through the woodland, until she was crouched behind a tree, fern and tall sage all about.

She peered around the tree.

A boat was pulled up on the bank. Snort the pony lay dead, blood soaking the ground from a wound in his neck, three men and a woman setting about butchering the animal with hand-axes and seaxes. They were all lean and hard-looking, wearing wool and fur and leather. Spears lay on the riverbank, and they all held sharp iron in their fists. A pile of offal steamed in the cool air. The river frothed and foamed, further on splitting into two channels as it forked around a slab of granite.

A deep, shuddering breath to still the tremors in her body, a whispered vow and then Orka stepped from behind the tree, hefted her spear and threw it. She was moving before it hit its mark, drawing her seax from its scabbard hanging across her stomach, slipping her axe from the hoop in her belt. There was a scream and gurgle as her spear pierced a man, tall and broad, wearing a green woollen tunic with a brown hood. The spear took him in the back, bursting out of his chest with a spray of blood as he crashed face down on to the dead horse.

The other three stopped, frozen for a heartbeat, one with her hand-axe raised in mid-stroke, chopping at the shoulder joints of Snort's hind legs. They looked from their companion to Orka, who was speeding towards them, snarling, her blades glinting in the spring sun.

The two men spread wide, one old and grey, one too young to grow more than a few wisps on his chin. The woman in front of Orka set her feet and dropped into a crouch, axe raised. Orka veered left, her speed and change of direction taking the older man by surprise. Her hand-axe parried the rushed thrust of his seax as he stabbed at her; a twist and her axe blade bit into his wrist; a yelp and she crashed into him, her seax plunging deep into his belly. They staggered back together, close as lovers, Orka ripping her seax up, slicing and sawing flesh until her blade bit into his lower ribs. She shoved him and the man fell away screaming, intestines spilling about his ankles, and Orka stumbled on, towards the river, turning, slipping and skidding and then falling to her knees.

With a hiss of air, the woman chopped her axe where Orka's head had just been. Orka hacked and sliced, axe and seax connecting with ankle and thigh and the woman screamed, wobbled, dropped to one knee, taking a backswing with her axe as she fell, slicing along Orka's back and shoulder. A spurt of blood; a line of heat, of fire and pain. Orka growled at the woman, launched herself into her and the two of them crashed back on to the riverbank, rolling, spitting, snarling. Orka glimpsed boots striding close, the young warrior rushing after them, looming, hesitating as he searched for an opening. Orka's axe went spinning and she grabbed the woman's wrist, headbutted her, the crunch of broken cartilage. A gush of blood over the woman's mouth and jaw as her eyes rolled back into her head, limbs flopping.

A searing pain ran across Orka's waist and she yelled, thrust the stunned woman away, rolled on the bank, the young man following, slashing wildly at her with his seax. Orka swung her blade, sparks flaring as the seaxes clashed and she kicked out, took the lad in the ankles, sending him crashing down beside her. She rolled and stabbed her seax into his thigh, deep; heard him scream; felt the blade grind on bone; pushed herself away as he swung at her.

Orka climbed unsteadily to her feet and spat blood, pain throbbing across her back and shoulder, her waist. She ignored it all, walked a few paces and bent and picked up her hand-axe.

The lad tried to climb to his feet, screamed and collapsed. He wrapped a fist around the hilt of Orka's seax, embedded in his leg.

The woman groaned, moving groggily.

Orka stumbled over to the waking woman and looked down at her.

"You killed my husband and took my *son*," Orka snarled, lifting her axe.

"Mercy," the woman blurted, raising a hand.

Orka chopped down, severed fingers spinning away, the axe blade crunching into the woman's face. A strangled scream cut short. Feet drummed on the grass.

Thorkel's blood-covered face hovered in Orka's mind, Breca's voice ringing out. At the Froa-tree, it had been his screams she had heard at the steading. She ripped her axe free, her mouth twisting, tears clouding her vision, and she chopped down again, and again, and again, arm rising and falling, the crunch of bone turning to a wet, pulped sound. Orka screamed, a feral, tortured noise of rage and grief, and all the while she chopped her axe into what remained of the woman on the ground. Blood and bone flew, spraying Orka, drenching her red.

A whimper came from behind her and she slowed, stopped, breathing hard. Turned.

She looked to the lad.

He was on the ground, one hand clenched around Orka's seax that was buried deep in his leg, his other holding his own blade, pointing it at Orka. He was staring at her with wide eyes, transfixed, trembling, his face pale as sour milk, twisted in pain and fear and revulsion. Tears cut lines through grime on his cheeks.

Orka threaded her axe haft into the loop on her belt and walked towards the corpse of the man draped over her slaughtered pony. She grabbed her spear shaft, put a boot on the dead man it was buried in, and heaved it free, then walked towards the boy.

"Back, stay back, or I'll gut you," he said desperately, face twitching, seax wavering.

"You couldn't gut a dead fish," Orka snarled, striding closer. Her spear darted out, around his clumsy parry and stabbed into his forearm. He shrieked, dropping his seax. Orka levelled the spear at him.

"Please," he squawked as he scrambled away, whimpering with pain as the seax in his leg shifted, realising he could go no further when he felt the river lapping at his back.

There was one boat pulled up on the riverbank, eight oar-stations in it. The ground along the riverbank was scored deeply with ruts from two other boats. Spatters of blood led up to one of the spaces a boat had occupied.

Injured among the survivors. Breca?

Orka looked north, downhill, saw the water foam white around a wedge of dark granite, the river splitting, forking into two channels. Two paths the *niðings* who had stolen her son could have taken. She looked back to the lad on the ground before her.

"Where is my son?" Orka asked him, spear pointed at his chest.

He looked at her, blood-drenched and grim, then at the spear. With a twist of his body he threw himself backwards, into the river.

Orka lunged forwards, grabbed an ankle and hauled him back out. She held her spear high, spun it into a reverse grip and stabbed down, into his shoulder, leaving the blade embedded in flesh and muscle.

He screamed, tears running down his cheeks, snot hanging from his nose.

"I am going to kill you," she said. "Your days are done." He screamed and begged as she stood over him, holding the spear in his flesh. "Tell me what I want to know, and it will be quick," she snarled at him. "Or you can have more pain." She paused and stared into his weeping face until his snivelling faded to a whimper and she was sure she had his attention. "Where is my son?"

"On the river. They took him," the lad squeaked.

Orka pushed down on the spear and the lad shrieked. The spear blade sliced deeper, through his shoulder and out into earth, pinning him to the ground.

"I know that, you little weasel-shite," Orka grunted. "*Where* are they taking him? What route did they take on the river where it forks?"

"I don't know, I don't know," he mumbled, "I came with my uncle." He glanced at the dead man flopped over the horse's carcass.

"You made the wrong choice," Orka said.

The lad nodded, whimpering. "He said I'd get paid in gold for climbing over a wall and opening a gate. I've got sharp eyes, long arms and quiet feet." His breath came in ragged spurts.

"You opened the gate to my steading," Orka said, voice cold. A flash of Thorkel's face, blood on his lips, hovered behind her eyes. She twisted her spear in the lad's arm.

He screamed, writhed, screamed again.

"Who took my son? Who is the chief, the gold-giver?"

"I . . . can't tell you," the boy wheezed, strings of spittle drooling from his mouth.

Orka's knuckles whitened on the spear.

"Please, no more," the lad sobbed.

"His name," Orka said.

"I . . . fear him," the lad begged, weeping. There was a sharp tang of ammonia as his bladder failed him, a dark stain spreading through his breeches.

"Fear *me*," Orka snarled. She twisted the spear again, leaned and grabbed the hilt of her seax still buried in his leg, dragging it slowly against the bone of his thigh.

She waited for his screams to fade. It took a while.

"His name," Orka said.

The lad looked up at her, eyes almost mad with pain.

"Drekr," he breathed.

Orka tugged her spear free and, as the lad opened his mouth to scream, she plunged it into his chest, put her weight into it, felt the blade pass between ribs and pierce his heart.

A gout of dark blood bubbled from the boy's mouth, choking his scream, and then the life was fading from his eyes.

Orka tugged the blade free and wiped it clean on the lad's tunic. She stared at the river, at the granite rock where the river foamed white, splitting and forking into two paths. Beyond the rock face the twin rivers twisted and disappeared as the land dipped, dropping towards the fjord and Fellur village.

"Drekr," Orka whispered to the cold blue sky.

CHAPTER EIGHTEEN

VARG

Varg walked through the streets of Liga, Svik and Røkia guiding him. In a short time and with their help he had acquired two linen under-tunics, wool breeches, a grey-wool tunic woven in a fine herringbone, *winnigas* leg-wraps with bronze hooks, goatskin turn-shoes, a nålbinding knitted cap and socks, leather gloves lined with sheepskin, a belt with bronze fittings, a seax in a plain leather scabbard with an elk-antler hilt, and a fine sealskin cloak. And a hemp sack to put it all in. He felt like a rich jarl, traders fawning over him. He knew it meant nothing, that they were doing it because of his coin and the two Bloodsworn warriors accompanying him, but part of him felt . . . good. That was a strange sensation, one that he had not felt for a long time.

He saw the trader who had given him the cleaver, and Varg gave him a coin because the man had shown him a kindness when he was a *niðing* thrall. And he bought Svik and Røkia a bowl of stew and a slice of bread.

"And a round of cheese?" Svik asked the trader.

"You like cheese, don't you?" Varg observed.

"Who does not?" Svik answered, frowning as he took the cheese.

They walked on, Røkia stopping at a stall with knives and axes laid out across a trestle table.

"You need this," Røkia said, hefting an axe. She held it out to Varg. He took it, felt the balance. The shaft was short, the axe head curved and unusually weighted. He was no stranger to working with axes, having felled much timber and chopped a mountain of firewood over the years on Kolskegg's farm, but he had never felt one like this.

"It's weighted for throwing," Svik said. "See the curve of the haft and blade."

"Ah," Varg said, patting the axe's poll in his palm.

"You ever fight with an axe?" Røkia asked him.

"No. I told you, only with my fists."

"Aye, well, you should have an axe, then. You'll have a spear, and you cannot afford to buy a sword."

"Or know how to use one," Svik added. "Most likely you'd end up chopping half your head off. Spear, seax and axe, they are a good place to start."

"And it is always good to have a few blades on your belt," Røkia said. "You never know what is around the bend in the road."

Varg wasn't sure how he felt about all this talk of warcraft. His driving thought had been revenge for Frøya: to make his sister's murderer scream. It felt strange, and disloyal, to allow anything else to take up room in his thought-cage.

This is my way to fulfilling my oath. A twisting path, but it is the only way forward.

"I'll have the axe, then," he told the trader, and fished out more coin. "How about that?" he asked, pointing to a fine *brynja* shirt of mail hanging on a rack, riveted rings gleaming with oil.

"You cannot afford it," Svik said.

"And besides, it is better to take one from the corpse of your enemy," Røkia said. "Better to win it in a scrap. How else are you going to earn your battle-fame?" She looked at him as if he was moon-touched.

The thought crossed his mind that if he fought a warrior already wearing a coat of mail, then the odds were that the warrior was skilled, certainly more skilled than him, and would have the extra benefit and protection of ring mail, so the likelihood of Varg surviving long enough to take the *brynja* off his enemy's dead body was not high. And besides, Varg had never thought about battle-fame in all his life. Even when he was fighting in the pugil-ring it had only ever been for the next meal, and then after that because Kolskegg had given him no choice.

"A coat of mail is a wonder," Svik said, "and very good at keeping sharp iron out of your body, but more important is this," he said, tapping a plain helm that sat on the table. Four plates of iron riveted with bands and a nasal guard.

"A stab to your body, you may live. A stab to the head . . ." he shrugged.

Varg picked it up and looked inside it, saw a sheepskin liner and leather strips to adjust the fit. He tried it on, buckling up the chinstrap.

"Good," Røkia said, rapping it with her knuckles.

"And it conceals your hair, which is also good," Svik said. "I suggest you keep it on until your hair is as long and beautiful as mine."

Røkia snorted.

"Here," Svik said, pointing at more goods laid out on the table. There were flints and iron for striking sparks, fishhooks and animal gut for the stitching of wounds, rolls of linen bandages, another flat piece of iron fixed to a curved grip of wood and leather.

"What's that?" Varg asked.

"An iron for the cauterisation of wounds," Røkia said, with another twist of her eyebrows at his ignorance.

"We have bought everything you need to put holes in other people," Svik smiled, "but you need to take some precautions in case someone else puts a hole in you."

"Sensible," Varg muttered, feeling like he was marching blindly down a track that he would not be able to return from.

"Good. We are done then," Røkia said, looking at the sun in the sky. "Best be getting back."

Varg had thrown his old tunic and breeches on a fire that was burning in a space outside near the back of the mead hall, beneath stooping cliffs and pine trees, along with his shoes that were more holes than leather. Then he scrubbed his body in ice-cold water from a barrel, using a brush of stiff horsehair lathered with soap of ash and fat. A trencher of cold mutton and pickle had been put in front of him by Svik as he'd dressed, and he had stuffed in mouthfuls of the smoked meat as he'd wrapped his *winnigas* tightly around his calves and buckled on his belt. Finally, he hooked the chinstrap of his iron helm through his belt and buckled it, so that it hung alongside his weapons. It felt strange, with the weight of axe, seax, helm and cleaver hanging at his belt alongside his pouch, and unimaginable that he could be dressing like this. But it felt good to be clean, to be wearing such fine clothes that he would never have worn to his dying day if he had stayed on Kolskegg's farm. He felt a smile twitching at the corners of his mouth and he wished that Frøya could see him. The thought of her cold in the ground withered his smile.

"Better," Svik said, regarding Varg as he stood straight. "You no longer look like a thrall or a *niðing* beggar. Oh, and this is yours: a gift from Glornir," he said, holding up the black-painted shield Varg had used in training the day before. He slung it across his back and picked up his sack with all else that he had purchased in Liga. Then a horn was blowing and Svik was hurrying Varg into the mead hall's courtyard, where Jarl Logur and his wife Sälla stood in the open doors, a dozen of his oath-guard around him. Glornir stood at the head of the Bloodsworn in a gleaming *brynja*, an iron helm hanging at his belt, his long-axe in his fists. Behind him a mass of warriors were gathered, with their black-and-red spattered shields slung over their backs, a mixture of *brynjas*, woollen tunics and boiled, hardened leather, spears and long-axes held in fists, resting on shoulders.

A nod passed between the two lords and then Glornir was leading them out of the courtyard. Glornir saw Varg and Svik standing at the courtyard's side; he said something and held his hand out, and Vol handed him a grey, ash-hafted spear with a leather cover over the spearhead.

"This is yours now," Glornir said, and threw the spear to Varg. He managed to catch it without fumbling it.

"It belonged to Aslog, whose seat on the oar-bench you will be filling. He was a fine man, though not fine enough to keep his head," Glornir said. "He won't be needing his spear any more, as he has taken the soul road. May it bring you battle-fame."

Varg nodded, not knowing what to say, and then Glornir was past him, leading the Bloodsworn into the streets of Liga. Varg and Svik joined the end of the marching warriors.

They strode down a wide street, people moving to the sides for the Bloodsworn to pass.

"How's your head?" a voice said: Torvik, the smith's apprentice.

"It feels like your smith is inside it, and trying hard to get out with a hammer," Varg said.

"Ha," Torvik laughed. "Mead is a double-edged sword, no?" he said, rubbing his own temple. "It makes the world better for a while, and then worse. Much, much worse."

They marched on, in loose order.

"Jarl Logur is good to the Bloodsworn," Varg said, thinking about the amount of food and mead the warriors must have consumed over seven or eight days.

"Aye, but the Bloodsworn have been good to him," Torvik said.

"How so?" Varg asked.

"The god-relic in Logur's mead hall: the Bloodsworn gave it to him."

"Relic?" Varg said.

"Aye, a sliver of the Vackna Horn, which summoned the gods to the Battle-Plain on the day of *Guðfalla*. It is set in the timber beam above Logur's high seat, and has helped to make him rich."

"Ah," Varg nodded, remembering seeing a bone-white sliver set in the beam, and feeling some strange sensation emanating from it. Relics had power: all knew that. Queen Helka had risen to her high seat in so short a time because she had unearthed Orna's skeleton, the wings of the giant eagle spreading wide over Helka's fortress at Darl.

"A generous gift that Glornir gave Logur," Varg said.

"Not Glornir," Torvik said. "It was Skullsplitter. Our old chief."

"Skullsplitter?" Varg said, remembering now campfire tales among the thralls of Kolskegg's farm, talking of a terrible, merciless warrior.

"Skullsplitter is dead, but the Bloodsworn live on," Svik said, "and the Bloodsworn have done more for Logur than give him a shattered piece of cow-horn."

"What do the Bloodsworn do, then?" Varg asked, wanting to find out more about this crew he was becoming a part of.

"We protect this port, from pirates and raiders," Svik said. "We are the wolves that protect the sheep."

"I thought wolves ate sheep," Varg said.

Svik smiled at him. "Sometimes we do." He shrugged. "But not sheep that are paying us."

The street spilled out on to the docks, and instantly Varg knew there was something wrong.

People were running: dockworkers, traders, merchants. A handful of Jarl Logur's guards with their blue shields in their fists were running the other way. Varg was one of the last of the Bloodsworn to leave the street and enter the dockside. There were screams, the slap of many feet on stone, and, above that, the sound of hooves.

Glornir led the Bloodsworn on, towards their ship the *Sea-Wolf*, people running and yelling, the sound of hooves growing louder. Varg strained, bouncing on his heels to see over the heads of warriors. And then a space cleared before the Bloodsworn, the stone docks empty as they approached the pier where the *Sea-Wolf* was moored.

A row of horses barred their way, wide and deep, warriors in iron helms with horsehair plumes and long coats of lamellar armour. Jaromir sat at their head, Ilia at his side. He held a curved bow in his fist, an arrow nocked.

Glornir walked on a few paces, then stopped and held up a hand. The Bloodsworn rippled to a halt behind him, spreading wide across the road. Shields were shrugged from backs, gripped in fists, helms buckled on to heads. Edel's wolfhounds growled.

Jaromir touched his heels to his mount and the horse walked forwards ahead of the massed *druzhina* behind them, their lances glittering in the spring sun.

"I was going to visit your Jarl Logur with my petition, and my evidence," he said, "but then I am told that your *drakkar* was preparing to sail." He sniffed. "Only the guilty flee."

Glornir said nothing, just regarded him with flat, emotionless eyes.

"Give me Sulich," Jaromir said. "Be a man of wisdom. Save your warriors, and your ship." He looked over his shoulder, at a pair of riders at the pier's entrance, both waiting, holding burning torches. Varg saw shapes moving on the *Sea-Wolf*.

"You have been out too long in the sun if you think I would hand over one of my own," Glornir growled, shaking his head. "No." He hefted his long-axe in two hands, holding it loose across his body, his blood-spattered shield slung across his back.

A twist of Jaromir's lips and then his bow was rising, drawing and loosing faster than Varg could follow. There was a hiss of iron through air, a crack, and the arrow fell splintered at Glornir's feet, his long-axe swinging in his hands.

A frozen moment as Jaromir and his *druzhina* stared, open-mouthed, then Jaromir was reaching for a fist full of arrows.

"LOOSE!" he cried, and forty or fifty arrows left their bows.

Bloodsworn warriors leaped forwards, shields closing around Glornir. Varg saw Einar and Røkia there, and many more, hunched behind their shields, protecting Glornir. Arrows fell like hail, rattling on to the linden-wood, then there was a scream. Einar stood tall and hurled a spear, which flew through the air and slammed into the chest of a *druzhina* warrior, sending them hurtling from their saddle in a spray of blood.

Jaromir slipped his bow back into its case at his hip and drew his sabre. He let out a wordless scream and spurred his horse on, the warriors behind him leaping forwards, lances lowering.

"SHIELD WALL!" Glornir bellowed.

All around Varg warriors moved, shuffling tight, shields rising, crunching together. Varg just stood there, lifting his shield, but he did not know what to do. A concussive crash sounded from the front of the wall, rippling back to where Varg stood, horses and warriors screaming, steel clashing.

The sound of hooves came from behind him, and he turned to see more mounted warriors riding hard at them across the dock, stone sparking under hooves.

"WARE!" Svik cried beside Varg, a row of warriors from the rear of the shield wall turning, re-forming to face this new foe.

"Helm," Svik yelled at him. Varg realised he was the only one in the Bloodsworn who hadn't buckled on his helmet.

He fumbled at his belt, couldn't unbuckle the chinstrap, and gave up. The thunder of hooves was not helping.

He looked up, realised he was standing in the open, riders charging towards him, and without thinking he raised his shield in front of him as Røkia had taught. A rider spurred their mount at him. A mountain of horseflesh hurtled towards him, the warrior on its back gleaming in scaled armour, a sabre rising high.

Varg stared up at his death, dimly aware of Svik yelling his name, calling him back into the shield wall. It was too late. All he could see was the warrior's snarling face, oiled beard, cold steel glinting. Time seemed to slow, the muscles in the horse's shoulder and chest contracting, expanding, and Varg slipped to the side, keeping his shield held high. The sabre crunched into it, a hollow *smack*, the power of the blow rattling through Varg's bones into his shoulder, numbing muscle. Then the rider was past him and instinctively Varg stabbed with his spear, a hard thrust angled up into the rider's waist. It should have pierced mail and flesh, stabbed deep under ribs, but instead the spear glanced away, Varg losing his grip and dropping it. He stared at the spear: saw he hadn't taken the leather cover off the blade.

Around him the other *druzhina* were crashing into Svik and the shield wall, with more yelling, screaming. A spray of blood flew across grey stone.

Then Varg's rider was dragging on his reins, turning his mount in a tight circle.

Without thinking, Varg dropped his shield and ran at the warrior. He leaped, grabbed a fistful of horse's mane and dragged himself up on to the animal's back, the *druzhina* warrior twisting, trying to hack at Varg with his sabre. A mail-clad elbow cracked into Varg's nose, sending blood gushing, but he hung on, one arm wrapped around the warrior, his other hand fumbling for his seax. He found the antler-hilt, dragged it free of its scabbard and stabbed into the small of the warrior's back, the blade deflected by the plates of his lamellar coat. The seax scraped along iron, grating sparks, finding the smallest of gaps where buckles and strips of leather tied the coat tight. The blade slipped in, sliced through wool and linen and into flesh. Varg thrust harder, the warrior arching in his saddle with a scream rising in pitch as Varg's blade sank deeper. He could feel the strength leak from the warrior, and with a final twist and shove Varg sent the rider toppling from his saddle, crunching on to the stone, where he lay twitching.

With a ragged breath Varg slipped into the saddle and sat there, not knowing what to do. He had never ridden a horse before. It felt much higher, upon its back, than it looked from the ground, and he could feel the animal's power beneath him, muscles flexing.

All around him combat was raging, horses rearing, neighing, the Bloodsworn standing solid in their shield wall. Here and there were a few fractured fights: Edel and her hounds bringing down a horse.

"Berser's hairy arse, what are you doing up there?" Svik called up to him, a savage grin on his blood-spattered face.

Varg just stared down at him.

Horns were blowing, warriors with blue-painted shields pouring on to the dockside. Jarl Logur was there, bellowing orders, but the fighting had already stopped, both Bloodsworn and *druzhina* standing and staring out into the fjord.

There, three huge, sleek *drakkar* were gliding across the water, horns blowing from their decks. Their black sails bore the image of an eagle, wings spread, beak and talons striking.

Even Varg knew whose banner that was.

Queen Helka had come to Liga.

CHAPTER NINETEEN

ORKA

Orka walked through the gates of her steading. The flames had burned out, much of the hall collapsed, some pillars and timbers still standing, black and twisted like diseased bones. Smoke hung in the air, churning sluggishly in a breeze. She walked to Thorkel's body, lying with his axe in his fist, his eyes staring and sightless. A fresh wave of grief wracked her, a spasm in her belly, and she turned and bent over, vomiting on to the ground.

"*Mistress*," a voice squeaked, and Orka saw a movement by the stream: Vesli the tennúr kneeling beside the limp form of Spert upon his rock. She spat, cuffing bile from her chin, and strode over to them, feeling the wounds in her back, shoulder and waist pulling. Small bodies littered the ground around the stream, a dozen tennúr lying twisted in death. There was one man, too, dressed like the ones Orka had fought by the river, in wool and leather. Woodsman's clothing. He lay upon the ground, a spear by his side, one foot in the stream, mouth open in a rictus scream. Half of his face was black and blistered, veins dark and protruding, spiralling out like a cobweb. At the swelling's centre there was a small, round wound, like a pinprick.

Spert's sting, Orka realised. She had seen what it did to intruders before.

"*Spert is alive*," Vesli said. She had cleaned the wound on her head and washed the blood away to reveal a ragged gash that stretched from her forehead up and along the crown of her skull. It had not been made with a sharp blade; it looked more like she had been chewed by razored teeth.

Orka looked at Spert. The chitinous segments of his long body were rising and falling with shallow breaths, the wound in his side covered with black congealing ichor. Orka frowned. The wound had been stitched, some kind of pale thread weaving through the segments around the gash, pulling them tighter. And a strange substance coated the wound, thick and opaque, like boiled glue. Vesli had soaked water into a linen bandage for Spert and was dripping it slowly into his mouth.

"You have stitched his wound?" Orka said.

Vesli nodded, looked at Orka and saw the bloodstains on her tunic.

"*Vesli help you, too. Vesli good at fixing wounds.*"

I am good at giving them, Orka thought.

Spert's bulbous eyes fluttered open at the sound of Orka's voice.

"*Mistress*," he wheezed.

Vesli shifted, wings spreading, and she fluttered around to Orka's back and shoulder, hovering, sharp fingers surprisingly gentle as she pulled back the tunic to inspect Orka's wound. She used the linen bandage in her hand to clean the deep laceration, then there was a spitting sound and Vesli was rubbing something into the wound. Whatever it was, in a few heartbeats the throbbing pain across Orka's back and shoulder began to fade.

Orka kneeled beside the vaesen, resting a hand on his head. "I am here," she said.

"*Spert sorry. Spert tried*," the creature croaked. "*Spert kill many vaesen, but nasty Maður stab Spert with a spear.*" He coughed, a ripple through his body, black ichor leaking from his mouth.

Orka glanced at the man's corpse by the stream.

You made him pay for that.

Vesli fluttered to the ground, sharp fingers tugging at Orka's tunic so that the vaesen could look at the cut along Orka's waist. She clicked her tongue, soaked and squeezed out the linen bandage in the stream and set about cleaning that wound, too.

"You did well, Spert," Orka said, letting Vesli work. "Rest, now. Recover."

"*Breca?*" Spert said, looking up at Orka. Vesli paused in her tending of Orka's wound.

Orka drew in a deep breath, then found that she couldn't say the words.

He is gone.

"What happened here?" she asked, instead.

Spert's mouth moved, sputtered a cough.

Vesli dropped her head. "*Maður and vaesen came over wall. Spert fought them, Thorkel barred the gates of the hall.*" She looked at the burned-out skeleton and put a hand with her spiked fingers to her throat. "*Fire and smoke, very bad, we all choke. Thorkel opened gates, fought.*" She made a clicking sound in her throat. "*Thorkel fierce. Thorkel change, become . . .*" She looked up at Orka, who just nodded. "*Warriors and vaesen break in, tennúr too.*" She paused, her face twisting in a snarl, and she spat on the ground. "*Oathless tennúr, and others.*"

"What others?" Orka grunted.

"*Skraeling, and . . . something else. Human, but not,*" she said. "*Like Thorkel, but . . . not,*" Vesli shrugged.

"One of the Tainted?" Orka prompted. "Human, but animal, as well."

"*Yes, yes,*" Vesli said. "*Man, with two long, sharp claws. He fought Thorkel. Nasty man, fierce.*"

Claws? The seaxes in Thorkel's body?

"Did you see his eyes?" Orka asked.

Vesli nodded. "*They glowed red, like embers in the fire.*"

A low growl from Orka.

"And then?" she said, knowing what must be coming, not wanting to hear it, but unable not to.

"*Tennúr flew in, try to take Breca,*" Vesli said with another savage twist of her lips. "*Vesli fight them.*" She put a hand to the wound on her head and shrugged, her wings rippling. "*Next thing Vesli know, Orka carrying her out of hall. Vesli grateful.*"

Orka nodded.

Vesli took a step away from Orka, to look at the wounds on Orka's waist and shoulder.

"*Vesli has helped?*" she asked, a thin smile spreading across her face, showing the hint of tiny, sharp teeth.

Orka stood and stretched, carefully rolled her shoulder and twisted to the side. Both of her wounds felt better. She could still feel them, but the pain was less. She brushed her fingertips across the gash in her waist and felt something sticky.

"*Orka heal quicker, now,*" Vesli said.

"How did you do that?" Orka said.

Vesli coughed and spat up a glob of glutinous spit, then began to knead it in her fingers. It congealed and became stringy, like tendon.

Orka decided she didn't want to know.

"You and Spert are free of your oaths," Orka said, looking from Vesli to Spert, at their wounds. "You have both earned it."

"*Vesli help you.*"

"Help me by looking after Spert." She looked up at the sky, tendrils of black smoke still in the air. "Take him away from the steading. People from the village may come. If they find you and Spert, they will kill you both." She walked back to Thorkel and stood over him, looking down at his pale, scarred face.

I would stay here with you and never leave you, my husband, if I could.

She blew out a long, ragged sigh, knowing what she must do. She walked to the barn and found a spade, then returned to the courtyard, counted paces across the ground and stopped near the western tip of the hall. Then she started digging. It was not long before the blade hit something solid with a dull thud. She carried on digging, uncovering a wooden chest. Once it was clear of earth, she reached in and grabbed a rope handle, dragged the chest free of soil, undid the bolt and opened the lid.

A flood of memories: of Thorkel, of battle, death, the screams of the dying. Old friends, old enemies. Some that had been both. She shook her head; a shudder rippled through her body. For so long she had fought these memories, turned away from them, tried to scatter them, or bury them like she had buried the chest.

But not this time.

Now she embraced them, let them grow and swirl behind her eyes, until all she could see was battle and blood.

Because that is what I am. It is my past, and my future, until Breca is safe at my side.

She reached in and took out a seax in a scabbard of polished leather, knotwork tooled into it, a hilt of walrus ivory, fittings and rings of silver. Reaching back in she pulled out a fist full of arm rings, silver and gold, twisted and wound together. Retrieving the spade, she walked back to Thorkel, setting the seax and arm rings beside him. First, she dug a shallow grave, then she paused and crouched by his side, just wanting to be close to him. When she was ready, she gripped the hilts of the two seaxes embedded in his body, and with a grunt and snarl pulled them free. She looked at them a long moment, then cast them aside on the ground, and dragged Thorkel's body into the grave.

With a whirr of wings Vesli joined her, trying to help by pulling on Thorkel's tunic. She was remarkably strong for her size.

Thorkel slid into the grave, his fist still wrapped around the haft of his long-axe. Orka arranged it on his chest, then placed the scabbarded seax beside him. She slipped the rings of gold over his wrists and up his arms. She stood and continued her work, gathering timber from about the yard, stones as well, and she built a barrow about him. Finally, there was only one space open to the sky, only Thorkel's face still visible. Orka paused and went back to the chest, reached in with both hands and pulled out a rolled sheepskin, laid it out on the ground and unrolled it, revealing a *brynja* of riveted mail. It had been inside a chest, buried in the ground for over ten years, but it glistened as if new, the grease and absence of air within the chest keeping it free of rust. Orka unbuckled her weapons belt that held her seax, axe and a pouch of tinder and kindling, and laid it on the ground. Then she lifted the *brynja* and threaded her arms into it, raising it high, her hands searching for the sleeves, and hoisted it over her head, the iron shirt slipping around her like the coils of a serpent. Orka shifted and wriggled and the coat slipped over her head and down her torso, hanging just above her knees. She twisted and shrugged, rolling her shoulders to settle it into place, adjusting to the weight, feeling it mostly upon her shoulders. It pulled at her wound. Crouching she reached back into the chest and pulled out a pouch that chinked with coin, then she picked up her weapons belt and buckled it tight, looped it, the belt helping to take some of the *brynja* weight from her shoulders.

A long moment, feeling the iron settle about her, as if it had never been gone. She turned and walked to the barn, found a hemp sack and filled it with provisions: a jar of oats, dried strips of salted pork and smoked trout wrapped in linen, a sealskin bag of whey and a round of hard cheese. A loaf of black bread. An iron pot and pan, a wood and leather water bottle. She filled that at the stream and packed everything into the sack, slung it over her shoulder and dropped it beside Thorkel's barrow.

The sun was dipping towards the sea, sending Orka's shadow stretching across the steading and she knew she had to go. But instead she stood and looked down upon Thorkel. With a sigh she stooped and picked up the seaxes that had taken his life. They were as long as her forearm, thick at the guard, single-edged and wide-bladed, with a sudden taper towards the blade's tips. The hilts were carved from ash, knotwork spiralling around them, a brass cap where a sword's pommel would be, a pin threaded with leather. Orka stared at them and slipped one into her belt. A coldness seeped through her blood like frost-touched iron, settling deep into her marrow. The other seax she held out and drew its blade across her forearm, a line of blood welling. She held her arm over the open barrow and watched as blood ran down her arm into her palm, and dripped from her fingertips on to Thorkel's face.

"I am blood. I am death, I am vengeance," she said, her voice flat, empty. Then she wiped the seax clean and slipped it into her belt, finally placing timber and stone on to the barrow, sealing Thorkel inside. She stooped, lifted her sack and picked up her spear, then strode out through the gateway.

With a hiss of wings Vesli flew around her, hovered over her.

"*Vesli come with you, help mistress get Breca back*," the tennúr said.

"No," Orka said. "Death is my only companion. Stay and help Spert."

Vesli looked at the two seaxes that had slain Thorkel, thrust inside Orka's belt.

"*What are you going to do with them, mistress?*" the tennúr asked.

Orka looked out, over the sloping hills and down to Fellur village, a smear far below.

"I'm going to find the owner of these blades, and give them back to him," Orka snarled.

CHAPTER TWENTY

VARG

Varg sat on the cold stone of the dockside and stared at his hands. They were shaking, blood spiralling a pattern across his skin.

People were moving all around him, Jarl Logur's *drengrs* filling the docks, a wall of blue-painted shields and bristling spears separating Glornir and the Bloodsworn from Prince Jaromir and his mounted *druzhina*. Voices were shouting, horses neighing. Varg looked down at the dead warrior on the ground before him. One of Jaromir's warriors, clothed in lamellar plate, his horsehair-plumed helm twisted at an angle where he had fallen from his horse. Blood bloomed from the wound in his side that Varg had given him, pooled on the stones. But all Varg could see was the man's eyes: flat and empty, staring at nothing.

Lifeless.

I took that life from him.

Varg had killed before, but he could not *remember* it. All he knew was that he'd come to his senses with his hands wrapped around the throat of one of Kolskegg's freedmen, then looked around to see another handful dead, Kolskegg among them, a ragged wound where his throat had been torn out.

This man on the ground before him, that had been different. He remembered *everything*, but most of all the sensation of his seax grating along the steel plates of the *druzhina*'s lamellar coat, finding the gap between plates and stabbing into it. Flesh parting; the hot rush of blood. It had been so easy, like slicing open a skin of wine. The man's strength was fading, emptying from him along with his blood.

Varg's guts spasmed and he vomited on to the stone.

"Huh," a voice said and Varg looked up and saw Røkia standing over him. She was blood-spattered, arrows embedded in her shield. Her gaze moved from Varg, to the dead *druzhina*, to the pile of vomit between Varg's feet.

"Your first kill then," she said.

He didn't feel like explaining, just spat bile from his mouth and looked back at her.

"It gets easier," she said with a shrug.

There was a blowing of horns and the scrape of timber on timber. Varg climbed to his feet and saw the first of three huge *drakkars* pulling in alongside a pier close by, ropes thrown and moored. The eagle-sail had been furled and lowered, now, but the sight of the ship still made Varg gasp. Out on the fjord the three dragon-ships had looked impressive, but it had been the eagle-inscribed sails that had stopped the fighting and silenced all on Liga's docks. The image of Orna the eagle-god spread in gold across the black sails: Orna, who had been slain on the day of *Guðfalla*, and was now the banner of Queen Helka. Now that the *drakkar* was close Varg saw it was almost twice the size of the *Sea-Wolf*. Figures leaped over the top-rail on to the pier, a gangplank laid out.

And then people were walking across the gangplank, passing from the ship to the pier. Six, eight, ten, twelve of them, spreading in a loose half-circle across the pier, facing Varg and the docks. Warriors, clothed in mail, men and women, the sides of their heads shaved, skin covered in flowing, swirling tattoos. Swords and seaxes hung from their belts, grey woollen cloaks upon them, edged in fur. Even from this distance Varg knew there was something different about these warriors, just by the way they walked. They had that warrior's confidence in their gait that Varg was becoming accustomed to in the Bloodsworn and Jarl Logur's *drengrs*, but there was something more to these warriors on the pier, something fluid. They moved like a flock of birds, or a pack of wolves, as if without looking each one knew where the others were. But the thing that stood out most to Varg was the thrall-collars about their throats. He had never seen a thralled warrior before.

After them a woman crossed the gangplank, tall, hair long and black as ravens' wings. It was pulled tight at her nape and braided, threads with gold wire curling through it, a red flowing cloak across her shoulders pinned with a brooch of gold. Arm rings glinted as her cloak blew and lifted in the breeze off the fjord. She, too, walked like a warrior, a sword at her hip, gold on the pommel and cross-guard, gold wire wrapped around the leather hilt, the scabbard ornately tooled, a throat and chape of gold.

Queen Helka.

Behind her followed a man, young, black-haired, tall and broad, his clothing almost as fine as Helka's, but where she wore gold, he wore silver. Beside him walked another man, equally as tall, dressed in a dark tunic and breeches, blond hair and beard braided with what looked like pewter or bone tied into and hanging from the braids. A thick, twisted torc coiled around his neck like a sleeping serpent. He wore no weapons upon his belt, just a gnarled staff in one fist, but he walked with the same confidence as one of the Bloodsworn. Behind him came more warriors in mail, spears in their fists and shields slung across their backs, though none of these wore thrall-collars.

Helka strode down the pier, her retinue keeping pace before and behind her.

Jarl Logur stepped out to meet her, and Varg saw Jaromir dismount, hand his reins to one of his *druzhina* and stride towards the queen.

"Well met, Queen Helka," Jarl Logur called out as he strode to her, two of his oathmen with him. Helka stopped, the warriors spread before her rippling to a halt, barring Logur's way. Helka said something and two of them stepped aside, allowing Logur to pass between them, but not Logur's warriors.

"A fine greeting for me," Varg heard Queen Helka say, looking at the warriors spread along the dockside: Bloodsworn, mounted *druzhina* and Logur's warriors.

"There was a disagreement," Logur said. "I was resolving it."

Helka looked at him a moment, then nodded.

Jaromir reached Queen Helka's thralled bodyguards. He walked as if he expected them to part for him. They did not, instead regarding him with cold, flat eyes. One of them sniffed him.

"I am Prince Jaromir, son of Kirill the Great, Khagan of all Iskidan," he said loud enough for all to hear.

Queen Helka's eyes flickered to Logur and then back to Jaromir.

"You have esteemed visitors," she said to Logur. "Welcome to my realm, Prince Jaromir. I hope that my jarl has made you comfortable."

"He has not," Jaromir said angrily. "I came to him with a reasonable request, and he has denied me. The blood of my warriors has been spilled on this . . . " His face twisted as he gestured to Liga's quayside.

"What do you expect if you attack the Bloodsworn?" Jarl Logur snapped. Queen Helka held a hand up, raising an eyebrow at Logur.

"This is not the place to discuss business such as this," she said. "Logur, lead us to your hall, where Prince Jaromir and I shall sit and he can tell me of his grievances."

"My queen," Logur said, dipping his head. He walked ahead of Helka, her bodyguards stepping aside for him. The jarl passed Jaromir, not looking at him, and strode from the pier on to the docks, a dozen of his blue shields settling around him. Another command from Helka as she followed, her guards allowing Jaromir to walk beside her, and then all of her retinue was in motion. Glornir and the Bloodsworn around him stepped back, opening a wider gap between them and Jaromir's *druzhina* so that Helka could pass between them. She saw Glornir and paused, then gestured for him to join her. He stepped out of the Bloodsworn, shield slung across his back and long-axe resting on his shoulder. He raised a hand as half a dozen made to follow him, muttered to Einar and then he was enveloped by Helka's bodyguard.

Varg stared at them as the procession passed him by, Helka's bodyguards striding ahead of her, heads swaying as they swept the crowds either side of them with predatory eyes. Varg found them unsettling, a tingling in his blood as they passed him by. An air of violence surrounded them, almost palpable, like a heat-haze on midsummer's day. One of them eyed the dead *druzhina* near Varg's feet, then looked up at him, as if it knew the kill belonged to Varg.

Their eyes met and Varg took an involuntary step backwards. He had expected arrogance, a cold, fierce haughtiness, but what he saw in the warrior's eyes shocked him.

Misery.

Then they had passed him by, the young man behind Queen Helka talking with the blond-haired man who walked with a staff. Varg saw small bones, what looked like rat and bird skulls, and pewter rings twisted in his hair and hanging from his braids, and his hands were covered in a knotwork of tattoos, disappearing up the sleeves of his tunic.

The whole procession passed them by, marched across the docks and into the street that led to Logur's mead hall.

"Thirsty?" Svik said in Varg's ear, offering him his unstoppered water bottle.

Varg realised he was and took the water bottle, drinking deeply.

"Some cheese?" Svik said, cutting a slice from a round he took from his pouch. He had blood on his hands, just like Varg.

"No," Varg grunted, the thought of food making his stomach churn. "Who are *they*?" he said.

"Who?" Svik mumbled through his cheese.

"Queen Helka's bodyguards."

Svik's general cheer withered. "Her wolf-pack," he scowled.

Varg frowned.

"They are *Úlfhéðnar*," Svik continued. "Tainted thralls, descended from Ulfrir, the wolf-god."

"They look fierce, and wretched," Varg said quietly.

"Aye, well, they are thralls. Treated well, given the finest of everything, but they are slaves, nevertheless," Svik said. "No one wants to live a life on their knees."

"No," Varg whispered, touching his neck. His thrall-collar was gone, but its mark was still there, like a weight on his soul.

"Good in a scrap, though," Svik said. "Vicious bastards."

I believe that.

"Who was the man behind Queen Helka?" Varg asked.

"That was her son, Hakon, talking with Helka's skáld and Galdurman, Skalk," Svik said.

A Galdurman . . .

Around them the Bloodsworn settled into waiting for Glornir, tending their wounds after the brief skirmish with Jaromir and his *druzhina*. Varg saw warriors cutting arrows from their shields, helping comrades clean and bind wounds. One of the Bloodsworn had fallen, an arrow through her eye.

The *druzhina* were doing the same, attending to their injured, all the while a row of Logur's blue shields separating them.

Varg strode over to his discarded shield and spear, which were still laying upon the ground, and picked them up. He leaned his shield against a wall and saw a slash through the black paint where the *druzhina* had struck at him with his sabre. He grimaced at the leather cover still on the blade of his spear.

I am an idiot.

"You are an idiot," a voice said behind him and he turned to see Røkia. She was snapping arrow shafts in her shield, then pulling the iron tips through the inner side. "You attacked a *druzhina* of Iskidan with the cover still on your spear."

"Yes," Varg grunted.

Svik laughed.

"And your helm is still hanging on your belt," Røkia added.

More laughter from Svik.

"No-Sense," Røkia muttered, shaking her head.

"Yet he lives, and his foe is walking the soul road," another voice said. Varg turned to see Sulich, the man this fight had been over. His shield was slung across his back, his sabre scabbarded at his hip. He walked to the dead *druzhina* and squatted, unbuckled the warrior's helm and lifted it clear.

Sulich clicked his tongue.

The dead man was young, younger than Varg, his black moustache bound with silver rings. Sulich placed the helm down on the ground and rolled the corpse over, hands moving to the wound in his side where Varg had stabbed his seax into the *druzhina*. Sulich inspected the plate, pulling at the stitching and gap where the seax had slipped through.

"Travel well, my brother," Sulich murmured, placing his palm over the dead man's eyes, then picked up the helm and stood.

"This is yours, now," Sulich said, holding the helm out.

Varg blinked and shook his head. The thought was repulsive to him.

"I am no carrion-crow, to steal from the dead," he said.

Sulich's face twisted. "Do not *insult* your victory," he said. "These are the spoils of battle. He knew that." Sulich looked down at the dead warrior. "Yes, he is dead, but all men die. Cattle die; all that draws breath will one day fail. He fought well, and so he died well. All that lives on is our battle-fame, and this . . ." He shook the helm at Varg. "This tells *your* tale. That on this day Varg No-Sense bested a mighty *druzhina* of Iskidan." His mouth twitched in a smile. "Even if his spear was still capped and his helm was on his belt and not his head. This is sounding like a saga-tale to be sung around the hearth fire, no?"

Some laughter around them; a few shouts of agreement.

Varg just stared at Sulich.

"He is right," Svik said. "Look around you."

Varg did, and saw the other few *druzhina* who had fallen being stripped of their war gear by Bloodsworn warriors. Even the Bloodsworn who had fallen was being stripped by a *druzhina*, other Bloodsworn standing by and allowing it to happen.

"This is the warrior's way," Svik said.

"Aye," Røkia grunted, "how else will you earn your battle-fame?"

"And it is fine war gear," Sulich said. "That coat of lamellar is a mighty prize."

"You have it, then," Varg said.

Sulich's face shifted, his good humour and smile evaporating, replaced by a scowl. He put the helm on the ground and walked away.

"What?" Varg said.

"You have insulted him," Svik said with a shrug. "No warrior would take from another's kill. That *is* stealing. That is not honour," Svik rapped his knuckles on Svik's head. "And Sulich is more honourable than most."

"There is too much to learn," Varg muttered.

"No one asked you to step into the ring with Einar Half-Troll," Svik said. "This is the world you have entered, that you have chosen. Best you learn how to live in it. Come, I'll help you." He squatted beside the dead *druzhina* and started unbuckling his lamellar coat, then looked up at Varg. "Come on, then, I'm not your thrall."

Varg crouched down and helped Svik strip the warrior of his kit: a belt with a long-handled knife and the sabre scabbard, the sword lying on the ground, which Varg retrieved. A bow case and curved bow, a quiver of grey-feathered arrows, and then they moved on to the coat of lamellar plate. It was heavy, and had extra panels to protect the upper legs, shoulders and upper arms. Beneath it the warrior wore a thick coat of quilted wool, but Varg left this on the *druzhina*.

"How do you carry all of this kit around?" Varg asked when he had it all piled in front of his shield, next to the hemp sack that stored all of the kit he'd purchased in the market earlier that day.

"We wear it," Svik said with a shrug, "it's easier to carry that way, or we store it in our sea-chest."

"Sea-chest?" Varg said.

"By the dead gods," Svik exclaimed, "don't you know anything? The chest you will sit on to pull an oar, once you are on the *Sea-Wolf*."

"Oh," Varg said.

A sound drew their attention and Glornir emerged from a street and came striding towards them, a glower seared into his brows. Three others walked close behind him. One was the blond-haired man with the staff who had walked with Helka's son. Skalk, Svik had called him, Helka's skáld and Galdurman. The other two were warriors in mail, a woman and man.

"Make ready to sail," Glornir called out as he reached them, striding on past Varg and the others, the Bloodsworn rising and falling in behind him.

Jarl Logur's bondsmen had pushed the *druzhina* back from the pier that led to the Bloodsworn's *drakkar*, and Glornir marched on to the wooden boards and down to the *Sea-Wolf*. Without pause he leaped over the top-rail and started shouting orders.

Varg tried to pick up all of his gear, buckling the horsehair-plumed helmet to his belt, slinging his shield across his back, the lamellar coat and weapons belt of the dead *druzhina* across one shoulder, his hemp sack of kit across the other, his spear clutched clumsily in his fist, and he set off after the Bloodsworn. Svik walked beside him, smiling.

They reached the *Sea-Wolf* and Svik stepped nimbly across, turned and waited for Varg to clamber over the top-rail. He was usually well balanced and agile, but carrying more than his own weight in kit did not help. He managed to climb on board without a slip or fall, the ship rising and falling on a gentle swell.

The *drakkar* was filling quickly, the mast heaved up and slotted into place, its woollen sail still furled, Einar wielding a huge mallet to hammer the mast-lock into place. Edel's wolfhounds found a mound of rope and curled up upon it.

"Your sea-chest," Svik said with a flourished bow as he led Varg along the deck, pointing to a chest between two ribs of the *drakkar*.

With a grunt of relief Varg dropped his hemp sack and shouldered the lamellar coat to the timber deck, then unbolted the sea-chest and opened it. It was big, and empty, so Varg quickly stored his kit inside, shutting and bolting it when it was done.

"Your shield here," Svik said, shrugging his from his back and slotting it into a rack nailed and pegged along the rim of the top-rail. Varg took his shield and pushed it in tight.

"Swap your spear for an oar," Svik said, pointing to a rack full of oars.

Varg took an oar, sat on his sea-chest, swivelled the shutter that closed off his oar-hole and threaded the oar through.

"Now, get comfortable. Your arse and that chest are about to become the best of friends." Svik smiled over the lid of his own chest, immediately in front of Varg. He frowned. "You do know how to row?"

"Yes," Varg grunted. He had rowed small fisher boats on the lake that bordered Kolskegg's farm, and hauled goods on the river. But never at sea.

Many of the Bloodsworn were sitting with oars ready. Glornir walked to the prow with Vol at his side, Skalk and Helka's two warriors behind them. Glornir stood in the prow and turned to face them all.

"Bloodsworn, we have work to do. Queen Helka has a problem in the north of her realm. A problem that is eating her people. We are going to find whatever it is, and kill it."

There were cheers from warriors. Varg felt a trickle of ice in his veins, and excitement.

Glornir looked at Skalk and the two warriors.

"Find an oar. You will work if you are going to add your weight to my ship." Then he turned and ushered Vol into the bow. She stepped into Glornir's place and rested a hand against the prow as Glornir vacated it, striding back down the deck to the steering oar at the stern.

Ropes were untied from mooring posts, looped and stored, Einar and a few others using oars to push away from the pier. The current of the fjord tugged them gently into open water.

"OARS!" Einar bellowed, and sixty oars hovered over the fjord's ice-black water.

"PULL!" Einar yelled, and Varg dipped his oar into the water with hardly a splash and pulled, watching Svik in front of him for his rhythm.

Lean and pull, lean and pull, and the *drakkar* moved away from the pier and Liga's harbour, sluggishly at first, but gaining speed.

Pine-cloaked peaks reared about them, distant waterfalls slicing through them like flowing tears as the *Sea-Wolf* cut through the fjord, Glornir steering them south and west, a white-foamed wake rippling from the prow, and someone began to sing. A steady, lilting kenning about the gods-fall, and Varg found himself joining in.

I cannot believe I am here, on a drakkar, one of the Bloodsworn, and sailing towards adventure and battle-fame.

The familiar seed of guilt bloomed inside him, but it could not overcome the flutter of excitement in his belly. A smile split his face as he rowed.

He was sailing the whale road with the Bloodsworn.

CHAPTER TWENTY-ONE

ELVAR

Elvar stared through the rain and mist towards the fortress of Snakavik. It was hidden from view, wrapped in murk and rain-soaked clouds, but she knew it was there. She was sat on her sea-chest, her oar banked and stowed, the *Wave-Jarl* gliding across the green-black of a wide fjord on a half-crew of oarsmen. Grey, mist-shrouded cliffs rose either side of them, thick with nesting gulls, shrieking their hunger. It was a constant chorus in spring that Elvar had once grown deaf to, but now she was back it was all that she could hear.

Ahead, a shadow appeared in the mist, tall and wide as a mountain, taking shape as if it were breaking through the clouds.

Bjarn hissed, the boy sitting close to Elvar, holding his mother's hand.

A snout and fangs longer than trees emerged from the mist high above them, eye sockets deep and dark, the mottled skull of a huge serpent taking shape.

"Mama," Bjarn breathed, a tremor in his voice.

"It's all right," Uspa said, squeezing Bjarn's hand. "It's dead. That is Snaka's skull, and the days of his dark deeds are long finished, though he has left his mark upon the land."

Snakavik loomed out of the mist before them. Elvar craned her neck to look up at its heights. The western extremity of the Boneback Mountains began here, sharp slopes and mist-wreathed peaks disappearing into the distance. Out of that slope protruded the upper half of an immense, bleached skull of a serpent, long fangs bared, eye sockets empty holes: Snaka's skull, its size impossible to comprehend unless you stood before it. Here it was that dread Snaka had fallen, oldest, father of the gods, slain on the day of *Guðfalla*, shattering the world in his ruin and remaking it. Snaka's fall had smashed the ground beneath him, allowing the sea to surge in and create the fjord they were now rowing upon. Earth had been hurled into the air and settled around his corpse, forming a mountain range that cut across the whole continent of Vigrið. The dead god's flesh had long rotted away beneath heaped earth and rock, but the serpent's skull, spine and ribs remained, a colossal and ever-present reminder of the legacy of the gods.

At least Snakavik is safe from vaesen, so we will be able to sleep at night without worry of being strangled by night-wyrms.

The bones of the gods were a shield against the vaesen, though Elvar was not sure why. Some latent power residing in the knit of bone and marrow. Whatever the reason, vaesen avoided any remnant or relic of the gods.

The sight of Snakavik made Elvar feel insignificant, like a rivet-nail tossed into a bucket of nails, and that was a feeling she'd fled Snakavik to escape. She sucked in a breath, trying to contain a swarm of memories long buried that were released by the sight of home, her eyes flickering to Grend. This had been his home, too, for more years than she had drawn breath, but if the sight of Snaka's skull stirred anything inside the old warrior, his face did not betray it.

At the skull's peak a fortress was built high upon a plateau of granite that the head emerged from, a mead hall and gate towers looking like horns and scales upon the snake-god's brow.

Within, below and around the skull and surrounding slopes a fortress and harbour had been built, over many decades a town spilling out around it. Elvar could just make out the timber towers and ramparts that wound around the skull, dark lines against the bleached bone, small as veins from her distance. The glow of a thousand torches from the town within the serpent's skull lit the eye sockets and open jaws as if ancient Snaka flickered with unholy fire.

The crew were silent as they rowed into the harbour of Snakavik, passing between the curved arches of fangs that burst from the water. The lower jaw of the dead serpent rested deep below the water line on the fjord's bed, but the tips of his lower fangs reared out of the water like the bleached bones of a dead whale, the space between them wide enough for twenty *drakkars* to row side by side.

Sound changed as they rowed into the cavernous skull, echoing and swirling, loud yet strangely muted. Ahead of the *Wave-Jarl* the harbour and town sprawled upon a slope that reared into the heights of Snaka's skull, bustling and teeming with life, more *drakkars*, *knarrs*, *snekkes* and fisher boats than Elvar could count moored to a snarl of piers and jetties. Behind her Agnar bellowed orders from the steering oar and guided them towards a pier with a free mooring space on it, Elvar seeing a fine-clothed harbour official striding down the pier towards them, a handful of well-armed guards at her back.

Jarl Störr's officials are as keen-eyed as ever for their coin.

"OARS!" Sighvat yelled and the rowers raised and banked their oars, the *Wave-Jarl* gliding towards the space on the pier. Warriors of the Battle-Grim leaped over the top-rail on to the pier, mooring ropes slung across to them and tied off, and then the strakes of the *Wave-Jarl* were grating against timber. Agnar climbed on to the pier and spoke to the harbour official, a woman wrapped in red wool edged with pine marten fur, a wool and fur hat on her head, rings of silver thick on her arms and around her neck. Her mail-clad guards stood close, eyeing Agnar and the crew of the Battle-Grim as bored warriors do, appraising. There was little trouble in Snakavik, at least not when Elvar had lived here. Jarl Störr was a stern master, and though his realm thrived, trade and wealth flowing, he was not a tolerant or forbearing man. Elvar's eyes flickered to a row of posts as tall as masts set along the dock-side, metal cages hanging from them, creaking on rusted hinges. Skeletons were wedged within them, bones picked clean by ravens and crows. In one of the cages a half-decomposed body was visible, male or female, it was impossible to tell. A half-gnawed arm flopped through the iron bars, tattered strips of a tunic flapping in the breeze.

A pouch of coin passed from Agnar to the harbour official, paying the *Wave-Jarl*'s harbour dues. The official handed Agnar a block of rune-carved wood, then she was walking away, her guards following.

Agnar called out a half-dozen names, a handful of warriors ordered to remain with the *Wave-Jarl* to guard the ship, and everyone else climbed over the top-rail on to the pier.

Elvar was already dressed in her *brynja*, her weapons belt buckled and looped at her waist, a brown woollen hood draped across her head and shoulders, holding off the rain. Out of habit she lifted her sword in its scabbard then let it slide back down. Her shield she had left wedged on the top-rail by her sea-chest, and her spear was still on the racks in the *Wave-Jarl*'s deck. Sighvat clambered on to the pier, chains rattling as he led their prize, the *Berserkir*, Berak. His wife and child followed behind them. Biórr and Thrud were their guards, Thrud still limping from the arrow he had taken in his calf back on the island of Iskalt. He was lean and knotted as walrus rope, his face scarred and pitted, his cheeks and bones all sharp angles. Finally, Kráka, the Tainted Seiðr-witch, and the *Hundur*-thrall stepped on to the pier and walked to Agnar.

Elvar stood quietly with Grend, her hand rising to close around the troll tusk that hung around her neck. She liked the feel of it in her fist, smooth and cold like walrus ivory. Grend wore his *brynja*, axe and seax on his weapons belt, a woollen hood pulled up over his black braided hair. Then Agnar was calling out and they set off along the pier, marching into the harbour town of Snakavik. They passed the creaking cages of criminals, each post with a rune-carved sign nailed to it. The one closest to Elvar read, "Worshipper of a dead god'. They passed through the docks, fish-houses and a score of taverns reeking of stale mead and urine. Elvar scowled at the narrow streets and walls, as if she could warn off the stench of fish, brine and humanity with a glare. By the looks of it Grend was trying the same tactic, but it wasn't working for either of them.

Even though the sun was still in the sky, the harbour town of

Snakavik existed in a permanent state of dusk or darkness, the serpent's skull only leaking light in through its open jaw, eye sockets and a few score cracked fissures that ran through its thick bone. Because of that, torches burned everywhere, smoke from whale and seal oil thick in the air, adding to the cloying sense of pressure all around. Elvar started to feel her skin crawl, realising how much she loved the open seas and life with the Battle-Grim.

Living a life where I could have died many times over is far more preferable to living one more day in this stinking turd of a town.

The road steepened, buildings rearing and leaning, crowds of people thick as flies: fishermen, warriors, merchants, traders, whores leaning in the entrances to alleys, sometimes the glint of iron deeper within the shadows, cut-throats waiting to relieve a whore's client of their coin or life.

They came to a crossroad and Agnar stopped.

"Find us a tavern with room enough for the Battle-Grim, one that sells good ale and mead," Agnar said to limping Thrud and gave him a bag of coin. Thrud grunted and shuffled off to the right, Biórr telling the prisoners to follow him.

"Sighvat, Huld, Sólín: with me," Agnar said, then strode on up the steep hill, Kráka and the *Hundur*-thrall accompanying them.

Elvar blew out a long breath, partly relieved, partly disappointed not to have been chosen. The rest of the Battle-Grim walked after Thrud and Biórr, Elvar standing there a moment then following after them.

"Elvar," a voice called. It was Sighvat, who was standing and looking back at her. "This way, with us, you halfwit."

Elvar shared a look with Grend and changed direction, following after Agnar and Sighvat and the others.

They climbed ever higher, winding through the streets of the town-in-the-skull, until Sighvat was red and blowing, sweat soaking him. They passed a tavern where a dozen or so warriors were stood outside, talking, leaning on a wall, drinking from horns. All of them were dressed well, in good war kit: mail and leather and wool, a few with swords at their hips, always the sign of a good gold-giving chief. Elvar noticed that each one of them had a black raven's feather tied into their hair. Some had shields slung across their backs or resting against the tavern wall. They were painted grey, black wings unfurled around the boss.

The Raven-Feeders. Elvar knew them. A crew with a ruthless reputation, led by Ilska Raven-Feeder, or Ilska the Cruel, some called her.

The warriors eyed Agnar and his companions as they walked past the tavern. Agnar was well known, a man of high battle-fame and reputation, and Huld and Sólín had their red shields with painted spear and axe over their backs, the known sigil of the Battle-Grim.

One of the Raven-Feeders, a fair-haired warrior with a beard patched with red and gold, leered at Elvar, smiling at her.

"Come join us," he said to her, gesturing with a horn of mead. He looked at fat-bellied Sighvat and grey-haired Grend. "I promise you a better time than you'll get from these old timers." He blew her a kiss, silver thick around his neck and arms.

Grend slowed, giving the man a dark look.

"Got something to say, old man?" the blond warrior said.

Elvar stepped between them, pushing Grend on, and looked the blond warrior up and down.

"I'd rather hump old Svin the dead boar," Elvar said, then turned and walked on.

A few laughs rippled among the blond warrior's companions, as well as a stream of insults that followed them up the street. Sighvat growled at Huld to ignore the taunts as she turned her head to glower at them.

They turned a corner and left the tavern and the Raven-Feeders behind them.

Checkpoints came and went, each time Agnar stopping to talk to guards at gate towers, showing the mooring rights the harbour official had given him, handing over more coin for a speedier passage to the fortress. Eventually they came to a levelled peak on the slope, and from here they began to climb the winding stair, built of timber thicker than masts, wide enough for a dozen to walk abreast. It hugged the back of Snaka's skull, spiralling high above the town, and then disappeared into one of the gaping fissures through the serpent's bone.

Elvar paused to look down over the thick railing posts, and saw the town spilling down the slope like too much porridge boiling over from a pot. Lights flickered through the smoke-smear, and her eyes picked out the *Wave-Jarl*, bobbing in the harbour, small as a rivet-nail from this height. Then Grend was grunting at her and she turned and walked into the bone tunnel, moisture dripping, the timber steps slick, smoke from oil braziers thick around her.

Elvar counted off the steps, as she had when she was a child.

"Two hundred and twelve," she breathed as she broke into daylight, the party emerging on to the crown of the skull like maggots from a wound. Cold wind scoured them, a fine rain swirling like mist. Elvar sucked in clean air, feeling its chill crackle in her lungs. The sun was sinking into the western horizon, spreading a diffuse glow through rain-bloated clouds.

A road of timber planks led eastwards across the skull towards a plateau of granite, upon which the fortress of Snakavik stood. Thick timber walls and a strong gatehouse were touched by the last light of day, the roofs of buildings visible within, a mead hall at the heart of the fortress. Even from here Elvar could see the curling, snake-carved beams of the mead hall's roof, the hall larger than some towns Elvar had seen on her travels. Behind the hall reared a Galdur tower, where Galdurmen learned their rune-dark ways.

Without a word they strode along the road, Grend ahead of her, his hood up, head down, shoulders hunched against the wind and rain. The gates were open, a dozen guards standing either side, more helmed warriors looking down on them from the gate tower's ramparts. They wore fine mail and held yellow shields with a knotted serpent coiled around the iron boss, jaws gaping. A woman stepped out to meet them, a captain judging by her war gear. A helm with dark eye sockets and etched with bronze was buckled on her head, and her hand rested on the pommel of a scabbarded sword.

Elvar stood at the back of their group and waited quietly as Agnar spoke to the captain, going through the same process as he had a dozen times already, showing her the harbour rights, handing her some coin, pointing to Berak.

She looked at the chained man, then nodded. She barked an order to one of her warriors, a young lad holding a spear, who turned and led them into the fortress.

They passed through wide streets rowed either side with longhouses, some of the garrison homes for Jarl Störr's *hird*, his oathsworn retinue of *drengrs*, then turned into another street where blacksmiths' forges belched smoke and the pounding of hammers rang in their ears. A courtyard opened wide before them: the mead hall of Snakavik, with wide steps and wooden pillars leading up to its deeply carved doors. A row of stables lined one edge of the courtyard, horses whinnying. Warriors stood at the top of the steps, before the doors, gleaming in polished *brynjas* and helms, bright spears in their fists.

The lad leading them hurried up the stairs and spoke to the warriors, one of them disappearing through the doors.

"You will wait here," the lad instructed Agnar as he climbed the steps and they all stuttered to a halt. Elvar looked around and saw the warriors regarding them with cool stares, most eyes drawn to Berak, who stood with his head down, long hair wet and hanging, casting his face in shadows.

Elvar's woollen hood sagged as the mist-like rain soaked into it, the courtyard shifting into darkness. Torches and braziers were lit, whipped by the wind.

The doors creaked and a warrior gestured for them to follow.

Agnar led them up the steps and into Jarl Störr's mead hall. Elvar passed beneath the archway and entered a high-vaulted chamber, crows roosting in the shadowed rafters. Long rows of tables and benches led towards the far end of the hall where Jarl Störr's high table was set. Behind that there was a dais, a single chair sitting upon it, and set a little behind that, what looked like a marble-carved head, huge as a boulder, tall as any man. The image of a man was carved upon it, with a high forehead, a broad, wide nose and thick lips. Its eyes were closed, dark veins running through the marble, which seemed to glow in the torchlight.

Agnar and his crew followed an escort of warriors, other warriors falling in around them, more warriors stationed around the periphery, where torches flickered on walls. Hearth fires burned down the centre of the hall, thralls turning carcasses of boar and deer on iron spits, fat dripping and sizzling in the flames as the evening's meal for Jarl Störr's freedmen and oathsworn was prepared.

A door at the far end of the hall opened and figures entered the room. A tall man led them, slim, clothed in a tunic of dark-blue wool, tablet weave around the neck and hems, a silver-buckled belt about his waist, a fine-wrought seax suspended upon it. A silver chain hung around his neck, a serpent's fang hanging from it, and a thick silver arm ring was coiled around his bicep, a serpent eating its tail. His hair was dark, touches of silver in it, pulled tight and tied at his neck, his beard neat, one braid running through it, bound at its tip with a silver ring. Heavy brows hung lidded over his eyes, shadowing them, his nose thin and sharp.

Jarl Störr.

He sat in the chair on the dais, other figures spilling through the door behind him, settling around him. Men and women, twelve, fourteen, all tall and broad, their necks and shoulders bunched with muscle beneath their tunics, thick-browed and glowering. Their hair was braided with gold and silver wire, the men's beards groomed and gleaming with oil. All of them wore pendants on thick chains around their necks, bear claws of iron hanging from them. Axes hung from their belts.

And all of them wore a thrall-collar.

They settled around Jarl Störr like hounds, some sitting at his feet, others stepping off the dais to prowl the space between the dais and high table, others leaning against walls, slipping into the shadows.

Three others stepped through the doorway on to the dais: two younger men and a woman. The men were both dark-haired and thick-browed, making dark shadows of their eyes, their noses thin, marking them out as close kin of Jarl Störr.

The woman was blonde-haired, tall and proud, older than the two men. A necklace of bones draped around her neck, tattoos of runes thick upon the backs of her hands and disappearing into the sleeves of her yellow wool tunic.

The three of them stood at Jarl Störr's shoulder.

The warriors leading Agnar drew to a halt as they reached the space between the mead benches and the high table, stepping aside to let Agnar face the jarl.

"Welcome, Agnar Broksson, chief of the Battle-Grim," Jarl Störr said. His eyes flickered over those behind Agnar, touching upon Elvar and passing over her, resting upon the bowed head of Berak, then returning to Agnar.

"Well met, Jarl Störr." Agnar bowed his head.

"I am told you have goods for sale, goods of interest to me," Jarl Störr said.

"Aye, my lord," Agnar said. Elvar was not used to hearing her chief talk so deferentially to another person. She didn't like it.

"I bring to you Berak Bjornasson," Agnar continued. "He is Tainted, *Berserkir*, wanted by three jarls for murder, blood-debt and weregild. I bring him first to you out of respect, and because I know your tastes."

Agnar signalled to Sighvat, who grunted an order and pulled on the chain in his fist. Berak took a stumbling step forwards, slowly raised his head and glowered at Jarl Störr.

A series of growls rippled through the *Berserkirs* ranged around Jarl Störr, a sudden tension in the air, like a gathering storm.

"You bring him first to me because you think I will pay the highest price," Jarl Störr snorted, waving a hand. He looked at Berak, silent a while. "And if what you say is true, then you are right. I will pay you well. I value *Berserkirs*."

"It is true," Agnar said. "My *Hundur*-thrall tracked him by scent, and my Seiðr-witch has confirmed his lineage."

"Hmm," Jarl Störr murmured, fingers drumming on the arm of his chair. "If only this were a world where I could trust in the truth of any man's word." He looked to the woman standing beside him. "Silrið," he said with a gesture of his hand.

The blonde woman stepped from the dais and walked towards them. She wore a tunic and breeches, *winnigas* wrapping her lower legs, leather cords criss-crossing them, a seax at her belt. It was shorter than most, not made for the shield wall. She drew it as she reached Berak, the steel blade glinting, and held it loosely. Berak towered over her, glared down at her.

"I need some of your blood," Silrið said. "Give it willingly, I advise."

Elvar saw Berak tense, the muscles in his back and legs abruptly taut. There was a long, drawn-out moment, and then he blew out a breath and raised an arm, pulling up the sleeve of his tunic to reveal a thick-muscled, hairy forearm.

Agnar had warned him what would happen to his child and wife if he caused any trouble.

"Good," Silrið murmured as she drew her seax across Berak's arm, a dark line of blood welling. She turned on her heel and strode back to Jarl Störr and walked past him to the statue of the head on the dais. She stood before it, the head taller than her.

"Wake up, Hrung," she said.

The statue was perfectly still.

Silrið kicked the statue's chin and a shuddering ripple passed through the head, like touching the still waters of a pond. Its mouth twitched.

"Hrung, *vaknaðu*," Silrið barked and the eyes snapped open. They were opaque and mist-like, pale as pearls and swirling sluggishly. Slowly they drew into focus and fixed on Silrið. The statue's lips moved.

"I was dreaming," the giant head said, his voice reverberating in the hall, Elvar feeling it pass through her body, like distant thunder.

"You can tell me of that later, ancient Hrung. But now, your jarl needs your service."

The cloudy eyes moved, looking at Jarl Störr in his chair, then back to Silrið.

"What would you have of me?" Hrung said.

"Some blood to taste. Tell us what you can," Silrið said, raising her blood-smeared seax.

Hrung sniffed, seeming to Elvar like he was drawing all of the air within the hall into his nostrils, then opened his mouth and stuck out his tongue, wide and fat and pale. Silrið placed the seax on to it and gently wiped the blood off, taking care not to cut the giant.

Hrung closed his mouth and his eyes then was silent a moment as Elvar saw his tongue moving, pressing into the sides of his cheeks. Then he opened his eyes and spat, a glob of red-smeared phlegm splattering on to the dais.

"Berser's blood, or I am a dwarf," the head said.

Jarl Störr smiled.

"Take him," he said, and Silrið walked back towards Berak, two of the hulking thralls at Jarl Störr's feet accompanying her, as well as a trio of warriors. Berak stood waiting.

Silrið held her hand out to Sighvat for the chain, but he just stared back at her.

"We have not discussed his price," Agnar said.

"Twice what you would have received anywhere else," Jarl Störr said. "I appreciate your business acumen, and, this way, if you find any more Tainted . . . "

Agnar dipped his head. "Your generosity is much appreciated, my lord, and my loyalty to you is guaranteed," he said, then nodded to Sighvat.

Your loyalty to Jarl Störr's coin, you mean, Elvar thought, unable to stop her lip curling.

Silrið took the chain and led Berak away, the two *Berserkirs* with her pushing close to Berak, snuffling and snorting.

"Well met, brother," one of them growled. Berak ignored them and followed Silrið with his head down, feet shuffling.

"Silrið will bring you your payment," Jarl Störr said. It was clearly a dismissal. Agnar dipped his head and turned, walking away, Elvar and his small crew following him.

"Hold." A voice rang out in the hall, vibrating through Elvar's body. The giant head Hrung's eyes were wide, nose twitching and sniffing. He stuck his tongue out, licked the air as if tasting it, then closed his mouth and smacked his lips.

"Elvar," he said into the hall.

Jarl Störr stared at Hrung, the two men at his shoulder taking a step forward.

"You must be mistaken," Jarl Störr said.

"Elvar is here," Hrung said, his bass voice filling the room.

Elvar stopped with a sigh and turned, dimly aware that Grend was turning beside her, Agnar's crew coming to a halt.

Elvar put her hands to her hood and pulled it back.

"Hello, Father," she said.

CHAPTER TWENTY-TWO

ORKA

Orka crept through thinning trees, Fellur village appearing ahead as a blacker shadow against the crow-dark of night. Wind soughed through the woodland about her, stirring branches and picking white foam on the fjord that reflected faint starlight and moonglow. The sound of boats creaking drifted on the wind.

She reached the last of the trees and waited, staring, then glanced to the east. Dawn was still little more than a thought, here in the dead of night where all were asleep.

Except for the hunters, Orka thought. *The prowlers and shadow-walkers*.

But she knew she would have to move, soon. The journey from her steading to Fellur had taken over half a day, and then she had taken more time to stow her spear and hemp sack. She did not need them for what she was about to do. But dawn would not wait for her, and she had dark work to do. Every moment away from Breca grated on her, like claws scraping bone, but something in her gut told her this was the wisest course, rather than choosing to follow one of the two river channels, not knowing which one Breca had been rowed down. She needed information and an image clawed insistently in her thought-cage. Of Jarl Sigrún's new thrall licking Thorkel's blood from her seax.

The open strip of land that lay between the woodland and village gates was filled with the tents of those who had come to attend the Althing. Here and there the orange-glow of embers from half burned-out fires leaked into the darkness. Orka whispered an oath, then stepped from the trees and picked her way through the tents. She took her time, letting her eyes adjust to the darkness, avoiding looking at any fire-glow, until she had passed through them all and stood before the barred gates.

There were no guards.

She took a few long strides and leaped up at the wall, grabbed the timber top and heaved herself up, swung one leg over, the momentum carrying the rest of her body after it. She dropped into mud, boots first, with a squelching thud, and stayed there, crouched, listening.

Ten heartbeats, twenty and there was no sound. She stood and padded into the village, disappearing into shadow.

All was silent in the village, not even dogs stirring at her passing. Soon the courtyard opened up before her, cold and still, the mead hall looming dark against starlight. Another long pause, Orka listening, eyes scouring the darkness. She spied something on the steps to the mead hall's doors: a deeper shadow. A guard sat sleeping, propped against a pillar, a thick fur pulled around their shoulders.

Orka slipped around the courtyard's edge, always keeping a wall to her back, then froze. A sound.

A groan, coming from the courtyard before the mead hall's steps.

She stared, shapes coalescing. Two figures were slumped on the ground, arms raised high, bound at the wrists and tied to a post. One of them was weeping, a sad, pathetic sound; the other looked to be asleep or unconscious.

The clouds parted, moonlight gilding the courtyard for a few heartbeats, then it was gone, hidden behind more cloud.

But Orka had seen who it was tied to the stake.

Mord and Lif, Virk's boys.

They went back to the Althing.

If they were staked out in the courtyard then they had committed a crime and would be awaiting trial, or the enforcement of a punishment.

Orka paused, looking at the sleeping guard on the steps. She should leave them, and was about to, when Breca's face appeared in her thought-cage.

"*I feel sad for Mord and Lif, Mama,*" he had said to her.

She ground her teeth, then she was creeping across the courtyard, bent low, coming up behind the two brothers. She slipped a hand around the mouth of the one who was awake, Lif, the younger of the two brothers. She felt him stiffen and struggle, hissed in his ear.

"It is Orka. Be still."

He froze.

"I'm going to let you go. Make a sound and I'll kill you myself," she breathed in his ear.

He nodded and she released him then crept around so that he was between her and the guard on the mead hall steps. She put a hand to Mord, who was slumped against the post. Blood trickled from a wound in his scalp, but he was breathing.

"We went back," Lif whispered. "Tried to kill Guðvarr. We failed. Tomorrow we will be tried: outlawry or execution, Sigrún said."

Orka put a finger to her lips, then crept away from Lif, towards the sleeping guard. As she slipped her seax from its scabbard she saw that the guard on the steps was a woman, strands of fair hair escaping the hood of her cloak and shimmering in tattered starlight.

Timber creaked as she put her weight on to the first step.

The guard stirred and opened her eyes.

Orka stabbed her seax into her throat, pushing deep, her other hand clamping over the woman's mouth as she felt her blade grind on the spine. She dragged the seax free with a surge of blood, black in the starlight, and the guard slumped, gave a gurgle and then she was still. Orka wiped her blade on the guard's fur cloak, propped her up so that she would remain in her sleeping position, then padded back to Lif.

He was staring, eyes wide.

Orka raised a finger to her lips, then sawed at the rope tying Lif and Mord to the post. Lif came free first and caught Mord as his arms flopped and his body teetered towards the mud.

Orka leaned close and whispered in Lif's ear.

"Take your brother to your boat, gather any provisions you can carry in a bag, and be waiting for me on the fjord, as close to the rear of the mead hall as you can get. If you see the first hint of dawn and I'm not there, leave."

Orka slipped away before Lif could say anything.

She eased around the side of the mead hall and crept silently through shadow, until she was close to the hall's rear. There were no openings along its length, only one shuttered window. That marked Jarl Sigrún's sleeping chamber. Orka knew *drengrs* would be sleeping in the main chamber of the hall, around the hearth fire, though not Jarl Sigrún's full strength of warriors. A party of riders had passed Orka on the path from the hills, six of Sigrún's oathsworn warriors, and a handful of others, some walking, some driving an oxen-pulled cart. Guðvarr had not been among them. They had been ordered to investigate the fire and smoke from Orka's steading, she guessed. But that would still leave at least a dozen *drengrs* at Fellur. Jarl Sigrún would want them around her to impose security at the Althing.

And Sigrún's thrall will be with her.

Orka stood beside the shuttered window, quietly slid her seax from its scabbard and worked at the lock, slowly, gently, until she felt the clip give. In one swift movement she pulled it open and climbed into the frame of the open window, stepping into the chamber.

Darkness, a hearth fire glow, a bed, two figures in it. Movement at the bed's foot as someone uncoiled from sleep around the hearth fire. The glint of fire-glow on iron: the thrall's collar.

Orka stepped into the chamber, the figures on the bed stirring, a wool blanket pushed back, revealing Jarl Sigrún and a lover lying naked, entwined together. The man was waking, disentangling his legs from Sigrún's and pushing himself up on to one elbow, his slim body pale, muscles etched in starlight and fire-glow. Orka slashed at his throat: a spurt of blood and he fell back gurgling. Orka clubbed the hilt of her seax into Sigrún's jaw as the jarl jolted awake and started to sit up, sending her crashing back to the mattress, and then Orka's seax was levelled at the thrall, who was on her feet, her seax half-drawn. The tip of Orka's blade touched the thrall's throat.

"Let it go," Orka hissed.

The thrall stared at her, a hint of amber in her eyes, tension in her muscles. An exhaled breath, then she let her seax slide back into its scabbard and lifted her hand clear.

"I need their names, and where they are going," Orka said.

The thrall's mouth opened to speak.

"Do not *lie* to me," Orka broke in. "I know it was you. I saw you taste my husband's blood." A tremor rippled through her, a wave of rage. She took a moment, controlling it, controlling the urge to stab and kill and destroy. "Their names, and a destination," Orka breathed.

A hesitation, then a curt nod from the thrall.

"I am a *niðing* thrall," the woman growled. "I do not give commands. I obey them."

"Who commanded this? The murder of my husband; the abduction of my son?"

A silence, the thrall's eyes fixed on Orka's. They glittered with amber.

"Wolf-kin, tell me," Orka growled.

"My name is Vafri," the thrall said, "and I am descended from Ulfrir, the great wolf-god, and Hundur the hound. Proud and strong we were." She shook her head with a twist of her lip. "If I am about to die, you will know my name, and my lineage."

"I care *nothing* for who you were. You are a thrall now, and have my pity for that, but you are the reason my husband is dead . . ." Her fist twitched, knuckles white around the hilt of her seax. "Who commanded this?" Orka growled. "I will not ask you again."

Vafri's lip curled, the glint of her teeth. "My master is Hakon, son of Queen Helka," she said. "I was ordered to report any sign of the Tainted."

"Report to who?" Orka hissed.

Another silence.

Orka's blade moved, a line of blood trickling down Vafri's neck.

"He is . . . not a man to cross," Vafri said.

"His name," Orka said.

"Drekr," the thrall grunted, a tremor in her voice.

Orka drew in a long breath, her thought-cage turning. She had heard that name from the lad by the river.

"And where is Drekr taking my son?" Orka said.

Vafri shrugged. "I am not told such things."

A twitch of Orka's wrist, and the seax sliced a deep line into flesh.

"I swear, I do not know," Vafri hissed.

"Guess, then," Orka said. "You are wolf-cunning. Where do you think they are taking my son?"

Another long silence. Their eyes locked.

"Darl, maybe," Vafri said. Her eyes flickered away, looking over Orka's shoulder for a moment, then returning to Orka. There was the creak of a bed and Orka turned and saw Jarl Sigrún reaching for her weapons belt.

A fist slammed into Orka's jaw, Vafri moving as soon as Orka's eyes were off her. Orka stumbled back, slashed with her seax to keep Vafri back, shook her head to clear the white spots dancing in her eyes. She took another shuffle-step, back and to the side, closer to Sigrún, at the same time drawing one of the seaxes in her belt: one of the blades she had pulled from Thorkel's body.

Sigrún had a fist around her sword hilt and was on her feet, drawing the blade from its scabbard. She yelled and was answered by the sound of movement beyond the chamber's door, in the mead hall. A voice called out. Orka slashed, diagonally from above, right to left, and Sigrún fell away with a scream, blood spraying from a red gash stark across her face, from forehead to chin.

Vafri snarled and rushed Orka, a seax in the thrall's fist. Her eyes glowed amber, the battle-joy bright in her. Orka remembered how the thrall had rushed and overwhelmed Virk. She snarled and ran at Vafri, taking her by surprise.

Vafri stabbed with her seax and Orka swayed to the side, letting her coat of mail take the seax's edge. She wrapped her left arm around Vafri's and heaved it into a lock, strained harder, hearing the *crack* of bone breaking. Vafri gasped, her momentum carrying her into Orka, jaws wide, teeth suddenly sharp, snapping for Orka's face and throat, her empty hand raking at her, nails razored as claws.

There was a burning pain across Orka's cheek. She slammed her head forwards, crunched into Vafri's nose and upper lip and heard the crackle of cartilage snapping, a gush of blood, lip mangled, teeth knocked loose. Vafri's legs buckled, the woman still conscious, snarling and spitting froth and blood as Orka plunged the seax in her right fist into the thrall's belly.

With a grunt and whine, Vafri curled over the blow.

The sound of boots and voices outside the door.

Orka shoved Vafri away, ripping her blade free, the thrall stumbling back and dropping to her knees, blood sluicing from her belly and nose. She toppled to her side, one hand clutching the wound in her gut, her other searching for the hilt of her seax, lying on the floor close to her.

Shouts outside; a kick and the door was hurled inwards, silhouettes filling it.

Jarl Sigrún stumbled towards Orka, swinging her sword overhead, her face a ruin of blood and gaping flesh. Orka caught the sword on her seax and swept it away. Sigrún was thrown off balance and tripped over the bed.

A wordless scream came from the doorway as *drengrs* pushed into the chamber, swords and axes in their fists. Guðvarr was first into the room, his shoulder bandaged from the wound Virk had given him, his sword held in front of him. He froze a moment, seeing blood and bodies in the fire-glow and moonlight, then his eyes fixed on Orka.

Orka threw her seax at him. Guðvarr leaped backwards into the *drengrs* thick behind him and they all fell tumbling. The seax slammed into the doorpost, quivering. With a quick step forwards, Orka swept Vafri's seax from her grasping fingers, the thrall's hand falling away.

"Walk the soul road without a blade," Orka snarled at the dying woman, then turned and ran at the window, hurling herself through into the darkness.

She landed on her shoulder, the soft ground breaking her fall, and rolled, managed to find her feet, a seax still in each fist, and ran. Shouts echoed out of Sigrún's window, then the sound of someone scrambling through, dropping to the ground. Other voices sounded further away: *drengrs* using the mead hall doors.

Orka sprinted through an alley, spilled into a street, skidded, righted herself and ran left, then turned right, back into another alley. Lights were flaring as torches were lit, heads poking from doorways as the yelling of Jarl Sigrún's *drengrs* woke the village.

Another street, figures stepping out of doorways, then another alley, and then Orka saw the glimmer of the fjord between buildings.

Horns blew out, loud and shrill, the village rippling to life.

Orka burst out of the alley into open ground, a gentle slope down to the fjord dotted with boats pulled up on to the beach, a small pier jutting out into the water. Orka's feet slapped on timber as she ran, eyes searching, looking past the boats moored to the pier for Lif and Mord.

Then she saw them, both of the young men sitting on benches in their small fisher boat, oars ready. Orka ran harder, skidded on timber and leaped into the boat, where she fell in a heap.

"Row," she gasped, pushing herself up. "Head south, for the sea."

Mord and Lif dipped their oars without a word, Mord with a bloodstained bandage around his head.

Feet drummed on the pier; voices shouted at them. A spear hissed through the air, then disappeared with hardly a splash to Orka's right. She saw Guðvarr on the pier, shouting insults, swearing vengeance, veins bursting in his neck. The boat picked up speed, cutting a silver-foamed wake as it took them into the darkness.

CHAPTER TWENTY-THREE

ELVAR

Elvar woke before dawn. For a moment she did not know where she was. The scent of mead and ale and urine helped her memory. She was in the hayloft of a tavern in Snakavik. Her head was full of memories and emotions, guilt, anger, pride, all swirling in her thought-cage as if caught in the current of a whirlpool. Rolling over she sat up, Grend close to her, his bulk a shadow as her eyes adjusted to the darkness. All about her lay the crammed, snoring bodies of the Battle-Grim. Pulling her boots on she stood, picked her rolled weapons belt up and made her way among them. A gentle glow showed her the opening to a steep ladder and she climbed down into the tavern.

Tables and benches were spread about a large room, the floor covered with dried rushes, dark patches of urine here and there, a flickering light coming from a hearth fire and an iron brazier of stinking whale oil.

Biórr and Thrud were down there and awake, Biórr stirring a pot of porridge over a small hearth fire and Thrud sitting with his legs stretched out, picking at his nails with a knife. Uspa and Bjarn were sitting on a bench in the corner of the room, a blanket across them both, a tafl board on the table in front of them. Bjarn smiled at her as she climbed down the ladder. So did Biórr.

There was a clatter of pots through a doorway and Elvar glimpsed the innkeeper and his wife.

"Porridge?" Biórr asked as she reached the ground and stretched. He was ladling some into two bowls, which he took over to Uspa and Bjarn. Elvar didn't much feel like company; she had hoped to sit at a dark table alone and sift through her thoughts. But the smile of the lad, Bjarn, drew her to him.

The bench scraped as she pulled it out to sit with them, laying her weapons belt on the table beside the tafl board, sword, seax and axe looped in the belt. Thrud's eyes rose from his nail-picking to follow her. He gave her a nod and a grunt, then went back to the dirt beneath his nails.

Biórr brought her a bowl and spoon, and put a clay jar of honey on the table, spooning some into Bjarn's bowl.

"My thanks," Uspa said to Biórr.

"Back to our game, then," Biórr said, picking up a pair of bone-carved dice. "Your jarl will not escape my warriors," he said, curling his lip in a false warrior-snarl.

"We shall see," Bjarn said, fingers twitching, eager for his next move.

Elvar dipped her spoon and blew on her porridge, shifting her weight in her *brynja*. She had slept in her coat of mail. Although she was home, after almost four years of travelling with the Battle-Grim she did not feel safe here. Especially after her words with her father last night.

He had been shocked to see her, though only his eyes had betrayed him. Thorun, her elder brother, had been more vocal about it, while Silrið the Galdurwoman had been as unreadable and indifferent as always. The only one showing anything close to happiness at Elvar's sudden return had been Hrung, the giant's head. He had smiled warmly at her.

He remembers all the ale and mead I used to pour into his big mouth.

Thorun had told her she was a disgrace to leave as she had, and worse to return unannounced. Broðir, her younger brother, had mostly just stared at her, looking disappointed. When Thorun had stuttered into silence her father had spoken.

"Why have you returned?" he had asked her. "I doubt it was out of *loyalty*."

If he had not added that last part, she would have stayed and talked. Instead she had turned on her heel and left, without uttering a single word. Closed the hall doors behind her to the renewed shouts of her eldest brother.

Strange, how we revert to the behaviour of our childhood, when back in the presence of our family.

I had so much to say: a fine speech planned.

But something about her father drove all rational thought from her mind. It had never been any different.

"Best eat it while it's hot," Biórr said to her.

"Huh?" Elvar grunted.

"The porridge. Best eat it while it's hot. Tastes like whale glue when it's cold." He looked into his own bowl. "Maybe it *is* whale glue."

Bjarn chuckled.

"You've tasted whale glue, then?" Elvar asked him.

"You'd be surprised what I've tasted. Starving does things to a man," Biórr said with his bright smile. "I have not always been this fine, healthy and successful example of a man you see before you this morning."

Elvar couldn't stop the smile from cracking her lips. Her eyes strayed to the tavern windows, where the darkness was shifting towards grey.

Morning it is, then.

"Mama, where's Papa?" Bjarn said, looking up from the tafl game, which he seemed to be winning.

Uspa looked down at him, her lips moving, but no words coming out.

"Your papa's had to go away for a while," Biórr said. "He's asked us to look after you while he's gone."

Thrud tutted and Elvar looked at Biórr.

Better a hard truth than a soft lie, my father always said, Elvar thought, but looking at Bjarn's face, and the tear running down Uspa's cheek, Elvar found herself surprisingly moved by Biórr's kindness.

Floorboards creaked above them and a form filled the hayloft's hatch, boots climbing down the ladder.

"You should have woken me," Grend said as he reached the ground, clicking his neck, buckling and looping his weapons belt, then stomping towards her. He looked at Uspa and Bjarn, then glowered at Biórr, who smiled back at him.

"Porridge?" Biórr said, starting to rise.

"I'll get my own," Grend grunted, walking to the pot over the hearth. He filled a bowl and sat down with them, filling the space between Elvar and Biórr.

More of the Battle-Grim were rising, figures climbing down the ladder and filling the tavern. The landlord and his wife appeared, bringing a fresh pot of oats to hang over the hearth fire, jugs of watered ale and horns and tankards to drink it from. Agnar came down the ladder, Kráka and the *Hundur*-thrall following him like faithful hounds. He looked at Elvar, nodded and walked to a table near the doorway. A muffled shout came from above and they looked up to see Sighvat's bulk stuck in the loft-hatch. Someone must have pushed from above, because there was a tearing sound and he fell through, grabbing the ladder to stop himself falling.

"How did he get up there in the first place?" Elvar frowned.

"All things are possible with enough mead in your belly," Biórr said. "At least, it feels so at the time. And mead is a fine killer of pain."

She smiled again.

Grend grunted.

Sighvat dropped the distance to the ground and stood there, pulling his tunic straight.

"Stupid loft," he muttered. "Must've been made for a dwarf."

He helped himself to porridge, emptying the pot and calling out for more. The landlord and his wife brought more oats, stirring in milk and water as more of the Battle-Grim crawled out of the hayloft. Soon the tavern was close to full, warriors filling most of the tables. Elvar sat quietly, eating her porridge, while Biórr and Bjarn went back to their game of tafl. It looked like Bjarn's bone-carved jarl and his remaining oathsworn were going to break through Biórr's guardsmen.

Uspa shifted on her bench, moving closer to Elvar.

"What next for us?" she said to Elvar, almost a whisper.

Elvar looked at her, feeling a stab of sympathy for the woman. She was a Seiðr-witch, her husband Tainted, and her son too, but she had gone from a life of freedom with her kin to losing her husband and wearing a thrall-collar around her neck. Agnar and the Battle-Grim excelled at hunting down the Tainted and Elvar had always kept herself distant from their prisoners – she knew it was her living and her reputation – but this time she felt the twist of some emotion within her. Perhaps because of saving the boy from the serpent.

That was a business decision, she told herself. *The boy will earn coin or be used as leverage against Uspa. A Seiðr-witch is a valuable asset.*

But part of her could sniff out the lie in her own reasoning. She looked at Uspa and could not keep the pity from rising within her.

A hard truth or a soft lie?

"I do not know," Elvar said, choosing the hard path. "Perhaps Agnar will sell you at the thrall-market, or keep you and sell Bjarn. Or sell you both, together or to different homes." She shrugged. "I am not chief of the Battle-Grim to make such decisions."

"But you are close to the chief," she said, her eyes flickering to the troll tusk about Elvar's neck, and the arm ring Agnar had gifted her.

Elvar just shrugged.

"We need to leave Snakavik," Uspa said, with a flare of her eyes and nostrils.

She is afraid. But I would be afraid, if I were in her place.

"Why would you be in such a hurry to leave, with your husband a thrall of Jarl Störr? He will only leave Snakavik for battle. At least if you remain here you will be close to him: may even see him, occasionally."

"We *need* to leave," Uspa repeated, a hiss.

The tavern door swung open, letting in the grey light of Snakavik, and a warrior walked in, a woman in fine war gear, her *brynja* gleaming as if freshly scrubbed with sand. Her dark hair was braided, a scar running through one cheek into her upper lip. Elvar recognised her.

Gytha, father's champion. Gytha's battle-fame was known to most; even now the landlord appeared in the kitchen doorway and half-bowed to her.

Gytha looked around and saw Elvar, and Grend sitting beside her. She dipped her head to Grend.

"Welcome home," she said to Elvar, though her eyes rested mostly on Grend.

Elvar nodded, not trusting the words her mouth might utter.

There was a moment's silence, Grend silent as a stone, then Gytha looked over her shoulder and gestured. Two more warriors walked in, carrying a chest.

"For Agnar," Gytha said.

The payment for Berak. My father spoke true, he pays well for Berserkir.

Agnar rose from his seat, where he had been hidden behind the tavern door. Elvar saw his hand drop from his sword hilt as he stood. He barked an order and Sighvat stepped forwards to take the chest from the two warriors.

"Jarl Störr is here to see his daughter," Gytha said to Agnar and all in the room. She looked around. Confused faces stared back at her. Only Agnar and a few others knew of Elvar's bloodline. Gytha's eyes came to rest upon Elvar. "He wishes for some privacy."

"A good time to take this to the *Wave-Jarl*, then," Agnar said, slapping the chest. "Battle-Grim, with me," he called as he walked through the tavern door. Sighvat followed him, and the rest of the Battle-Grim stood and filed out of the tavern.

Biórr looked at Elvar, noting that she made no move to leave the room. She could see the candle-light flickering to life in his thought-cage.

"That means you as well," Grend told Biórr with a frown.

Biórr rose slowly.

"You will be . . . all right?" he asked Elvar. "I can stay."

Grend snorted and put his hands on the table to rise.

Elvar touched Grend's arm.

"I have earned my place in the Battle-Grim's shield wall," she scowled at Biórr, clutching the troll tusk at her neck. "Why would I need you to stay? You think me some *niðing* who needs protecting?"

He shrugged, holding his hands up, then gestured for Uspa and Bjarn to follow him. Thrud rose and put his knife away, falling in behind the woman and child. They were the last to leave.

More warriors entered the tavern: Jarl Störr's oathsworn guard. They spread around the tavern, checking the room was empty. Two climbed the loft-ladder and shouted down that all was clear.

Jarl Störr entered the room. He saw Elvar and walked to her, figures filing in behind him: her brothers Thorun and Broðir, and finally Silrið, one of the few Galdurwomen in all of Vigrið, her necklace of animal skulls clinking as she walked. Jarl Störr sat down opposite Elvar, Thorun and Broðir either side of him. Silrið stood behind him.

"Daughter," Jarl Störr said. He looked at her, a long and appraising look. Elvar felt like he was reading the secrets of her soul. "You should not have left," he said into the silence.

Elvar curled her lip as she felt her anger building, a shapeless, bile-filled thing. She drew in a breath, trying to control it. Trying to break the patterns of her childhood where her father would admonish her and she would rage back at him, achieving nothing, always walking away feeling useless, and angry with herself, that she could not master her emotions and speak the truth of her heart.

"I do not regret leaving," she eventually said. "I have earned my reputation, my battle-fame."

"Battle-fame? In the employ of some merchant," Jarl Störr said.

"Agnar and the Battle-Grim are great warriors, famed throughout all Vigrið, and in the wide world beyond. Places you have never set foot. Places where *your* name is not known," Elvar said.

Her father sniffed. "He might be a capable warrior, but that does not change the fact that he makes his coin by dealing in flesh and blood. He is nothing more than a *niðing* merchant, a whore who will lie down for whoever shows him the most coin."

Elvar felt her blood race, anger bubbling at the insults thrown at her chief. Again, she took a moment to master it and bite back the words that formed on her tongue like the first spears hurled in a battle.

"You are happy enough to pay him," Elvar said instead. "What does that make you?"

"Sensible," her father said with a shrug, "if he is selling something I want. But enough of Agnar and his band of mercenaries. I have come here to talk about you. About your kin, about your future." He drummed his fingers on the table. "When you left, the way you did: it brought shame on me. You made people doubt me. The whisperers revelled in it. If he cannot control his own daughter, they said, how can he control the future of Snakavik?" He sighed. "I had to spill blood to regain my control of this realm. A lot of blood."

"This is where you do not understand me," Elvar said. "You do not control me. No one does, or ever will."

"You are a jarl's daughter," her elder brother, Thorun exclaimed. "Father gave you everything, and in return you have *responsibilities*."

"What, to be a pawn in his politics?" Elvar snapped. "To be traded, to be sold like some thrall-whore to a worthy husband for a piece of land? To lie back and be ploughed like a field, to have their seed sown in my belly and spend my life rearing little piglets like a fat sow?"

Thorun sucked in an angry breath.

"Yes," he said, "if that is what Father wants."

"I wonder if you would be so quick to agree if it were you that were being bartered, if it were you that would have to be humped by some sweating pig and turned into a brood bitch."

"I would be happy to obey my father, whatever he asked," Thorun snapped.

"Well, then *you* can wed Helka's piglet and have a good humping, and I'll lead the warband," Elvar said.

Grend snorted, the closest he came to laughing, and Thorun frowned.

Jarl Störr gave a thin smile.

"Ahhh," he sighed, leaning back in his chair, "it is harder managing my children than the rest of Snakavik and all my realm combined." He shook his head. "I want you back with me, daughter. With us. It is where you should be."

"I will not wed Hakon, just to spread your border a little wider."

"A little?" Thorun said. "Father's realm and Helka's combined would cover more than half of all Vigrið."

"I do not care," Elvar shrugged. "I am born for the battle-storm and shield wall. I will make my own reputation, not be wed into someone else's."

"Reputation?" Thorun sneered. "You? More likely you are riding on Grend's reputation. He stands at your shoulder in every conflict, I do not doubt, to protect you. He was ever mother's hound, and now he is yours."

Without realising it, Elvar was on her feet, her fist wrapping around her sword hilt.

"I will show you the sharp edge of my reputation, brother, and Grend can stay here sitting on his arse," she said.

Thorun flushed red.

I had just seen my seventeenth name-day when I saw you last. You used to enjoy humiliating me in the practice court then. It would be different, now.

"Elvar fights her own battles," Grend's voice grated through the tension. "She has won her own renown, and is a name to be respected, and feared."

Elvar looked at Grend and blinked. The old warrior rarely praised anyone or anything, and all in the room knew it.

Grend looked at Thorun. "I would sit down, if I were you."

Thorun's hand moved to the hilt of his sword.

Jarl Störr gave Thorun a dark look. "You will stop your bleating," he said quietly, "or you will leave."

Thorun's glare flickered from Elvar to Grend to his father, finally withering, and he dropped his eyes.

"Good." Jarl Störr fixed his heavy-lidded gaze on Elvar. "I came here to speak with you, daughter, of reconciliation. I would have you back at my side." She opened her mouth, but he held a hand up, silencing her. "Perhaps a marriage alliance with Helka is not the only road to consider. There are other ways to fulfil our ambitions." He shrugged, his eyes touching on Silrið.

"There is always more than one path through the forest," Silrið said. "If one is brave enough to search for it, and perhaps strong enough to cut down a few trees."

Jarl Störr grunted. "Either way," he said, "I would have you with me, Elvar Störrsdottir. Perhaps it is time for you to be given your own *drengrs*, to lead your own warband."

Elvar blinked at that, surprise washing away all her anger.

Her father stood.

"Think on that," he said, "and come to me when you have an answer."

Elvar stared dumbly at him.

He turned away and walked from the room, Thorun, Broðir, Silrið and his guards following. Broðir hesitated at the doorway, looking back at Elvar.

"Come back to us, sister," he said, a shy smile spreading across his face. "Thorun's an arseling, and I have missed you." Then he was gone.

Gytha snapped an order and the remaining *drengrs* left the tavern room. She looking at Grend, then closed the tavern door behind her.

Elvar stared down at Grend. She sat down on abruptly weak legs, and then she started laughing.

CHAPTER TWENTY-FOUR

ORKA

"There," Orka said, pointing at a bank of tall reeds growing thick on the riverbank, little more than a collection of different shadows in the first grey of dawn.

Mord and Lif bent their backs, changing course on the river and rowing their fisher boat towards the reeds. The two brothers were soaked with sweat, exhaustion heavy upon them, though Orka was just as sweat-soaked. She had taken shifts on the oar through the long dark before dawn.

The boat's prow cut into the reeds and ground on silt, Orka jumping from the prow on to the bank with a splash. She searched a few moments, then saw what she was looking for, her spear shaft pale and grey and straight among the wind-bent reads. She pulled it from the ground and hefted her hemp sack, tied around the shaft, then clambered back into the boat.

Lif looked at her with dark, wide eyes. He was crow-haired and as tall as Virk, his father, but slim and lithe where Virk had been thickset and solid. His beard was patchy, pale skin showing his youth. He could not have seen more than seventeen or eighteen winters.

"What?" Orka grunted.

"Are you hurt?" he said. "You are covered in blood."

Orka looked over the boat's side and saw her reflection in the river. Her face and hair were thick with crusted blood. Sweat had carved grooves through it, looking like some runic knotwork. She reached up and pulled a fragment of bone from her hair.

"It is not mine," she said, remembering her axe and the woman she had slain at the riverbank less than a day ago. It felt like much longer.

"Oh," Lif breathed. He chose not to give voice to the questions in his eyes.

Mord was slumped across his oar, fresh blood seeping through the bandage around his head. He was more like his father, fair-haired, broad-faced and solid, a thick hedge of beard on his chin. Orka stepped over their stowed mast and touched his shoulder.

He looked up at her. "We need to talk," he mumbled. "Why have we rowed in one big circle around the fjord?"

"We will talk later," Orka said. "No time, now. Move," she grunted, helping him to stand and guiding him on to a pile of rope and net at the stern of the boat. She pushed them out of the reed-bank with her spear, then sat at the bench and hefted Mord's oar, looking at Lif.

"How much longer? Where are we going?" Lif muttered.

"A little further, then we can look for somewhere safe to camp," Orka said.

He looked at her with black-rimmed eyes, but only nodded. Together they dipped their oars into the river and pulled.

The boat grated as Orka and Lif dragged it up on to the riverbank, pausing to help Mord clamber out and collapse beneath a willow, then the two of them hauled the boat higher up the riverbank, into a stand of bog myrtle and juniper, almost covering it from sight. Mist curled sluggishly across the river, the morning sun slowly burning it away. Orka stood and looked back the way they had come, the river wide, curling like a serpent through a steep-sided valley before it spilled into the fjord where Fellur village squatted. Beyond the river she saw hills rising towards cliffs; she could still see the spot where her steading lay.

It is a barrow, now, not a home.

A flare of grief and anger bubbled up inside her. It had been kept at bay by the confrontation with Sigrún and the thrall, then the escape, hard rowing and burning muscles and exhaustion suppressing all else for a while.

Orka carried her bag and dropped it beside Mord, then sat with her back to the wide tree and began to rummage through it.

Lif kneeled beside his brother, undid the blood-soaked bandage around Mord's head and took it to the riverbank to clean.

Mord sat and stared at Orka.

"Here," she said, handing him a strip of salted pork. He reached out and took it, and chewed.

"Why have we rowed a circle around the fjord?" Mord asked Orka.

Lif joined them, wringing out the bandage.

"To deceive that *niðing* Guðvarr?" Lif said, looking to Orka.

"Aye," she grunted, chewing on a strip of pork. She passed some to Lif. "He watched us row away south, towards the sea," she said.

"So, when dawn came that is the way he would go to search for us," Lif said, a smile creasing his face.

"I hope so," Orka said. "He is idiot enough."

"Jarl Sigrún is no idiot, though," Mord said. "She would send boats and scouts in all directions, out on the fjord and along the fjord bank."

"Aye," Orka nodded, "maybe. Though Jarl Sigrún may be too busy having her face stitched back together to think on anything else."

Lif raised an eyebrow. He cleaned Mord's wound, which looked like it had come from some kind of blunt weapon, a club, a spear butt or sword hilt, and re-tied the linen bandage around it.

"Why are you helping us?" Lif asked Orka as he worked. "What grievance has caused Jarl Sigrún's face to need stitching? And where are Thorkel and Breca?"

Orka said nothing, just chewed her meat. She drew the three seaxes at her belt, two that she had taken from Thorkel's body and one from Sigrún's thrall. She had left her own seax buried in the timber doorpost of Jarl Sigrún's sleeping chamber. She turned the thrall's seax in her hand, looking at the knotwork carved into the horn hilt. Wolf heads, jaws gaping.

Fitting, for an Úlfhéðnar.

Two of the seaxes had blood on them, dried to black stains now. She opened her pouch, took out a cloth and some oil and set about cleaning them.

"Thorkel is dead. Slain," she said flatly as she worked, "and Breca has been taken. I went to Jarl Sigrún to talk to her about it."

"And opened her face with a blade?" Lif said.

Orka ignored him.

A silence settled between them as Orka cleaned her blades, then she set them down and went back to her sack, where she pulled out the loaf of bread and the round of hard cheese and sawed off slices for the three of them.

"What now?" Lif said as he chewed on black bread.

"We sneak back to Fellur and kill that *niðing* Guðvarr," Mord said.

Orka looked at him.

"Orka?" Lif said.

"Do as you wish," she said with a shrug.

"Where are you going?" Lif asked her.

"Not back to Fellur village," she grunted.

"Where, then?" Lif pressed.

Orka gave him a flat look. "I am going to find my son."

"And we are going to kill Guðvarr," Mord repeated.

Lif looked at his brother with sorrow. "How?" he asked.

Mord opened his mouth, but no words followed.

"Help us," Lif asked Orka.

"No," Orka said.

"We do not need anyone's help," Mord said angrily. "Guðvarr is for us to kill. It is our father who is a corpse because of him, us who owe him blood feud, and that filthy thrall of Jarl Sigrún's."

"You only need to kill Guðvarr," Orka told them.

"No, Guðvarr *and* the thrall," Mord said. "Our father's death is Guðvarr's fault, but the thrall dealt him his death wounds."

"Sigrún's thrall has a hole in her belly. She may already be dead," Orka said, chewing on some cheese.

Mord and Lif both stared at Orka, eyes wide, mouths flapping like fish.

"She may yet live, but most die of a gut-wound," Orka added.

A silence settled between them, Lif staring at Orka with a mixture of fear and awe.

"Guðvarr, then," Mord said eventually.

"But, we tried to kill him, and ended up tied to a post," Lif pointed out.

Lif looked at Orka. "You have some clever about you, and some stones," he said, "to sneak into Jarl Sigrún's bedchamber. And some weapons craft, to cut her up and put a hole in her thrall's belly. How would you advise us to go about our revenge?"

Orka sighed, a long exhalation.

"Wait," she said. "No point rushing back with all of Fellur seething like a kicked wasp nest. Wait until things are quiet, when they have given up searching and are getting on with planting their fields, or reaping the harvest. That is the time to strike."

"I like it," Lif said, nodding. "See, Mord, now that is some deep-cunning."

"Too long," Mord snarled. "I want Guðvarr dead *today*. Or on the morrow at the latest."

Orka turned her flat stare on him. "Have you not learned already, what you want has little to do with it?" She shrugged again. "You asked for my advice. You don't have to take it."

"I think we should listen to her," Lif said. He chewed his bread slowly. Clearly his thought-cage was turning over in his head. "And we need to learn some weapons craft."

Mord's face twisted. "I know weapons craft," he said.

"Aye, as that lump on your head declares," Lif said.

"I was outnumbered," Mord muttered.

"You could teach us," Lif said to Orka.

Orka blinked.

"No," she said.

"You fought Jarl Sigrún and her warrior-thrall, defeated them both. We are not good enough to do this, and our father's bones cry out for vengeance," Lif said. "I would not let him down."

"I am about my own vengeance. I have no time for yours," Orka grated.

"We could help you," Lif said.

"No," said Orka and Mord together.

"Why not?" Lif said.

Orka looked at them both. "I do not want your help. I do not need it. Come with me and you will most likely get yourselves killed. Or me."

"We could help you," Lif said stubbornly. "Where are you going, on this vengeance of yours?"

"North, and west," Orka muttered, looking to the north, towards the fortress and town of Darl, where the snow-tipped peaks of the Boneback Mountains glittered.

"Wherever it is you are going, you would get there faster if we were rowing you," Lif said. "If you leave us, then you are walking, as that is our boat."

Orka stared at him. "I could take your boat," she said.

Lif's face twitched at that, a flicker of fear and hurt. Mord growled a curse, his hand reaching for the axe loop at his belt. It was empty, their hastily gathered weapons slung in the boat.

"I will not take your boat," Orka told them. "I will walk."

"Those who took Breca, do you think they are walking?" Lif asked.

A twist of pain, like a knife in Orka's belly, at the mention of her son's name.

"No," she said. "I followed their tracks to the river. They took him from there by boat."

There was a long silence as she chewed that over in her thought-cage.

"Fine. Row me to Darl," she said into the silence, "and I will teach you what I can."

CHAPTER TWENTY-FIVE

ELVAR

Elvar took another draught from her mead horn and swallowed, feeling some of it trickle down her chin.

"You've had enough," Grend said.

She gave him a dark look, one that she had learned from him on the many occasions he had inflicted it upon her. Grend shrugged and leaned back in his bench.

They were still sat in the tavern in Snakavik, Elvar drinking an endless river of mead and ale. It was growing dark outside, torches lit and smoke thick in the air, though it always grew darker in Snakavik before the rest of the world, the sun blotted out by the serpent's skull. Agnar and many of the Battle-Grim had returned, filtering in like mist-wraiths as Elvar's thought-cage was consumed with all that her father had said to her, picking over his words like a carrion-crow over old bones.

You should not have left, he said, I want you back at my side, he said. Agnar of the Battle-Grim is a mercenary whore, he said . . .

She ground her teeth.

"What are you going to do?" Grend said quietly, his voice sinking into the hum of the tavern. "I mean besides grinding your teeth to dust."

"Don't know," Elvar muttered sullenly.

Shock had shifted to anger as Elvar sifted through her father's words. As ever, he said more in the words unspoken. Their meeting had not been what she had expected.

Judgement, disappointment and a sense of my own inadequacy are my most vivid memories of growing up with Jarl Störr as a father.

"He offered you *drengrs* of your own. A warband of your own," Grend said.

Elvar nodded. That was what she had wanted, to lead, to prove herself, but her father had wanted her to be sold off as a prize brood bitch to Queen Helka's son, Hakon, so that her children would rule all Vigrið. That was why she had left, to escape such a fate.

It would have been a thrall's life, no matter if the collar were gilded with gold.

"What would you have me do?" she asked Grend.

The old warrior snorted. "As if you have ever taken my advice."

"I might," she said.

Grend shrugged. "He is offering you what you wanted, so take it. But I am no deep-thinker, and all know that Jarl Störr does not say all: for every plan spoken, there is another hidden within it." He shrugged again. "Whatever you do, I will follow you." He looked at the palm of his hand, at a white scar that ran along it. Elvar remembered seeing the blood well, remembered the words he had spoken, the oath he had sworn.

"It is . . . confusing," Grend said. "When a thing does not go as you expected."

"Aye," Elvar said, nodding and drinking.

"At least Thorun has remained the same," Grend said.

"He can always be relied upon," Elvar grumbled. Thorun had only ever made things worse. "Thorun was born an arseling and just grew bigger."

Both of them snorted laughter.

"Something funny?" a voice said beside her. She looked and saw Biórr sitting and playing tafl with the boy, Bjarn. She had not noticed them return to the tavern or sit so close to her.

Elvar shrugged, not knowing where to start.

"You are Elvar Störrsdottir, then," Biórr said to her, his voice remaining steady, eyes fixed on the board and wooden carved pieces.

She took another drink from her mead horn.

"Yes," she breathed.

"Why would a jarl's daughter leave a life of privilege behind her, a life of wealth and power, and trade it for an oar-bench, for a life of violence and death?" he said to no one in particular.

Grend shifted beside her.

"To prove my worth," Elvar said before Grend had a chance to threaten the young warrior. "To earn my reputation."

"You have done that, right enough," Biórr said, eyes flickering to the troll tusk around Elvar's neck.

"Elvar is the bravest warrior I know," Bjarn said, looking up at her with his large, dark eyes. "She saved me from the serpent."

"Grend saved us both," Elvar said.

"So, you left Snakavik in search of a reputation?" Biórr asked.

"Yes," Elvar said. "And to live free, to be my own master, not some play-piece on a tafl board that my father can manoeuvre and sacrifice." She waved a hand at the board between Biórr and Bjarn. The boy moved his jarl-piece, making a break for a gap his oathsworn guards had carved through the ranks of their attackers. Biórr's carved wooden warriors were circled around the jarl, a net drawing tight to capture and kill him.

That is how I feel, Elvar thought. *No matter how far I travel, the weave of my life tugs me back here. To Snakavik and my father's web of plans. Should I leave the Battle-Grim and take a place at my father's shoulder, involve myself in his politics and struggles, involve myself in the war for Vigrið?* She blew out a long breath and realised that Biórr was staring at her.

"What?" she said, glaring.

"I am thinking that you have a pleasing face," he said, with a twitch of his lips, showing his white teeth. "Fine cheeks, eyes that snatch my breath, and such lips . . . "

Grend's chair scraped as he shifted his weight, turning to glare at Biórr.

"But there is far more to you than just what the eye can see," Biórr finished.

Elvar's brows knotted.

"You are fighting a battle in your thought-cage, one that I cannot see, but it is a great struggle; one that is heavy on your shoulders." He leaned forwards. "I could help you."

Grend growled deep in his throat. "She is not for the likes of you," the old warrior said, his voice like a slow-drawn blade.

Biórr shrugged. "From what I am learning of this shieldmaiden, that is a choice you cannot make for her, old warrior."

Thrud was sat close by, sitting at his usual pastime, picking his nails with a small seax. A sliver of bone hung from a leather cord around his wrist, hacked from the skull of a wight he had slain when he had first joined the Battle-Grim. He huffed a laugh.

"Something funny?" Grend asked him.

"Just waiting to see if the young cub is fast enough to escape the old wolf's teeth and claws," Thrud said.

Grend reached out and put a hand on Biórr's wrist.

"You are right, Elvar will choose her own path. She always has. But I am there to stamp on the rats in the shadows, those that smile at her and hide their intentions. I am the one who crushes their skulls before they can scratch or bite."

Biórr took his gaze from the tafl game and looked at Grend, then at Grend's fist clamped around his wrist, Elvar seeing a shift in the young man's eyes. The smile and hint of humour that seemed ever-present was gone, replaced with something hard and cold.

There was a slap of boots and Sighvat was looming over them.

"Chief wants a word," he said to Elvar.

Elvar stood and took a moment as the world swayed around her. Grend stood too.

"Didn't hear the chief ask for you, big man," Biórr said.

"Where Elvar goes, I go," Grend growled. "Agnar knows this, and the sooner you understand that, the better."

Sighvat nodded an agreement, and then he was leading Elvar and Grend across the tavern, winding between tables and benches, his bulk bashing the elbows and shoulders of all in their path, warriors of the Battle-Grim mingled with locals, fisherfolk, traders and craftsmen, warriors, whores. Agnar was sitting in a corner, his bearskin cloak cast over a chair behind him. Like Elvar, he still wore his coat of mail, his weapons belt unbuckled and lying upon the table, beside a horn carved cup and a jug of ale.

Agnar gestured for Elvar and Grend to sit, Sighvat stomping off in search of food.

"I am not prying; your business is your own," Agnar said. "I just wanted to check that you are . . . well." He looked from the mead horn in her hand to the mead that glistened on her chin.

"I am well enough," Elvar said with a twist of her lips as she sat heavily, Grend pulling up a chair.

Agnar nodded, as if she had said much more than her words.

Above them the roof rafters creaked rhythmically. When Agnar rented the hayloft of the tavern the landlord had evicted half a dozen whores who rented the space. By the sounds of it they were making up for their lost coin, most of it from the Battle-Grim now that they had been paid.

Sighvat returned and slammed a trencher of food on the table: a joint of cured ham, cheese and flatbread, a bowl of butter, cream and strawberries.

Elvar moved to cut herself a slice of ham.

"That's mine," Sighvat said, waving a protective hand over the food. "I'll get yours now."

He stomped off again.

"Sighvat doesn't share food," Agnar smiled.

Sighvat returned with another plate of ham and flatbread.

"That's yours," Sighvat said as he sat, the bench creaking. He carved himself a thick slice of ham, chopped some cheese and wrapped it all in the flatbread, then took a huge bite.

"What?" he said to Elvar's staring.

"Nothing," Elvar said and reached for her own plate.

Agnar smiled and shrugged.

"My father has asked me to take my place at his side, offered me *drengrs* and a warband," Elvar said.

I owe him the truth.

Agnar had been good to her, taking her in when she had only seventeen winters on her back. She had told him the truth then, and he had kept his lips closed about it for almost four years. He had promised her no special treatment, that she would earn her place in his shield wall or be cast out, for which she had been grateful. That was all she had ever wanted, the chance to be judged on her own merits. Her own skill, her own courage. Her hand drifted up to the troll tusk around her neck.

And I am still here.

Agnar opened the chest beside him, pulled out two pouches and thrust them across the table at Elvar and Grend.

"Your share of the Battle-Grim's spoils," Agnar said. "Your father pays well for *Berserkir*, and troll meat fetches a good price in Snakavik's markets."

Elvar just looked at the bags of money.

Grend took the two pouches and slipped them into his cloak.

Agnar leaned across the table.

"Follow where your heart and thought-cage lead you," he said, "but know this. Whatever your choice, whatever your road, you will always have an oar-bench on the *Wave-Jarl*. You have proved your worth, Elvar Troll-Slayer."

He offered her his arm, one warrior to another.

She felt a flush of pride swell her chest at Agnar's words, reaching her face to twitch a smile. She leaned forwards and took his arm.

He is a merchant whore. Her father's words spiralled through her head.

He is my friend, Elvar snarled back at her imaginary father, though the memory of Agnar in Jarl Störr's mead hall, negotiating over the *Berserkir*, lingered in her memory.

"Tell me your decision when you are ready," Agnar said, then reached for some food.

Elvar sat back with a sigh.

In truth, she did not know what to do.

And then it came to her.

She stood, her chair tumbling over behind her. "My thanks, chief," she said over her shoulder as she made for the tavern's door. A hand grabbed her as she reached it.

It was Uspa, her hood pulled up over her head. Thrud was leaning in the shadows, watching her.

"When are we leaving Snakavik?" Uspa asked her pleadingly.

Elvar blinked and shook Uspa's hand off her.

"I don't know," Elvar said.

"I told you, I need to leave," Uspa hissed.

"Tell me why, and I'll talk to the chief," Elvar said.

Uspa looked into Elvar's eyes.

"You are mead-drunk," Uspa said with disgust. "When you are sober, I will tell you."

Elvar shrugged. "You may be waiting a long while," she said and pushed her way through into the twilit town. She took a few swaying steps before she paused for a moment, sucking in cleaner air.

"Where are we going?" Grend said as he stepped out of the tavern behind her.

"I'm going to speak to Hrung's head," Elvar said.

Elvar climbed the steps of her father's mead hall. Gytha led her, Grend following behind. The climb through Snakavik and the skull tunnel had cleared her head, and the searing winds that howled about the fortress had seemed to scour the alcohol from her veins.

Gytha led her into the mead hall. The tables were being made ready for the evening meal, thralls bringing out trenchers of meat and jugs of mead, tending to the hearth fires. Elvar reached out and grabbed a jug, Gytha raising a hand to the thrall who was trying to take it.

Elvar stepped up on to the dais and walked past her father's high seat, empty now. Gytha stopped before the head of Hrung, whose eyes were closed, the muscles of his face slack, his mouth drooping like his long moustache in what looked like sleep.

"He is sleeping," Gytha said. "I said I would bring you here, but I told you there would be no point. The giant sleeps longer and more heavily than he used to. Though your father may still flay me for it."

"He will not," Elvar said. "I am Elvar Störrsdottir, how could you refuse me?"

Gytha raised an eyebrow. "I have not sent him word, for which I will be judged."

"Then send him word that I am here now," Elvar shrugged. "Just, wait a little longer before you do. Give me a few moments with Hrung and then I shall be gone."

"The ancient one is asleep, anyway," Gytha said as she turned. She paused beside Grend, her fingertips brushing his arm. Grend looked straight ahead and Gytha walked away.

"You should talk with Gytha," Elvar said. "Spend time with her, while we are in Snakavik."

"No," Grend grunted.

Elvar looked at him and sighed.

"Hrung," she said, but the giant head did not move.

Elvar held the jug beneath the giant's huge nose, dipped her fingertips into the mead and flicked droplets on to his lips.

A ripple passed through the head, a tremor of flesh. An inhaled breath through the nose, the lips parting and Hrung's fat tongue tasted the mead. The eyelids flickered, opening to reveal Hrung's clouded eyes.

"Elvar," he rumbled.

"I brought you a gift," she said, holding the jug up.

"Ah, but you were always my favourite," the head said, a grin spreading across his face.

"Not much of a compliment, when you are choosing between my father, brothers and me," Elvar said. She tipped some of the jug into Hrung's mouth, mead trickling over his tongue and down his throat. She watched as a stain spread slowly through the wood at her feet.

"Ah, but it tastes good, even if it does not have the effect it once did," Hrung sighed.

"That is because you are only a head," Elvar said, looking at the stain seeping about her feet.

"You are still full of wisdom, then," Hrung rumbled.

"I've missed you," Elvar smiled, only realising the truth of it as her words left her mouth. Few of her memories from Snakavik had any warmth to them, save for some scattered moments with her younger brother, Broðir, and her conversations with Hrung.

"I have missed you, too, little one," Hrung said. "It has been dull without you." He licked his lips. "And dry."

Elvar poured some more mead on to Hrung's tongue and his throat rumbled his pleasure.

"Ah, but the years have been parched and empty since you left. Not a day has passed since then that I haven't wished Jarl Störr and Silrið had left me dead in Snaka's throat."

"I remember the day you were hoisted from the fjord," Elvar said, though she had only seen three winters, then. She had been sitting upon Grend's shoulders, down on one of the harbour piers. "I thought you looked sad. There was red algae covering your eyes and cheeks. It made you look as if you had wept blood."

"Perhaps I had," Hrung said. "It is no pleasant thing, being swallowed by a serpent-god and having your head bitten clean from your body. Worse still that a small fragment of Snaka's dying power seeped into me and condemned me to life when I would rather rest in death with my giant-kin. As bad as this life can be, though, it is better than the three hundred years I spent sitting in the deep fjord, only Snaka's fangs and fish to count." His eyes took her in, lingering on the troll tusk and rings draped about her. He took a deep breath through his large nostrils, strong enough to stir Elvar's braided hair.

"You have found what you sought, then," he said. "You reek of battle-fame and great deeds."

Elvar shrugged.

"And you have not managed to rid yourself of old loose-lips," Hrung said, his cloudy eyes shifting to Grend. The old warrior just stared flatly at the giant.

The sound of voices echoed in the corridor beyond the mead hall, the slap of many feet on timber.

Gytha has told my father of my presence here, then.

"I would stay longer, but my father is coming to spoil our reunion," she said.

"Ask your question, then," Hrung said.

"Is it so obvious?" Elvar said.

Hrung chuckled, a sound that vibrated through Elvar's chest. "As much as you like my company, I think need has driven you to me. Ask, little one," he said.

"My father has bid me return to Snakavik, to stand at his side. He has offered me warriors, a warband. Everything that I wanted."

Hrung's head shifted, severed muscles in his neck contracting. A nod.

"This is known," he said, "but that is no question."

"My question is: Should I take his offer?"

Gytha appeared at the mead hall's entrance, gesturing for Elvar to leave.

Hrung stared at Elvar, his opaque eyes swirling like storm clouds.

"I have to go," Elvar said.

"Silent and thoughtful and bold in strife, the jarl's bairn should be," Hrung intoned.

Elvar frowned. "Silent, thoughtful, bold, I strive to be those things," Elvar said. "But that does not answer my question. When to be bold, that is at the heart of my question. Are my father's words strife? Is that what you are saying? Or, should I be bold in the battle for Vigrið and join my father as he moves against Queen Helka?"

Hrung was silent, only the clouds in his eyes moving.

Voices in the corridor.

"*Please*," Elvar hissed. "Give me a straight answer, just once."

Hrung's mouth twisted in a grin. "That is not my way, little one," he said. "Blame old Snaka, he made me and my giant-kin with a love for words and riddles. You must sift through my gift to you and find the gold in it."

"A riddle, then, anything," Elvar said, her eyes flickering between Hrung and the doorway.

"To answer your question, I will ask you another. Can the sun be cold, or the sea be dry, or the wolf become a lamb?"

Grend growled in his throat. "What use is a talking head, if it only ever spouts shite?"

Hrung's eyes fixed on to Grend.

"Eyes are for seeing, ears for hearing, and a thought-cage for understanding. Unless your thought-cage is already stuffed full of straw, such as yours, Grend the Talker," Hrung rumbled.

Grend's eyes narrowed, his hand moving to the axe at his belt.

"What are you going to do, offended warrior, cut off my head?" Hrung laughed, the sound echoing, filling the hall.

Elvar laughed too as she tipped the rest of the mead on to Hrung's tongue, then turned and ran, Grend following her. She flew through the doors, past Gytha and out into the sunset as the shadow of her father filled the corridor behind her.

CHAPTER TWENTY-SIX

VARG

Varg stood in the stern of the *Sea-Wolf*, behind Torvik and a handful of other warriors. More stood behind Varg, all of them jostling and laughing and singing as figures leaped over the starboard top-rail and ran the oar-dance, leaping from oar to oar as the *Sea-Wolf* was rowed into a sharp-sloped fjord. Surviving a summer storm seemed to be something worth celebrating among the Bloodsworn. Varg agreed, a faint echo of the fear still lingering in the pit of his belly that he had felt as the waves had risen and the lightning-scarred skies had unleashed a torrent so heavy he could not see his hand in front of his nose. He had been certain his death was at hand, fragmented memories seared into his thought-cage like the incandescent bursts of lightning that had crackled through the heavens above him, the sound of Einar bellowing orders and the dimly glimpsed figure of Glornir strapping himself to the top-rail so that he could keep his grip on the tiller without being hurled overboard. The skies were clear, now, as if the storm had never been, the air fresh, and the sun was sinking into the rim of the world, turning the now calm ocean and fjord to molten bronze.

Torvik climbed on to the top-rail, looked back at Varg and the others, then leaped on to the first oar, teetered for a moment, then found his balance and leaped to the next. Only two days had passed since they left Liga, but to Varg it had felt like a lifetime.

Like a new life, as if I have been reborn.

His hands were raw and blistered from rowing and handling what felt like leagues of sea-soaked rigging, his face red and burned by the sun, his clothing sodden from the sudden storm that had swept out of the north, and yet he felt . . . happy. It was a strange sensation, when all he had known his whole life was toil and misery, the only light in his life during the long dark of servitude being Frøya. He tensed just at the memory of her name, a flutter of happiness and guilt in his belly, a reminder of why he was here, of the oath he had sworn. To find her body and avenge her murder. To rip and tear his sister's killers. He had sworn it as he had stood blood-drenched over Kolskegg's still-warm corpse and his oath hovered now in his mind and blood like a dark-winged raven, croaking that time was passing.

I have not forgotten you. I will never forget you. And my oath stands, I will make it happen. But if I feel some moments of cheer as I walk that path, or find some friends, is that so bad a thing? Should it feel so . . . wrong?

"Go on, No-Sense," a voice said behind him, Svik pushing him, and Varg blinked, shook his head and saw that there was no one between him and the top-rail. He jumped up on to the rail and stood there a moment. Around half the crew were rowing the *Sea-Wolf*, thirty oars rising and falling, the other half taking part in this oar-dance. Ahead of him Torvik leaped from oar to oar, grinning and whooping. Varg sucked in a deep breath and leaped on to the first oar, timed it so that it was dipping as he landed, his feet spread, knees bending as the oar began to rise. He felt the air churn around him, swirled his arms and then he was stable, standing on the oar, a grin splitting his face.

"Get on with you," Svik yelled, the warrior standing on the top-rail now, waiting his turn at the first oar. Varg grinned and leaped, landing on the next oar with his left foot, dipping and pushing off, leaping to the next one, moving on as if the oars were stepping stones across a river that were too small to take both of his feet.

There was a cry and a splash ahead of him, and Varg glanced to see Torvik disappear into the fjord's ice-blue embrace, an explosion of sun-flecked foam as he resurfaced. Varg ran on, along the entire starboard length of the ship until he was leaping on to the rail before the prow. A smile and dip of her head from Vol the Seiðr-witch from her usual place in the prow, one of Edel's wolfhounds there, panting and watching Varg, nudging him for a neck-scratch. He quickly obliged and then he was leaping back on to the portside rail, one foot slipping and then he was leaping again, airborne, weightless, landing with a thump on the first oar. There was a flash of a black beard and teeth as Jökul the smith grinned over his oar at Varg.

Varg grinned back as he bent his legs and leaped onwards. There were many things that he was learning in his short time with the Bloodsworn, shield and spear under the merciless tutelage of Røkia, ship craft from seemingly everyone, but some skills came naturally to Varg and did not need teaching. Endurance, determination, and balance. He was light on his feet. On Kolskegg's farm during the Winternight celebration that followed the harvest Varg had taken part in the tree-run, where those willing had to run across a river full of cut timber trunks that spun and moved under your feet. It was not unknown for men and women to be crushed or drowned during the trial, but Varg had won it every year since his first attempt, when he had only eleven winters on his shoulders. And so, he was enjoying this trial and faring better than many of the other Bloodsworn, as attested by the shrieks and splashes occurring around him.

The stern was in sight, a handful of oars dipping and rising between him and Glornir, who stood at the tiller. Varg landed on an oar, his leg bending to go with the oar's flow, but it jerked beneath him, dipping when it should be rising. He swung his arms, balanced for a heartbeat, then his foot was sliding and he was falling, plummeting to the water below. He glimpsed a snarl of red beard staring over the oar-port, Einar Half-Troll grinning as he watched Varg fall, and then he hit the water.

It was cold as ice, snatching his breath away. He sank, turning, thrashing for a moment, unsure which way was up. He expelled some air and tracked the bubbles, followed them, and then his head was bursting from the water and he was gasping in air.

The hull of the *Sea-Wolf* was gliding away, Glornir steering the ship towards a shallow bank on the fjord. A few figures were still leaping across the oars, Svik among them. Varg swam for shore, along with a dozen or so others.

Shouts drifted from the *Sea-Wolf* and the anchor-stone in its wooden frame was heaved on to the top-rail and dropped overboard, Glornir choosing to get his feet wet rather than scrape the hull on the fjord's bank. Bloodsworn were leaping over the side and splashing ashore as Varg's feet touched the ground and he began to wade to shore. A figure appeared, standing on the bank, waiting for him.

It was Røkia, a shield and spear in her hands.

Varg shook his head as he emerged from the water, a wind blowing across him and causing him to shiver, despite the lingering warmth of the setting sun.

"You are not serious?" Varg said to her. "I am soaked to the skin – unfairly, I might add, as Einar Half-Troll threw me from his oar."

"I am always serious," Røkia said, stone-faced.

This is a truth, Varg thought. He sighed. "Give me a few moments to change my tunic and breeches and dry off in what is left of this sun."

"Ha, just what I would have expected from a warrior with No-Sense," Røkia said. "Do you think your enemy will kindly wait for you to dry your feet and arse if they come upon you in a fjord or river? No, they will fall upon you like wolves and seek to carve you into small pieces, using their good fortune of finding you unprepared. You must learn to fight and survive under the worst of conditions, not the *best*."

"That is what I have done all my life," Varg muttered under his breath.

Røkia threw his shield to him and strode away, either not hearing or choosing to ignore his words. Varg caught the shield rather than let it empty his mouth of teeth, and trudged after her, dripping on the fjord's grassy bank. He glimpsed Svik on the *Sea-Wolf*'s top-rail, holding his arms up and dancing a jig.

He must have won the oar-dance.

Røkia turned again, this time throwing him his spear, which he caught deftly, its leather sheath in place over the blade.

"Come and kill me then," Røkia said, a cold smile on her lips as she raised her shield and set her feet.

There was a smell of woodsmoke as fires were kindled and iron pots hung for supper, the crackle of butter melting in pans. Varg's belly growled.

He sighed, shoulders slumped, then sucked in a deep breath and straightened.

Might as well get on with it. Getting beaten up by Røkia is the only path to food.

He lifted his shield and checked the grip on his spear, as Røkia had taught him. They were only a few days away from Liga, but each night Røkia had put his shield and spear in his fists and continued with his training. At first, she had continued teaching him shield work, adding the principle of treating the shield as a weapon as well as a form of defence, using both the iron boss and the hide-bound rim. The second night she had put a spear in his hand and taught him the two main grips. He approached Røkia now with an overhand grip, the shaft angled down, his blade pointed at her shield boss. This gave him a longer reach than the reverse grip, with which he noted Røkia held her own spear, though he knew his overhand grip was weaker.

Best to use the longer reach as I approach, a chance to draw blood before I am in range of her own strikes.

Røkia grunted as he approached and he took that as her approval of his choice, and then he was jabbing at her, aiming at shoulders, legs, trying to find a weakness around her shield.

"Side steps," she grunted at him over her shield rim. "You'll not find an opening by coming straight at me like a stupid old boar."

Varg listened, shuffling left and right, keeping his spear shaft jabbing, in and out, his strikes almost finding her flesh, but always ending with the dull thud of his leather-bound blade meeting her linen-wrapped shield. And then Røkia was stepping in, using her reverse grip on her spear to sweep his own away, stepping closer still, her blade slipping inside his shield and raking across his chest, her sharp-angled face close enough that he could smell the apple and onions on her breath.

"You now have a wound," she said, then smiled at him as she shoved her shield into his chest. He took a step back, stumbled over her foot that she had sneakily placed behind his, and then his arse was on the grass and he was looking up at her, her leather-wrapped blade touching his throat.

A position he was becoming all too familiar with.

"A good start," she said, "but when you failed to strike me, you should have broken away and shifted your grip. And never stop fighting until one of us is dead. I wounded you with my strike, but it would not have been a killing blow. Not immediately, anyway."

She offered him an arm and heaved him to his feet.

"Again," she said.

Varg stood in a line of the Bloodsworn, a bowl in hand. It was dark now, the summer sun long disappeared beyond the horizon, the sky a scattering of stars above him. He had changed out of his sweat- and fjord-soaked clothes into a fresh tunic and breeches from his sea-chest. Hearth fires flickered, sending shadows dancing, the sound of the fjord lapping at the shore and the creak of the *Sea-Wolf* on the water. He reached the pot hanging over the fire and ladled fish stew into his bowl, then turned and walked away, looking for somewhere to sit. He saw Svik stooping to speak to Einar Half-Troll, who was as big as the boulder he was sitting against. Svik pulled a loaf of bread from beneath his cloak and handed it to Einar, then sat down with the big man.

"Congratulations for your victory on the oars," Varg said to Svik as he approached them.

"It is all in the reflexes," Svik smiled and dipped his head at Varg. "I do not like getting wet," he said. "It makes a mess of my beard, so I have learned to have light feet and fine balance."

"That is something I do not have to worry about," Varg said, rubbing his head and chin. Although, to his surprise, he found that his stubble had grown and it was no longer scratching and itching his palm.

"No, but it will grow," Svik said solemnly. "Soon you will have hair as pretty as mine. You did well on the oars. It is a shame you . . . slipped."

"I did not *slip*. I was thrown," Varg grunted, not able to stop himself looking at Einar. "As I think you may know." He looked pointedly at the loaf of bread that Einar was ripping chunks from. "And as Einar well knows."

"I like bread," Einar grunted.

"Are we even, now?" Varg asked the big man.

"No," Einar said, not looking at Varg. He tore another chunk of bread from the loaf Svik had given him and dipped it in his fish stew, slurped on it, then slowly looked up at Varg. "You got wet, but I see that you are already dry. Me, I can count your teeth by their imprints in my leg, and will be able to do so for all the years of my life."

"It was a fight," Varg shrugged.

"That is a fair point, Half-Troll," Svik said. "You were trying to smash his bones with your fists."

"I was holding back," Einar sniffed. "I was being kind. I even told him to stay down, and how does he repay my kindness? By *biting* me." He pulled a face. "I do not like to be bitten."

"I am now most clearly aware of that," Varg assured him, "and I swear that I will never put my teeth in you again."

"Hhmmm," Einar rumbled, his brows knitting. Varg thought he could almost see the big man's thought-cage churning as he turned Varg's words over. With another rumbling breath Einar tore a chunk of bread from his loaf and offered it to Varg. "Sit and eat, then," Einar said.

"My thanks," Varg said, thinking that this was as close to a truce as he was likely to get. He sat beside Einar, as Torvik appeared and joined them.

"I hear Einar threw you in the fjord," the young apprentice scout and blacksmith said, a big grin on his face. Varg looked from Torvik to Einar.

"I . . . slipped," Varg said.

Einar nodded, a rumble of what Varg took to be approval reverberating in his chest.

Torvik looked at the three of them.

"You slipped on Einar's oar, along with an *uncommon* number of others, and Svik won," Torvik said. "Hmmm."

Varg slurped on his bread.

"It is true, I am blessed with good fortune," Svik said, twirling his red moustache. "And also, I am a remarkable oar-dancer. What can I say? Some bread for your fish stew?" Svik offered to Torvik, smiling.

"I hear the Skullsplitter was a remarkable oar-dancer," Torvik said as he took Svik up on his offer of bread.

"Skullsplitter?" Svik said, raising an eyebrow. "No, the chief was big and heavy as a bear. Dancing on oars was not one of Skullsplitter's skills. Splitting skulls with a long-axe, however . . . "

"How did a warrior like that fall?" Torvik muttered. "I heard it was in a sea-battle, falling from the *Sea-Wolf*'s rail in a coat of mail and drowning." Torvik shook his head.

"Aye," Svik said, his face unusually melancholy. He sighed and shook his head. "It was a hard-fought battle, and no denying." He looked around at their camp, the Bloodsworn going about their evening meal. "If I were you," Svik said in hushed tones, "I would not speak so loudly of Skullsplitter's fall around Glornir. He still mourns the death of his brother; it is a grief that sits heavy on his shoulders."

Torvik nodded.

Footfalls and the murmuring of conversation stilled. Glornir walked towards the hearth fire, Vol at his side, and Skalk, Queen Helka's Galdurman followed them, his knotted staff in his fist. The two warriors from Queen Helka's retinue were with him, gleaming in their fine *brynjas*. The man Varg had learned was named Olvir, a scar over one eyebrow shifting the set of his eyes, and the proud-faced, thin-lipped woman was called Yrsa. They both wore swords at their hips and dark cloaks over their shoulders, both pinned with brooches of silver fashioned into the likeness of eagle wings. Wherever Skalk went, they were close behind him. Varg had seen them all taking shifts on the oar-bench, and glimpsed them bailing water furiously during the sea storm that had swept over them.

"Your ears, Bloodsworn," Glornir said as he came to stand by the hearth fire. "For those who do not know, this is Skalk, famed skáld and Galdurman of Queen Helka. He has some words for us, about our mission."

Varg stared at Skalk. He was a tall man with an honest face, laughter lines thick as crow's talons at his eyes. His shoulders and chest were broad, everything about him suggesting a warrior's bearing, not a sorcerer's.

He is a Galdurman . . . I could ask him to perform an akáll *and save myself much time. Who knows how long it will be before Glornir is satisfied that I have proven myself?*

"It is always good to know what lies ahead, no?" Skalk said, nodding and smiling at the Bloodsworn. "So, I will tell you why my queen has hired you, and what I know of the task she wishes you to perform. We are travelling to the source of the River Slågen, from which this fjord flows." He gestured to the glossy-dark of the fjord behind them, glittering in the starlight. "That river will take us to the foothills of the Boneback Mountains, on the north-western border of my queen's lands. Something there is killing her people."

"A lusty ram or aggrieved goat, perhaps," Svik called out, laughter spreading around him. "We have all heard the tales of loneliness among those who live within the shadow of the Bonebacks, and what that can do to a man."

"This is no laughing matter," Skalk said, pausing to stare at Svik. "Not if it were your kin that were being . . . consumed. At first, people were disappearing from farms and more remote places, and we thought it was on account of raids from Jarl Störr across the river." A frown creased his brow as he mentioned the jarl's name, a flicker of fire-glow in his eyes. "The region shares a border with Jarl Störr's land, and though there is officially peace between the jarl and my queen," he looked around them and smiled knowingly, showing small white teeth behind his blond beard, "we all know that a jarl teaches his *drengrs* the art of war through raiding." Warriors among the Bloodsworn nodded, seeming to Varg as if they were remembering their own pasts.

"But then, we began to find those who had disappeared," Skalk continued. "Or, find *parts* of them." Another frown. "They were being eaten. Or at least, some of them were." He shook his head. "A queen must protect her people, and so action must be taken. But the queen's *hird* are spread thinly along her borders, and so she thought of you, the Bloodsworn, known for their fair-fame reputation, and she heard news that you were within her own lands, at Liga." He spread his arms, gave another smile. "There are vaesen loose in Queen Helka's domain, killing and eating her people, and they must be stopped."

"What vaesen?" a voice called out. It was Røkia, Varg saw.

Skalk shrugged. "That I do not know. There have been no witnesses. Ones with big teeth and long claws, I would guess, judging by the bite marks and wounds on the remains we have found. Trolls, or *Huldra*-folk, maybe *Vittor*, or wights? I do not know. But whatever they are, I suspect that there are more than one or two of them."

"How many dead have you found?" Svik called out.

Skalk looked at him.

"It is hard to tell exactly, you understand," Skalk said. "Here a leg, there an arm, elsewhere just a bloodstain." He looked up at the star-flecked sky. "Perhaps as many as thirty."

Murmurs rippled around the Bloodsworn.

"That is a lot of dead, which means a lot of vaesen, most likely," a new voice said, quiet and sinuous. It was Vol, standing beside Glornir. "They must have crossed from beyond the Bonebacks, and that means finding a way past the Grimholt. Past your tower of guards. How is that possible?"

Skalk turned a heavy-browed look upon Vol, eyes abruptly cold and hard.

"I am not accustomed to answering the questions of thralls," he said, "or hearing their criticisms."

Glornir straightened, and Varg felt a shift around him, a sudden tension in the air that made the hairs on his arms stand on end.

"It is not a criticism," Vol said, speaking slowly and ignoring Skalk's insults, "just an observation. If vaesen have found a way through the Bonebacks . . . "

"I am not being *clear*," Skalk said, glowering at Vol. "You are a thrall. Do not speak to me unless I give you permission."

"Vol has saved my ship and my crew more times than I can count," Glornir said with a glare. "Thrall, freedman, all on my ship risk their lives, and *will* be respected for that. If you choose to travel on my ship, with my crew, you will give her the same respect as any other of my Bloodsworn. Or we are going to have a problem. Do I make myself clear?"

Skalk stiffened, and his guards, Olvir and Yrsa, shifted. Fingertips twitched, brushed a sword hilt.

"She is a Tainted thrall," Skalk said with a sneer.

Glornir shrugged. "I am not in the habit of repeating my words," he said.

"Neither am I."

"It is my ship, and my crew. You can always walk from here," Glornir said.

"It's my coin," Skalk said, his voice quiet now, cold.

"Queen Helka's coin," Glornir replied. "If you want to pay someone else for your vaesen-hunting." Glornir gave a thin smile, holding Skalk's gaze.

There was a long, drawn-out moment, and then Skalk smiled. "As you wish. You will do the fighting, and the dying if there is any to be done, so . . . " A shift in his shoulders suggested the matter meant nothing to him. "I will ignore the collar about your thrall's throat." He looked around at the gathered Bloodsworn, his easy smile back on his face. "That is all I know. We shall travel there together and root out the vaesen-filth. And Queen Helka will show her gratitude to you with a chest of silver."

Skalk stepped around Glornir to the iron cookpot hanging over the fire and ladled some fish stew into a bowl, then walked away, Olvir and Yrsa following.

Varg sat and stared at his own bowl, his thought-cage whirling.

Galdurmen and vaesen. I am sailing into an adventure, hunting trolls or wights or whatever the Boneback Mountains are hiding.

A shiver ran through him.

Troll-hunting is a long way from Kolskegg's farm.

There was a humming in his blood: fear or excitement, he was not sure.

CHAPTER TWENTY-SEVEN

ELVAR

Elvar sat on a patch of wind-blasted bone high on Snaka's skull, staring out over the fjord of Snakavik far below as the sun rose behind her. Tendrils of mist coiled like serpents around the cliffs that edged the fjord, gulls swirling small as motes of dust, and the fjord glistened in the new sun.

Grend lay snoring beside her, wrapped in his cloak.

Elvar stood, breathing out a long sigh, and buckled on her weapons belt, the familiar weight of sword and seax settling around her waist and hips.

"Come on," she said, nudging Grend with her toe.

"Could have chosen somewhere warmer to sit and think," he muttered as he climbed to his feet, then looked at her. "I hope it has helped?"

"It has," she said, striding off.

They made their way over thick ridges of bone, until they came to the skull tunnel. Grend nodded to guards bearing Jarl Störr's yellow shields as smoke and firelight wrapped around them and they descended through Snaka's thick skull into the town below.

Elvar walked in silence, chewing over her thoughts, working through all that Hrung had said. Like her father, he said far more with the words he did not speak, but with Hrung Elvar knew that there was an impartial truth wrapped within his words that she had never been able to uncover in her father's.

Grend walked quietly beside her, something that Elvar always valued in his company. He never pushed or hurried her, always followed, whether he agreed or not.

They turned a corner and the tavern appeared before them, a painted sign creaking over the door, a soft fire-glow leaking from shuttered windows and the open door.

Grend's hand touched her shoulder.

"Wait," he breathed, the rasp of leather on wood as his axe slid into his fist.

"What?" Elvar said, frowning. Then she realised.

There were shouts from within the tavern, the clang of iron, a scream.

She reached for her sword hilt and broke into a run, Grend a few steps behind her.

A voice: loud, female, shouting. A flash of searing light exploded through the door and threw the window shutters open. Elvar and Grend stumbled, blinded for a moment. Elvar blinked and rubbed her eyes, her vision returning quickly, dappled with white spots. She ran on.

Figures burst through the open doorway: five, six, seven, one with something draped over their shoulder. All had sharp iron in their fists, some glittered in mail. They were not the Battle-Grim.

Elvar was close. She drew her sword in one fist, her seax in the other.

One saw her, a blond-haired warrior, tall and broad with a thick beard, silver rings about his neck and arms. A black raven's wing was braided into his hair. He wore a *brynja* and had a sword in his fist, and he turned to meet her as Elvar ran at them.

Their swords met, sparks grating, the clangour loud in the silent streets, Elvar holding the warrior's sword in a bind and slashing at his belly with her seax. More sparks, the man grunting, though the iron links of his *brynja* held. Another warrior turned on Elvar, a woman, axe and seax in her hands. The rest ran on, downhill and away from the tavern.

The woman lunged at Elvar, who stumbled away, sweeping the blond warrior's sword wide with her seax, chopping down into his calf with her sword, slicing the blade deep through leg-wraps and breeches into flesh as she stepped away.

Grend slammed into the woman lunging at Elvar, the two of them crashing into the tavern wall.

The blond warrior yelled and swayed, and dropped to one knee as his injured leg gave way. He glared at Elvar, his face twisting, muscles twitching, and his lips drew back, revealing jagged teeth, sharp canines. Elvar stabbed at him but he moved, faster than Elvar thought possible, an arm swinging to bat Elvar's sword away. She stepped forwards, off balance, close to the blond warrior, looking straight into his eyes. A hissed breath as she met his eyes causing her to freeze a moment. They were grey, colours shifting like sun and rain through clouds, the pupil narrowed to a pinprick.

He is Tainted, she thought. He was snarling at her, trying to rise, but his wounded leg was failing him. He staggered and Elvar stabbed with her seax, fear giving her speed and strength, and her blade punched deep into his throat. She pulled away and ripped it out. There was a spurt of arterial blood, black in the half-light, and he toppled to the ground.

Elvar stood over him, chest heaving, and saw Grend push away from the tavern wall, his axe swinging. With a spurt of blood and a gurgled scream the woman sank down the wall, leaving a smeared trail of blood on the whitewashed wattle and daub.

They stood there, staring at each other.

Shouts sounded from inside the tavern and Elvar ran through the door.

She was met with the stink of blood and voided bowels, burned flesh.

Thrud lay across a table, a red gash across his throat, another wound in his back, blank eyes staring. Biórr was slumped unconscious against a wall, blood pulsing from a wound in his shoulder, more blood sheeting his face. Uspa lay on her face on the ground, three or four bodies piled around her. Their hair and clothes were smoking, the flesh on their faces and hands charred and blackened.

Grend checked the room, as Elvar ran to Biórr and crouched beside him.

The loft-ladder had been moved, wedging the loft-hatch closed, blows from above shaking the roof. Elsewhere in the roof an axe head burst through timber with the sound of cracking and a form crashed through in an explosion of timber and straw, landing in a cloud of dust.

Sighvat stood, axe raised, spitting and sputtering, a half-formed battle-cry on his lips. He frowned when he saw Elvar.

"Where are they?" he said.

"Dead or fled," Elvar told him.

Grend kicked the ladder away, freeing the loft-hatch.

Agnar dropped from the hatch to the ground, his face a snarl, sword in his fist. He took in the scene as Elvar had done, and strode to Uspa as other Battle-Grim dropped down to the ground and turned one of the dead with his boot. Heat still radiated from the corpse.

"More escaped," Elvar called to Agnar as her fingers found Biórr's pulse in his neck. He groaned, eyelids flickering.

"They took something," Elvar frowned, picturing in her thought-cage the figures who had fled. At first she had thought it was one of the chests Agnar's payment had been held in, but it had been too supple, slumped across a warrior's shoulder.

"They took the boy," she said, standing and looking at Uspa. She was breathing, a bruise already purpling along one side of her jaw as Sighvat lifted her.

"Who are they?" Agnar growled.

"Ilska's Raven-Feeders," Elvar said. She walked out of the tavern, back to the warrior she had slain. He was blond-haired, with a thick beard now slick with his own blood. His war kit was good: a fine sword and *brynja*. She lifted the raven feather in his hair with her boot.

"The Raven-Feeders," she called out. He was the warrior who had spoken to her as she had followed Agnar to see Jarl Störr.

Agnar joined her, frowning. No words were spoken, but Elvar knew what he was thinking.

Why did they take the boy? Tainted children were worth coin, but not like an adult *Berserkir* or *Úlfhéðnar*. But whatever the reason, such an insult could not stand.

Agnar yelled a few orders and in a dozen heartbeats Elvar, having snatched up her shield, was following him into the snarl of Snakavik, Grend, Sighvat with the *Hundur*-thrall and a score of Battle-Grim behind them.

"There it is." Elvar pointed with her sword at a tavern that came into view as they turned a corner. Agnar barked a command and a handful of the Battle-Grim peeled away, Sighvat leading them, slipping into side streets to check for other entrances and exits to the building.

Without waiting, Agnar shrugged his shield from his back into his fist and kicked the door in, throwing himself into the tavern, ducking and turning, shield raised, sword ready. Elvar followed behind him, covering his back, Grend and other forms pouring through the doorway.

A man cowered over the hearth fire, stirring the embers with an iron poker.

"Where are they?" Agnar snarled at him.

The man froze a moment, mouth open, Elvar seeing his eyes measuring Agnar and the Battle-Grim.

Everything is a choice, her father had said to her once. *Truth or lie, fight or flight, love or hate.*

"They are gone," the man said.

Sighvat crashed into the room through a back doorway, timber splintering, the *Hundur*-thrall at his side. Footsteps drummed on stairs, voices shouting.

"Empty, chief," Sighvat said.

"Where?" Agnar said to the landlord, striding towards him.

"The docks." The man pointed with his iron poker.

"If you're lying to me, I'll be back to cut your tongue from your mouth and throw it on the fire," Agnar said, then turned and left the tavern.

Sighvat growled at the thrall, who spent a few moments on all fours sniffing the tavern floor and benches, then straightened and hurried after Agnar.

They hurried through Snakavik's streets, winding ever downwards, towards the harbour. The streets were filling, now, but all parted to let the stern-faced warriors with naked steel in their fists through. The *Hundur*-thrall led them on, pausing as they reached the docks and the road split. Grend peeled away to speak to a handful of harbour guards.

"That way," Grend pointed, even as the thrall loped off in the same direction. They ran now, feet slapping on stone, past the pier that the *Wave-Jarl* was moored upon, a score of the Battle-Grim aboard it, guarding the ship and what was left of the coin Agnar had been paid by Jarl Störr. The shrieking of gulls was louder, the reek of fish and salt heavy in the air.

Elvar saw a ship pulling out into the harbour, a sleek-lined *drakkar*, mast upright, sail hoisted on the yardarm but not unfurled. Oars dipped and pulled as the ship moved towards the fangs of Snaka that breached the water. Agnar and the Battle-Grim sprinted, only stopping when the pier met the green-blue water of the fjord, waves lapping against timber. Elvar and Grend halted at Agnar's shoulder, the Battle-Grim spreading in a line beside them, all staring at the *drakkar* as it cut a white wake through the harbour. Grey shields with black wings painted upon them lined the *drakkar*'s top-rail, a figure standing at the stern holding the tiller: a woman. Elvar could see her clearly, shafts of light piercing through the eye sockets and cracks in Snaka's skull to illuminate her. She was looking back at them, hair dark as a raven's wings, bound with silver at her nape, a woollen tunic of grey, a sword at her hip, hilt and buckle glinting with gold.

"Ilska," Agnar murmured beside Elvar.

Ilska the Ruthless. Ilska the Cruel. Elvar knew of her battle-fame, had heard many a tale of her around the hearth fire. Ilska was a woman who had risen fast and far, carving her reputation in blood and steel.

Beside her stood a man, tall and hulking, a wolf pelt draped across his shoulders. He leaned upon a long-axe, the sides of his head shaved like Agnar's, but where Agnar's hair was yellow as ripe corn, this man's was black as the grave. Like Ilska, he was looking back at the Battle-Grim as they lined along the pier.

Agnar thumped his sword hilt into his shield with a rhythmic pounding. Elvar joined him, and in heartbeats all of the Battle-Grim were beating upon their shields: a rowing rhythm, a battle rhythm. A promise.

Elvar saw the flash of white teeth as Ilska grinned. She raised an arm to Agnar, saluting or mocking, Elvar did not know.

"She will come to regret stealing from me," Agnar said and spat at the lapping waves.

Elvar laid out a wool blanket on a table and laid her battle-gains upon it. A sword and scabbard, belt, a *brynja*, a pouch with bone dice and a few copper coins. A silver torc and three silver arm rings. Boots, breeches and a bloodstained tunic. She had stripped it all from the blond warrior's corpse outside their tavern, as was her right.

The sword and brynja will fetch a good price, and the boots, breeches and tunic look like they will fit Grend, she thought.

Deeper inside the tavern Biórr was being tended by Kráka. Sighvat was asking Biórr questions, but the young warrior was just staring and mumbling. On the table next to him Thrud's corpse had been wrapped in his cloak. They would take his body to the *Sea-Wolf* and drop it into the sea, once they were out on the ocean currents. The corpses of the Raven-Feeders were thrown naked into the street. Now that the blood-quickening that battle brings had left her, Elvar felt her stomach lurch at the sight of the burned corpses that had been found collapsed around Uspa.

That is power I have never seen from a Seiðr-witch before, she thought, *and I have grown up around Silrið and then Kráka.*

Uspa was still unconscious, laid upon a table close to Biórr and Kráka.

Agnar was talking to the landlord, counting out coin from a pouch to pay for the damage the Battle-Grim had brought upon the tavern.

"It is not Agnar's fault," Elvar said.

"No, but it is deep-cunning," Grend said as he rolled up the items he had stripped from his kill. A hand-axe and seax, a fine-tooled belt, tunic and boots. "If Agnar leaves Snakavik known for the destruction of his resting place," Grend continued, "and a reputation for not paying, then the next time he is here the Battle-Grim will most likely be sleeping on the deck of the *Wave-Jarl*."

Elvar grunted at that wisdom. She did not mind sleeping on a ship's deck, but recognised the pleasures of a straw bed and a hearth fire. She was about to tie her newfound treasure in the wool blanket when she paused and lifted one of the silver arm rings. It was thick and heavy, torchlight flickering where the metal twisted and flowed, the terminals carved into the likeness of a snarling wolf or hound.

Elvar held it out to Grend.

He looked at the arm ring, then at her.

"I do not follow you for wealth or prizes," he said with a frown.

"I know," Elvar said. "This is a gift, in recognition of your friendship. You would insult me if you refuse it."

Grend frowned, then reached out hesitantly and took the silver ring from her. He threaded it over his large fist, up his forearm and about his bicep, then squeezed it tight. He looked at Elvar and she saw his eyes were bright. He said nothing, just dipped his head to her.

Uspa groaned, shifting on the table, and Elvar hurried to her. As she did so she saw Agnar's eyes upon her, his face unreadable.

Kráka helped Uspa to sit up and offered her a cup of watered ale.

"Where is Bjarn?" Uspa croaked, her eyes searching the room. She grabbed Kráka's wrist. "Tell me, sister," she whispered.

"He is taken," Kráka said.

Uspa let out a wail, her hands clawing at her face.

Elvar grabbed Uspa's wrists and pulled her hands away, leaving blood smeared on Uspa's cheeks.

"I told you," Uspa hissed at Elvar. "I *told* you we needed to leave Snakavik."

"This was why? You knew?" Elvar asked.

"Uspa spoke to you of this?" Agnar said as he reached them, his brows knotted in a frown. "Thrud died. He was a good warrior, a friend." He looked from Uspa to Elvar. "I should have been told."

Elvar blinked, looking at the corpse of Thrud, tied in his cloak. *Could I have averted this*, she thought. *Saved Thrud's life?*

"I . . . " she muttered, but bit back the words gathering on her tongue. She had stopped making excuses to her father a long time ago. She would not choose that path again.

"Get him back. Get Bjarn back for me," Uspa pleaded, talking to Agnar but with her eyes fixed on Elvar.

"We tried," Agnar said. "Ilska and the Raven-Feeders have him. They have sailed on their *drakkar*." He shrugged. "I went after your son because I will not be attacked, robbed, have my warriors murdered. But there is no tracking Ilska now. Even if I wanted to, it would be a long, hard task to find her, and one that would end without coin. I am chief of the Battle-Grim; I am their gold-giver, their ring-giver." His eyes flickered to Elvar. "Chasing after your son would not feed my crew. If I come across Ilska again, I will settle my grievance with her, but other than that . . . " he shrugged. "The question in my thought-cage, though, is, why did they take your son? He is worth a few coins in the thrall-market." Agnar looked out at the naked corpses of Ilska's warriors who had died in their raid and sniffed. "He was *not* worth this."

Uspa looked around the room, finally fixing her eyes upon Agnar.

"They did not want Bjarn," she said. "They wanted me."

"Why?" Agnar asked her. "You are useful: a Seiðr-witch is always useful. But to risk a raid on me and my Battle-Grim, to start a blood feud. Why?"

"If I tell you, will you get my son back for me?"

"That would depend on how much coin I can make from what you tell me."

"Coin? Is that the sum of your soul, Agnar, chief of the Battle-Grim? Coin?"

"Coin feeds bellies and is the weighing scale of a warrior's reputation," Agnar said.

Uspa nodded. "More coin than you can imagine, and more fame than you could ever wish for," she sighed.

"Tell me, then," Agnar said.

Uspa looked away, her face twitching. Fear deep in her eyes.

Agnar took a step closer to her, his fingertips brushing the hilt of his seax. "My oathman died because of you. I will know why."

"Threats do not work on me, Agnar Coin-Seeker. I do not fear death, or pain."

"I could put those words to the test," Agnar said.

Uspa shrugged. "And waste both our time," she answered.

Agnar blew out a breath. "But you do fear your son's death. You fear a life parted from him. So, Bjarn, then. Your secret for your son."

Uspa chewed her lip, then nodded. She leaned forwards, her lips touching Agnar's ear, and whispered something. Agnar jumped back, as if stung.

"You lie," he said.

Uspa just stared at Agnar.

Elvar felt her heart pound and blood surge through her veins, because she had heard the words Uspa had whispered.

I know the way to Oskutreð.

CHAPTER TWENTY-EIGHT

ORKA

What do they want with my Breca? Orka thought as she rowed. *Why would they go to such lengths to steal bairns? My son. Harek. The others Virk spoke of. And why did they slay the Froa-spirit?* Orka muttered to herself as she rowed. She knew that some of these questions could not be answered and that gnawing on them would only cause her pain and break her focus. Any thought of Breca caused her pain, not knowing where he was, if he was in pain, being mistreated. But the questions would not stay locked away. Instead they circled and spiralled through her thought-cage, like crows drawn to the scent of death. And the last question that loomed over them all.

Thorkel said one was dragon-born. Tainted seed of Lik-Rifa. But they do not exist. Was it a death-haze mistake? Thorkel was not one for mistakes. The thought of Thorkel felt like a fist squeezing her heart and she snarled and spat, imagining pushing a seax into her invisible enemy. She bent and rowed, bent and rowed, the questions swirling.

The Froa-spirit because we had bowed the knee to her, swore we would dwell in peace in her land, and so we were under her protection? To take Breca they had to break her power first. But why? Why is Breca so important to them? In a way it did not matter. It would not change what Orka intended to do: get her son back and kill everyone who was involved in his taking. But unravelling the answers to these questions might help her find him, and then it did matter. But the answers would not come.

She lifted her head, blinking sweat from her eyes. She had been lost in the heave and pull of the oar, and the swelling waves of emotion in her thought-cage and veins as well; she felt like a small, solitary figure drifting in a sea of grief. Images of Thorkel and Breca swirled around her. Hate consumed her.

"What is it?" Lif asked, sitting on the bench beside her and pulling on the other oar. He was sweating with the rowing and the summer sun, both of them stripped to linen tunics, Orka's *brynja* and woollen tunic rolled and tied beneath the oar-bench. Mord was in the stern sitting on a pile of rope and weaving coppiced willow branches into a fish trap. They had spied plentiful trout and salmon in the river as they had rowed upstream but had little luck with their spears in skewering any for their supper.

"For fishermen, you are not very good at catching fish," Orka had remarked.

"We fish the fjords and deep seas," Mord had snapped. "Our nets are too big for this river. Not even a river, more like a stream."

They had left the river they had fled Fellur upon, for fear of Jarl Sigrún sending larger, faster *snekkes* in search of them, and so were now using a tapestry of smaller rivers and streams that threaded the land like veins.

Orka had just shrugged at Mord's response, and now Mord was building a basket-trap to set in the river once they made camp for the night, in the hope that they would rise to a basket of fresh fish to fry and break their fast with.

The water ahead was white-foamed, cutting through a steep-sloped spur of land, rocks breaching the flow like the knuckles of a giant's fist. Orka had felt the struggle against the current growing in the fibres of her back and shoulders, but the realisation had not registered properly.

They were approaching rapids.

"We should set ashore," Orka said, "and walk around these rapids."

"Why walk when we can row through it," Mord called out behind them.

Orka looked around. They were into their second day of hard rowing since escaping Fellur, the land shifting around them, leaving the cliffs and waterfalls of the fjord behind them and moving into a land of rolling hills and dense woodland. As the day had passed, the river they were rowing upon had quickened, the currents tugging at them as the banks had closed in and steepened. Now hills rose all around, the river cutting through sharp slopes dotted with holly and purple heather, the sky a cloudless, searing blue. The hiss and roar of water churning around rocks in the water drowned out all else, sounding like shattered crystals, a sweet, ice-touched music. All looked calm, the world empty and peaceful, but something gnawed at Orka, a tickling on the nape of her neck, like the prickle of frost's first morning touch.

They were close to the first rocks, and Mord was right, with some care they could navigate their way among the white-foaming boulders.

Orka saw something poking from behind a boulder, sharp and jagged. It looked like the shattered, rotting strake of a boat's hull.

The roar of water grew louder, something lurking deep within it, the hint of a tinkling melody that reminded Orka of better days, like a sun-kissed scent or the memory that a birdsong can evoke. The music was a gentle but insistent hand that tugged her into memories of the past, of spring sunshine and Thorkel's voice and Breca's laughter.

The boat bucked beneath them.

Orka looked at Lif and saw he was staring ahead, a smile touching his lips, frozen in mid-stroke of his oar. Orka shook her head, trying to rid the music that was spreading through her body, muting all else like a fog.

A boulder reared close, hidden by a swell in their course. Orka slapped Lif and dragged on her oar. Lif started and stared wide-eyed, tugging on his own oar. They swerved around the boulder, the hull scraping against granite, and then they were past it, a plume of white foam exploding around their prow. Orka glanced down, the river water clear and pure, and she glimpsed something on the shingle bed. The glint of bone.

"Row for shore," she cried, heaving on her oar.

"What's happening?" Lif called to her.

"NÄCKEN," Orka yelled.

Something smashed into the keel with a crunch and the boat rocked, the prow lifted clear of the river, Orka and Lif hurled from the oar-bench. A shout sounded from behind them and Orka twisted to see Mord's boots as he disappeared over the side with a splash and gurgle. The prow of the boat crashed back into the water, slamming into a boulder and rolling, water pouring in. Orka staggered to her feet, ripped her oar free of the hole and rammed it into the river, pushing away from rocks, then scraping on the bottom, shoving them towards the bank. Behind her she heard the truncated screams of Mord as he rose above and slipped below the water. A snatched glance and she saw the hint of something below him, a shadow beneath the foaming water, and a thick, green-flecked arm wrapped around Mord's throat.

"Here," Orka shouted, thrusting her oar at Lif, "get the boat to shore. Do not get into the water."

"What are you doing?" Lif said as he took the oar, standing and setting his feet.

She drew a seax and leaped over the side.

The water was cold as ice, snatching her breath away. She resisted the involuntary urge to gasp, kicking with her legs and swimming beneath the surface. Her head cleared, the lulling melody abruptly gone, and she saw a greenish shadow ahead, dense as oil, wrapping around a thrashing Mord. Orka kicked harder, swerved around a boulder and then she was upon them. Air bubbled from Mord's mouth as the shape of a man dragged him beneath the water. A hate-filled face, hair floating like clumps of rotting reeds, dark eyes glinting like jade, his mouth and jaw distended, too big for his face, rows of needle-long teeth gnashing. He had long fingers that were wrapped around Mord's throat, thick arms slick with green slime, his body a striated shadow amid the oil that seemed to coil and curl around him like smoke. Mord was thrashing in the water, beating upon the creature to no effect.

Orka kicked, her head breaking water, and she sucked in a deep breath, hearing that ice-cold melody seep into her like mead, lulling, intoxicating, and then she was diving beneath the water again and the music in her head evaporated like sun-touched mist.

Below Mord and the Näcken Orka saw a pile of bones, elk, bear, wolf and human, and upon it all sat a huge lyre with long strings of rotted gut. Thick branches of crumbling, sunken trees wove together around and above the lair of bones.

The Näcken's mouth opened wide and bit down into Mord's shoulder, a pulse of blood seeping into the water, and Mord's mouth opened in a scream, an explosion of bubbles.

Orka kicked her legs, reached the two figures and slashed with her seax, at the same time grunting out words, expelling precious air.

"*Járn og stál, skorið og brennt*," she murmured through a burst of bubbles as her seax bit into the Näcken's side, slicing, green-tinged flesh parting, oily blood flowing like the pulp of grass and leaves.

The creature spasmed and jerked in the water, its jaws releasing Mord and opening wide in an unheard scream. Orka grabbed Mord by the tunic and dragged him away, letting her feet sink to the bone-thick riverbed as she bunched her legs, then she was pushing up and away, heaving Mord through the water, the two of them bursting into fresh air, gulping and gasping. Mord coughed and hacked, floundering in the water, Lif on the riverbank dragging their fisher boat on to the shore and yelling his brother's name. Orka kicked and swam, pulling Mord through the white-foaming water, and then she felt something wrap around her ankle. She shoved Mord away, towards the riverbank, and then she was being dragged beneath the water. She twisted and slashed with her seax and saw her blade bounce off the green-scaled skin of the Näcken's wrist.

Words and deed together, you hálfviti idiot.

The Näcken's jaws opened wide, a black maw filled with silver-sharp teeth, and Orka struggled, jerking away with a flush of panic and she slashed her blade across the vaesen's mouth.

"*Skörp járn brenna og bíta*," Orka snarled as the seax connected and the blade sliced through skin and flesh into the creature's mouth, teeth spraying, green blood gushing like oil. "*Brenna og bíta*," she repeated as she stabbed into its shoulder. A shriek erupted from the Näcken that Orka felt rather than heard, the force of it pulsing through the water, filling Orka's body and ears with pressure, hurling her away, though she somehow managed to keep a grip upon her seax. Another shriek behind her, of pain and rage, but she did not look back. She used the momentum to keep kicking, swimming towards the shore until her feet touched shingle and her head and shoulders were bursting into daylight. Lif ran along the bank and held a spear out. Orka grabbed the shaft and hauled herself to the shore. She glanced back at the river, saw a dark cloud boiling beneath the surface, speeding away, fading from sight. She stumbled on to land, coughing and spluttering, Lif trying to support her, and they staggered to where the boat and Mord lay upon the bank. He was pale-faced, his shoulder lacerated and bleeding.

"What was *that*?" he breathed.

Orka stabbed her seax into the ground, then took the spear from Lif, tugged off the leather sheath and strode to the other side of Mord and the boat, where she buried the iron blade into the ground.

"A Näcken," she said. "Sneaky, slimy bastards."

"What are you doing?" Lif asked her, staring at the seax and the quivering shaft of the spear, both stabbed into the riverbank.

"Näcken don't like iron. They can sense it, feel it through the earth," Orka said, then dropped to her hands and knees, vomiting water and slime.

CHAPTER TWENTY-NINE

ELVAR

Elvar watched as Agnar walked away, beckoning for Uspa, Sighvat and Kráka to follow him. They walked through a doorway into the landlord's kitchen and chambers.

"Out," Elvar heard Agnar say, and the landlord and his wife appeared in the doorway, moving into the tavern's main room.

Oskutreð, Elvar thought. *Uspa said she knows the way to Oskutreð. The great Ash Tree, where the gods-fall battle raged hottest, where Ulfrir and Berser fell.* That thought was almost too big for Elvar to comprehend, or to believe. Without realising it she found she was walking after Uspa and Sighvat, Grend following her. She reached the doorway and saw Agnar was seated at a table, Kráka beside him, Uspa sitting opposite him, Sighvat hovering inside the door. Agnar looked up as Elvar tried to walk into the room, Sighvat moving to block her way.

"This is not for you," Agnar said to her.

Elvar stood and just looked at Agnar.

"I heard her," Elvar said. "I heard what Uspa told you." A heartbeat after those words had left her lips the thought crossed her mind that she should have kept them to herself.

Agnar's face shifted, a flat look filling his eyes, reinforcing that thought. *He does not trust me*, she realised.

"Come in," he said.

Elvar stepped into the room, Grend making to follow her, but Sighvat stepped in front of him.

"Him, too," Agnar said and Sighvat moved to the side, allowing Grend in.

It was a small room, one window and door, the table Agnar was sat at surrounded by clay ovens and a hearth fire with an iron pot hanging over it. A few dozen barrels of ale and various foods were stacked against the walls, jugs of mead on shelves, and there was a long bench with chopping boards, knives and cleavers, and two straw mattresses laid out on cots.

"You heard?" Agnar said.

Elvar nodded. She opened her mouth to say the name, but Agnar held a hand up.

"Are you staying, or are you going?" he asked her.

Elvar frowned, confused.

"Your father's offer, of a warband if you return to his side. Are you staying with me, or are you going to join him? I told you to tell me when you are ready, but this . . . " He waved a hand at Uspa. "This changes things."

There was a tension in the room, Agnar staring at her intently, and she heard Sighvat's feet shuffle behind her.

Elvar sucked in a breath. She had forgotten all about her father's offer with the events of the day.

"I am staying with you. With the Battle-Grim," she said.

A silence fell, all of them staring at her. She felt Grend's eyes boring into her back.

"You are certain? If you are to be a part of this conversation, then there is no going back from it," Agnar said. "No leaving me to tell all that you learn here to your father."

"I am certain," she said. "A wolf cannot become a lamb." She looked at Grend as she said those words. They were Hrung's last words to her. She had pondered it in her thought-cage all through the night, and was certain she had the right of it. Her father had never been trustworthy, not with her. All her life he had tricked her with clever words and half-truths. Even though his offer seemed all she had ever dreamed of, there must be more to it. He would not just give her all she asked for. It was not in his nature, and the wolf could not become a lamb.

Agnar held her gaze, the silence lengthening, and then he nodded. "Then sit down," he said, gesturing to a chair.

Uspa was looking down at her hands.

"Oskutreð," Agnar said to her, "is a myth, a fair-fame tale that warriors like me tell around a hearth fire, to fill our dreams with gold."

"It is real," Uspa said, her head snapping up, a twist of her lips. "Look at this world around you, filled with *Berserkir* and *Úlfhéðnar.* Look at where we are: sat in a town and fortress built within and upon a serpent's skull. Of course Oskutreð is real."

Agnar looked at Kráka.

"All the Tainted know Oskutreð to be true," Kráka said. "The great tree was at the heart of the gods-fall where our ancestors fell; the *Guðfalla* is like a song in our blood."

Agnar looked between the two Seiðr-witches.

"The tales tell of it being beyond the vaesen pit, beyond the Isbrún Bridge, beyond Dark-of-Moon Hills," Elvar said.

"That is a truth," Uspa nodded. "It is no tale."

"And if it is a truth, how is it that *you* know the way?" Agnar asked her. "Two hundred and ninety-seven years are said to have passed since that day when the gods fell, and yet none have ever found it, despite the tales of relics and riches and power."

"The *Graskinna,*" Uspa said. "The Grey Skin, a Galdrabok full of dark magic. It tells the way, for those with understanding."

"Those with understanding?" Agnar questioned.

"Galdurmen, Seiðr-witches," Uspa said. "Those who understand the old ways, those who can bend the world with rune and spell."

"And where is this *Graskinna*, then?" Agnar said. "Kráka could look at it, confirm to me whether you are telling me the truth, or just some tempting lies to get your son back."

Kráka nodded. Elvar saw the woman tense, a tremor in her flesh. *She is excited.*

"Kráka cannot look at it. No one can," Uspa said. "I destroyed it."

Agnar just stared at her. Kráka let out a sharp hiss.

"When you found us on Iskalt Island, we were there for a reason.

As my husband fought the troll, I was casting the book into the pool of fire and speaking the words of unbinding. The *Graskinna* is gone."

"I saw you," Elvar breathed.

Uspa just looked at her.

"So, how did Ilska and her Raven-Feeders know of you and this *Graskinna*, and how did they know to come here after you?" Agnar asked Uspa.

"My husband and me, we stole the *Graskinna* from them. They have been hunting us a long while. You hunted us, too, because of the price put on our heads. Berak slew some of Ilska's crew, and others as we fled her and her Raven-Feeders. He had to. And then, when you brought us here, I saw some of Ilska's warriors outside that tavern. We all did. I tried to hide myself and Bjarn," she shrugged. "But they must have seen me and told Ilska." She looked at Elvar. "I kept telling you that I needed to leave Snakavik."

"You did," Elvar said, "but you failed to mention it was because you knew the way to fabled Oskutreð, or that Ilska the Cruel and her Raven-Feeders were hunting you."

Uspa shrugged. "I had to know that I could trust you, before I told you such things."

Agnar sat back in his chair, puffing out his cheeks.

"I do not like it," he muttered. "You are asking me to chase after Ilska the Cruel and her Raven-Feeders, find them, and steal back your son." He shook his head. "Just the finding of them is task enough, and could take many months. Then there is taking your son back from them. That could be no easy thing. The Raven-Feeders, they have a reputation."

"Is Agnar Battle-Grim afraid of Ilska and her Raven-Feeders?" Uspa said.

Agnar gave her a cold smile. "Do not try to provoke or manipulate me," he said. "I am a practical man and am afraid of losing good warriors, yes. I am chief of the Battle-Grim; I am like a jarl to them. I am their gold-giver. I choose our course, the battles we fight, and, aye, death perches on our shoulders like an old raven and all in the Battle-Grim have made their peace with that, but I will not throw their lives away." He tugged on the blond braid in his beard. "And all the while we are chasing Ilska, we are earning no coin or silver."

"Coin is your god, then," Uspa said, a sneer on her lips.

"Don't be a fool, woman," Agnar snapped. "Coin buys food and mead; we would starve without coin, and silver is a battle-won prize, a symbol of our battle-fame and reputation. Why do you think we wear rings of silver and gold? To make our mark on this world. What else is there?"

"With the finding of Oskutreð your battle-fame would live for ever," Uspa said.

"Then why did you burn the book?" Elvar asked.

"To stop fair-fame hungry fools like you from finding it," Uspa snapped. "There are the remains of gods there. And other things." She did not need to say any more. In her thought-cage Elvar was seeing the bones of Ulfrir and Berser, of Svin and Rotta and Hundur, their battle gear and treasures, and the weapons of their children. A silence settled on them, and Elvar saw the same thoughts in Agnar's eyes.

"Vigrið is no peace-loving land, but if the way to Oskutreð was made known, new powers would rise in this land, and most likely a new war with them," Uspa said with a shiver. "Best that the way is shut and can never be found."

"Then why show me the way?" Agnar breathed, the lure of power and riches heavy in his eyes.

"For my son," Uspa said. "For *love.* When you weigh this life on the scales, you realise that is everything. The things you seek . . ." She shook her head.

Agnar leaned forward.

"I could put a thrall-collar on you and order you to show me the way, and save myself a lot of hard and dangerous work trying to get your son back."

"I will die before I wear the thrall's collar," Uspa said. Her eyes flickered to Kráka. "I mean you no insult, sister. Those of the Tainted who wear the collar, they still cling to life. It is part of being human. Survival. To bear hardship and trial, in the hope of it ending. But

I do not care for my life. I care for my husband, whom I have lost, and I care for my son, who is taken. If you put the thrall-collar on me, then my life would be over, for I would never see my son again." She shrugged. "That is no choice to me: better death. And you saw what I did to Ilska's warriors. Do not doubt that I could take my own life, if I set my will to it."

Something in the way Uspa spoke convinced Elvar it was the truth. Agnar leaned back in his chair, fingers tugging at his beard.

He believes her, too.

Agnar leaned forwards.

"You will take me to Oskutreð first, and then I shall find your son for you," he said.

Uspa barked a laugh. "Do you think me such a fool? I would be worthless to you once you set eyes on Oskutreð. My son first."

"It could take a year to find him, and I do not have the coin and silver to fund a search of great length."

"Then find him quickly," Uspa said.

"There are no guarantees," Agnar said. "Oskutreð first. I will swear to you an oath."

Uspa opened her mouth, then paused, her face shifting.

"An oath," she murmured. "Perhaps. There is an oath that you can make. That we can all make to one another. But it is not just words. Our lives would be bound, and the breaking of the oath would have . . . consequences. Swear on it and I shall take you to Oskutreð first." She held Agnar's gaze. "The *blóð svarið*," she said.

Elvar felt a chill in her blood at Uspa's words, though she did not know what they meant.

"What is that?" Sighvat rumbled. He was standing close to the doorway, ensuring there were no prying ears.

"The blood oath," Kráka said. "It is made with blood, runes and words of power. To make the *blóð svarið* is to bind yourself to your vow, and to those who take it with you. It is a seal in your body unto death and to break it is to die." Kráka looked at them all in turn. "Painfully."

"If all here make the oath, I will show you the way to Oskutreð," Uspa said, looking from Agnar to Elvar, then Sighvat, Grend and Kráka.

"What do you mean, painfully?" Sighvat said, frowning. One hand crept up to the pendant at his throat, the clawed foot of a frost-spider, Sighvat's first kill in the Battle-Grim.

"We will swear the oath and seal it with our blood and Seiðr-magic," Uspa said. "That will bind us so long as blood flows in our veins."

"Painfully?" Sighvat repeated, glowering at Uspa.

"If you break the oath before you die, then your blood shall boil in your veins. You will die screaming," Uspa said. She looked at them all. "This is the only way I will agree to take you to Oskutreð before you search for my Bjarn."

Sighvat blew out a long breath. "Don't like the sound of that," he muttered.

"I have made one oath. I shall not make another," Grend said, breaking his silence. He looked at the white scar etched across his left palm.

"All of you must take the oath," Uspa said. "You have all heard Oskutreð spoken of. It is the only way that we can trust one another."

"No," Grend said.

"Uspa is right," Agnar said, leaning back in his chair. He looked from Grend to Elvar.

"Grend is oathsworn to me," Elvar said. "Wherever I go, whatever path I choose, Grend will follow. He can be trusted with or without your oath."

"No," Uspa said, a crack to her voice like a leather whip. "All or none. This is the greatest secret in all of Vigrið. I will *not* share it without your oath and your blood."

Elvar looked at Grend, knowing the circumstances and significance of his last oath. He stared back into her eyes, seeing the hope and desire within her. Muscles in his cheek twitched. Eventually he nodded. "I will take your oath," he said, "but only for Elvar. None of this matters to me."

Sighvat snorted.

"Close the door," Uspa said to Sighvat as she stood and walked to one of the benches. Agnar nodded and the big man did, shutting out the light and noise from the tavern. Uspa picked up a chopping board and a sharp knife, then sat back down at the table.

"Gather close," she said, Sighvat and Grend stepping up to the table, and Uspa set to carving runes into the chopping board. Three, four of them, a series of straight lines, some angled, all deep into the wood. At the sight of them Elvar felt a thrumming in her blood, a buzzing building in her head.

Do I want to do this? Bind myself to the fate of a Tainted child? Go up against Ilska the Cruel and her Raven-Feeders? She could see Bjarn's face: remembered when he had been hurled from the *Wave-Jarl* into the sea, how she had leaped after him.

I am bound to him already.

And the thought of Oskutreð swirled through her like mead in her blood. Intoxicating, overwhelming. Fear and excitement fluttered in her veins, blending into a heady mix.

Those who find Oskutreð, and all the treasures that are there, their names will live for ever. Long after my father's name and bones have faded to dust.

A silence settled over them, heavy as a rain-soaked cloak.

"Life," Uspa whispered, pointing to the first rune. She drew the knife across the heel of her hand and let the blood drip on to the rune, filling the deep-carved lines.

"*Líf*," Kráka breathed.

"Death," Uspa said, her blood tracing the second rune.

"*Dauða*," Kráka whispered.

"Blood oath," Uspa muttered as her blood flowed into the third rune.

"*Blóð svarið*," Kráka echoed.

"Torment," Uspa said, her blood filling the last rune.

"*Kvöl*," Kráka croaked, the word sounding like a drumbeat in Elvar's head, or a door slamming shut.

"All of you," Uspa said, "join your blood to mine."

There was a rasp of seaxes leaving their scabbards. Elvar sliced her blade across her palm and held her hand out. She saw Grend do the same, saw his blood flow and she held his hand, knowing the sacrifice he was making for her, knowing that he did not want to do this, knowing that his oath to Elvar's dead mother drove him. Their blood mingled and dripped on to the runes.

Agnar held his hand out, blood dripping, then Sighvat, and finally Kráka. All of them with hands held over the runes, their blood falling, mingling.

Uspa opened her mouth and spoke.

"Blóð eið munum við gera,
að binda hver við annan með rúnir af krafti,
hurðir að gömlu leiðunum, innsiglaðar og bundnar með blóði."

Uspa spoke in little more than a whisper, but her voice seemed to fill the room, echoing in Elvar's head.

"Blood oath we make, binding one to the other with runes of power, door to the old ways," Kráka said, her voice scratching.

"Eið okkar innsigluð með blóði okkar, lífi, dauða og kvalum,
bundin með blóði okkar," Uspa said.

"Our oath sealed with our blood, life, death and torment, bound with our blood," Kráka intoned.

A wind swept through the room, a chill rippling through Elvar. The blood that filled the runes hissed and sizzled, steam rising from them, and then the blood rose into the air, hovering, like long strands of tendon or red string, painting the runes in the air. Sighvat gasped. With a crackle the blood runes moved together, merging into one long strand, and it floated up, higher, towards all of their hands, which were still held stretched over the runes. The strand of blood wrapped around them, binding hands and wrists together, pulling them tight, Elvar flinching as it touched her skin. It was hot, pain jolting up her arm, but she could not pull away. She heard Grend hiss beside her, saw Sighvat's arm jerk, but none of them pulled away.

The smell of burning flesh, the crackle of skin sizzling.

"*Svo skal það vera,*" Uspa growled. "Say it with me."

"*Svo skal það vera,*" Elvar and the others intoned.

"So be it," Kráka said and the blood-cord around their hands and wrists writhed and hissed and sizzled, then evaporated into steam.

Elvar's arm fell away, a red weal wrapped around her hand and wrist like a red tattoo.

They all looked at one another, fear and awe reflected in each other's eyes.

Agnar smiled.

"To Oskutreð," he said, and Elvar could not stop the thrill in her veins or the laughter bubbling out of her throat.

CHAPTER THIRTY

VARG

Varg banked and shipped his oar as the *Sea-Wolf* cut across the current towards the east bank of the River Slågen. Strakes bumped on timber as the ship grated against a pier, Svik and Røkia leaping from the top-rail on to wooden boards and tying off mooring ropes. Beyond the riverbank was a farm. A stockade wall with a single gate surrounded a turf-roofed longhouse and outbuildings, and beyond the timber wall fields of barley and rye rippled across a meadow that stretched towards tree-shrouded foothills.

They had rowed hard up the river for five long days, the muscles in Varg's back and shoulders coming to feel like they were in a permanent state of spasm, his hands raw, but now it seemed that the time for rowing was over. Glornir had announced a little earlier that they were about to make landfall and continue their journey by foot, moving into the foothills of the Boneback Mountains in their quest.

Glornir slotted the tiller and shouted orders, Einar Half-Troll echoing them, and then all was movement, warriors stacking oars in racks and delving into their sea-chests. Svik appeared at Varg's shoulder as he sat on his sea-chest, still staring at the farmstead. Between the pier and the stockade wall was an area of ground dotted with moss and grass-covered mounds.

Barrows, of the thralls who died in the service of this farm, most likely. The sight of it stirred memories in Varg's thought-cage, dark memories that felt more like long-clawed nightmares, now he was free of them.

How did I live so long with a collar around my neck?

A wyrm of anger uncoiled in his gut, slithering through his veins.

"Hurry up, or you'll be left behind to guard the ship," Svik said as he rummaged in his own sea-chest.

Varg blinked and shook his head, trying to banish the memories of Kolskegg's farm, but they clung to him, like flies to a rotting corpse.

"What should I bring?" Varg asked Svik.

"Your war gear," Svik said. "We are marching to a fight, so wear all that you can. Leave behind what you can't fit on your body. You will soon get tired of carrying a sack over your shoulder."

Varg shrugged on a grey woollen tunic over the linen one he'd been rowing in, then lifted out his weapons belt, with seax, throwing axe and cleaver hanging from belt loops and scabbard, and buckled it around his waist. He looked at the war gear he had taken from the *druzhina* warrior back in Liga, the horsehair helm and coat of lamellar plate. Somehow it felt wrong to wear it.

I did not win it through any great act of skill, just a desperate, lucky thrust in the man's back with my seax, he thought. Instead he lifted out the simple iron helm he'd bought from a trader in Liga, along with a leather pouch, and last of all his sealskin cloak. Then he closed the chest and bolted it. He buckled the pouch and helm to his belt and slung the cloak around his shoulders, fixing it with an iron brooch. His shield was set in the top-rail rack and he prised it free, slung it over his shoulder and then returned his oar to a rack close to the central mast-lock, exchanging it for his spear. He followed Svik over the top-rail and on to the pier, his legs unsteady as they tried to adjust to being on solid ground. He was glad to have the earth under his feet again. Svik was gleaming in his bright *brynja*, a sword and seax hanging from his weapons belt along with a buckled helm. He looked at Varg in his linen tunic and cloak, and shook his head.

"You may regret not wearing that fine coat of plate you have stowed away," he said. "Most likely half a moment after you get punched in the chest by an angry troll."

"It's too heavy," Varg said, at the same time noticing almost all of the Bloodsworn had shrugged their way into coats of mail, only a handful in wool or leather. He looked at his feet, feeling foolish.

"No-Sense," Svik said, then shrugged. "You'll learn the hard way, *if* you live long enough."

A horn rang out, deep and braying, Einar standing on the riverbank with a horn at his lips, Glornir and Vol there, along with Skalk and his two warriors.

"Bloodsworn, with me," Glornir cried out, then turned and walked away, his shield over his back and a long-axe in his fist, using it like a walking staff. Mail clinked and leather boots slapped on timber as fifty warriors strode along the wooden pier, leaving ten of their band behind to guard the ship.

They marched across a hard-packed path and through the barrowfield, Varg setting his eyes ahead, determined not to look at the mounds of stone and earth, fearing the memories they would unleash. Einar called out to the farm as they approached, but there was no answer, no sign of movement. Varg had known the farm was deserted as soon as he'd seen it: no plumes of smoke to mark any hearth fire or forge, no movement in the fields where there should be workers and animals, and the gates were creaking in the breeze, half-open.

"Set a shield-line," Glornir ordered Svik, then marched through the gates, Edel and her two hounds behind him, followed by Einar, Røkia, Vol, Sulich and a handful of others. Skalk followed, with Olvir and Yrsa in his wake. Olvir had shrugged his shield from his back, his sword drawn, and Yrsa held a spear over her shield rim. Varg stared after them and looked at the longhouse beyond them, its roof green with turf, its doors closed.

Svik called out an order and the remaining Bloodsworn moved into an open line around the farm wall, looking out towards the rye and barley-filled fields, weeds thick among them.

These crops have not been tended for a good long while.

To the east of the farmstead a fenced paddock stood with grass grown long, the gate open. Two shaggy-haired ponies stood staring at the Bloodsworn.

They have decided the grass here is tasty enough, Varg thought, seeing that the gate was open and no ropes tethered them to the paddock rails.

Jökul the smith walked towards them, signalling for a few others to follow him.

Varg stood in silence, the only sound the wind soughing through the barley and Jökul trying to catch the ponies in the paddock. Eventually he enticed them with a few apples, and in short time they were harnessed up with tack found in a stable block and being loaded with food barrels and kit for the Bloodsworn.

There were footsteps behind Varg and he turned to see Glornir marching out of the farm gates, his face twisted in a scowl.

"Empty," the Bloodsworn's chief said to Svik. "No bodies, no blood." He paused and rubbed a hand over his bald head.

Edel walked out of the gates, a tunic in her hands. She drew her seax and sliced the tunic into two, then offered the two halves to her wolfhounds. They took deep snorting sniffs of the fabric.

"Bloodsworn," Glornir called out, lifting a hand in the air and turning it in a tight circle, one finger pointed skywards. Torvik and a handful of other scouts stepped forwards, moving north, halting before the field of barley and rye. They were all young men and women clothed in wool and leather, apart from Edel in her *brynja*. She loped past Glornir and joined the other scouts, taking their lead, her hounds at her side. Edel stepped into the field of barley, Torvik and the others following her.

"Let's go and earn our coin," Glornir called out, and set off after Edel and the scouts.

Varg sucked in a deep breath. Beyond the fields of abandoned crops, meadows rolled into foothills that glittered with streams and were draped with birch and rowan, and beyond them the towering heights of the Boneback Mountains reared, their peaks wreathed in cloud and snow. Varg fell in alongside Svik, but before they reached the barley Varg looked back over his shoulder and saw sullen faces staring out from the *Sea-Wolf*, watching them. Lots had been drawn to decide who would stay with the ship, for it seemed that none wanted to. They were the Bloodsworn and were marching into danger, where no doubt fair battle-fame and silver awaited them. No one wanted to hear tell of the great deeds after the fight was won.

Apart from me.

I just want to survive long enough to find out how my sister died, and avenge her, Varg thought, his hand brushing the pouch on his belt as he walked towards the Boneback Mountains.

CHAPTER THIRTY-ONE

ORKA

"Kill me," Orka said, standing with her feet spread in the grass, her hands loose and ready at her sides.

Lif lunged at her, his seax wrapped with a strip of wool, stabbing at Orka's belly.

She slapped the blade away with the flat of one hand, side-stepped and punched Lif on the jaw. He stumbled away a few steps, then his legs gave way and he sank to the ground, looking up at Orka with a dazed expression.

Mord laughed, sitting on a boulder as he filleted a salmon as long as his arm.

"I thought you were teaching us weapons craft," Mord said. "This looks more like beating us up for fun. Not fun for us, I feel I should point out," he added.

"I *am* teaching you," Orka said, offering Lif her arm and pulling him back to his feet. "That if you do a foolish thing, pain will follow. Or death." She scowled at Lif. "You took too large a step, which left you off balance. Small steps in, small steps out," she said. "Never lunge. Never over-extend. It's the same rule, whether you are using your fists, a seax, a spear or a sword. And never charge straight in. That only works for bulls and boars." She paused. "And for trolls. Side steps: look for the openings; find the gaps in your opponent's defence. And strike in flurries: two, three, four blows. Often the blow that ends a fight is the one your enemy did not see coming."

Lif rubbed his chin, a bruise already mottling.

"Pain and bruises reinforce a lesson," Orka said.

"Heya, agreed," Lif mumbled.

"Then we must have learned much from you already," Mord barked a laugh as he looked at her through one swollen, blackened eye. Other bruises speckled the faces and bodies of both brothers, varying from purple to green to yellow, telling the tale of how old the bruises were, and how long the brothers had been receiving such lessons from Orka during their journey north. Mord's shoulder was still bound with linen where the Näcken had bitten him, though that wound was healing well, and his head still bore a red scar where he had been clubbed by Guðvarr at Fellur village. Orka had been silently impressed with the way he had thrown himself into the weapons craft lessons she had given the two brothers, despite Mord's more serious wounds.

"By the number of your bruises you should be fit to fight a *holmganga* against Ilska the Cruel soon," Lif said to Mord.

"Huh," Mord snorted. "I hope never to meet her for any reason," he said. "The tales tell how she fought three men in the *holmganga*, and cut the stones from each one of them." He winced.

"Ilska has slain more than a few men in the *holmganga*," Lif said. "Vaesen, Iskidan warbands, a *Berserkir*. But I am not so scared of her, now that Orka has taught me some weapons craft." He smiled at his brother. "Ilska the Cruel, Agnar Battle-Grim, even the Skullsplitter. I feel like I could fight them all."

"Then you are a *hálfviti* idiot," Orka muttered.

"Who is the best?" Lif said, ignoring the dour twist of Orka's lips.

"There is no such thing as the best," Orka muttered. "And the Skullsplitter is dead."

"I'll fight Skullsplitter, then," Mord said and Lif sat on the floor, laughing and holding his belly.

"Time to go," Orka said, ignoring them and squinting at the sky. The sun was low on the horizon, newly risen, the air fresh and clean. An eagle soared high above them, wings spread. They were stood on the slope of a gentle hill, their boat pulled up and hidden in a reed bank below them. It had taken them close to fifteen days of hard rowing to reach this point, longer than the journey from Fellur to Darl should have taken, because they had left the wide and busy River Drammur for fear of pursuit, and so had threaded their way east and then north in a looping half-circle, rowing then pushing and dragging their boat across land to the next river, rowing again, then travelling across land for the next river again. It had been hard, back-breaking work, but they had not been followed, and the countryside was mostly deserted.

No one to see us, no one to sell information about us to any who might follow.

Only yesterday had they started to pass homesteads and farms, faces staring at them as they rowed on by. Orka's eyes tracked the glitter of the river, one of a dozen that carved their way through the hills around her. At the edge of Orka's sight a shadow spread across the high ground that overlooked its far bank: a town, smoke from a hundred hearth fires curling up into the sky above it.

Darl.

And Breca. A spark of hope flared in her chest, of longing, the possibility of finding her son blazing so bright within her that it was painful. Her hand brushed against one of the seaxes thrust into her belt. One of the blades that she had found in Thorkel's body.

And if I do not find him, then I shall have my vengeance.

I am blood. I am vengeance, I am death.

Without looking at Mord or Lif, Orka picked her way down to the boat and waded through the reeds, leaped into it and hefted an oar. She heard the brothers following behind her, but her eyes were fixed on the river and the course ahead.

Orka shipped her oar, Mord doing the same, and their boat coasted over the river. They were both staring at the sight before them, Lif, too.

Darl, fortress and seat of power of Queen Helka.

The river was wide and deep, dark and brown, unlike the crystal rivers and streams they had used to make their way here. Ships and boats of all sizes thronged on the river and clustered around a hundred wooden piers and jetties. Orka saw at least a dozen *drakkars* sitting sleek and wolfish at the docks, their hulls low in the water with proud eagle-carved prows.

Beyond the piers, taverns and buildings rose in a cluttered crush upon the slope of a gentle hill, rising towards a timbered wall, and beyond it a fortress. It was a swarming hive of motion, of sounds and smells, but Orka's, Mord's and Lif's eyes were drawn to the fortress atop the hill. A mead hall crowned the fortress, and out of its walls swept the skeleton of a giant eagle. Two huge, skeletal wings, each one the size of a small hill, spread wide like protective hands, a skull and razored beak rearing above the mead hall thatch. Orka felt the pulse of a headache beginning in the knot of muscles about her neck.

No vaesen will ever bother the people of Darl, with Orna's remains guarding it. One the size of this eagle skeleton would keep vaesen away for many leagues.

Behind the mead hall and eagle skeleton Orka glimpsed the Galdur tower of Darl, where Galdurmen learned their rune-dark arts. She hawked and spat into the river.

"Jarl Sigrún spoke true, then," Lif finally said, "when she talked of the eagle-god protecting the fortress. I thought she was telling falsehoods to convince Fellur to give their oath to Queen Helka."

"Aye," Orka sniffed.

"What do we do now?" Lif asked her.

"Find a space to dock on one of those piers," Orka said.

They reached for their oars and threaded a way through the boats on the river, so busy that it was like moving cattle on market day.

Eventually they found a small pier on the eastern fringe of the docks, Lif tying off the boat and Orka climbing a ladder on to the pier. She found a harbourmaster waiting for her, a fat man with a felt cap and numerous chins beneath his thin, wispy beard. His tunic spoke of wealth, edged in fine tablet weave, and his guard was kitted out well, a tall woman with a bored look on her long-nosed face.

"How much?" Orka asked, and she paid the sweating man from her pouch of coin. She did not haggle, did not want to be remembered. Lif gasped as he clambered up the ladder and saw the coin exchanging hands, but the man and his guard had turned and were striding away from them before he managed to blurt out any words.

"We would fish the fjord a whole month to earn that amount of coin," Lif said to Orka.

She ignored him, climbing back down the ladder into the boat. Her *brynja* was rolled beneath the oar-bench. She heaved it up and slithered into the coat of mail, the boat swaying as she did so, then buckled her weapons belt about her waist, feeling the weight of axe and seax settle. Finally she hefted her hemp sack and threw it up on to the pier, gripped her spear and climbed back up the ladder.

Mord followed her up. Lif stood and waited for her.

A horn call rang out, high above them, echoing down from the walls of the fortress. Other horns joined it, blaring, spreading throughout the fortress and town, people on the docks stopping and staring.

An answering horn rang out, distant, and Orka looked downriver.

Three *drakkars* were on the river, tall-prowed, oars dipping and rising in perfect time, water falling from the rising oars glistening in the sunlight. As they drew closer to the docks Orka realised they were huge, seventy or eighty oars, at least. Activity exploded on the dockside as they curled in towards a large pier, noticeably empty of ships despite being in prime docking location. Voices shouted and ropes were thrown from the first *drakkar*, men and women on the pier catching them and tying the ropes around mooring posts. A gangplank was dropped over the *drakkar*'s top-rail to the pier and figures were disembarking: ten or twelve warriors, clothed in mail, men and women, the sides of their heads shaved and covered in flowing, swirling tattoos. Swords and seaxes hung from their belts, grey woollen cloaks upon them, edged in fur. They spread across the pier in a half-circle, a protective fist.

"*Úlfhéðnar*," Orka muttered and spat on the pier.

"What!" Lif said, his eyes wide.

"Tainted, descendants of Ulfrir, the wolf-god," Orka said. "Like Vafri, the warrior who slew your father."

And then a woman was crossing the gangplank to the pier, tall, her hair long and black, braided with threads of gold wire. A red cloak was draped across her shoulders and gold arm rings glittered in the sun. She wore a sword at her hip with gold on the pommel and crossguard, gold wire wrapped around the leather hilt, the scabbard ornately tooled, a throat and chape of gold.

"Who is that?" Lif breathed beside Orka.

"I am guessing Queen Helka, as this is her fortress," Orka said.

The queen stopped and turned, waiting for two men to cross the gangplank. One was a raven-haired young man, tall and broad, his clothing all fine wools and silks, rings of silver on his arms and about his neck. The other stood out as different. He was as tall as the younger man, but his head was shaven clean apart from a thick blond braid that stretched down his back, his face angular with a short, neatly cropped beard. Instead of a tunic he wore a fine wool kaftan and breeches that were baggy above the knee and striped, wrapped tight with *winnigas* from ankle to knee. He wore a curved sword on one hip, and a bow case and quiver of arrows on the other.

"And them?" Mord said.

"Helka has a son called Hakon," Lif said.

"That is most likely him, then," said Orka.

"What about the other one?" Mord asked.

"A guest from oversea, I am guessing," Orka said. "I have seen others dressed similarly. They were from Iskidan."

Lif whistled.

The three of them watched in silence as more warriors disembarked from the *drakkar*, and Queen Helka and her companions strode down the pier. People close to her dropped to their knees, bowing. There was the sound of many feet, and warriors emerged from a street, spreading on to the docks, an honour-guard come to greet Queen Helka. They wrapped around her and her retinue, and then they were all marching into the streets of Darl and disappearing from view.

Slowly people on the dockside climbed back to their feet and returned to their normal business.

"What now?" Lif said.

"Now we say farewell," Orka said as she bent and rummaged in her sack. She took out Thorkel's nålbinding wool cap, which she pulled on to her head. She looked at the two brothers. They were staring at her, open-mouthed.

"What?" she said.

"You can't just *leave*," Lif said.

"That was our agreement," Orka said. "You row me to Darl; I teach you some weapons craft." She looked at their bruised faces. "I have done my best."

"But what shall we do?" Lif said.

"That is up to you," Orka said. "Not my business." She took a few steps, then paused.

"Do you have any coin?" she asked them.

"A little," Lif said.

Orka walked back to them, took her pouch from her belt and opened the drawstring, before sifting through it. "Here," she said, holding out a few coins. "This will buy you food for a while, long enough for you to make some more."

Mord scowled at her.

"We cannot take that," Lif said. "Our father, he taught us . . . "

"Be in no one's debt," Mord said. "Earn your own keep; pay your own way, he always said."

Orka shrugged. "Take it, or don't," she said. "It is nothing to me. Though I think you have earned it. You have rowed me here, and I have taught you a few things that might help you in a scrap. The scales are not even, to my thinking." She pressed the coins into Lif's palm and closed his fingers over them. "Your life is your own," she said, quietly, "as is your vengeance. I have told you already, I think you should wait, earn some coin, make a home for yourself somewhere quiet and let some time pass." She looked at the town and fortress, her mouth twisting. "Far from this stink, if you ask me. And when the time is right, go back to Fellur and put sharp steel in Guðvarr's belly. But it is your choice, the two of you. If you wish to rush back in search of your vengeance and practise your newfound skills on Guðvarr now," she shrugged.

Mord and Lif looked at one another.

"Keep your wits about you and your blades sharp," Orka said to them and then she was turning and striding down the pier and on to the dockside. She did not look back, her thought-cage filled with the task ahead of her.

My son, if you are here, I will find you. And anyone who stands in my way will wish they hadn't.

CHAPTER THIRTY-TWO

ELVAR

Elvar banked her oar as the square sail of the *Wave-Jarl* was unfurled, the wool stinking of mutton-tallow and grease. The sail sagged for a moment and Sighvat bellowed orders, Biórr and a handful of others dragging on the rigging, and then the sail billowed and filled with a south-easterly that hurled them slicing through the waves like a fresh-cast spear.

They were sailing across Lake Horndal, wide as a small sea, the water deep, night-black and impenetrable, and land was just a thin smudge on the edge of Elvar's vision. She twisted on her sea-chest and looked back over her shoulder at the trading town of Starl shrinking behind them. They had stayed there two days, long enough to restock their provisions: fresh barrels of water, mead, stock fish and smoked meats, as well as re-caulking weathered strakes with pine-tar and horsehair, a coat of fresh tallow to protect the sails and scraping the hull of seaweed, algae and slime. The *Wave-Jarl* leaped across the white-tipped waves like a horse after a long sleep and a good meal. Elvar heard Agnar laughing and saw him standing at the steering oar, feet spread. Rising from her bench she stumbled a step, then found her sea-footing and walked down the deck towards him. A hand gripped her wrist. It was Grend, looking up at her from his sea-chest. A lattice of thin red scars was laced around his hand and wrist, not yet healed, the same as Elvar bore, a reminder of their oath to one another and to Uspa. That had been twelve days ago, and since then they had packed and left the tavern, loaded the *Wave-Jarl* and rowed almost a hundred leagues.

"Going to see the chief," Elvar said with a scowl to the question in Grend's eyes.

Grend nodded and let go of her wrist. If anything, he had become more protective over her since they had sworn their new oath. Elvar didn't like it.

She threaded her way across the deck, packed with provisions for what could be a long journey on foot, past a stack of wheels and axles and dismantled carts, five of them and eight pack-ponies that Agnar had purchased in Starl. They were tough beasts, tethered and munching on hay, seemingly unconcerned about the fact that they were no longer on dry land.

Agnar smiled at Elvar as she reached him.

"Something I wanted to tell you, chief," she said.

"Aye, what is it, then?" Agnar said. He gave her a hard look, a warning to take care over what came out of her lips. They had sworn to keep silent about their destination, the few of them who had sworn the oath, not even telling the rest of the Battle-Grim.

"Not until we are on the north shore of Lake Horndal," Agnar had said. "With the Boneback Mountains behind us and the Battle-Plain all that we can see before us. There will be no going back, then, no chance of desertion or betrayal."

So, they had kept their silence, Agnar only telling the Battle-Grim that they had a new job and that it would pay well.

Pay better than any other job imaginable, Elvar thought. *Finding Oskutreð will change our lives. It may change all of Vigrið.*

"That day Bjarn was taken," she said.

"Aye," Agnar said, his frown thickening, eyes flickering to see if anyone was close, or pausing in their tasks to flap their ears.

"I fought one of Ilska's Raven-Feeders as they fled the tavern with the boy," Elvar continued.

Agnar nodded, his frown fading now that he knew she was not talking about what had happened or been said inside the tavern kitchen.

"I think he was Tainted," Elvar said. "He . . . changed. When he saw death looming. His teeth, his eyes."

"Are you sure?" Agnar said.

Elvar took a moment. "No," she said, thinking of the blond warrior, his beard and *brynja*, their combat lasting little more than a dozen heartbeats. And it had been dark, dawn only a hint in the perpetual gloom of Snakavik. "It was dark, and over too quickly. But I have lived around the Tainted, my father and his *Berserkir*-thralls. I have seen them *turn*."

"Aye," Agnar grunted, "I don't doubt you have." He tugged on his beard. "Tainted among Ilska's Raven-Feeders," he murmured. "If he was, which you say is not certain, then the question is: Did Ilska the Cruel know?"

Elvar shrugged.

"The Tainted can live among us and go unnoticed," Agnar said. "Many do. That is the safer path for them. But to be a warrior in a crew like the Raven-Feeders, to live with death's talons in your shoulder, her breath on your neck, and still manage to control that wildness of the blood . . . "

"Not so easy," Elvar said.

"Aye," Agnar grunted. "And if Ilska knew, then why wasn't the warrior wearing a thrall-collar? Better to do her bidding, then, and she wouldn't have to pay him as much. Or she could have sold him?" He looked at Elvar. "I do not know if this is important or not, but it is good to know, and good that you remembered. A fine quality to have, to be able to go back over the details and pick out the thread of a thing." He patted her arm, saw the red and white scars spiralled around her wrist, then smiled.

"Look about you, Elvar Störrsdottir. Did you ever think that you would be travelling on such a journey, such an adventure?"

"No," Elvar smiled back, the thought of what they were doing, of where they were going, sparking a constant glow of excitement in the pit of her belly.

Oskutreð, the great tree, centre of the dead god's realm. To be part of a quest that will live on in songs and saga-tales for ever.

She grinned, wider, and turned to look out over the prow of

the *Wave-Jarl*, over the green-black of the lake, a cold wind whipping white-flecked foam on wave tips. To the east and west the Boneback Mountains reared, green slopes thick with pine and the glitter of waterfalls. Here and there a sheer cliff face showed yellow or grey, the hint of colossal, ancient bones. Starl was built in the shadow of a high-curling rib of Snaka's that arched high as the clouds, one of the few places where his ancient skeleton could still be seen. The rib cast a long shadow arcing across the wide water. The lake was one of two places where a handful of Snaka's ribs had not been overlaid with rock and earth. Perhaps there had been a lake here before the death of the great serpent, denying a solid foundation for the upheaval and resettling that Snaka's death caused. Elvar did not know, but whatever the reason, this was one of only two passes through the Boneback Mountains to the northern side. To the Battle-Plain, where the battle had raged the hardest on that dread day, the *Guðfalla*, when the gods fell, and where vaesen prowled now in greater numbers. Looking up she saw the silhouettes of osprey in the sky, and further east an eagle. The *Wave-Jarl* cut through the waves, the speed of it tugging Elvar's braid out behind her.

This is freedom, to sail with shield-brothers and sisters on a journey for fair battle-fame and dragon-hoarded treasure. In search of fabled Oskutreð. The joy of it bubbled in her veins and she laughed out loud.

Elvar sat with her back to a hawthorn tree with a trencher balanced on her knees. She used a small skinning seax to cut and skewer a fillet of still steaming oat-wrapped cod from the pan. She blew on it and huffed as she put it in her mouth, the flesh and fried oats too hot, but too delicious to wait for.

They had made landfall soon after midday of their second day on the lake and had searched for a suitable place to anchor and moor the *Wave-Jarl*. They were in a secluded inlet now, flanked with alder, birch and hawthorn. The wagons had been brought ashore and constructed with mallets and dowel-pins, the ponies hobbled close by. Elvar could hear the boat creaking on the water, and through the trees she glimpsed starlight reflecting silver around the ship and on the newly tarred hull. Lots had been drawn for who would stay to guard the ship, Elvar not feeling her usual fear at that possibility, because she knew that all who had sworn the oath to Uspa had no choice but to continue on the journey to Oskutreð.

All the Battle-Grim were gathered together, apart from Grend and Sighvat, who were first to take watch. They were not too far away, though, lurking on the outer edge of the copse of trees that the company had made camp within. Agnar stood beside a firepit scratched into the ground, flames flaring and crackling, branches swaying above him. A pot hung over the fire, a barley stew simmering in it, and a flat iron pan lay over hot embers, with more of the cod Elvar was eating frying in oats and butter.

A silence had settled over the gathering, because Agnar had just told them why they had ventured north, through the Boneback Mountains and into the heart of the Battle-Plain.

"Oskutreð?" Huld said. She was the next youngest in the warband, after Elvar, her hair black as night. She reached up and tugged on the bear-claw that hung from a leather cord about her neck. Elvar saw her own emotions flickering across Huld's face: disbelief, followed by fear and excitement.

"Aye," Agnar said.

"How?" another voice asked. It was lean, grey-haired Sólín, who had been picking her teeth with a seax. Her arm hung at her side now.

"There is much to the tale," Agnar said. "Uspa stole a book of magic, a Galdrabok, from Ilska the Cruel."

"The *Graskinna*," Uspa said, her voice a hiss from where she sat at the edge of the shadows. Kráka and the *Hundur*-thrall were sitting with her.

"Uspa was destroying it when we found her, throwing it into the molten fires of Iskalt Island. But not before she had read it and learned its secrets," Agnar smiled.

"So Ilska's attack was not for the boy. It was for her," Huld said, looking at Uspa.

"Aye," Agnar said, "that is what we think. They took the boy in their rush to flee. Perhaps to trade or bargain with us, with Uspa."

"Ilska could be following us, then," Elvar said, voicing a possibility that had been lurking in her thought-cage.

Biórr came and sat beside her, a bowl of barley stew and black bread in his hand.

"She could," Agnar agreed. "Though there has been no sign of her." He shrugged. "I hope that she does. It will make fulfilling my oath easier." He pulled back the sleeve of his tunic to show the spiralling scars around his hand, wrist and forearm. In the flame-glow they looked like rings of fire. "I swore the *blóð svarið*, the blood oath, to Uspa the Seiðr-witch. She will guide us to Oskutreð, and I will get her son back or die in the trying." He looked around. "Others swore it, too. Sighvat. Elvar. Grend. Kráka."

A jerk of Biórr's head as he looked at her.

"And even though you do not bear these marks," Agnar continued, raising his scarred fist, "if you follow me to Oskutreð, then you are bound by it too." He blew out a long breath. "Oskutreð, the great Ash Tree, where the gods fought and fell. Ulfrir, Orna, Berser, Rotta, all of them. Their remains, their riches, their war gear. Their captains . . . " His words spun a saga-tale of gold and wealth, of fame and fortune unimaginable. Elvar could see the fire of it sparking to life in the eyes of everyone around her.

"Will you follow me?" Agnar said, his voice little more than a whisper.

"We will follow you, Agnar Fire-Fist," Biórr said.

Voices rang out, a chorus of heya's, oaths and cheers.

"Then let us seal it with some mead," Agnar cried, laughing and rolling a barrel into view.

The cheers were louder as the barrel was opened and horns were dipped. Agnar gave full drinking horns to all of his Battle-Grim, laughing and smiling as he did, people raising their horns and drinking, to Agnar, to Oskutreð, to the Battle-Grim. Elvar lifted her horn and took a deep draught of mead, feeling the honey-sweet trickle down her throat and send a warm glow through her belly. Agnar smiled at her and walked on.

Biórr drank beside her, quietly sipping.

"So, we are to Oskutreð, then," he said, nodding to himself. "That is quite a thing."

"Heya, so it is," Elvar agreed, holding her mead horn up and clinking his, then drinking some more.

"A toast," Biórr said, smiling at her. "To finding Oskutreð and changing the world."

Elvar echoed him and they drank together.

"I am glad you, *we*, are sworn to be finding Bjarn," Biórr said.

"There is a kindness in you," Elvar said, liking how Biórr often mentioned Bjarn.

Biórr shrugged, looking away. "It is because I need a rematch of tafl board with him. He beat me the last time, and I need my revenge."

Elvar smiled. "I have been thinking about that day, when Bjarn was taken," she said. "Why did Ilska run? She fled Snakavik, fled from us. If she wanted to trade the boy, why did she do that?"

"Who knows the mind of Ilska the Cruel?" Biórr said. "I doubt that she was running because she was scared of us. But maybe she wanted to avoid a scrap. Let things calm down before she tried to trade with us. It is not so easy to bargain and trade with people when you have a blood feud with them."

"Aye," Elvar nodded. "And they had killed Thrud."

A twist of Biórr's lips and he looked away.

"He was your friend," Elvar said.

"His death, it was my fault," Biórr said heaving a sigh.

"It was an ambush and a fight," Elvar said. "Lucky that you and Uspa came out of it breathing." She thought about Agnar's words to her, as they were crossing the lake. "We all live with death's talons in our shoulder, her breath on our neck," she said. "Thrud knew that as well as we do."

"That is a truth," Biórr said, looking into the hearth fire. They were silent for a while, sipping at their mead.

"It cannot have been easy leaving Snakavik behind," Biórr eventually said, startling Elvar. "Leaving your kin behind," he added at the twist of her eyebrow.

"It was not so hard," Elvar said. "My father is not an easy man to like, and my brother Thorun is an arseling."

"You have another brother, though," Biórr said.

"Aye, Broðir." She smiled. "I *do* like him. But, he is . . . content, with his lot in Snakavik."

"And you are not?"

"No," Elvar said. "My father would have sold me off as a brood bitch to Queen Helka's spawn. I would not have been content with that."

"Some would think that a fine life," Biórr said, "not wanting for anything: warmth, food, silver in plenty. Power."

"Not me," Elvar snarled as she sipped her mead. "I want to earn my own battle-fame and silver, not be given it, or ride on the reputation of those before me." She thought of her father, and the ever-fading memories of her mother, just fractured images now, of her smile, her laugh, her touch. She felt eyes upon her and shivered, looked at Biórr.

He was staring at her, his eyes glittering in the firelight.

"What?" Elvar said.

"You are a rare thing," Biórr smiled. He reached out, his fingertips brushing the marks on the back of Elvar's hand, sending a shiver through her. Gently he gripped her hand and held it up to the firelight, turning it so that the lattice of scars glowed like red rivers from Eldrafell, the fire mountain. "I follow Agnar Battle-Grim, but I will also follow you, Elvar Troll-Slayer, Elvar Fire-Fist," he said quietly. Then he leaned forwards and touched his lips to hers. It was just a caress, but it sent a tremor through Elvar, as if ice had trickled down her spine. She pulled away, startled, and he smiled at her.

The sound of footsteps approached, twigs cracking in the darkness behind them, and then Grend was looming above Elvar, looking down at them with a deep scowl on his face.

"Your watch," he said, his eyes shifting from Elvar to Biórr and then back to Elvar.

Elvar stood hurriedly, nodded and walked off into the darkness.

CHAPTER THIRTY-THREE

ORKA

Orka sat in the corner of a tavern with a jug of watered ale and a drinking cup. It had not helped to relieve the headache that pounded and pulsed. Smoke from a hearth fire was slowly filling the room, too much of it to filter through the smoke hole in the vaulted roof, the reek of whale oil and hops and urine thick in the air. She had chosen the darkest corner of the tavern, wrapped a new cloak that she had purchased from one of the many traders lined along the dockside streets of Darl about her and pulled up the hood. The cloak was a grey wool herringbone that covered her *brynja* and weapons, and the hood was brown homespun wool, casting her face in shadow. This was the eleventh tavern she had visited in little more than a day since she had walked away from Mord and Lif, mostly just sitting and listening, sometimes asking a barkeep or serving girl a question or two. In return, so far, she had received only silence or dark looks.

A dozen or so people sat at tables, mostly sailors from docked ships and a couple of whores smiling at men deep in their cups. Closest to her was a man sitting and stirring a bowl of stew. One side of his head was burn-scarred, what hair he had left on his head tied back tight at his neck. A short-axe and seax hung from his belt, and Orka spied the hilt of another seax poking from his boot.

"Want something to eat?" a serving girl asked her, a young girl in a dirty hangerock over a threadbare tunic.

"No," Orka said. The girl moved to turn away, but Orka pulled her hand from her belt and rolled a bronze coin on the table. The sound of it drew the girl's gaze like carrion calls to crows.

"If you want a man, or a woman, I can find one for you," the serving girl said. A pause. "I finish soon . . . "

"I'm looking for someone," Orka said.

"Who?"

"Drekr," Orka said, loudly enough to fill the room.

The serving girl blinked; other heads turned, looking Orka's way for a moment.

"Don't know anyone that goes by that name," she muttered, turning and hurrying off. She glanced at the burned man as she passed him, but he continued to stare at his bowl of stew. Slowly he lifted the spoon and slurped a mouthful. The girl reached the bar, where what looked like the landlord dragged her close and had a hissing conversation with her.

Orka took a sip from her cup.

The landlord strode around the bar towards her. He was balding, with a flat nose and red veined cheeks. On his belt he wore a seax in a worn leather scabbard.

"You should go," he said.

"I'm minding my own business," Orka said, "and I haven't drunk this jar of horse-piss that I have paid for, yet." She lifted the cup and sipped, twisting her lips.

"Have your coin back," he said, flipping her a half-copper. "Don't need your sort round here."

"My sort?" Orka said.

"Out," he grunted, his hand going to the hilt of his seax.

Orka stood, her chair scraping, and rose to her full height, looking down at him. She was a head taller, and wider as well. He took a step back, a ripple of fear crossing his face, his eyes flickering to the burned man and then back to Orka.

"Don't want no trouble," he said sullenly.

Orka walked past him and out through the tavern door into a face full of hissing rain. It was dark, which meant it was somewhere between midnight and dawn, as the summer nights were lengthening towards solstice. Orka turned left and walked on twenty or thirty paces, then turned into a shadowed alley that ran between the tavern and the next building. She stood and waited, hidden in darkness, leaning against a wattle and daub wall at an angle where she could see the street in front of the tavern's entrance. After a count of a hundred the tavern door creaked and a figure stepped out, looked both ways, then turned right and walked away. It was the burned man.

Orka followed him.

She kept at a distance, clinging to the shadows. Despite the hour the streets were busy, song and laughter echoing out from numerous taverns, drunks stumbling, traders shouting to sell their wares, spits of rabbit and squirrel turning over fires that hissed in the rain, soups and stews steaming in cauldrons. The burned man walked through a series of wide, bustling streets, seemingly in a half-circle around the base of the hill the fortress of Darl was built upon. Canals had been carved into the land, feeding from the river like leeches, and the burned man led Orka past a host of moored ships, boathouses and barns. The acrid stench of a tanner's yard clawed up her nose and she saw a courtyard with skins pinned and stretched upon frames ready for scraping. It was quieter here. The burned man was turning again and they were soon back in a street full of taverns, torchlight flickering, deeper shadows in the alleys, whores and cutpurses plying their trades. Mud sucked at Orka's boots.

The burned man stopped at a large tavern, a sign creaking above the entrance painted with a red-wounded warrior and runes. Orka moved a few steps closer to see through the rain, then stopped, merging with the shadows at the entrance to an alley. The tavern was called *The Dead Drengr.* Three figures stood outside, two of them men in wool and leather, both tall and thickset, one bald and with a cudgel in his hand. He nodded to the burned man.

The other figure was a woman, clothed in a *brynja* and cloak, the bulk of a sword visible beneath the cloak. She had a shield slung over her back, painted black with gold eagle wings spread.

One of Helka's drengrs.

She stepped in front of the burned man, but the bald man with the cudgel said something and she moved aside.

The burned man entered the tavern.

Orka stood in the shadows, watching, waiting, thinking, the rain soaking into her hood and cloak. Grey light began to leak into the street, the herald of dawn.

Then she was slipping into an alley. It was empty apart from rats, and she emerged on the far side to see the glitter of an oil-black canal dappled with rainfall, boats moored and bumping gently on the water. She crept along the back wall of a building, and then she was at the rear of *The Dead Drengr.* A high wattle wall and gates enclosed a courtyard, stables and other outbuildings. Orka heard the whicker of horses. A voice.

"Move," the voice said, and then a figure emerged from the open gate. It was a man, tall and thickset like the two on the tavern's front door, a hood pulled up over his head, a wooden staff in his hands. Behind him walked a line of children: seven, eight, more, all in cloaks and hoods, their hands bound at the wrists. Orka could hear some of the children crying. Another man followed at their rear.

The first man reached a boat moored on the canal and jumped in, ushering the children after him, spitting out sharp commands. An awning had been rigged across the rear half of the boat behind the oar-bench, and the first children clambered underneath the woollen sheet. One refused to climb on to the boat and just fell to her knees, sobbing. The man at the rear cuffed the child and hoisted her up by her hair, throwing her into the boat.

Orka cursed herself for leaving her spear in the room she'd rented earlier, but she had wanted to look as inconspicuous as possible. Her hands checked over her other weapons, an old habit. She had bought plain scabbards for the two seaxes she had pulled from Thorkel's body, and now one of them was hanging from the front of her belt across her hips, and the other was nestled in the small of her back. She checked the draw on both, that they would not stick, and then lifted her hand-axe from the loop on her belt.

Without conscious thought she was moving, running across a

mud-slick path to the canal, her axe in one fist, a seax hissing into the other.

The man on the boat must have glimpsed movement because he stopped pushing children into the boat and looked up at her. Orka's arm swung and her axe was spinning through the air. It took the man in the face with a wet slap like splitting wood. He fell back and disappeared into the canal with a splash.

The second man stared, frozen for a moment, then turned. He was reaching for an axe at his belt and opening his mouth as Orka hit him. Her seax punched into his belly and she headbutted him across the nose. He gave a grunt and muffled cry as she ripped her blade across his torso, then shoved him hard. He stumbled backwards, blood and intestines spilling at his feet, tripped over the edge of the canal and then he was gone, too, just a widening ripple in the canal to mark his existence.

There was a frozen moment as Orka looked back at the tavern gates, waiting to see if anyone had heard. No movement, no sound.

"Breca?" Orka asked desperately to the children who stood staring at her from the boat, more shadows beneath the awning peering out at her.

"Breca?" she said again, then a child opened her mouth to scream.

"No," Orka pleaded. "I won't hurt you. They took my son, Breca. Is he here?"

Another silence, all of the children staring. One snuffled, started to cry again.

"No one called Breca here," a boy said, with dark curly hair and large eyes. He looked older than the others, with maybe twelve or thirteen winters on his back.

"Are you sure?" Orka said, stepping into the boat. Children cowered away from her and she froze, then pulled her rain-soaked hood back. She was wearing Thorkel's nålbinding cap, her blonde hair braided, a coil across one shoulder.

"Anyone here called Breca?" the boy said, looking at his companions. They were all grime-streaked and hollow-eyed. Some shook their heads; others just stared.

"There are others," a girl said. "Like us."

"What do you mean?" Orka said. "Where? Here? Come close. I'll cut your bonds," she added and squatted down.

The girl took a hesitant step towards her and held her arms out, tied at the wrists. "I heard Bersi talking about them."

"Bersi?" Orka said as she raised her seax to the leather cord around the girl's wrist.

The girl nodded over the side of the boat, a twist of revulsion creasing her face and she spat where the man who had received Orka's axe in the face had fallen. Orka lamented the loss of her axe.

I will find another.

"Bersi was talking about others like us, that had been kept in there." The girl looked at the tavern. "They're gone now."

Orka sliced through the leather cord, freeing the girl's arms. She rubbed her wrists and gave a hesitant smile.

"You're free now," Orka said.

Others held their wrists out and Orka sawed at them until all were free of the leather bindings.

"Why have they taken you?" she asked the older lad. "What do they want you all for?"

"Don't know," the lad shrugged.

"One last thing," Orka said. "Do you know a man named Drekr?"

Looks of fear.

"Where is he?" Orka said, a snarl.

"In there," the first boy who had spoken to her said. He pointed at the tavern.

Orka stood and stepped off the boat on to the canal side, then looked back at the older boy.

"You're free now," she said. "Will you help these others?" She gestured to the rest of the children, who were sniffling, wide-eyed with fear.

"I will," he nodded.

"Good. If you can row a boat, take this one. If not, run, fast and far, and do not look back."

She walked towards the tavern.

CHAPTER THIRTY-FOUR

VARG

Varg dropped a ladleful of cold porridge into his bowl.

"Don't look so disappointed," Svik said to him. The warrior was sitting against a tree, the first hint of dawn lancing through branches into the glade they had camped within and tinting his features with gold.

"It's cold," Varg complained.

"There are worse things than cold porridge in this world." Svik smiled up at him. "You will most likely be meeting some of them soon."

"That does not make me happier, if that is what you were trying to do," Varg told him, still staring at the porridge.

Glornir had ordered no fires as they had moved into the foothills before the Bonebacks.

In truth Varg was used to eating much worse: the food and rations on Kolskegg's farm that had been given to the thralled farmworkers had been little better than the slop fed to the pigs.

It is strange how quickly we become accustomed to better things. It was not so long ago that hot porridge with cream and honey was a feast beyond compare. Now it is . . . normal.

"Here, have some of my cheese," Svik said, slicing a wedge from a hard round sitting on a trencher at his side. "Please take it, before your mood infects me and I cut my own throat."

"In that case, don't eat the cheese," Røkia said to Varg, nudging him with her elbow as she slopped cold porridge into her own bowl. "This could be the answer to my dreams." She gave Svik a cold smile.

"She loves me really," Svik said as he shook the cheese at Varg, who took it and sat beside the slim, gleaming warrior.

"You *really* do like cheese, don't you?" Varg observed.

"Cheese saved my life," Svik said.

"Oh no, not that story again," Røkia said, rolling her eyes. "Do not ask him *how.*"

"How?" Varg asked Svik.

Svik grinned and shifted, making himself comfortable. Other Bloodsworn were gathering around, Einar pushing through them to sit close to Svik and Varg.

"I love this story," Einar said.

"That is only because one of your kin is in it," Røkia said.

"I am not a troll," Einar said, giving Røkia a hurt look, "I just have big bones."

Røkia raised an eyebrow.

Torvik came and joined them.

"Svik is a great tale-teller," Torvik whispered to Varg.

"When I was young," Svik said, "I had two older brothers, and we lived in a steading on the eaves of a forest. One day when it was still early my two brothers came running out of the trees, frightened for their lives. They had gone to cut wood for our winter store, but a troll had come upon them and threatened to eat them."

"Trolls are nasty like that," Einar whispered to Varg.

"Being both proud and practical, even if I was only young, I thought that this was not an acceptable situation," Svik said. "We needed the wood stores for winter or we would freeze, and also I did not like the thought of someone threatening my family. So, I set off into the woods, remembering to take a round of cheese with me in a small hemp sack, as I might be gone a while and become hungry."

"Sensible," Einar commented.

"I found the dead wood and cut timber that my brothers had begun working on, their axes and saws and other tools left where they had dropped them. There was no sign of a troll, so I picked up an axe and continued with the hard work. Before long I grew tired and so stopped for a break. I sat on a log and took out the cheese to eat some, but as I did so I felt the ground tremble and heard branches snapping, and turned to see a troll striding towards me, his antlers and tusks lowered."

"As all know, that means the troll was angry and wanted a fight," Einar whispered to Varg. "Trolls are very territorial."

Varg nodded.

"I must confess," Svik said, "I was scared at the sight of this troll. I had only seen fourteen or fifteen winters, and this troll was bigger than Einar, and I could clearly see that he meant me harm. In my fright I just stood and stared at the creature, still holding on to the cheese."

Varg looked around. There was at least a score of Bloodsworn gathered close, more joining them, eating their porridge and listening with smiles on their faces. Skalk was there, with Olvir and Yrsa, the three of them listening intently.

"The troll was striding towards me, but then it stopped," Svik continued. "It just stood there, staring at me. More precisely, staring at my hand. I looked down and saw that in my fright I had made a fist, and in my fist was the cheese. I was squeezing it. In fact, I had squeezed it so hard that the whey was pouring from it, making a pool about my feet. The troll blinked. 'You are strong for a small one,' he said. 'I have never seen someone crush a rock to dust with their bare hands." Svik smiled at them all. "Trolls do not have the most clever about them," he said, tapping his temple with one finger, "and this one thought that I had crushed a rock in my fist. Thinking that this could work to my advantage I did not enlighten him to the truth. Instead I explained, very politely, that I was cutting wood for my winter store and that it was best not to make me angry, or late. The troll was so scared that I would turn my rock-crushing fists upon him that he offered to help me."

Laughter rippled around the ring of warriors, loudest from Olvir and Yrsa. Varg found a smile splitting his own lips.

"What happened then?" Einar asked, excited as a bairn the morning of his name-day.

"You know what happens next, you oaf," Røkia said rolling her eyes.

"I like the way Svik tells it," Einar grunted.

"After we had cut and split all of the wood the troll invited me back to his cave for some porridge," Svik said. "I feared to insult him by saying no, and so I went with him. His cave was big and dark and damp, but there was a store of treasure within it: weapons, coins, rings of bronze and silver that he had taken from the warriors he had slain. The troll put a pot of porridge over the fire, and soon it was ready to eat. 'How do you fancy a competition?' the troll says to me, a cunning look to his eyes. 'Let us see who can eat the most porridge?'"

"'Of course,' I answered, knowing that if I declined I would insult the troll and enrage him, but inside I was shaking, as I knew that if I lost the competition the troll would see that as weakness and most likely kill me." He looked around; all were leaning forward now, their bowls of porridge forgotten.

"When the troll went about finding two bowls and spoons for us to eat from, I quickly took the hemp sack that my cheese had been in and stuffed it up my tunic, the bag's mouth hidden close to my neck. The troll returned with two bowls, each as big as that pot there." Svik pointed to their porridge pot, as big as Varg's shield. Warriors whistled and shook their heads. "The troll filled mine and gave it to me. It was so heavy I could not lift it, so I let the troll just set it between my legs on the ground. And then we began to eat," Svik said. "I could see the troll was enjoying his meal very much, making all kinds of slurping sounds, and soon I was feeling full. So, I checked that he was not keeping a close eye on me, and then I poured a spoonful into the hemp sack under my tunic. I did this time and time again, until the hemp sack was bulging, and still the troll continued to eat." Svik pulled a face. "I was at a loss, frightened for my life, and full to bursting as well. And then I had an idea." He held a finger up, looking at each face around him.

"'I am so full,' I said to the troll, 'I do not think I can eat another mouthful.'

"The troll smiled at me, porridge dripping from his teeth. 'There is a fate for winners, and one for losers,' the troll said, and I knew full well what he meant by that. Slowly, I put my hand to my belt, where I had a small sharp knife. I drew it. The troll frowned at me and tensed, ready for my attack. But instead I turned the knife on myself and stabbed myself in the belly."

There were gasps around the circle and Svik re-enacted the strike, pretending to plunge a blade into his gut and saw it across his belly, doubling over, his face twisted in pain. Then he sat straight and smiled. "But instead of my entrails falling out, all that spilled on to my hands was porridge. I had stabbed through my tunic into the hemp sack below, then sliced it so that porridge poured out."

Murmurs of approval around the glade.

"'Ah, that feels better,' I said, and immediately began to eat more porridge from my pot, cunningly spooning it into the top of the sack. With each pretend mouthful more porridge would leak from the hole in my tunic."

Einar smiled broader than the sun, nodding at the clever of it.

"The troll stared at me with eyes wide and big as two plates. He nodded respectfully. 'You are a man who takes his porridge-eating seriously,' he said, and then with a sigh and a shake of his head he went back to eating from his own bowl. Eventually I could see that he was becoming full. He started to wriggle and shift and pull faces. 'I cannot believe this,' the troll said at last, 'but I think I am to be out-eaten by a human. My belly is so full it feels like it will burst.'

"'Ah,' I said, 'I understand how you feel. No one likes to lose an eating competition. Especially to such a small and inconsequential human such as me.' The troll nodded and scowled, agreeing. 'It all depends on how much you want to win, and how far you are prepared to go,' I said, and looked down at the knife-slash across my tunic, and the porridge that was still leaking from it.

"The troll stared at me, and his scowl turned to a smile. 'I am as brave as you, little man, and I am prepared to do what I must to win.' And with that the troll pulled his own knife of flint from his belt and slashed his belly open. To this day I can still see the confusion on his face as his guts spilled out on to his lap, instead of his porridge."

There was a silence around the glade, and then laughter erupted, Varg's voice joining them all, though Einar laughed the loudest, slapping the ground with a big slab of a hand. Olvir and Yrsa wiped tears of laughter from their eyes, Olvir bending over, hands on knees.

"And so, that is why I try never to go anywhere without a round of cheese," Svik said as the laughter died.

"Ah, but that is deep-cunning," Einar said, still rocking back and forth with mirth.

Glornir strode into the glade, his *brynja* gleaming in the fractured sunlight. "Are you trying to announce to every vaesen for a hundred leagues that we are here?" he frowned. "On your feet. We are moving out."

The camp burst into movement. Torvik jumped up and offered Varg his hand.

"Come on, brother, there's no lamb for the lazy wolf," Torvik said to him with a grin.

"I'm not lazy," Varg said as he climbed to his feet, though he was thinking on the fact that Torvik had just called him *brother*. It flooded his thought-cage with memories of Frøya, who had called him *brother* their whole life together. She had been his only friend, the only person he could trust, and now she was gone. Torvik calling him *brother* reminded him of her, and sent conflicting emotions swirling through him. Part of him felt guilt at the reminder of his sister and his unfulfilled oath. Another part of him liked it. It made him feel as if he were no longer alone in this hard world.

Varg helped break camp and get kit and camp gear packed and loaded on to the three ponies they had taken from the farm. As the sun clawed over the rim of the world they moved out, Torvik and the other scouts following Edel into the foothills ahead of

Glornir and the Bloodsworn. Varg walked with his shield slung across his back and his spear in his fist. Shadows stretched long and dark through the wooded hill, the Bloodsworn falling into a loose column both before and behind Varg. They were moving through a land of tree-cloaked hills and shadow-dark valleys, of sun-drenched meadows and rivers winding and glistening like jewel-crusted serpents that coiled through the land. The new-risen sun blazed bright as Varg stepped out on to a hillside of rolling meadow and left the trees behind him. It had been eight days since they had left the ship and deserted farm behind and now the Boneback Mountains filled the horizon, towering high and wide as far as he could see. Snow-capped peaks and dark-green slopes of thick-forested pine looked like white hair and a moss-covered cloak across the shoulders of an ancient, colossal giant. The days were becoming longer as they moved further north and the year approached the summer solstice, when daylight would hold the darkness at bay for a whole month.

In the distance he saw Edel and her hounds leading the scouts, crossing a stream and disappearing into the woodland beyond. Closer ahead of him he saw Glornir walking with Vol. He increased his pace, striding through green grass and purple heather and, as he drew closer to them, he saw that Vol was leaning towards Glornir, her jaw moving.

"She should have reached us by now," Vol was saying, Varg catching the words snatched on the wind. Glornir just marched on and said nothing in response, using the shaft of his long-axe as a walking stick.

"We should be *looking* for her, not walking into the Bonebacks with Helka's whoremaster," Vol said, louder.

Glornir looked at her. "We are the Bloodsworn, warriors for hire. This is what we do." He tugged on his grey beard. "I worry for her, too, but Vigrið is a large place, and we do not know where to look. She will have to find us. I have made no secret of our path, where we have stayed—"

Varg slipped on a patch of sun-dried grass, the ground dusty, then righted himself, Glornir and Vol turning to look at him.

"What?" Glornir said to him.

Varg increased his pace until he was walking alongside them.

"The *akáll* I spoke of," he said.

"No," Glornir said. "Perhaps there will be a time, if you have what it takes to become one of us, but that time is not now." He glowered at Varg. "I have explained this to you. Do not ask me again."

Varg opened his mouth, feeling anger stir in him, urged on by the urgency in his gut, the *need* that he felt every waking moment. To honour his oath. To honour and avenge his sister.

"Do not," Vol said to him, raising a hand. She stared at Varg, too, but without Glornir's anger. If anything, he saw pity in her eyes. His footsteps faltered and he dropped back, walking alone, his head downcast. The anger in his gut stirred, frustration fanning its flame. It was like a sleeping forge, the coals hot beneath the ash, waiting to flare with a fresh blast of air from the bellows.

Perhaps there will be a time, you say. But when will that time come, if ever? Am I wasting what little time I have left on a task that means nothing to me? What are Jarl Helka's people to me? I never knew them, never cared for them, he thought. A knot of emotion rose into his throat. *Frøya is all that I ever cared for.*

He heard voices behind him, turned and saw Skalk striding through the meadow with Olvir and Yrsa. He blinked tears from his eyes, and with an act of will pushed the emotion bubbling within him away, into the deep dark corners of his soul.

A Galdurman, a voice said in his thought-cage. *One who can perform an* akáll . . .

Skalk must have felt Varg's eyes, for he looked at him, and Varg returned the gaze.

This time Varg did not tell that insistent voice in his head to be silent.

CHAPTER THIRTY-FIVE

ORKA

Orka slipped into the courtyard of *The Dead Drengr.* Above her rainclouds shredded and blew across the sky like tattered banners. Shadows stretched and faded as dawn leaked into the world, a quiet stillness in the air. Behind her she heard the splash of oars dipping into water, the children she had freed rowing away. A horse looked out over its stable door at her and whinnied. Orka followed the curve of the wattle fence, one seax in her fist, the other still sheathed across the small of her back. There was one door to the tavern and Orka reached it, stood and listened a moment. She could hear the muffled sound of voices. Gently she lifted the latch and pulled the door open a little. Light bled out through the gap, voices louder: the general hum of conversation in a tavern, some drunken song. Orka could see a small room with cupboards, a clay oven glowing with fading heat, tables and shelves with cups, trenchers, eating boards. Knives and half-carved joints of meat. A door on the far side opened into the tavern. Orka glimpsed tables and chairs, people sitting and talking.

She stepped into the small room and pulled the door to behind her, taking care that the latch did not slip back into place. She took a look around and saw a set of wooden stairs leading up to a loft space. Another glance into the tavern. No one had heard her. She looked back to the steps.

I need to know if there is anyone in that loft, she thought. *Don't want an enemy at my back or blocking the only exit once I'm in the tavern.*

She walked to the steps and slowly and carefully climbed them, testing each foot, letting her weight settle, until she was in the loft. It was empty and dark; there were no windows, only the glow from a recently extinguished torch of rushes still seeping into the room. Water dripped from thick thatch. She stood and sucked in a breath. It was a room the size of the tavern below, rafters crisscrossed, cobwebs draping them. A score of small reed mattresses filled the floor space, the smell of urine and faeces thick in the air. Orka was about to turn when something caught her eye: a thread of leather disappearing into the reeds of the mattress closest to her. She reached out and pulled it, and held in a gasp.

It was a small, wooden-carved sword dangling on a snapped leather cord.

Her heart pounded, feeling like a drum in her chest, and her stomach lurched.

She remembered seeing the carving around Breca's neck, on their last night together in their home. A flood of memories tore through her thought-cage, of sitting and eating together, Breca angry about Virk's death, wanting to learn sword craft. Thorkel was talking about the right path, about choices. She felt a savage rush of emotion, her throat constricting and tears prickling her eyes.

He was here. My Breca was here. Alive.

Hope flared.

Where is he now? Where have they taken him? What do they want with him?

She thought of what to do next, of the choices before her.

Sometimes there are no choices. We are swept along in a current not of our own choosing.

She clenched her jaw, teeth grinding.

I will be the current. I will be the course.

Muted laughter filtered through floorboards from the tavern below. Orka pushed back the swell of emotion in her chest. Blinked away the tears. Made a fist around the wooden pendant, her knuckles whitening.

Made a fist of her heart.

She looked down at the floorboards, light filtering through cracks from the room below, and heard voices, laughter.

Drekr. The ones who stole my boy: who murdered my husband.

I will be their death.

She pushed the pendant and cord into a pocket in her belt pouch. Then she turned and stepped carefully down the steps, back into the small room, and walked to the door that looked into the tavern.

A man stood behind a bar, grey-haired and balding, a bronze ring binding his beard. He was pouring ale into jugs. Most of the tables in the tavern were empty, one near the entrance beneath a shuttered window filled with six or seven people, men and women, all playing knucklebone. The burned man was sitting with them, smiling as he threw the bones. His face was thin and angular, his mouth wide, his upper teeth too long for his lips to cover them.

Closer to Orka stood a woman, her back to Orka as she faced into the room. She was tall, wearing a quilted tunic, axe and seax hanging at her belt. Her gaze was fixed upon a table. Two figures sat there, heads close together, deep in conversation, and another man, a dark-haired warrior in mail with a shield upon his back, stood behind them. One of those sitting had a fine cloak pulled about them, a brooch fashioned as an eagle-wing, their face in shadow with a woollen hood pulled up high. The other man at the table was huge and hulking, his muscles bunched thick on his shoulders and back, looking like he had no neck. He wore a dark tunic, with knot-weave embroidery around the neck and chest, raven-hair pulled tight and braided down his back; his black beard had silver rings in it and his face was handsome, thick-browed and sharp-lined, or would have been but for the claw marks that scarred him. Four raking lines carved through him from forehead to chin, twisting his face and mouth. They were recent, judging by the rawness of the wounds, by the stitches and the scabbing.

Orka stepped into the room and grabbed the female guard by the hair, dragged her back. She stabbed her seax into the woman's throat, sawing through cartilage and flesh to slice the blade free. The woman's arms flailed as a hiss and gurgle escaped her mouth, an explosion of arterial blood.

The man at the bar saw Orka first, his mouth dropping open, ale pouring over the rim of a jug and pooling on the bar as he stood frozen, staring.

Chairs scraped and shouts erupted from the knucklebone table. The hiss of steel dragged from leather. At the closer table the hooded figure looked from Orka to the bleeding woman in Orka's grasp and stood, stumbling back, their chair falling over, the hood falling clear to reveal a black-haired man, young and proud-faced.

Orka recognised him from the dockside.

Helka's son, Hakon.

Behind him the *drengr* in mail stepped forwards, shrugged the shield off his back and into his fist, drew his sword and stood in front of Hakon.

"That's her, that's her: the one asking questions," the burned man shouted, pointing at Orka. Those around him spread wide, drawn steel in their fists.

The scar-faced man still sat in his chair, turning to regard Orka with a scowl.

"That's my friend you've just put a blade through," he growled, his voice like gravel.

Orka held the dying woman up by her hair. She wiped her seax on the woman's quilted tunic and let her drop, grabbing the axe from her belt as she slid to the ground.

"Do you recognise this?" Orka said, holding the seax for the scar-faced man to see.

He blinked and lifted a hand to his face. His mouth twisted in what once would have passed for a smile.

"You are Drekr, then," Orka breathed.

"He was your man?" Drekr asked as he stood slowly, his eyes still on the seax. He was taller and wider than Orka, seemed big enough to blot out the sky in this dark tavern. An axe hung from his belt. "He fought well, your man. But he squealed like a pig when I stuck him."

"Where is my son?" Orka growled as she strode forwards into the room, her rage a white-hot flare, burning through her limbs.

The *drengr* guarding Hakon tried to guide the prince backwards but Hakon pushed the warrior forwards, towards Orka.

"Kill her," Hakon screeched. The *drengr* shrugged and stepped to meet Orka, shield raised, sword tip hovering over the rim, blocking Orka's way to Drekr and Hakon.

Orka bent her knees and lifted her seax and axe, shuffling right as the *drengr* took a quick step forwards and stabbed at her, high over his shield rim like a striking adder, the sword blade hissing past her face. Her axe darted out, hooking the *drengr*'s shield and tugging the warrior forwards. He stumbled and swung his sword at Orka's head but she ducked, stepped in and punched the seax into his side, hard enough to burst the iron riveted rings asunder, stabbing deep, blood sluicing over her fist. She twisted the blade and the *drengr* gasped and stiffened, and Orka shoved him away, sending him tumbling into a table that cracked and splintered, collapsing beneath him.

Hakon yelled.

Men and women from the knucklebone table came at Orka, six or seven of them, the burned man hovering behind them, shouting. The bartender leaped over the bar and drew a seax.

The door opened, the two guards from the street silhouetted by daylight, along with the other *drengr*.

Drekr had his axe in his fist, part snarl, part smile on his face. He stepped around a chair.

Orka ran at him and ducked his axe swing, her shoulder crashing into his chest, lifting him from the ground and throwing him into an empty table, shattering it, splinters flying. She stumbled after him, chopping her axe at his face, but he rolled away, the axe crunching into wood. Movement to her left: a woman rushing in. Orka ripped her axe free, spun and sliced with her seax, cutting into the woman's arm as she chopped down at Orka. A scream rang out, followed by another as Orka hacked her axe into the woman's torso, felt ribs break and spun again, dragging the woman with her. There was a crunch as someone's seax slammed into the woman's head, the blow intended for Orka, a spurt of blood and bone in her face. Orka grabbed the collapsing woman, heaved her up with both hands and hurled her through the air into those behind her, sending them hurtling backwards into the shuttered window, wood splintering and light pouring in as they fell out into the street beyond.

A blow to Orka's back, the sound of links from her *brynja* splintering, a line of hot fire, and she staggered forwards, tripped over a chair, twisted as she fell, feeling air hiss where her head should be, Drekr looming behind her swinging his axe. The bartender was there, slashing at her with his seax, and Orka rolled, chopped with her axe, felt it bite into an ankle, heard a scream and the bartender fell. She kicked out with her legs, sending a ruined table crashing into Drekr's shins. He snarled and hacked it to splinters with his axe, strode after her.

Orka scrambled away, pulled herself up on the bar, threw herself backwards under the hissing arc of Drekr's axe, twisting and slashing with her seax, and felt it bite, slicing through wool and flesh.

A cry from Drekr and then she crashed into him, the two of them stumbling back, Drekr tripping over a table and both of them falling out through the smashed window. People yelled and leaped out of the way as Orka and Drekr rolled together in the muddy street, Orka ending up on top, her axe arm pinned beneath Drekr, her seax pulling back to stab him. They were close, spitting and snarling in each other's faces.

"Where is my *son*?" Orka grunted, her seax hovering.

Drekr headbutted her. There was a burst of white light in her head, her strength leaking away, her limbs abruptly loose, and he heaved her off him, sent her rolling across the street. Spitting blood, she pushed up on to all fours and saw him rise, blood staining a cut across his torso as he strode towards her. A line of pain from the wound across her back as she staggered to her feet, swept up the axe and seax where she'd dropped them, set her feet and snarled at him.

Drekr smiled and hefted his axe in his fist. It was not a long-axe, as Thorkel had favoured, but the haft was still long enough for Drekr to grip it two-handed, like a long club.

Figures burst out of the tavern, rushing at Orka, including the burned man.

"She's *mine*," Drekr snarled.

They slowed and formed a rough ring around Orka and Drekr instead, others in the street joining them. People emerged from other buildings, swelling the crowd. Orka heard shouts, bets of coin. She glimpsed Hakon in the gathering crowd, his *drengr* at his side.

"Where is my son?" Orka grunted as Drekr drew near.

"He is gone," Drekr said with a shrug.

Orka moved on him and feinted left with her axe, a side-step and stab with the seax. There was a clang of steel as Drekr's axe blade deflected it. She stepped out of his range before he could counter. They circled each other a few moments, gauging, assessing. Drekr's footwork and balance were good: impressive for such a big man. But he had one weapon where Orka had two, and he was wearing wool while Orka wore a coat of mail.

He will tell me where Breca is, if I have to carve the answer from his flesh.

Then she was moving in again, her two weapons a blur, striking in flurries. Sparks rang out, Drekr retreating, using his axe like a short staff, blocking, slicing, Orka swaying, stabbing, chopping, eyes fixed on his as she sought his life. An exchange of blows, strikes, parries and counters, and then they were stepping away from each other, both of them breathing hard. Orka felt a pain across her leg, below the knee, and glanced down to see blood soaking into her leg wrap. The pain arrived a few moments later, throbbing, burning.

She ignored it.

Drekr scowled at her, a red line across his torso, another wound across his shoulder, his tunic torn and hanging. Orka glimpsed a tattoo across his shoulder and chest, a serpent with jaws open and fangs bared, its body all writhing knotwork.

He strode at her and she moved to meet him, axe high, seax low. He caught an overhand swing of her axe on his own axe shaft, wood *clacking*, a twist of his wrist and his axe blade sliced her forearm, her axe spinning from her grip. At the same time, she was stabbing her seax at his belly, but somehow he was twisting to the side, her seax stabbing into air, just nicking his tunic. He gave a short, stamping kick to her wounded leg and she staggered, dropped to one knee and then he was behind her, his axe shaft around her throat, squeezing.

She grabbed the shaft with her free hand and swung her seax behind her, wildly trying to find Drekr's flesh but slicing only air. Black dots floated in front of her eyes.

"A good scrap," Drekr grunted behind her, the muscles in his arms straining and bulging like eels in a sack, "but you are finished now. Know this as you take the soul road: your son will change the world."

He gave a savage wrench on the axe shaft, Orka feeling muscle and tendon tear in her neck, her vision greying, like a curtain of fog rising up all around her. Strength was draining from her limbs, her breath a ragged, burning gasp.

Dimly she heard distant sounds: the blowing of a horn, the thumping of hooves, all of it fading, falling away.

Thorkel. Breca. Their faces floated in her thought-cage, both of them staring at her, sombre-eyed, accusing.

"*Avenge me*," Thorkel whispered.

"*Find me*," Breca pleaded.

Something shifted, deep inside Orka, her consciousness and clarity returning with a snap. She felt her blood churn through her veins, the heat of anger changing, abruptly cold, primal, sweeping her body, fire and ice mingled. A flush of strength flooded her muscles, her vision returning in a rush, sharper, senses keener.

The horn was blaring louder, voices shouting commands, the tramp of many feet.

She let go of the axe shaft crushing her throat and grabbed Drekr's fist that was gripping the shaft, tore at it and felt the crackle of bone: a finger or thumb breaking.

A snarl came from behind her as Drekr's grip loosened, and in a snapping, snarling burst Orka ripped herself free, threw herself forwards, twisting and turning, slashing with her seax. Drekr stumbled away, blood blossoming across one thigh, holding his axe clumsily, the knuckle around his thumb purpling and swelling.

Orka found her axe in the mud and stood.

"You will tell me where my son is," she snarled, a savage hate pulsing through her. She wanted to tear, rip, kill, to shred Drekr's flesh and pound his skull into the ground.

Shouts and screams sounded among the crowd, one man running between Orka and Drekr, then others. Orka saw Hakon in the crowd, pulling his hood up, turning and running, his *drengr* guard shielding him from the crush. She glanced away and saw a company of *drengrs* marching down the street, thirty or forty warriors with shields ready, spears pounding a steady rhythm on their shields as they advanced. A warrior rode at their rear, blowing on a horn.

"Can't have you getting out of this," Drekr said. "My thought-cage tells me you will be a pain in the arse." He gestured and men stepped out of the crowd, those from inside the tavern, and the two that had stood guard outside. They moved in on Orka, a tightening circle of axes, cudgels, seaxes, all pointed at her.

Orka set her feet and growled at them, turning slowly.

"Who wants to die first?" she snarled.

There was a pounding of hooves and a horse appeared in the crowd, hurling people away. It rode closer, neighing and stamping, its rider stabbing down at one of the guards in the circle around Orka. The man fell away with a scream, a red gash down his chest and the horse pressed into the ring, the other guard raising his cudgel to swing at the rider, but a second horse and rider appeared, crashing into him, sending him flying.

"Come on," the first rider shouted, a man leaning in their saddle and waving a hand at Orka.

She blinked, the red haze in her head fading a fraction, melting enough to realise who it was.

"Come on!" Lif yelled again. He grabbed the neck of Orka's mail coat, his horse pounding on, dragging her with it, and together they crashed through the circle around her, sending the burned man reeling. Orka gripped Lif's forearm and jumped, heaving herself into the saddle behind him, Mord riding hard behind them.

They rode down the mud-slick street, people leaping out of their way, and then Lif was dragging on his reins and they were veering right into an alley. Orka looked back and caught a glimpse of Drekr standing and staring at her. He lifted his axe in a salute, a promise, and then Orka was plunging into the shadows.

CHAPTER THIRTY-SIX

VARG

Varg paused and wiped sweat from his brow. The terrain around them had shifted over the last few days of travel, from gentle hills and meadows to sharp slopes and twisting valleys. He was climbing a steep, rock-littered ravine, the Bloodsworn stretched out in a long line behind him. Above him Glornir and Vol climbed together, and ahead of them he could just make out the forms of Torvik, Edel and the other scouts reaching the lip of this dried-out river and disappearing into a fringe of pinewoods. Edel's two wolfhounds stood at the ravine's rim, one of them looking down at Edel, barking and wagging its tail. To Varg it looked like level ground lay beyond the ravine's lip.

At least, that is what he hoped.

"Get moving, Varg No-Sense," Røkia called up to him. "Or are you waiting for an eagle to swoop down and carry you the rest of the way?"

"My sore feet are wishing exactly that," Varg muttered, blisters throbbing on the soles of his feet. He rolled his shoulders and shrugged his shield upon his back, shifting the leather strap that bit into him, and walked on, using his spear like a walking staff. Sweat steamed from his body, the temperature palpably dropping as they climbed ever higher towards the Boneback Mountains, despite the clear skies and summer sun. Varg finally clambered over the rim of the riverbed, more like the gradient of a dried-out waterfall now, and looked ahead. He saw an open, rocky space and then trees looming tall, the scent of pine sap thick in the air.

He heard a grunt, the sound of rocks skittering behind him, and he turned to see Sulich stumble, his long warrior-braid swinging wildly as scree shifted beneath his feet. Varg thrust his spear shaft out and Sulich grabbed it to steady himself.

"Hold tight," Varg said, and pulled Sulich up the rest of the slope and on to the rim.

"My thanks," Sulich said to him as he clambered on to level ground.

"And my apology," Varg said, "for insulting you in Liga. About your kinsman's war gear." It was something that had chewed at Varg's thought-cage, but every time he had looked at Sulich the warrior had ignored him, or his brows had been knitted in a way that discouraged any conversation.

Sulich looked at him and gave him a long and appraising gaze, a hint of a frown.

"I am . . . *was*, a thrall," Varg continued. "Have been one all of my life. This warrior's way, it is a mystery to me. I meant you no insult."

Sulich maintained his gaze, then gave a curt nod.

"We will think on it no more," he said.

"Thank you," Varg said.

The two of them stood and looked at the trees. Something about the shadowed gloom set Varg's hairs standing on end. The air was colder, Varg feeling it in his chest as he sucked in deep breaths, and he could see the glimmer of frost patches on tree bark. His breath misted.

They set off into the trees together. The ground was spongy with needles and stiff with frost. Varg heard grunting behind them, turned and saw Skalk climbing over the ravine's rim. The Galdurman stopped, waiting while Olvir and Yrsa appeared over the rim behind him. They stood together in silence, staring at the woodland.

A decision was made in Varg's thought-cage, and he stopped to take a drink from his water bottle, letting Sulich walk on ahead, and waited for Skalk and his two guards to draw near. The

Galdurman glanced at him as Varg fell in beside him. Olvir the guard frowned and stepped closer to Skalk, while Yrsa's eyes were searching the shadows of the pinewood.

"Your shield, it is unfinished," Skalk said as they walked along together. "There is no blood-spatter upon it."

"I am recently come to the Bloodsworn," Varg said. "I am not yet one of them, have not yet taken their oath."

"Ah, that is how they do things, then," Skalk said, nodding to himself. "Like an apprenticeship to a blacksmith, or a farrier." He paused, a smile twitching his lips. "Or to a Galdurman."

"Aye," Varg said.

"And what is it you wish of me?" Skalk said. "You have a question, or a request?"

"You see straight to the heart of it," Varg said, a tremor in his veins. Fear. Hope.

"Time is a gift, not for wasting," Skalk said.

"Straight to it, then," Varg said. "I wish for an *akáll* to be done. It is important to me."

"Hmmm," Skalk said, nodding as they walked among the pine trees. "That is no small thing. The Bloodsworn have a Seiðr-witch. As you are one of them, or soon to be, why do you not ask her?"

"Because time is a gift, not for wasting," Varg said, "and Glornir will not allow Vol to perform an *akáll* until I have sworn my oath to them."

"Then swear your oath."

"Glornir says I am not ready. And there is no time set upon it: it could be a day or a year. Or never. Glornir will only tell me when he deems me ready," Varg said with a bitter twist of his lips.

"Ah, and time is beating like a drum," Skalk said, nodding. "Rushing by. Oaths bind us, drive us, do they not?"

"They do," Varg said, a tremor in his voice.

"I could perform this *akáll* for you. But there would be a cost. One part of which is that I suspect you would lose your place in the Bloodsworn. I do not think Glornir is the kind of man to look favourably on acts of . . . impatience."

"It is not impatience," Varg said. "It is the fulfilment of an oath."

"Yes, to you this is important. To Glornir," Skalk shrugged. "Trust me, he will not think well on you doing this. You must recognise this, before you go any further."

Varg nodded, blew out a slow breath.

"I acknowledge it," he said.

"And Glornir would most likely not look too kindly on me if I were to perform this *akáll*, with me knowing that it would take you from the Bloodsworn. I have to ask myself, is that something I want? Glornir and the Bloodsworn are an ally to Queen Helka, and this task is important to her."

"It is nobody's business but ours," Varg said.

"That is . . . naive," Skalk said.

"I can pay," Varg said, his hand going to his coin pouch on his belt.

"I would want paying, of course. An *akáll* is no easy thing, and it takes its toll," Skalk said, looking at Varg and the coin pouch. He frowned. "I do not need your coin. But there are other ways of paying: you would owe me a debt, as and when I call for it. I would require your oath. Your blood oath."

"I see," Varg said.

"Do not answer me now," Skalk said. "It is too great a thing to decide in an instant. Think on it, and perhaps we shall talk more. Yes?"

Varg nodded. The weight of his oath pressed down upon him, the need to honour and avenge his sister heavier with every day. It gnawed at his soul. He knew Skalk was speaking wisdom, and he also disliked the thought of being indebted to this man, to anyone. But in Varg's heart he knew that he had no choice at all. He drew in a deep breath.

Paused.

Something around him had changed. A tingling in the air, a silence, heavy as unforged iron. No birdsong or hum of insects. He frowned, slowing, and saw that Glornir and Vol had slowed ahead of them, Sulich catching up with the chief and Seiðr-witch. They were all walking slowly, heads turning, eyes searching the forest.

A whistle came from up ahead, deep in the woodland.

A warning from Edel? Varg thought.

He heard the hiss of a sword leaving its scabbard, Yrsa drawing her blade and shrugging her shield into her fist.

A figure appeared out of the forest gloom: Torvik, running back to Glornir. A hushed conversation between them.

Glornir held his hand in the air.

"Bloodsworn, on me," he called out.

Varg quickened his pace and joined Sulich. The warrior had shrugged his shield from his back, his other hand resting on the hilt of the sabre at his hip. Instinctively Varg gripped his shield and slipped the leather cover from his spear blade, tucking it in his belt.

Røkia will be proud of me, he thought.

"What is it?" Skalk said as he joined them. Olvir and Yrsa both had shields and swords in their fists, and were scanning the gloom around them. More of the Bloodsworn were joining them, jogging through the forest, shields moving from backs to fists. In a score of heartbeats all of them were gathered, over fifty warriors forming a loose line behind Glornir.

"Show us," Glornir said to Torvik, and the young scout turned and led them on.

They walked in silence, Glornir at their head, his long-axe held in both hands, Vol just behind him. Skalk, Olvir and Yrsa strode behind them, and then the rest of the Bloodsworn in a loose formation, shields ready.

Varg walked beside Sulich and Røkia, behind him the heavy tread of Einar Half-Troll.

"Stealth is never a possibility with you, Half-Troll," Varg heard Svik mutter.

"I am doing my best," Einar grunted.

Varg looked about him, his skin prickling. The pine forest felt strange, a sickly scent seeping through the air, creeping into Varg's nose and sticking in his throat.

Glornir slowed to look up at a tree as they passed it. Varg saw it had a rune carved into it. Sap leaked down the bark and the rune was stained with something dark. Just the sight of it set Varg's hairs standing on his neck.

They moved on and Torvik led them along a path that ran through an old stream bed. Banks of earth reared either side of them, roots of trees bursting free of the soil, twisted and knotted like arthritic limbs, draped with moss and lichen.

Varg saw shadowed figures ahead, Edel standing with her two wolfhounds, a few other scouts with her. Others stood on the streambanks. They were all staring in the same direction.

Fear trickled into Varg like seawater into a cracked hull.

Trees loomed around them, thick-trunked and grey-barked. Bodies hung from their boughs; rope was knotted about their ankles. Men and women were trussed like hogs for slaughter, arms stretched and dangling as if trying to reach the ground. They had been gutted and skinned, their flesh torn at by carrion, eye sockets dark and empty where they had been pecked clean, lips and tongues shredded. Piles of offal were heaped beneath each body, flies a swarm.

Varg counted twenty-four of them.

A rune had been carved into the meat of their chests.

Varg felt his gut lurch and he took a step out of line, bent over and vomited on to a moss-green bank.

"How long?" Glornir asked Edel.

"A month?" Edel said frowning. "It is hard to tell; the cold has preserved them."

Some of Edel's scouts were sifting through the offal with their spears. One called out and lifted a boot, and then a seax scabbard. Another speared a piece of fabric and raised it into the air. It was pinned with a cloak-brooch that glinted gold, fashioned in the shape of eagle wings.

Yrsa let out a hiss. Olvir strode towards the bodies, staring at the brooch on the cloak that the scout had lifted, then up at the corpses. His face was twisted, but it wasn't fear that Varg saw there. It was grief.

"You knew them," Vol said to Olvir. It wasn't a question. She looked at Skalk, a frown creasing her face. "You *sent* them."

Glornir looked at Skalk. Strode towards him. The Galdurman took a step away, shifting the grip on his walking staff.

"These are Helka's *drengrs*," Glornir growled. "You said she was stretched too thinly to send any of her warriors."

A long moment passed as the two men stared at one another.

"I meant, any *more* of her warriors," Skalk said with a shrug, breaking the silence. He walked around Glornir and stood beneath one of the corpses, prodding it with his staff, setting it turning. The rope binding its ankles creaked and frayed, and then the body dropped to the ground in a heap. Skalk turned it over with his staff, grunting with the effort, and squatted and stared at the rune carved on the torso. He frowned.

"*Bannað jörð*," Vol murmured as she stood over him.

Skalk looked up at her.

"Forbidden ground," she said.

I do not *like this*, Varg thought, wiping bile from his mouth and turning in a slow circle, his eyes trying to pierce the gloom.

He heard footsteps as Svik came to stand beside him, Røkia the other side.

"You all right?" Svik asked him.

"No," Varg said. "I'm scared."

"Fear is good," Røkia said. "It sharpens the senses, makes you faster, stronger. It is the forge of your courage and will help you kill your enemies."

Svik frowned at her. "It makes me want to piss my breeches and run away," he said. Then he looked back at Varg. "We all feel fear." He shrugged. "But we fight anyway. And we guard each other's back. We are the Bloodsworn."

"Edel," Glornir said, "search the bodies. Search this ground. I would know all we can of who or *what* it is we are hunting."

"Aye, chief," she said.

"Bloodsworn, make ready to move out," Glornir called out, his words setting crows flapping and squawking in the branches above them. He looked from Skalk to Vol, then at the Bloodsworn gathered behind him. "We have not been told the full truth, that is clear, but it makes no difference. We are the Bloodsworn, and we are here. We will rid these hills of whatever is lurking here, and we will earn our coin."

They waited in silence as Edel and her scouts cut down the corpses, examined them and then scoured the land. Soon she was signalling a way forward, into the gloom. Glornir gave Skalk one last glower as he raised his hand and then he was marching after Edel and her hounds, the Bloodsworn following. Varg looked back at the corpses piled now beneath the trees and saw Olvir standing, staring at the first who had been cut down. Skalk barked a command and the *drengr* followed after them.

Tears were rolling down Olvir's cheeks.

CHAPTER THIRTY-SEVEN

ORKA

Orka grunted and drank a draught of mead from a horn as Lif pushed a curved bone fishhook through skin and flesh in her back.

"Sorry," Lif muttered as he stitched the wound Drekr had given her. He paused to pour more water over it, then snatched the horn of mead from Orka and poured some of that over the wound as well, wiping the blood away with a strip of linen. Orka stiffened, giving another huff of pain.

"Sorry," Lif said again.

"Just get on with it," Orka growled as she took the mead horn back, her voice an abrasive rasp, her throat sore and swollen from where Drekr had tried to crush her windpipe. The mead soothed the pain. A little.

They were sat in a small room, a divided hayloft above a steading that looked out over a pigpen, fields of wheat and rye beyond. Mord had opened a shutter to let some light in for Lif to work by, but the stench came in with the light. Orka heard raised voices outside, and the braying of a donkey that was refusing to pull a cart of hay. She heard the crack of a whip. They were in a barn on a farm on the outskirts of Darl.

"Why are you here?" Orka said as Lif stitched her wound. "Why were you still in Darl? I told you to leave."

"Looking for you," Lif murmured.

"And a good thing we were," Mord said from the window, "judging by the giant who was throttling the life from you when we arrived." He was watching the track that led to the farm, checking to see if they had been followed, and at the same time crushing some yarrow leaves in a bowl and mixing them with honey.

"I had it under control," Orka muttered.

"Ha," Mord laughed. "I would hate to see what out of control looks like to you."

"What were you doing?" Lif asked. "Apart from fighting half of Darl, or so it looked."

Orka sucked in a deep breath. A dark mood had settled over her, seeping through her like poison in the blood.

"The giant, Drekr," Orka breathed. "He killed Thorkel. Took my Breca." She felt a flare of rage, and of shame, as she said the words out loud, that she had been so close to him and come away without her son, or her vengeance.

"Oh," Lif said.

"If you don't mind me asking, what was your plan?" Mord asked. "When we arrived, you were surrounded by six men and women, all with sharp steel in their fists," He paused. "How were you hoping to come out of that alive?"

"There were more of them to begin with," Orka said.

"What, in the tavern with the smashed window?"

"Yes," Orka snapped.

"So, you didn't attack seven on your own? You attacked more? How many?"

"What does it matter?" Orka said.

"I am intrigued. You tell us to have patience. To wait until the time is right for our vengeance. But you walk into a tavern and try to attack . . . "

" . . . twelve people," Orka sighed.

Mord just looked at her blankly.

"What was your plan again?"

"To kill them all, save one."

"To kill eleven warriors?"

"I wouldn't call them warriors," Orka snarled.

"All right, not *drengrs*, maybe, but they still looked handy in a scrap to me. And you planned on killing them *all*, except for one."

"Yes, that's right."

Mord laughed. "How did you think you were going to walk out of there alive?"

Orka took another long sip of her mead and felt the sweet liquid spreading through her belly, into her limbs.

"Killing doesn't come easy to most people," Orka said. "Even if they tell you it does. Oh, the ones that brag about it, like Guðvarr, they can kill easy enough, if someone is holding their enemy down for them. But in a fight . . . " She shrugged. "When it comes to it, most people care more about staying alive. They hesitate."

"And you don't?" Mord asked.

"Killing's always come easy to me," Orka said. She sniffed. "Not something I'm proud of, but there it is. And I don't hesitate."

A silence settled over the room. Outside, pigs snorted and the wheels of a cart turned, the donkey finally deciding to move. Orka emptied her drinking horn.

"Why kill them all but one?" Lif said into the quiet as he stitched.

"The one would tell me where my Breca is. They would see what I have done to their friends and comrades, would know what I could do to them. They would be likely to tell me the truth."

"See," Lif said, "I told you she was a deep-cunning thinker."

"Doesn't sound like wolf-cunning to me," Mord muttered, staring out the window.

Nor to me, now it's had a chance to work its way around my thought-cage.

"That's done," Lif said, dropping his fishhook into a bowl of boiled water that was cooling now; they'd used it to sterilise the hook before stitching Orka's wound. Lif poured more water over Orka's back and Mord passed him the bowl of yarrow and honey. Lif dripped the herbs and honey on to Orka's wound and then placed a patch of linen over it, finally wrapping a longer linen bandage around Orka's shoulder and chest.

"How is that?" Lif asked her.

Orka stood and rolled her shoulder. She felt a twinge of pain, and the stitches tugged a little. She swirled mead around her mouth and spat out blood into the bowl. Put her hand to her nose and blew a clot of blood out. Her lip and nose were split and swollen from where Drekr had headbutted her.

"Good," Orka said. "My thanks." She reached for her linen tunic, but Mord thrust another at her.

"Have mine," he said. "Yours has got a hole in it."

"Huh," Orka grunted and took his tunic, shrugging it on. It was a little tight, but she could manage.

"Why were you looking for me?" Orka asked them. "I told you to leave Darl."

"That is what we planned to do," Lif said. "We were buying food from traders on Darl's dockside as you advised, planning to row further north and find some land to farm, fish from the river, and make our deep-cunning plan to end Guðvarr next spring." He looked at Mord.

"And then we saw a ship rowing into Darl's harbour. Jarl Sigrún's *drakkar*, and she was stood at the prow," Mord said.

"You are sure it was her?" Orka said, frowning.

"Aye," Lif nodded.

"She had a red-cleaved wound through her face," Mord added, tugging on his blond beard.

Orka grunted.

"That still does not explain why you came galloping through a street on two horses and dragged me from a fight," Orka said.

"She is looking for all of us," Lif said, Mord nodding. "That must be why she is here. So, we sold our boat and bought some horses. Thought that if we could find you and ride inland, away from the River Drammur, where they are clearly searching for us, then we might escape them."

"You sold your boat and came looking for me, to *save* me?" Orka said slowly.

"Aye, of course," Lif said. "You did not know Jarl Sigrún was in Darl. You could have just walked into her and her *drengrs*."

"At this point we did not know that you were happy to try killing entire warbands all on your own, you understand," Mord said.

"And Guðvarr could be with her," Lif added.

"We were trying to think of a plan with more deep-cunning than just walking into a tavern where we would be outnumbered twelve to one and try to put some steel in his belly," Mord added, a smile twitching his mouth.

"Huh," Orka said. "It seemed like a good idea at the time." She sighed and picked at a cut on her forearm, another reminder of Drekr and his axe. She looked at her *brynja*. It was draped over a chair, a rent across its back, rings shattered and twisted by Drekr's axe blow.

"I need some rings and rivets," she said. "And a hammer and tongs."

Lif and Mord frowned at her. "What for?" Mord asked.

"I don't want a hole in my *brynja* if we are going to go back into Darl and try to kill them," Orka said.

"Kill who?" Lif said.

"All of them."

Orka stood in a shadowed alley and waited, leaning on her spear, her hood pulled up over her head. She had crept back to the room she had rented alongside a stinking canal, climbed up a wall and through an open shutter to find, to her surprise, that her spear was still there, along with the rest of her kit. Not that there had been much of it.

Lif stood beside her, leaning against a wattle and daub wall and peering around a corner, into the street. Rush torches burned outside a tavern door, pushing back the darkness. It was a crow-dark night, cloud blotting out the moon and stars. People walked in the street, indiscriminate shadows, red-tinged when they passed close to the torchlight.

"Get back," Orka growled at him and the young man stepped back into the shadows.

"He's been in there a long time," Lif muttered. "Too long."

Orka ignored him.

Three days had passed since Lif and Mord had carried her from the fight with Drekr, during which she had bought rings and rivets from the farmer they were lodging with, repaired her *brynja*, sharpened her blades, and plotted with the two brothers. A seed of doubt lurked deep in her gut about their abilities, about whether they had the skills and hardness of hearts to do what had to be done. Also, she did not want their deaths on her shoulders. She carried enough of that weight with her already. Some nights she thought she heard the voices of dead friends muttering to her and she would wake with a start, her heart thumping and sheened in sweat. Sometimes she heard Thorkel's voice, or Breca's.

And another voice whispered that Mord and Lif would slow her down, pull her away from what she had to do. That she was better off alone.

But they stayed to warn me of Sigrún, even sold their boat in an attempt to save me when they could have just rowed away and saved themselves, she thought. On the scales of honour, Orka owed them a debt. And she did not like that, either.

It is what it is. I will take one step at a time, kill one enemy at a time. They have made their choice and are in this, now. They know the path we are walking, the steel-edge of it, where life and death are closer than lovers.

The tavern door opposite her opened, and Mord came out into the street, his fair hair and beard glowing amber in the rush-light. It was the tavern that Orka had first seen the burned man in. Mord looked both ways, then walked right, taking a quick glance at the alley Orka and Lif were in, giving a curt nod even though he could not see them and then he was walking past them, on down the street.

Orka waited.

"He's not coming," Lif whispered.

Orka made a sound in her throat, like a wolf would growl at an annoying cub.

The tavern door creaked and a figure stepped out, looking both ways then focusing on Mord's back.

The burned man.

He walked after Mord.

Orka and Lif watched him as he strode past the alley they were in, Orka gripping Lif's shoulder as he started to move.

She tutted at him.

The burned man walked on, fading into the shadow-filled street.

Orka let go of Lif and stepped out into the street, making sure her cloak was tight about her, hiding any glint or gleam of her *brynja*, and her hood was pulled to hide her face in shadow. She walked along the street, limping a little, more from the kick Drekr had given her than the axe-cut below her knee. She had washed and stitched her *winnigas* so there was no sign of blood and used her spear as a staff to speed her walking.

People in the road thinned as they moved through the streets of Darl towards the canal district where Orka had found Drekr. She followed the burned man, slowly catching up with him until she could see the shape of Mord beyond him. Mord turned into an alley, disappearing, and the burned man followed.

Orka picked up her pace. Heard voices. A scuffle. She broke into a limping run and turned into the alley, gesturing at Lif to stand guard.

Mord was standing with his back to a wall, clutching his right arm to his chest, a seax at his feet. The burned man stood in front of him, a short axe in his fist.

"I won't be asking you again," the burned man said. "Who are you?"

"He's a friend of mine," Orka grunted, pulling her hood back, and the axe man spun around. His eyes flared in recognition and he swung his axe as Orka lunged, but she dipped her blade beneath his wild parry and stabbed on, her spear blade slicing his bicep. The burned man squealed in pain as his axe fell from his fingers and he stepped back, reaching clumsily with his left hand for the hilt of the seax at his belt.

Orka drew back with her spear, carving a red line across his cheek, and then Mord clubbed him across the shoulders, sending him to his knees.

Orka stood over him, spun her spear and punched the butt into his jaw. He toppled into the mud like a sack. With a quick step forward, Orka kicked the axe away.

"Pick it up," she grunted to Mord as she crouched and drew the seax from the burned man's belt, tossed it to Mord, then bound the unconscious man's wrists and ankles with twine. She stood and dragged his limp body deeper into the alley, Mord and Lif following.

"Wake up," Orka said as she sat the burned man against a wall. They were close to the far end of the alley, open ground beyond and then the ripple of the canal. Clouds parted, starlight leaking out, silvering the burned man's scarred face. His front teeth were too big for his mouth, protruding from his lips. Orka slapped him and he blinked.

"You should not have come back. You are a fool," the burned man said.

"A fool who has you trussed like a hog," Orka said.

"Drekr said you would be a pain in the arse," he muttered.

"Your name?" Orka asked him.

He glowered at her.

"The axe," Orka said, holding her hand out to Mord. He passed her the burned man's fallen weapon. Orka took it, thumbed the blade and then cut a strip of linen from the burned man's tunic. She folded and rolled it, grabbed his face and started stuffing the linen into his mouth, filling it. He struggled and twisted, strings of spittle flying from his mouth, but Orka's grip was iron.

Only when his mouth was full to bursting and he was making choking sounds did Orka stop. She showed him the axe again, and then chopped into his knee. There was a crack and a spurt of blood.

His body spasmed and he retched and gagged, thrashing and panting muffled screams, shaking and thrashing like a trapped animal. His body seemed to swell, his face twitching, and Orka saw the teeth protruding from his mouth change shape, growing longer, sharper. She grabbed his flailing arms and looked at his fingers. The nails were darkening, growing.

"What is happening to him?" Mord hissed.

"He is Tainted," Orka said. "Sometimes they cannot control the beast in their blood, especially when experiencing sudden pain or shock. He is one of Rotta's kin." She spat on the ground.

"Rotta, the rat?"

"Aye, the betrayer."

"What shall we do?" Mord said.

"We wait. He cannot escape. He could gnaw through his bonds, but I will smash his teeth with his own axe if he tries to do that."

The burned man slowed in his thrashing, breathing hard.

"Your name," Orka said, holding his gaze.

He glared at her, shook his head and snapped his sharp rodent teeth.

Orka raised the axe and chopped into his other knee.

The burned man's eyes bulged as he hissed and gagged, flailed and floundered in his bonds, banging his head against the wall. Bloodied froth dripped from the linen in his mouth where his long teeth gnashed into his lower lip, blood dribbling down his chin.

Orka waited.

Lif made a sound behind her.

"What?" she said, looking up at him. "Is anyone coming?"

"No," Lif said with a quick shake of his head. He was staring at the burned man, eyes wide and his face pale.

"Harden your heart," Orka growled at him. "He is not a man any more. He is a stepping stone on the path to our vengeance. To me finding my son. Now see to your task." She turned her back on Lif and focused back on her prisoner. He was weeping, snot hanging from his nose, but his eyes glared hate and defiance. Orka showed him the axe again, dripping with his blood, and then began to pull one of his boots off.

He convulsed, kicking and writhing, but Mord held him and Orka tugged his boot free and held his foot on the ground. She paused, looking at his pale flesh. A tattoo wound around his ankle and calf: a curled, knotted serpent. She frowned and raised the axe, then looked the burned man in the eye.

"I can do this until the sun comes up," she said, then looked at the sky. "Long enough to go through your toes, your feet and up to your stones. Answer my questions, or this will only get worse."

The burned man was weeping. He sagged, like a sail with no wind, and nodded.

"Call for help and you lose your foot," Orka said and tugged the linen from his mouth.

"What is your name?"

"Skefil," the burned man said, his voice shaking with pain, or fury, or shame.

Probably all of them.

"Where is Drekr?"

"He will rip your head from your shoulders," Skefil wheezed.

"I would like to give him the opportunity to try," Orka said. "Where is he?"

"Gone," Skefil muttered.

"Gone where?" Orka said.

Silence. A hate-filled gaze.

Orka raised the axe.

"North," Skefil blurted. Another twitch of Orka's wrist. "To the Grimholt Pass."

"Why?" Orka asked him.

Skefil clamped his teeth tight.

Orka swung the axe, blood and toes sprayed and Skefil sucked in a gasp of air, ready to scream. Orka pressed the axe into his mouth, the hooked blade drawing blood at the corners. Skefil froze, a tremor passing through him.

"I can make your mouth bigger, if you wish."

A long, slow-tremored exhalation.

"Good. Why is Drekr travelling north?" Orka asked. She removed the axe blade a handspan.

Skefil sucked in a long, ragged breath, more tremors rippling through his whole body. "He is taking more Tainted children to the Grimholt," he finally moaned.

Orka's breath caught in her chest.

Was Breca in Darl, then? Is he one of the children with Drekr?

"Was my son, Breca, with him?"

"I don't know," Skefil said.

"Be careful how you answer. What is left of your life will be decided here, by your next words." She lifted the axe.

"I swear, I do not *know*. I never saw any of the bairns, only their backs as Drekr rode away. I am just eyes and ears in Darl. I watch, I listen. I tell Drekr what I learn. Drekr does not tell *me* anything."

Orka let out a long, deep breath as she studied him, thinking. There was terror and pain in his eyes, his defiance crushed. She believed him.

"Your son will change the world: that is what Drekr said to me. What did he mean?"

Skefil shrugged, "I only know Drekr and his crew have been swiping Tainted bairns and sending them north. That's all I know, nothing else, I swear."

Orka nodded.

"All right." She glanced at Mord, who was standing over them, watching against anyone passing along the canal. "Jarl Sigrún is in Darl, you know this?"

"Aye," Skefil said.

"Tell me what you know."

"She is searching for outlaws from her village. Someone who slew Queen Helka's *Úlfhéðnar* and put a scar in Sigrún's face . . . Ah," Skefil nodded, the flicker of a knowing smile. "It was you."

"And us," Mord grunted. "She is searching for us, too."

Skefil gave Mord a disdainful look. "I am no *Úlfhéðnar* and yet look at your arm."

"Where is Jarl Sigrún lodging?" Orka pressed.

Skefil shook his head and let out a wheezing laugh, drool hanging from his lip. "You wish for death. Or are moon-touched. Jarl Sigrún is a guest of Queen Helka. She is staying in the Eagle-Hall." He nodded his head, gesturing to the winged fortress that loomed on the crest of the hill that Darl was built upon.

Orka blew out a breath.

"One last question, and then you are free," Orka said. "What was Hakon Helkasson doing in a tavern with Drekr?"

Skefil shrugged. "He is involved with the Tainted bairns, but how, I do not know."

"And Queen Helka does not know?"

"That would be my guess," Skefil said, "from the cloaks and hoods and shadows."

"Mine, too," Orka murmured. She looked at Skefil. "You have been helpful. My thanks." And then she lifted the axe and slammed it down into Skefil's head. A crunching crack into his skull, a gasp and spasm, his tied feet drumming and then Orka was ripping the axe free, fragments of bone and brain spraying. Skefil sagged into the mud.

A hiss came from Lif and Mord.

"You said he was going to be free," Lif breathed.

"Aye, free of this life," Orka grated.

"Why did you kill him, when he answered everything?" Mord pressed.

"Because a cleaved head no longer plots," Orka growled.

CHAPTER THIRTY-EIGHT

ELVAR

Elvar stood beside a gloss-black boulder, staring as the sun rose in the east, banishing the darkness and bringing colour to life in the world of ash and shadow. She wiped sweat from her brows, not quite believing what she could see, even though she was stood here, looking at it with her own eyes.

"So that is the vaesen pit," Grend said beside her.

They were stood on what felt like a cliff edge, the ground covered in thin soil and yellowed grass, here and there patches of gloss-black rock shining through. And before them a chasm opened, wide and deep, and within it a river of fire flowed, black-crusted, glowing orange, flares of white heat here and there. Hot thermals rose out of the pit, covering Elvar in a sheen of sweat. For days now, the temperature had been rising. Initially after leaving Lake Horndal and walking north it had become colder each day, and by the third day they had been travelling through snow-covered lands. Grend had woken to ice in his beard. But later that day the snow on the ground had begun to thin, even though they were trudging through a blizzard. Cold winds still blew, and snow still fell, but the ground had become warmer. Elvar had felt it through her boots. The snow and ice on the ground had just begun to melt away. And then, late yesterday, Elvar had seen patches of grass and black rock through the melting snow. Soon after, Elvar had stripped off her sealskin cloak and wolf pelt and strapped them to one of the pack ponies that already carried her helm and spear, though she still wore her mail coat and weapons belt, her shield slung across her back. Snow still fell around her, but it hissed and evaporated in the air, the ground pulsing with heat like a fresh-baked loaf just taken from the oven.

"Have you ever seen such a thing?" Elvar breathed.

"No," Grend muttered. "And then there is *that*." He pointed north, beyond the chasm that was the vaesen pit, towards a mountain, its top sheer and almost level, as if a giant had taken a huge axe to the mountain and chopped its head off. Veins of red latticed the mountainside, where streams of fire leaked from its crust like pus from festering wounds.

"Eldrafell, the fire mountain," Elvar said. "Growing up in Snakavik and Snaka's skull, you become used to the wondrous. I never thought I would see something that made me feel . . . awe."

"Ha, that is a truth," Grend barked a laugh, which was rare for him.

The tales told that Mount Eldrafell had been broken in the fall of Snaka and that an ocean of fire had burst from its throat, spewing over the land and pouring into the vaesen pit, a huge rent in the land where the vaesen dwelled. They had fled the flames, all manner of creatures that had dwelled in the world below, clawing and climbing their way out of the pit into the world of sky and air and flesh.

Lights danced and flickered in the sky, silhouetting Mount Eldrafell and the horizon. They were fading with the arrival of the sun, but still bright enough for Elvar to see. There were lights of all colours and hues: amber and red and purple spiralled and swirled around blues and greens and pinks. During the brief night the whole horizon had been lit with the undulating incandescence of the *guðljós*, the god-light. Some said it was the souls of the gods who had fallen in battle, unable to rest, still waging their eternal war.

"It is . . . beautiful," Elvar breathed.

"Heya," Grend agreed. He looked at Elvar. "Following you has been . . . " He paused, looking intently at her. "Eventful."

Elvar smiled. "Better than growing a belly and watching over a spoiled jarl's daughter in Snakavik," she said.

Grend shrugged and pulled a face, as if he were unsure about that.

Elvar slapped his arm.

"You should have spoken to Gytha, while we were in Snakavik," Elvar said.

Grend's face changed, the humour and warmth evaporating, his jaw a tight line.

"It would only have caused pain. To stir the embers of a hearth fire that cannot blaze."

"It *could* blaze," Elvar said. "Gytha could join us." She looked at him, saw that settle into his thoughts. A ripple of hope flickered across his features followed by pain, a pinching of his eyes.

"She would not come. She made an oath to your father."

"You never asked her. She would do it for you."

He let out a long, exhaled breath.

"And then I would be the cause of her oath-breaking." A muscle twitched in his jaw.

"You are a stubborn mule," Elvar said. "Life is for the living, happiness for the taking." An image of Biórr's face appeared in her thought-cage. It was not the first time she had thought of him during the journey into the north, since he had kissed her.

Grend shook his head.

Footsteps sounded behind them and Agnar joined them, Uspa and Kráka with him.

"It is a sight, and no denying," Agnar said, a grin on his face as he looked out over the vaesen pit.

The Battle-Grim had made camp on a small hillock fifty or sixty paces away from the pit's edge. They had arrived a short while ago, just before nightfall, or, more accurately, twilight, because as they approached the summer solstice the darkness of night had faded into a long, extended and mist-like twilight. Uspa had strode to the brink of the vaesen pit and then prowled along its edge, the whole of the Battle-Grim following her. Elvar had been about ready to drop with exhaustion when Uspa had declared they were at the right place, and then all had set about making camp, much to Agnar's frustration. He had wanted to cross over to the other side, but Uspa had said that it was impossible, and that they would have to wait for the right time.

For today.

"We must find the bridge and move on," Agnar said, staring across the vaesen pit and scanning the northern horizon. Elvar stared, too, wondering where the famed bridge was. She could see no sign of it, only molten fire and smoke.

"And where is Oskutreð?" Agnar murmured. "It is supposed to be the greatest of all trees, its boughs holding up the sky. Surely we should be able to see it?"

"Much was destroyed on the *Guðfalla*," Uspa said. "Do not expect it to appear as it does in the tales." She pointed at a series of rolling hills to the east of Eldrafell. "Dark-of-Moon Hills," she said. "We are close."

"We must find the Isbrún Bridge and move on, then," Agnar repeated, turning and looking back, to the south. Elvar followed his gaze but could see nothing but blue skies and in the distance the white glare of sun on snow. She squinted. Was that something, on the edge of her vision? A smudge of movement on the horizon?

They had travelled north with surprisingly little opposition from vaesen, considering that the vaesen prowled the plains north of the Boneback Mountains with far more boldness than they trod the lands to the south. Fewer humankind lived on this side of the mountains, and those who did dwelled in isolated, stockaded steadings, rune-marked and defended by stout-hearted men and women. A day ago, they had come across the carcasses of an entire herd of elk in the snow, over fifty animals laying in the blood-spattered snow, strips of flesh and fur frozen and ragged among the bones.

It was difficult to tell what had killed them, as they had been visited and gnawed upon by all kind of predators and carrion-feeders, including tennúr who had stripped the skulls of all their teeth. But to trap and bring fifty elk down, that required a fearsome amount of vaesen, and not just a feat of strength, but of cunning as well.

"Have you found the elk-slayers with your keen eyes?" Kráka asked Agnar.

"What are they? Wights, skraelings, Huldra-folk?" Elvar asked, that familiar tremor in her gut, in her blood, where she longed to prove her worth, to earn her battle-fame. To prove her father wrong.

"Ach, it might be nothing," Agnar said, blinking and looking away, rubbing his eyes from the snow-glare. "Either way, whether it is something or nothing, we need to be moving on."

"Today is the day," Uspa said, looking up at the sky. "It is *sólstöður*, the beginning of the long day, when night is banished from the sky for thirty days."

"Good," Agnar said, laughing and clapping his hands. "Let's be on with it, then."

Elvar stood in silence, Grend one side of her, Biórr the other. The Battle-Grim were lined together on the slope of the hill they had camped upon, silent and grim in the light of the rising sun, all of them looking north at the vaesen pit and what lay beyond. One of the pack ponies stamped its feet and whickered.

Uspa stepped forwards and walked the twenty paces to the black granite boulder Elvar had stood beside earlier. The Seiðr-witch drew a seax at her belt and sliced it across the heel of her palm, blood welling. She made a fist, then opened her hand and touched her bloody fingertips to the black boulder, slowly pressing her palm upon it.

"*Isbrú, opinberaðu þig, blóð guðanna skipar þér,*" Uspa chanted. Her blood gathered in cracks in the rock, trickling down to the ground. A tremor passed through the boulder, as if it were breathing, and then the imprint of a hand appeared, huge, dwarfing Uspa's. Elvar blinked and stared harder.

No, she thought. *Not a handprint, a pawprint.* Claws the length of Elvar's seax were carved into the gloss-black rock.

A wolf or bear print. Is that the mark of Ulfrir, or Berser? The mark of a god? She felt a flutter of excitement and fear in the pit of her belly.

"*Isbrú, opinberaðu þig, blóð guðanna skipar þér,*" Uspa called out again, stepping away from the boulder and walking towards the vaesen pit, five paces from its edge, four, three, two, until it looked as if she would step over the edge and plummet to her death.

"No," Agnar cried out.

And Uspa stepped over the chasm's edge into thin air.

Gasps and shouts came from among the Battle-Grim, Agnar stumbling forwards.

Uspa's foot came down on something solid.

The air before Uspa shimmered, like a heat haze, but filled with flickering colours, as if the *guðljós* lights that Elvar had seen shimmering in the night sky had fallen to the earth. They formed into a shape, wide and long, a writhing, twisting bridge that arced over the vaesen pit to the land beyond.

"Behold, the Isbrún Bridge," Uspa called out as she turned and looked back at the Battle-Grim.

Elvar felt a smile split her lips, excitement a tremor in her bones. The saga-tales were coming to life, and she was a part of it.

"Ha," Agnar shouted, punching his fist into the air and laughing, jumping on the spot.

"Battle-Grim, there lies the bridge to Oskutreð. The last feet to tread upon it belonged to the gods," Agnar cried out, grinning at them all, and a cheer rang out from them, feet stamping, spear butts thumping on the ground, Elvar joining her voice with theirs.

A sensation in Elvar's feet, a vibration through her boots. She frowned, looked down and saw that the ground of the slope she was standing upon was shuddering, a tremor in the grass, the soil vibrating. Her weight shifted and she stepped back, frowning.

Something moved in the earth where she had been standing. A shape appeared, like a handful of pale, pink wyrms, glistening and writhing.

No, not wyrms. Fingers. Or claws.

A hand thrust out of the ground, small as a child's, but the fingers were long, thin and sharp, then another hand reached out, a face appearing, fragile and sharp-featured: a narrow line of a nose and chin, hairless with large, dark eyes. It hauled itself out of the ground, standing as tall as her knee. Ink-dark veins threaded pale-pink skin, wings on its back shaking, a cloud of soil in the air. It looked up at Elvar and opened its mouth wide, revealing two rows of teeth, the outer one sharp, the inner row flat, like grindstones, and it hissed at her.

A tennúr!

All along the slope the ground was trembling and shifting, more of the small creatures appearing. Thirty, forty, fifty of them, more than Elvar could count, and more still clawing their way from the ground. It was as if the hillock they had camped upon were some huge nest. Their wings snapped out behind them, soil spraying in small clouds, and they were leaping into the air, hurling themselves at the Battle-Grim. Shouts of shock and warning rippled along the line of warriors. Elvar staggered away as the tennúr that had emerged at her feet flew at her, claws reaching, jaws gaping wide. She fumbled for her sword, trying to shrug her shield off her back and into her fist. Sharp claws raked her face and she cried out, her sword half out of its scabbard. The tennúr's claws hooked into her cheeks and it pulled itself on to her, jaws gaping wide, its teeth far too close.

Elvar shook her head, her sword clearing her scabbard, then she stumbled and fell backwards. The tennúr still clung to her; its jaws lunged forwards.

A shower of blood and bone exploded over Elvar's face, the tennúr abruptly gone, Grend standing over her with his axe. Elvar lay on the ground, staring up at him, then there was movement beneath her and small hands were clawing out of the ground to reach around one leg, more movement around her arm. She thrashed and heaved but could not pull herself free. Grend's axe rose and fell, rose and fell, tennúr screeching, more blood like a mist in the air and Elvar was free, lurching to her feet, Grend chopping at another tennúr in the air as it flitted down upon Elvar, wings buzzing. She realised that Grend had two tennúr clawing their way up his legs, claws raking bloody grooves through his breeches, and that he was ignoring them to defend her. She stabbed one through the back and skewered it. The creature shrieked and flailed, letting go of Grend's leg, and she threw it spinning from her blade to slam into another tennúr in the air, both of them crashing to the ground.

More tennúr were on Grend, one hanging on to his back, jaws opening wide and crunching down on his shoulder, the sound of mail grating on teeth. Elvar stabbed it through one eye and it fell away, loose-limbed.

Elvar had her shield in her fist, now, and she punched the boss into a tennúr as it flew at her, sending it spiralling away. Grend grunted, more tennúr swarming around him. Blood flowed from wounds on his legs, claw marks on his neck and chin, and sheeted down his face from a wound on his scalp. Elvar stabbed and chopped at the creatures upon him, a red-blood harvest. When he was clear they moved back to back, shields raised, sword and axe slashing and stabbing against the swirling blizzard of wings and teeth and claws, guarding each other. Elvar wished she had not left her spear and helm strapped to one of the pack ponies.

Agnar was bellowing, battle-cries or orders, Elvar was not quite sure. She glimpsed warriors around her running to him, their shields slamming together, forming a small circle, spears and swords stabbing out. The shield wall began to move towards the Isbrún Bridge. A horse screamed, reared and collapsed, swamped with tennúr. A woman on the ground, Sólín, Elvar thought, was rolling in the heaving grass and soil, fighting a trio of tennúr as they tried to prise her jaws apart and rip her teeth from her gums.

We need to move, to join Agnar's shield wall.

There was a grunt from Grend, and Elvar felt his weight shift from her back, falling away. She turned and saw a tennúr perched on Grend's shoulder, a gloss-black stone in its hands, red and dripping. Grend lay sprawled upon the ground, the black hair on the back of his head matted with blood, the tennúr dragging at his head, trying to get long-clawed fingers into his mouth.

Grend, the only constant in her life, the man who had given her his oath and never broken it, the man who had sacrificed everything to protect her.

Elvar screamed, fury and fear mingled, and chopped at the tennúr with the rock, sending its head spinning through the air. She stepped over Grend's motionless body, shield raised, sword stabbing and hacking as tennúr tried to fall upon him.

She was the only one standing on the slope. Agnar and his shield wall were halfway to the bridge, and further away Sighvat, Kráka, Huld and the *Hundur*-thrall were dragging the surviving ponies in a half-circle away from the hillock and the swarming tennúr.

A spark of fear rose in her belly at being left with these vermin. To have her teeth and eyes ripped out. To be so close to Oskutreð and to fail.

"AGNAR!" Elvar bellowed, and she saw the shield wall ripple to a halt in its passage towards the bridge. She glimpsed Agnar's face looking over a shield rim at her. And then he was shouting, the words lost in the din of shrieking tennúr, but the shield wall started to move back towards her. She felt a flare of hope in her belly.

Many of the tennúr saw the shield wall moving too, and flew into a frenzy, more and more of them hurling themselves at Elvar until she could see nothing but wings and teeth and claws. She felt blows raking her, hot fire as claws scratched rents in her flesh, her mail grating, her sword and shield red and battered, arms leaden, muscles burning. Weakness seeped through her body.

From blood loss, dimly she realised, knowing that she could not stay on her feet much longer.

And then tennúr were shrieking and wailing, falling around her, wings and arms limp. A figure appeared through the curtain of wings and bodies, a man, wielding a spear with *Berserkir* speed, stabbing and slicing in great arcs. A gap opened among the tennúr and Elvar saw him: Biórr, his lips drawn back in a snarl, as he waded through the flying creatures, using his spear and shield to carve and force his way into the maelstrom of vaesen. He saw Elvar and grinned, then looked down at Grend.

The sight of Biórr gave Elvar a burst of new strength and she raised her shield, stabbed and hacked and slashed. Biórr reached her and they stood over Grend and fought until a gap opened around them, the tennúr retreating, hovering, staring at Elvar with malice and hunger in their eyes. Biórr used the respite to throw his shield across his back and squat, pulling Grend up with a grunt and heaving the big man on to his shoulders, then he stood.

The tennúr swarmed back upon them, but Elvar raised her shield and forged a path through them, shielding Biórr and Grend as best she could. She tripped over something, managed to stay on her feet and saw a bloodied corpse on the ground, unrecognisable as tennúr shredded its flesh, fighting over teeth as they were ripped from a lacerated mouth. Shouts and yells filtered through to her, and then the boiling storm of vaesen were thinning and she saw shields, a wall of them marching towards her. She broke into more open ground as she left the slope, the land levelling, tennúr still buzzing around her, but glimpses of the sky among them. She saw Sólín rolling on the ground, trying to hold a tennúr with one hand, her seax in her other fist, stabbing at the creature. Elvar swerved and sliced, hacking into the tennúr's shoulder. It squeaked and fell away. Elvar grabbed Sólín's wrist and hauled the grey-haired warrior to her feet. Agnar's voice bellowed and she saw his face among the shield wall. A gap opened in the shields, Elvar pushing Sólín on, through the gap and falling back to cover Biórr. After a few more heartbeats Biórr stumbled and staggered into the Battle-Grim, Grend across his shoulders, Elvar behind him. Shields snapped tight, protecting them, and then the shield wall was moving, away from the hillock and towards the Isbrún Bridge.

Elvar heard a buzzing above her, a sharp pain in her ear and scalp, as a tennúr fell upon her head, fingers clawing into her and entwining in her braided hair. Agnar grabbed the creature by the throat, its jaws snapping, and ripped it off Elvar, throwing it to the ground where it was stamped and trampled upon. The shield wall moved on, the buzz of tennúr falling away, and Elvar shoved her way to Biórr's side, her hand going to Grend's throat, checking for a pulse.

She sighed with relief as she found it, slow and rhythmic.

"My thanks," she said, squeezing Biórr's arm. He gave a half-smile, grunting under the weight of Grend.

Elvar glanced back over her shoulder as the shield wall continued its march and saw a cloud of the vaesen hovering and whirling above the hillock, clusters of them on the ground where they crawled and buzzed thick as ants over what must be corpses: one pony and a handful of warriors.

And then the ground changed beneath Elvar's feet, from grass and soil to something solid as rock. Elvar looked down and saw that she was upon the Isbrún Bridge. Agnar hissed a breath in and the shield wall opened up, warriors stuttering to a stop and staring.

The bridge was wide enough for fifty warriors to walk abreast, and made of ice, thick and solid, a crunch and crackle under Elvar's feet, like walking on frost-touched grass. Light shimmered within the ice, captured and fractured from the molten river that Elvar could see through the bridge, bubbling far below.

How does the ice not melt?

"This is not the place to stop," Uspa called out, standing at the arch of the bridge. Behind her lay land that had not been seen or trodden upon by humankind for three hundred years.

"Ha, the Seiðr-witch speaks truth," Agnar called out. "Onwards," he bellowed, "to Oskutreð."

CHAPTER THIRTY-NINE

VARG

Varg sat with his back to a tree and chewed on a strip of hard mutton. His jaw was aching and he was certain it would be easier to chew through the leather sole of his turn-shoes. It was late in the night, or at least Varg thought it was. *Sólstöður* had begun, the month of day, where night was banished for thirty days. It was not full light, twilight hovering in the air like motes of dust, their camp set in a small glade among pinewoods. Faintly Varg could see the line of the moon, pale in a pale sky. But his body told him it was night and he pulled his cloak tighter about him.

He sat alone. Torvik was on guard duty, as were Svik and Røkia, all of them scattered through the woodland. Glornir sat with Vol, his long-axe cradled on his lap as he ran a whetstone along its edge. Einar Half-Troll was sitting with Sulich, grumbling about the hole in his belly that needed filling. Sulich was shaving the stubble from his head with his seax.

"A hot meal is all I can think of," Einar muttered.

"No fire," Glornir said through the scrape and rasp of his whetstone, not raising his eyes from his axe blade.

They all knew the rule by now, and the sense of it, but chewing on strips of cold hard mutton did not help to ease the absence of hot food.

Skalk sat nearby, Olvir and Yrsa beside him. The two warriors spoke in hushed voices, a strain etched upon Olvir's face that had not left him since they had found the mutilated bodies hanging in the pine trees. Skalk's head was bowed, his face a shadow. Varg still felt unsettled by those bodies and had dreamed of them each night since then, skinned carcasses swaying, ropes creaking. He thought of his conversation with Skalk before they had found the bodies, of how Skalk could perform an *akáll*, if Varg were prepared to leave the Bloodsworn and swear an oath to the Galdurman. Without thinking his hand strayed to the pouch on his belt and he thought of Frøya, his dead sister, murdered. He did not know where her body was or who had killed her. It gnawed at his soul like a rat chewing marrow from a bone.

Footsteps sounded, and Torvik appeared through the trees, saw Varg and strode to him, smiling as he sat beside him.

Varg offered him a strip of mutton.

"What is it you have in that pouch?" Torvik asked him, taking the mutton.

Varg pulled his hand away as if he'd been caught stealing.

"You protect it like it was filled with gold," Torvik said. The young man shrugged. "It is your business, but if I can help you, I would."

Varg blew out a long, tremulous breath. Then he reached back to the pouch, unhooked it and put his hand in, pulling out a lock of black hair.

"It is my sister's," Varg said. "I need it for the *akáll* which will show me who murdered her."

Torvik nodded. "I will help you," he said.

"Help with what?" Varg asked him, frowning.

"When Glornir grants you the *akáll*," Torvik said, "I will help you hunt your sister's killers. Edel tells me I have a good nose, that I will make a decent huntsman. I will help you find your sister's murderers, and help you kill them."

Varg just stared at Torvik. He opened his mouth to say something but found there was a pressure in his chest and a lump in his throat that words could not squeeze past. All his life he had been alone, Frøya his only companion, his only friend, the only one he had ever trusted. As he sat and stared at Torvik he knew that this lad before him meant what he said.

If Glornir ever deems me worthy, a voice in his thought-cage said.

Whether Glornir grants the akáll *or not, that does not change what Torvik has just offered*, he answered that voice.

He looked away and swiped a tear from his eye.

"My . . . thanks," Varg muttered.

It will be hard to leave these people. Torvik, Svik, Einar, even Røkia, he thought. *I have grown to . . . like them*. But after talking to Skalk he knew what he should do, for Frøya, to fulfil his oath.

Torvik shrugged and smiled.

"*Bannað jörð*," a voice called out and Varg turned to see that it was Skalk who had spoken. The Galdurman had raised his head and was staring at Vol. "Forbidden ground," Skalk said. "That was the rune carved into the corpses of my *drengrs*."

"It was," Vol agreed.

"What does it mean?" Skalk asked her.

Vol frowned. "A warning, to stay away," she said, then shrugged. "I don't know."

"It sounds like some gods-tainted warning to me," Skalk said. "I am a Galdurman, have studied the rune lore and Galdur-law all my life, have travelled all Vigrið and beyond, and bent the knee at a score of Galdur towers, and that was a rune I have never seen before. And yet you knew what it said. It is part of your Tainted Seiðr filth, yes?"

Glornir raised his eyes from sharpening his whetstone and fixed Skalk with a hard look.

"Do not threaten me," Skalk said with a wave of his hand. "I am no child or thrall to be cowed with a look or a reputation." His gaze shifted to Einar, whose brows were knotted like a thunderhead. "You want a fire for your porridge, Half-Troll?" Skalk said. He held his hand out. "*Eldur*," he breathed, and a spark ignited in his palm, a solitary flame crackling into existence.

Varg felt a chill slither through his veins. He had never seen Galdur-magic, and now that he had, he felt that he did not like it much. He could feel the power radiating from Skalk in waves, like heat from a fire.

Glornir looked from Skalk to the flame crackling in his hand.

"Put it out," he said.

"No fires," Einar muttered.

Skalk closed his hand into a fist, the flame stuttering and dying.

"Is this sacred ground, to you Tainted?" Skalk asked, eyes moving back to Vol.

She shrugged. "We are walking across Snaka's bones. I can feel them even now, like a song in the ground, deep beneath us. He made us, made the world; of course this is sacred ground. But that is no reason to string and gut a warband of *drengrs*."

Varg saw Olvir shift, his mouth twisting.

"But the rune did not say *sacred*. It said *forbidden*," Vol said.

"Sometimes the two walk hand in hand," Skalk mused. "Then why is this forbidden ground?" Skalk asked again.

"I do not know," Vol said.

"No doubt we shall find that out, when we find whatever did that to your warriors," Glornir said.

A silence settled between them.

"What is the difference between a Galdurman and a Seiðr-witch?" Varg asked into that silence. The thought had formed in his thought-cage and he had not realised he asked it out loud.

Skalk turned his gaze on to Varg, staring at him as if he had just uttered the greatest insult.

"I have worked on a farm my whole life," Varg said with a shrug. "Magic is magic to me, regardless of who performs it."

"Galdur-magic is taught by the wise, by scholars, to the worthy. *Years* of learning, of truth-seeking. It is honour and skill and patience. But Seiðr-magic, it is a pollution in the Tainted's blood. A glimmer of old Snaka in their veins, the bloated god. It is not *earned*, like my power." Skalk shook his head. "There is no honour in it, no skill. It is just *in them*."

"And why is that so bad?" Varg said.

Yrsa snorted, giving a twist of her lips, and Skalk just stared, speechless for long moments. He sat up straighter. "The gods almost destroyed this earth," he said, as if speaking to a child. "Almost destroyed us, mankind. And their offspring are no better. They fought in that war too."

"So did humankind," Sulich said, not breaking the scrape of his seax across his head.

"They were forced, little different than thralls," Skalk said. "But the Tainted, they chose to fight, wanted to fight, just as their cursed parents did." He stared at Vol as he spoke. "Cursed blood flows in them. That is why when mankind rose from the ashes of the *Guðfalla* they swore to hunt out any of the gods who survived the gods-fall, and to hunt out their seed, their mingling with humankind. It was only when Ulfrir's chain was found that we began to thrall the Tainted, rather than execute them."

"Ulfrir's chain?" Varg asked. Tales had been told at Kolskegg's farm, round the fire pit and food table, but from an early age he and Frøya had learned it was best to keep apart from the others. He only knew some of the tales.

"Ulfrir the wolf-god was chained on the last day," Yrsa said. "A rune-wrought chain, filled with Seiðr-magic by Lik-Rifa, the dragon, Ulfrir's sister. It bound him tight and cast him down, and then Lik-Rifa's followers swarmed upon him and slew him with many wounds."

"Aye, I have heard that tale," Varg said.

"And when Snaka was slain and fell, he broke the world," Yrsa said. "The chain was broken, links and shards hurled in a thousand different directions."

"That is right," Skalk agreed, taking up the tale again. "And many years later, as humankind began to spread through the world again, we found some of those links, buried in the ground, half-submerged in rivers or fjords, and we used Galdur-magic to break them down, to mix them with iron and forge the thrall-collars. Wherever they were found, that is where the first fortresses grew. Darl, Snakavik, Svelgarth in the east. That thrall-collar around Vol's neck, there is a remnant of Ulfrir's chain forged into it. That is how she is controlled. The same with Queen Helka's *Úlfhéðnar*, and with Jarl Störr's *Berserkir*. And the Galdur-tongue is used to command them. Glornir will have been taught the words of power when he bought that collar."

"This is true." Glornir nodded his agreement.

"I have always thought it a strange thing, to judge a man or woman by their parentage," Sulich said, stopping the shaving of his head and sheathing his seax. "Far better to judge them on their deeds, to my mind."

Skalk's eyes snapped from Vol to Sulich.

"A strange thing for an escaped murderer to say," Skalk said. "Am I to judge you on your deeds?"

Sulich looked at him, stood and strode towards Skalk.

"I am no murderer," he said, his voice cold and hard.

Olvir and Yrsa stood, their hands hovering over their sword hilts.

"That is not what Prince Jaromir said," Skalk answered, still sitting, calm and relaxed.

Sulich stood a few paces from him, Olvir and Yrsa ready.

"I am no murderer," he repeated.

Skalk shrugged. "A matter we shall resolve, when this is done and we are back in Darl."

"Sulich," Glornir said. "Sit down."

The shaven-haired warrior turned and looked at Glornir, then strode back to Einar.

Varg felt the hairs on his arms prickling. He knew that violence had been a hair's breadth away.

They heard the sound of footsteps in the trees and all of them looked, hands reaching for weapons, an expression of the tension bubbling within the camp.

Svik walked out of the woods and stopped.

"What?" he said, looking around.

CHAPTER FORTY

ORKA

Orka walked along a dirt track, leading her horse by the reins, a solidly built skewbald gelding called Trúr. Mord and Lif walked either side of her with their own mounts, Mord with his injured arm bound from the wound Skefil had given him. Blood seeped into a linen bandage and he held the arm close to his body. The sun was climbing into the sky, the fresh chill of dawn still lingering. Wisps of mist curled upon the stream they were following, the fortress and town of Darl behind them.

They were travelling back to the farm they were lodging at, which lay nestled in the curl of a valley up ahead.

"What now, then?" Lif asked Orka. He had been mostly silent since the questioning and killing of Skefil.

"We think," Orka said. "About our choices, what is possible, what is not, and then we come up with a deep-cunning plan that will put sharp steel into Guðvarr and Jarl Sigrún, and see your father avenged."

In truth all that Orka wanted to do was pack some provisions in a bag, leave Mord and Lif behind and ride north after Drekr. But she owed these brothers a blood-debt and that was weighing on her soul. She knew that she should help them achieve their vengeance, especially while Drekr was no longer in Darl to kill but Guðvarr and Jarl Sigrún were, so it made sense in her thought-cage to put them in the ground first, before she went in pursuit of Drekr.

But the thought of Breca was like a splinter in her heart. His face haunted her; his voice whispered in her ear. Her son: taken, scared, hurt. It set a wolf snarling in her blood.

"What is wrong?" Mord asked her.

"What?" Orka said.

"You were growling, and your face was twitching."

Orka blew out a long breath.

I will find you, Breca, I swear it, she thought. Every moment away from him clawed at her.

But I owe these two brothers.

As long as we can do it soon. I must be away from here soon.

"We must kill Guðvarr and Sigrún, and quickly," Orka said.

"Aye, I know that part," Lif said. "It is the *how* that I am wondering about."

Orka looked back over her shoulder. Darl lay behind them, the fortress silhouetted on the hill with the great eagle-wings spread wide, catching the risen sun and blazing golden, the River Drammur coiling about the town's feet like a sleeping serpent. Meadows and rolling hills lay between the fortress and the farm they were staying upon, the meadows filled with fields of ripening barley and the hills dotted with herds of goats and sheep.

After throwing Skefil's corpse into the canal they had used what was left of the night to scout out the Eagle-fortress. It was frustratingly well guarded, with plentiful *drengrs* on the gates and patrolling the high timber walls that ringed Queen Helka's mead hall. They had also made their way to the docks and looked at Jarl Sigrún's *drakkar*, which was guarded by a handful of Sigrún's *drengrs*, but also under the protection of the harbour officials and their guards. An attack on Jarl Sigrún when she returned to her *drakkar* looked as unlikely to be successful as trying to infiltrate the fortress.

"I am thinking the best path will be to lure Guðvarr and Jarl Sigrún out of the fortress, rather than try and sneak into it," Orka said.

"And how would we do that?"

"When you want to catch a wolf or a fox, you bait a trap," Orka said.

"Bait? What bait?" Lif said.

"Me," Orka shrugged. "I slew Vafri, Helka's *Úlfhéðnar* thrall that she gifted to Sigrún, and I slew Sigrún's lover and left a scar on her face, so it is me that Sigrún and Helka most want to see in the ground. Anger blinds some people, makes them more likely to make mistakes. To rush. So, we find a busy place. You and Mord hidden in the press of a crowd. I sow some chaos and Jarl Sigrún and Guðvarr come to take their vengeance on me. That will be when you put steel in Guðvarr's belly, but first whisper a word in his ear, so he knows who his killer is, and why he's dying." She shrugged. "Then you slip away into the crowd."

"I like it," Mord said, nodding. "Let's do it." He had been surly since taking the wound from Skefil, his pride hurt, Orka thought. He had been keen to assault Helka's fortress, though he probably couldn't even climb the walls with his injured arm.

Pride and shame, she thought. *Both enemies of a long life. He needs some ice in his blood, to see more clearly.*

"Sounds like there are many ways for that plan to go wrong," Lif said. "Like, how will you get away?"

"All plans go wrong," Orka said with a shrug. "And when this one does, we will improvise."

"No hesitation," Mord said, looking at Orka.

"Exactly," Orka grunted.

They walked on, turning a corner in the dirt track and passing around a spur of land, the farm appearing in a valley below. The longhouse was built alongside a narrow river, barns and paddocks around it, a field of barley beyond. A gentle breeze lifted the blended smell of smoke, barley and pig-shite up out of the vale. The sound of geese squawking rose on the breeze.

Orka frowned, felt a tingling in her blood.

She stopped.

Mord and Lif carried on a few paces, their horses' hooves a rhythmic thud on the ground. They realised Orka had stopped and slowed to a standstill.

"What is it?" Lif said.

"Come on, my belly needs filling," Mord grumbled.

Orka frowned, sniffing.

They were a few hundred paces from the farm, and at a glance all seemed well. But Orka's skin prickled. The donkey wasn't braying, as he seemed to do from dawn until dusk, and there was no smoke rising from the green-turfed roof of the longhouse's smoke hole.

"Get on your horses," Orka said, slipping a foot into an iron stirrup and swinging herself up into her saddle, her spear gripped in one fist. She shifted her weight, settling on to Trúr's back. The horse whickered.

"Why?" Mord frowned.

"The plan has already gone wrong," Orka muttered.

Figures appeared in the farm courtyard: mounted figures. Lots of them. Ten, twelve, fifteen, more still hidden. The glint of weapons and *brynjas*. One of them rode to the farm's entrance, drew his sword and pointed at Orka and the brothers.

"It's Guðvarr," Lif said.

"Stay and fight, or flee and fight another day?" Orka asked them. Her blood was thrumming, the imminence of violence calling to her, dancing in her veins. But a distant part of her thought-cage whispered that the numbers were too great, that Mord and Lif would likely die. Part of her didn't care.

"Over a score of them," Lif said.

"Sigrún's *drengrs*, and some of Helka's, too," Orka said, seeing the glint of gold eagle-wings on cloak brooches. She looked at Mord and Lif and saw the gleam of vengeance bright in their eyes as they stared at Guðvarr, but also the hesitation that hovers like raven's wings over impending battle, when the possibility of death looks you in the eye. Fear can be ice or fire in the veins, freezing the body or setting a blaze within it.

Guðvarr had started to ride up the track towards them, Orka able to see his dripping, pointed nose, and close behind him rode Arild, the *drengr* who always seemed to accompany Guðvarr. She wore a *brynja* that gleamed in the sun, whereas Orka had only seen her in wool and leather before. The warriors that followed behind them were also clothed in mail with iron helms, all *drengrs* with sword skill and weapons craft.

Orka looked back to Mord and Lif, still standing, holding their horses by their reins, just staring. They wore wool and leather, armed with seaxes and axes, Mord with a fishing spear, no helms. And they were hesitating.

Orka made the decision for them.

"We ride," she said, dragging on her reins and touching Trúr's ribs with her heels. She saw Lif clamber into his saddle and Mord lingered a moment, his face twitching, then he was heaving himself on to his horse's back with a grimace of pain at his injured arm and the three of them were riding away, back along the track they'd been travelling on.

The sound of hooves came behind them, like rumbling thunder, and Guðvarr's squeaking voice. Orka rounded the spur that hid the farm from view, her gelding moving at a fast canter, Mord and Lif catching her up. Ahead Darl reared, the river massed with a forest of masts. Soon the farm track joined a road with a few people upon it: carts pulled by oxen, other travellers.

Going back to Darl is not a good idea. It would be like riding into the wolf's jaws, with Helka's drengrs *before us and Guðvarr and his crew behind us.*

A crossroad loomed ahead, straight on to Darl, south to the river, north to . . .

The Boneback Mountains.

They reared in the distance like jagged teeth, a gap in their profile marking where the Grimholt Pass lay.

Orka pulled on her reins and nudged with her leg and Trúr turned, heading north. Mord shouted after Orka, but the wind dragged the words away and Orka ignored them, seeing that he and his brother followed her. There were more shouts behind them as Guðvarr cleared the spur of land and saw them. He was only two hundred paces behind now, screeching and kicking his horse into a lathered gallop. *Drengrs* swarmed behind him.

Orka lifted her weight in her saddle and kicked Trúr on. He was a strong, big-boned gelding, built more for the plough or battle rather than speed, but he had a big heart and Orka could feel the joy in him at the gallop. Trúr's stride opened up and it felt to Orka like she was flying, wind whipping tears from her eyes as they sped across rolling meadows of heather and gorse.

This is what it must have felt like to be one of Orna's daughters, Orka thought, *to fly and rule the skies*, and she *whooped* with the joy of it. They rode on, the terrain changing about them as they moved away from the River Drammur. A gap widened between them and Guðvarr's crew, four hundred paces, five hundred, the *drengrs* riding more carefully than Orka and the two brothers. The land rose, hills swelling around them, covered in fern and heather and patches of woodland, dissected by a myriad of streams. The path narrowed, slopes rising, and Orka heard the sound of rushing water. Then a wooden bridge was before them, narrow, crossing over a ravine. Orka pulled on her reins, shifting her position, and Trúr slowed, moving from a gallop to a canter. She heard the thunder of hooves on timber as she crossed the bridge, Mord and Lif slowing, taking the bridge one at a time.

Orka looked down and saw steep-sided slopes and a white-foaming river perhaps forty or fifty paces below her. She reached the far side of the bridge and dragged on her reins, leaped from her saddle and ran to a lightning-blasted hawthorn tree. She swept her axe into her fist and chopped at wood, dry-splintering as branches snapped.

Mord and Lif reached the far side of the bridge and reined their horses in, Lif calling to Orka, Mord staring back over his shoulder. Hooves thundered, the sound of Guðvarr and his *drengrs* far closer than Orka wanted them to be.

Orka swept the splintered branches up into her arms, ran back to the bridge and threw them down on the timber, then crouched and took her tinder and kindling from a pouch on her belt, her striking iron. Sparks leaped, the kindling hissing into flame among the dry branches. Fire crackled, flames clawing, and the hawthorn branches burst into fire, the timber of the bridge beginning to blacken and smoke. Orka stood, looking between the new-kindled flames and the far side of the bridge. Guðvarr appeared around a bend in the slope. He saw Orka and the others and spurred his mount on. It was sweat-soaked and salt-streaked, foam flying from its mouth. Guðvarr yelled a victory cry, grinning as he looked at Orka, Mord and Lif. Then he saw the flames. They were spreading now, along the timber walkway and up the posts and rails. Black clouds of smoke billowed, obscuring Guðvarr and the *drengrs* from view. Hooves thudded on timber as Guðvarr attempted to cross, but timber creaked, weakened by the flames, followed by a splintering, cracking sound, and Guðvarr retreated. He sat on his horse and hurled insults across the bridge at them. A spear hissed from one of his *drengrs*, and it thumped into the ground close to Lif's mount.

"Take it," Orka told Lif as she climbed back into her saddle, leaned and patted her gelding's neck, then clicked him on.

"That's bought us some time," Orka said, looking east and west along the ravine as Mord and Lif rode up alongside her, Lif holding his new spear. The ravine curled into the distance, meaning Guðvarr and his *drengrs* would have to travel some distance to find another crossing point, and then travel back here to pick up their trail.

"Will they give up?" Lif asked.

"I hope not," Orka said.

Behind them, from beyond the flames and smoke they heard a frustrated, furious screech.

"Why not?" Lif asked.

"Because I want Guðvarr to follow us, so that you can kill him," she said.

"I like it," Mord said, a smile spreading across his face. He frowned. "Follow us where?"

"North, to chase my vengeance, as your vengeance chases us," she said, a cold smile touching her lips. "We are riding there. To the Boneback Mountains; to the Grimholt Pass."

To find Drekr and my son.

CHAPTER FORTY-ONE

VARG

Varg crawled up a slope of patchy, frost-hard grass and thin soil, the Bloodsworn all about him. Ahead Edel, Torvik and her scouts were all crouched behind a rock. Edel was whispering to Glornir as they peered over the slope's rim. The sun hovered over the peaks of the Boneback Mountains, but its touch had not yet reached the valley they were crawling through, shadows clinging to the valley floor, thick as mist.

The slope's rim was close and Varg shuffled for a space as the Bloodsworn spread along it, all looking down into the valley beyond. Crawling up a slope like a lizard was not so easy to do with a shield on your back, a weapons belt about your waist and a spear in your fist. Einar Half-Troll took up more space than a boulder on the slope's rim, but he looked back and beckoned to Varg, glowering at another Bloodsworn who was about to fill the space at Einar's right. Varg scrambled up the remaining distance and settled beside Einar, who smiled at Varg and put a big finger to his lips. Einar had seemed to take a liking to him, ever since the oar-dance and Varg's apology. He had even offered to share his loaf of bread at their last meal. Varg had gratefully accepted: anything was better than leather-hard mutton.

A valley opened up, steep-sloped, running north to south, with what looked like a well-used track cutting away to the east. A waterfall filled the northern edge of the valley, cascading down from a cliff face that Varg had to twist his head to see. A permanent cloud of mist swirled and churned at the waterfall's foot, a pool spreading wide and breaking off into a handful of channels.

Three days had passed since Edel had found the corpses hanging from the trees, and with every step Varg had felt a mounting tension. There had been a war going on in his thought-cage about whether to talk to Skalk again about the conduction of an *akáll*, or whether he should wait for Glornir's approval. Seeing Skalk's conjuring of fire in his fist had only added to his confusion. It was only a single flame, but to Varg it had chilled his blood. But as they had travelled deeper into the Boneback Mountains that conflict had faded in his mind, overwhelmed by a growing sensation: a trembling in his blood. It was almost as if he could smell or sense a growing danger, like drawing closer to a rotting corpse.

The valley's floor was in twilight shadow, but as Varg lay there the sun rose higher and light slid down the slopes like liquid gold, and the darkness retreated before it. The streams in the valley burst into glittering, blinding light. Varg heard Edel speaking in hushed tones to Glornir and Vol. Edel's two wolfhounds were crouched, ears pricked forwards. One was growling. Edel pointed.

Varg saw movement: a figure appearing deep in the valley close to the waterfall. Even from this height Varg could tell that it was big. Muscled and antlered, with thick tusks jutting from its lower jaw, it emerged from a stand of pine trees and walked to the pool.

"What *is* that?" Varg hissed.

"Troll," Einar said in his rumbling whisper.

The troll stopped at the pool's edge and looked around, scanning the valley's sides. It seemed to sniff the air and Varg felt a moment of fear, that they would be seen or that somehow this creature would pick up their scent. Then it was looking back to the pine trees and gesturing. A line of people emerged from the treeline, smaller than the troll. They were humans, and Varg saw the glint of sunlight on iron, chains about their necks and ankles, binding them to each other. Maybe thirty or forty people filed out from the trees to the pool, all with buckets in their hands. More figures appeared, a few manlike in shape, with spears in their hands, the glint of sunlight on mail. Others were clearly not human: thick-muscled and elongated, crouched and stooped, walking upright but bent over, using knuckles on unnaturally long arms. Weapons hung from baldrics slung across their shoulders.

"Skraelings, before you ask," Svik said from Varg's other side.

The thralls kneeled at the poolside and filled their buckets, and then the troll was making a snorting, barking sound and they were standing and moving back towards the treeline. In a dozen heartbeats they were gone, the troll, warriors and skraelings all following after, and a moment later the valley was empty, as if they had never been there.

Echoed commands rippled along the line of Bloodsworn, Glornir summoning his captains, and Svik scrambled away, keeping his head below the ridgeline and across the slope to Glornir. Røkia went, as well, along with Sulich. Glornir spoke to them, gestured into the valley a dozen times, and then Svik was scrambling back. Torvik came with him.

"Half-Troll, No-Sense, Hammer-Hand, you're with me," Svik said, "and you, Halja Flat-Nose, and you, Vali Horse-Breath," he said to a woman and man, sister and brother, both of them quiet and stern-faced. And then Svik was scuttling along the slope below the ridgeline, moving south towards a stand of pine that crested the slope. Varg looked at the others, Torvik grinning at him, and then they were all moving, following Svik. The rest of the Bloodsworn were breaking up into smaller groups, each one led by one of Glornir's captains, and accompanied by one of Edel's scouts. Varg glimpsed Skalk and his two guards staying close to Glornir, and then Svik was leading them into the stand of pine that crowned the edge and over the other side. The slope was steep and soon they had to break from the cover of the trees. Torvik took the lead, choosing a winding path down the slope, using boulders and bushes for cover. Soil and stone shifted beneath Varg's feet, but he was sure-footed and kept up easily with Torvik. Einar slipped once, his huge bulk starting a small landslide of soil, but Svik steadied him and then the ground was levelling, and they were on the valley floor.

Torvik allowed them a moment to gather and then he was moving on, across the valley floor, splashing through a shallow stream and then up the far bank, into the cover of more pine woodland. They veered north, following the line of the valley, towards the waterfall. The din of its cascading waters grew, until Varg could see the shimmer of salmon-scales in the pool. They were close enough now to see a path through the trees that the troll and thralls had taken. Torvik turned eastward and led them higher up the valley slope, shadowing the path, always keeping it in view. They moved silently and as fast as wolves, the ground thick with pine needles that soaked up the sound of their footfall. Varg thought he saw the flitting shadows of movement on the far side of the path, shadows among the trees. He picked up his pace and drew level with Torvik, touched his shoulder and pointed.

"They're Bloodsworn," Torvik whispered after a frozen moment of silence, and then they were moving on.

Varg became aware of a change around him, almost like a vibration in the air, in the ground. He looked down; he half expected to see the carpet of pine needles they were crossing to be shaking, but all was still. It grew as they moved on, a pressure all around, like a gathering storm, a tingling in his blood.

Torvik stopped, held a fist up and they gathered around him.

The path they were following spilled into an open glade, the ground trampled to mud, a cliff face at its far end. There was an arched entrance in the cliff, tall and wide, the flicker of torchlight within it like pinpricks. People were walking in and out of the entrance, their bodies skeletal, clothes ragged, a constant stream of thralls in iron collars leading ponies harnessed to carts, and the carts were full of rubble. They filed north out of the tunnel entrance and led the ponies and carts to the far edge of the glade, where there was a newly made mountain of boulders and rubble. Here they unloaded their carts and then led them back into the tunnel entrance, swallowed by the darkness as if they were walking willingly into a sleeping serpent's mouth.

Torvik pointed at different spots in the glade, and Varg saw other figures: warriors with spears, and a few of the skraelings. Varg did not like the look of them, clothed in thick tunics like a warrior, with weapons on their belts, though they looked crude and heavy, but their arms were long and knotted with striated muscle, their necks thick, and even from this distance something seemed . . . wrong, with their faces.

I have lived on a farm my whole life, he thought. *The worst I have seen of vaesen is a mischievous fetch who cursed the milk one yuletide, and a knot of newly hatched serpents in the river, and they were not much bigger than eels.*

The troll was nowhere to be seen, though the cave entrance was more than large enough for him to have entered the tunnel.

"Good job, lad," Svik said to Torvik, patting his shoulder. "I'll take things from here." He stabbed his spear butt into the ground and ran his fingers through his red beard, pulling out knots, and twirled his moustaches and began braiding them.

"What are you doing?" Varg whispered.

"Getting ready," Svik said.

"For what?" Varg said.

"The signal. There's going to be a scrap, of course. Blood will be spilled, and I want to look my best for battle. It's important." He looked Varg up and down. "I suggest you make yourself ready." Svik grinned. "Time for us to earn our silver and battle-fame."

He finished tidying his beard, then unbuckled his helm from his belt and tugged it on to his head, shrugged his shield from his back, settled his hand into the grip and let it hang at his side, before pulling his spear out of the soft earth.

Around him the others were all doing the same, Halja and Vali setting their shields against a tree, buckling on helms, taking leather covers from spearheads, checking the draw of seax and sword from their scabbards. When they were satisfied, they gripped their shields and stood beside Svik. Jökul Hammer-Hand squatted, scooping up a handful of pine needles and soil, rubbed it between his palms and let it filter through his fingers. Then he stood, pulled his helm on tight and slipped a hammer from a hoop in his belt, the black-iron head pitted and stained, the haft longer than a normal hammer's, more like an axe. He shrugged his shield from his back and stood, his brows heavy and dour, glowering down at the skraelings in the glade.

Einar's shield was as big as a table. He pulled it from his back and hefted it, then drew an axe from his belt, the blade hooked and bearded.

Torvik loosened his seax in its scabbard and lifted his shield from his back. Stood with shield and spear ready.

Varg blinked and realised he should be doing the same. He unbuckled his helm from his belt and pulled it over the nålbinding cap he was wearing, tugged the buckle tight under his chin. Next he checked the draw of his seax, axe and cleaver, all of them hanging on his weapons belt, letting them slip back into place. Then he took the leather cover from his spear blade, threading it through his belt, and finally he shrugged his shield from his back and gripped the wooden handle, his fist and knuckles fitting into the space of the iron boss.

He looked up, feeling his heart beating hard in his chest, and saw Svik looking at him.

"Brothers, sisters, are we ready?" Svik said to them, all humour gone from him. "Remember, we are Bloodsworn, bound to one another. Stand or fall, we are sworn to each other. That is our strength."

Nods, grunts.

Svik looked at Varg and Torvik. "Well, not you two, but if you survive this . . ." He shrugged and grinned.

That's comforting, Varg thought. He felt the strong urge to empty his bladder.

"With me," Svik said, and led them through the trees, down the slope and closer to the glade and cave entrance. He stopped before the trees thinned, still on the slope, maybe forty or fifty paces to level ground and the muddy glade. Svik rested his shield on the ground and kneeled behind it, all the others settling around him, except for Einar, who stayed standing. They all wore *brynjas*, except for Varg and Torvik. Jökul wore a pitted leather apron over his coat of mail.

Varg looked into the glade over his shield rim. The thrumming in his blood was stronger here, pulsing in his bones like the beat of a drum. And at the same time, fear slithered through his belly, turning his legs weak, making his mouth dry. He was looking at vaesen and warriors, all with sharp iron or steel on their belts or in their fists. And he was going to fight them.

He swallowed, no spit in his mouth, wanted to stand and move, a voice in his thought-cage whispering to him.

Just walk away. How can you fulfil your oath to Frøya if you are dead? Who are these people to you? You should wait until battle is joined, and then just slip away.

Instead he just stood there, waiting for death's wings to settle over the glade.

There was a movement at the edge of the glade, and Glornir stepped out into the sunlight.

"Move," Svik said, his voice a growl, rising and striding down the rest of the slope. They all followed, Einar and Jökul moving to the wings, Torvik, Halja and Vali immediately behind Svik. Varg stood, hovered a moment, hefted his shield and then he was following them.

CHAPTER FORTY-TWO

ELVAR

Elvar undid knots in the walrus-rope that she had used to strap Grend to the back of an empty cart, her fingers numb and swollen. She swore and cursed as she struggled with a knot, eventually tugging it free.

"When you're ready, girl," Sighvat grunted and together they slipped Grend from the cart's back, Elvar taking the weight of Grend's ankles and Sighvat gripping the unconscious warrior under the shoulders. Together they placed him upon a woollen cloak that Elvar had laid on the ground, and Elvar checked his wounds.

After they had crossed the Isbrún Bridge they had stopped to tend to injuries and take a tally of the wounded and their losses. One wagon and two ponies had been lost, loaded with bundled spears and an assortment of barrels of ale and of horsemeat and whey. Three of the Battle-Grim had fallen on the hillock to the tennúr swarm.

Almost everyone was injured, from a few scratches to gaping wounds torn by the vaesen's claws. All had needed to clean their wounds with boiled water and vinegar; some were stitched, and poultices of yarrow and honey were applied, draped in moss and wrapped in linen bandages. Agnar had ordered a fire to be lit as some wounds had needed to be cauterised.

"My thanks, Sighvat," Elvar said as she kneeled beside Grend. The big man stood and looked at Grend, then patted her shoulder, almost sending her sprawling, and walked away.

Fresh blood had seeped into the bandage around Grend's head. He was scratched and gouged across his legs and face, but the worst injury was the blow to the back of his head that a tennúr had dealt him with a lump of black rock. Uspa had come to Elvar's aid when they had stopped after crossing the bridge. Elvar had been trying to clean the wound and examine how bad it was. Tears had been blurring her eyes. The Seiðr-witch cut away Grend's blood-matted hair with a sharp knife, then helped Elvar wash the area clean. All the while Elvar had felt as if a fist of fear was clenched in her belly, twisting her innards and making her movements too quick and jolting. The feeling intensified as Uspa probed Grend's skull with her fingertips.

"His skull is not broken," Uspa had pronounced, after what felt like a lifetime.

Elvar had sagged with relief.

Uspa helped her to finish cleaning the wound, then to apply a poultice of herbs and moss and bind it with a bandage.

"When he wakes up, he will need to drink some peppermint and valerian," Uspa had said as she'd left to tend the wounds of other injured Battle-Grim.

Grend had remained unconscious through the whole process, and so when Agnar had shouted for all to make ready and move out, Grend had been strapped within an empty cart.

Then they had moved out, Uspa leading them into an untouched world. Elvar was not sure how long they'd been marching through this land, the perpetual daylight playing tricks in her thought-cage, but she guessed it was about half a day.

"How is he?" a voice said behind her and Elvar looked up to see Agnar. His face and the side of his shaved head was raked with claw marks. They were not too deep and were clotting now. He kneeled down beside her, offering a plate of pickled herring and fried cabbage, and a pot of skyr.

"He hasn't woken," Elvar said as she untied the linen bandage from around Grend's head and checked the wound. The poultice was still in place.

Agnar leaned forward, close to Grend, and sniffed.

"Doesn't smell bad," he said, "which is always a good sign." He patted Elvar's arm. "He'll wake when his body is ready."

Elvar sniffed and blinked away a tear that threatened to spill out of her eye.

"We are the Battle-Grim," Agnar said quietly. "Our life is blood and battle. None of us are likely to die old and grey in our beds." His words were gentle, and Elvar knew the truth of them, but she struggled to keep a sob from forcing its way out of her throat.

"I know that," she murmured, speaking slowly to keep her voice steady. "I have travelled and fought with the Battle-Grim for years now, and seen death's wings hover over us a thousand times. I know that the raven-wings do not care who they take, do not distinguish between rich or poor, kind or cruel. But always Grend has been at my side or guarding my back. He has never been injured once, not even a scratch, so to see him like this, so fragile . . . "

"Aye," Agnar nodded. "Death is our constant companion, a whisper in our ear, but when you see a friend fall . . . " He shook his head. "Nothing prepares us for it, even though we've waded through a river of the dead."

He looked at her. "That is why we fight so hard for each other. We do not abandon the living. We do not abandon those we have sworn oaths to."

"You were coming back for me," Elvar said, "when Grend fell and I stood over him, I thought that our death was upon us."

"Aye, I was coming back," Agnar said, "but someone beat me to it." He smiled. "We cannot choose our kin, but us . . . " He waved a hand at the warriors around him, going about the task of setting camp and tending to the wounded and horses. "These are my kin, closer than blood. My sword-brothers, my shield-sisters. I would give my life for them, and I think they would give their lives for me."

"We would," Elvar said. "I would."

Agnar grinned at that and nodded his head.

They sat in silence a while as Elvar continued to check all of Grend's bandages and wounds.

"You have never spoken of your kin," Elvar eventually said.

Agnar stared into nowhere, the silence stretching so that Elvar thought he was not going to answer her. Then he sighed.

"There is nothing to tell. My mother died of the wasting disease when I was ten winters old. My father sold me as a thrall when I was eleven, because the crops had blighted, and he needed food for the winter." A twist of his mouth, part grimace, part smile. "Or he *tried* to sell me. I put a wood-axe between the eyes of the slaver trying to buy me and ran." He laughed, though there was little humour in it. "I ran a long time, until I forged a new family around me; one that I can *trust*."

He squeezed her hand, then stood up.

"Are we moving out, soon?"

"No. We will rest, lick our wounds, sleep." He looked up at the sky, bright with sunlight, a few thin clouds translucent as silk. "No point waiting for dark in this perpetual day. We will march when we are rested, stop when we are tired." He looked down at Grend.

"He will wake soon," he said, and walked away.

Elvar sat beside Grend and ate the pickled herring and cabbage that Agnar had brought her. There was still heat in the ground, not as hot as the camp beside the Isbrún Bridge, but they had made half a day's march from the molten river of the vaesen pit and were now camped alongside a stream, on the edge of woodland and hills. Alder grew close as well as birch and elm.

The Dark-of-Moon Hills, Elvar thought as she stared at them. *I have heard of them sung about by skálds in my father's mead hall. Never did I think I would be looking at them, one sleep away from walking among them.* Despite the fatigue in her bones and her distress over Grend, she felt that familiar flicker of excitement. *To walk in the land of the gods . . .*

There was a groan and Grend stirred. Elvar jumped and kneeled over him, stroking his scratched face. His eyelids fluttered open, stared at her, unfocused. Then he saw her.

"Following you into the Battle-Plain," he breathed, "may not have been the *wisest* of decisions."

"Wise? Of course it wasn't wise," Elvar said, her jaw aching from her sudden smile, tears spilling down her cheeks, dropping on to Grend's face. She stroked his forehead. "I feared . . . " she whispered.

"Feared what?" Grend mumbled.

"A life without you in it," Elvar said.

A smile softened Grend's hard-cragged face. He reached out a hand and cupped Elvar's cheek, strikingly gentle for this man of violence.

"Ha, it will take more than a few winged rats to rid yourself of me," he said as his hand fell away.

"Good," Elvar laughed.

"Thirsty," Grend muttered.

Elvar unstoppered her water bottle and held his head up to pour a few sips into his mouth.

"I'll be up in a moment," Grend whispered, then closed his eyes and went to sleep.

Elvar leaned against him, smiling and eating her supper.

She heard footsteps as a warrior strode towards her. It was Sólín, two horns of ale in her hands. The grey-haired woman sat beside Elvar and offered her one of the horns.

"I owe you a blood-debt," Sólín lisped, spit spraying from her mouth.

"Are you well?" Elvar asked as she put her bowl of skyr down and took the horn.

"Thothe little vaethen bathterds took thum of my teeth," Sólín lisped, opening her mouth to show red, bloody gums, three of her front teeth torn out.

"A nasty business," Elvar said.

"I am alive," Sólín said with a shrug. "Bether to looth a few teeth than my life. And for that I have you to thank."

"We are shield-sisters," Elvar said. "There is nothing to thank. You would have done the same for me."

"I would, I hope," Sólín said, "though you do not know until you are in the battle-fray. That ith the time of telling, when a warrioth heart and boneth are truly known." She looked at Elvar, a swirl of tattoos across one cheek and brow, and offered her arm in the warrior grip. "I thaw your warrior heart, your battle-thtrength, and am proud to call you thithter."

Elvar took Sólín's arm with a grin.

They sat and drank their ale together.

Laughter drew Elvar's eye, and she saw Biórr with Uspa, Kráka and the *Hundur*-thrall. He walked away from them, to the iron food pot hanging over the hearth fire.

"Would you watch Grend for me?" Elvar said as she drained her mead horn. "I have some thanks of my own that needs saying."

"Aye," Sólín said.

Elvar stood and walked through the camp, and saw that Biórr had left the food pot and was walking away. She followed him, weaving through the camp, past a dug-out pit fire and warriors sitting and talking. Sighvat was humming to himself. She raised a hand to their calls and shook her head at their invitations to sit and drink with them, and she walked on to the far edge of camp that ran along the stream's edge. Here the wagons were drawn tightly together, and the surviving ponies had been unharnessed and picketed.

Biórr was handing bowls of food to Uspa, Kráka and the *Hundur*-thrall, all four of them laughing at some unheard jest. He sat down and began to eat with them. They looked up at Elvar as she stood over them.

"I wanted to thank you," Elvar said, the words abruptly evaporating, her mouth dry.

"Well, go on, then," Biórr said with a smile.

"My thanks," Elvar said. "You saved my life, and Grend's. We would be food for tennúr now, if you had not come back for us."

"Heya, you would," Uspa agreed.

"The tennúr would be making a fine feast of your young, white teeth by now," Kráka said, and they all laughed and cackled.

She stood there a few moments, the laughter fading, and a silence settled.

"You are welcome, Elvar Fire-Fist," Biórr said.

"Why did you do it?" Elvar asked him. "Break ranks from the shield wall? Risk your life for me?"

He smiled at her. "You have to ask?" he said.

Elvar reached down and gripped his hand, pulled him upright

and dragged him close, kissed him, soft and long, tasting sour skyr on his breath. When they parted, Biórr was blinking at her, his cheeks flushed, and she could feel her heart thumping in her chest. She turned, still holding his wrist, and led him along the streambank, away from the camp. Kráka's cackling laughter drifted after them. An old willow squatted ahead of them, branches a curtain that floated on the stream and loamy ground. Elvar pushed a way through the branches, into a hidden space around the trunk where the ground was moss-covered and soft, then turned and looked at Biórr. He stood there, gazing back at her. She brushed a strand of dark hair from his face where it had fallen from his braid, traced the line of his freckled cheek, then her hand slipped behind his neck and she dragged him to her and kissed him again. Harder than before. Slowly she pulled him to the ground.

CHAPTER FORTY-THREE

VARG

Varg followed Svik and the others down the tree-shadowed slope. The ground levelled as he caught up with them. He could hear his heart pounding in his head, beating time like a drum, and everything around seemed to become brighter, sharper, louder. He saw Glornir striding down the centre of the glade, his eyes dark pools in his socketed helm, his long-axe held across his body. Edel was with him, her wolfhounds either side of her, and a handful of other Bloodsworn. Skalk, Olvir and Yrsa were behind them, hovering at the treeline. All around the glade other groups of the Bloodsworn emerged, each one led by one of Glornir's captains: Røkia, Sulich and Vol.

The thralls in the glade were staring open-mouthed, the warriors there shouting, some frozen, staring, others moving together. The skraelings were unnaturally still, heads twitching like predatory birds as they looked at the various groups of the Bloodsworn emerging from the trees. As Varg drew closer to them he saw they bore the rough features of a man or woman, with small dark eyes, mouth and nose, but they were uneven, like a melted candle, and small tusks grew from their lower jaws.

A woman in mail raised a horn to her lips and blew it, long and loud.

The thralls screamed, many of them breaking away from their carts and running in all directions, chains clinking.

One of the skraelings drew a short, wide-bladed weapon from its belt, looking like something between a sword and a cleaver, and hacked at a thrall. She gave a scream as she collapsed, blood spurting from a gaping wound between her shoulder and neck. Others tried to steer the fleeing thralls back into the tunnel, grouping together, facing out at the Bloodsworn.

It looked like the glade had burst into madness.

"On me," Svik grunted, and Varg shuffled to Svik's left, the group forming a loose line, shields raised but not locked together. Mud sucked at Varg's shoes. All of the Bloodsworn were moving into the glade, a net drawing tight upon the tunnel entrance. They outnumbered their enemy, maybe a score of warriors milling in the glade, and ten or twelve of the skraelings.

Spears hissed, hurled by warriors among the Bloodsworn. There were screams as warriors fell, blood spurting. One of the skraelings let out an inhuman screech and staggered, pierced through the torso. It plucked at the spear, blood blooming around the wound, soaking into its hide tunic. It gripped the shaft with a long-fingered fist and ripped the spear free; looked at the Bloodsworn and opened its jaws wide, shrieking.

They are hard to kill.

"WALL!" the woman who had blown the horn yelled, the warriors about her drawing tight, shields rising together.

The warriors moved into a curved line, shields coming together with a snap as the last of the thralls disappeared. The skraelings erupted into motion, charging at the Bloodsworn. Two came at Svik's group.

"SHIELDS!" Svik yelled.

Varg shuffled tight to Svik as Røkia had taught him, shoulders touching, and their shields came together with a crack, Varg's overlapping Svik's, the rim tight to Svik's iron boss. Torvik was on Varg's left and his shield did the same, the seven of them forming a solid wall of linden wood and iron. The two skraelings were charging at them, screeching and grunting in inhuman voices, faster than Varg would have thought possible, moving in a loping, four-limbed run with their knuckled fists.

"Ready," Svik yelled and he set his feet, his left arm and shoulder braced into his shield. Varg did the same, looking over the rim, holding his spear high in a reverse grip.

The first skraeling slammed into their small shield wall, Svik, Halja and Vali taking the brunt of it. The full weight of the skraeling crashed into them with a dull thud and the shields rippled and bucked, soaking up and spreading the force of the impact. The skraeling fell backwards, rebounding from the shields to fall sprawling into the mud. Spears stabbed downwards.

And then the second skraeling was upon them, crashing into Varg and Torvik. There was an ear-shattering *crack*, an explosive pain in Varg's shoulder and he was weightless, flying through the air. He crashed to the ground, all the air driven from his lungs, and he rolled, tangled in his shield and losing his spear. He came to a halt, flopping in the mud and gasping for breath, pushed himself on to hands and knees.

Torvik was yelling, thrown twenty paces away from Varg but scrambling back to his feet and brandishing his spear. The skraeling was stood between them, crouched, snarling, saliva dripping from its tusks. It reached to its belt and drew a thick-bladed weapon, shorter than a sword but longer than a seax, and wide as a cleaver. It hissed at them both, head snapping between Torvik and Varg like a hawk, and then it was leaping at Torvik, emitting a high-pitched screech.

A spark of rage bloomed in Varg's belly, pure and white-hot, like when he was in the pugil-ring and had been floored, like when Einar had knocked him down. An instinctive response to losing. Most people would not get back up.

The red mist, Frøya had called it. Whatever it was, it surged through Varg now, flooding his veins, his body, his mind. The pain in his shoulder evaporated. He pushed himself upright and ran at the skraeling, snarling incoherent threats.

Torvik took a blow from the skraeling's weapon on his shield, wood splintering, and stumbled back a few steps. He stabbed out with his spear and scored a red line across the skraeling's shoulder, but it shrugged it off, screeched again and swung its blade. Torvik brought his shield around and the skraeling's blade crunched into it with an explosion of splinters.

Varg ploughed into the skraeling's back, the creature grunting, and both of them crashed to the ground. The skraeling bucked and twisted beneath Varg, who slammed the boss of his shield into its head and shoulder. Long arms flailed and punched him in the head and he fell away, then he saw the skraeling stumble upright, blood sheeting one side of its melted face, and raise its weapon.

Varg tried to rise and slipped in the mud.

The skraeling loomed over him.

A spear point burst through its belly and it screamed, arching its back, Torvik's snarling face behind it. The skraeling grabbed the spear and wrenched it through its own body, turning on Torvik, who stared at it, open-mouthed.

There was a tremor in the ground, a shadow, and an axe hacked into the skraeling, opening it up from shoulder to ribs. An explosion of blood and bone. It collapsed with a gurgled sigh.

Einar stood over them, put his boot on the dead skraeling and ripped his axe free.

"On your feet," he said to Varg.

"Take my hand, brother," Torvik said and pulled Varg up, both of them breathing hard, eyes wild and faces blood-spattered.

The din of battle was overwhelming. Varg saw Svik and the others were pressing forwards against a shield wall of warriors, six or seven strong, shields clashing, steel stabbing. Elsewhere Glornir was stood swinging his axe two-handed, a skraeling falling away in a spray of blood. Røkia was yelling a battle-cry and leading her band of Bloodsworn as they broke through another shield wall of mail-clad warriors, Røkia thrusting her spear into a man's belly. Everywhere was death, the air thick with the iron tang of blood and faeces. And everywhere the Bloodsworn went, their enemies looked to be falling.

"Not the time for a rest," Einar grunted at them as he strode towards Svik.

Varg shared a look with Torvik, who grinned at him, and then they were following Einar, Varg hefting his shield and drawing his seax, the two of them rejoining Svik's line and pushing into the wall of shields. Varg locked his shield with Vali's, Torvik moving to the far end of the line.

There were seven warriors facing them, men and women spitting and shoving, snarling and stabbing from behind their wall of shields. Varg dipped his shoulder and put his weight behind his shield and shoved, glimpsing a blond beard and the glint of a spearhead. He jerked his head to the side, felt the iron blade grate against his helmet, magnified and deafening inside the helm, and stabbed his seax low, under his shield rim, felt the blade bite, heard a grunt and the pressure on his shield lessened. He pulled his seax back, blood-slick, and shoved forwards, stabbed high and it grated across the riveted rings of a *brynja*.

A shouted command rang out and the warriors they were facing took a step back. Varg's limbs heavy, muscles burning, sweat dripping in his eyes.

This shield work is harder than a bout of fists between the hazel rods.

"AT THEM," Svik yelled and he took a step forward, closing the gap, the rest of the line following. Beside Varg, Vali hissed like an enraged serpent at their enemies, his face twisted in snarling fury. He had left his spear in the body of a skraeling and was wielding a bearded axe. Hooking the blade over the shield rim opposite him he tugged, the warrior holding the shield stumbling forwards a step. It was a man, dark-haired with a wrong-set broken nose and spitting insults at Vali. Jökul slammed his hammer on to the warrior's helm, putting a fist-sized dent into it. The distinct sound of bone cracking could be heard and the man collapsed.

Svik stepped over the fallen man's body, stabbing down with his spear, and pushed into the gap in their wall of shields, Vali, Halja and Jökul close behind and the enemy shield wall split apart like a cracked egg. One fought on, Einar making short work of him, and the others broke and ran.

Varg stood there, blinking, exhaustion and fury fighting within him, still feeling the anger pulsing through him like cold fire, like a distant drumbeat, his body twitching with the need to fight.

A bellowing, louder than a tree falling, echoed out from the tunnel entrance and filled the glade. Varg winced with the noise of it.

A shape lumbered from the tunnel, almost as tall and wide as the entrance: the troll they had seen at the waterfall. Varg had not realised how big it was. Tall as two men, wide as three, it thundered into the clearing, mud squelching and flying between its thick-clawed toes. It was naked and muscled as a bull, its hide scaled, patches of moss upon it, testicles swinging like two boulders between its legs. It gripped an iron-banded club in its fists. Yellowed tusks jutted from its lower jaw and small, pinprick eyes glared out from beneath thick-slabbed brows.

Figures moved behind it: a dozen warriors led by a grey-haired man in an oil-dark *brynja*. He wore an iron helm with a mail neck-guard, his grey beard bound into a thick braid and a dark cloak billowing out behind him like wings. Arm rings of silver and gold were thick upon him. He had no shield, but held in his hands a long, two-handed curved sword. Not a sword of iron or steel, it was yellowed with veins of grey, like old bone. And it seemed to shimmer in the man's hands, waves of power rippling out from it like a heat haze. The tingling in Varg's blood grew, louder and wilder, calling to him, giving him life and energy and at the same time suppressing and squeezing him, as if he had dived deep into a mountain pool and the weight of water above was crushing him.

The man strode to stand in front of the troll, a dozen warriors spread behind him, all mailed with sharp steel in their fists. He raised the bone sword over his head. Red eyes flickered like embers within the shadows of his helm as he glowered at the Bloodsworn.

"You should not have come here," he said, and marched forwards.

Glornir stepped out to meet him, Bloodsworn spreading wide behind their chief.

The troll bellowed and lumbered forwards.

Spears hissed through the air, Bloodsworn hurling them at the troll. Some pierced its thick hide, blood welling; others skittered away. The troll roared, swiping at the spears, snapping shafts.

Glornir swung his long-axe around his head and aimed a great, looping blow at the red-eyed man, who stepped forwards to meet Glornir, the bone sword slicing down. The weapons connected and there was a concussive *crash*, Glornir hurled through the air. The red-eyed man paused a moment, then strode after him.

Svik yelled a war cry and ran at the red-eyed man, his whole crew following: Halja and Vali, Einar, Jökul and Torvik. Varg stood there a moment, battling with the pulsing waves of pain that emanated from the bone sword, and then he was running, too.

There were little more than forty paces between Svik and Glornir, who was back on his feet, shaking his head, blood running from his nose. He still gripped his long-axe, and he stood and faced the red-eyed man, hefted the axe. The stranger strode at him, the bone sword rising.

Svik screamed, Varg and the others echoing him, other Bloodsworn running. Varg heard Røkia shout a war cry and glimpsed her hurling her spear at the red-eyed man. It was a powerful throw and it flew true and fast, straight at the old man's chest.

He cut the spear from the air with his bone sword, the two halves falling splintered at his feet.

Svik and his crew sped across the mud and blood-spattered glade.

A shadow loomed over them, a roar, and Vali was abruptly gone, flying through the air in an explosion of blood. Halja screamed. The troll lurched in front of them, filling Varg's vision, cutting Glornir from sight, his iron-banded club swinging at Svik. The red-haired warrior leaped forwards into a diving roll, passing beneath the pendulous arc of the club and back on to his feet, mud-spattered, still running, and hurled his spear at the troll, drawing his sword before the spear landed. There was a bellow of pain as the spear sank deep into the troll's thigh. Svik swerved, avoiding a stamping kick and slashing at the troll's leg. Einar and Jökul swept wide around the enraged creature, both hacking and hammering. Torvik ran straight at it, and threw his spear, the blade piercing the troll's shoulder, sinking deep. Another bellow of pain and the troll's club was swinging, all of them leaping away, even Einar, the club clipping Svik and sending him flying, rolling in the mud.

Varg bounced on his toes, then ran in, behind the swing of the club, swaying out of the way of a punch that hammered into the ground, mud spraying, and rammed his shield rim down on to the troll's foot. It was like punching stone, the impact juddering up through his arm. He lost his grip on the shield and leaped, grabbed Svik's spear shaft, still buried in the troll's thigh, and heaved himself up the troll's body, slashing with his seax across the creature's belly. The blade sliced through a few layers of tough, hide-like skin, blood welling, but not deeply enough to spill its guts. The troll roared at Varg and grabbed him around the throat in a boulder-sized fist, lifted him into the air and squeezed.

Pain, bones close to cracking, no air even to scream. His vision blurred, bright spots erupting, darkness. A bubbling fear merged with his rage, flooding him, and he snarled and struggled and spat, stabbing his seax into the troll's fist.

Then he was weightless, falling, losing his grip on his seax, crunching to the ground, rolling. Still. He inhaled a mouthful of mud. Spitting, he took ragged gasps as he tried to rise, air rushing into his lungs. He pushed himself up in the mud and saw Svik was on the troll's back, stabbing furiously with his seax into the meat of the muscle between neck and shoulder. Einar was swinging his axe, opening a great red wound down the troll's thigh, and Jökul had stepped in close and was hammering the creature's toes. The troll screamed, enraged.

Varg pushed himself up and shook his head. It hurt to swallow, but that was far better than being dead.

The troll let out a thundering howl and dropped its club, spinning and slapping at its back, trying to dislodge Svik. Dark blood was spurting in fountains. One of its flailing limbs caught Jökul and sent him spinning through the air, crunching to the ground, limbs twisted.

A scream came from behind Varg and he spun round and froze for a moment at what he saw.

Glornir was on one knee, blood flowing from a wound across his shoulder and chest, his *brynja* rent and hanging in tatters. The red-eyed man was standing over Glornir, bodies heaped around him, raising his pale sword.

Varg realised where the scream had come from.

Vol stepped forwards, one hand raised. She moved in front of Glornir, drawing a seax and slicing it across her hand, shouting words Varg did not understand.

"*Bein af því gamla, þú munt ekki fara framhjá,*" she screamed, spittle flying from her mouth, at the same time her bloodied hand tracing shapes in the air. Glowing fire flickered and rippled into life, sharp, straight lines appearing in the air, a Seiðr-rune forming in blood and flame above Glornir, glowing red and orange as the bone sword sliced towards his head. The bone blade met the rune and there was a burst of incandescent light, blinding Varg for a moment. He blinked, his vision returning to see that the bone sword had slowed, as if moving through water, then stopped, stuck halfway through the flaming Seiðr-rune, as if the red-eyed man had chopped his blade deep into timber and could not wrench it free. His body strained with the blade, muscles in his arms bunching, and Varg saw him grunting and hissing words that Varg could not hear.

Vol snarled back at him, leaning into the Seiðr-rune as if it were her shield in a shield wall, her hand up, palm pressed flat to it, her face twisted in a grimace of pain, lips moving, words pouring from her in a constant flow.

All around them Bloodsworn were trying to reach them, fighting furiously with the handful of warriors who had followed the red-eyed man.

The bone sword shifted, ripples of power washing out from it. The Seiðr-rune flickered and flared, like a stuttering torch as the bone sword began to move again, cutting through the flames.

"*Guðir bein brjóta þig, kló tæta þig,*" the red-eyed man bellowed, spittle flying from his mouth, muscles in his face twitching and writhing, veins bulging, and the Seiðr-rune exploded. Vol was hurled backwards, crashing into Glornir, both of them thrown to the ground, and the red-eyed man stepped over them and raised his sword again.

The rage that had pulsed in Varg's belly flared bright, fuelled by his fear, white and blinding in his head. He snarled and ran, hands grasping at his weapons belt, drawing his axe and cleaver. Leaped.

The red-eyed man paused, sword held high, and looked back over his shoulder. Saw Varg hurtling towards him, twisted.

Varg slammed into him, chopping and hacking with axe and cleaver, the two of them falling, rolling. Varg came to a stop, scrabbling for purchase, the fire in his blood sweeping him, burning in his veins. The red-eyed man bellowed, heaved Varg away and stumbled to his feet.

Varg rolled to a halt, the red mist in his head pulsing with his every heartbeat, urging him to kill and rend. When he fought in the pugil-ring the red mist had energised him, given him a rush of adrenalin-fuelled strength and speed, a clarity of thought and an instinctive knowledge that he would never give in. But he had always restrained it, known that to surrender to it would mean the death of his opponent. It was as if he kept a pit-hound on a leash. But here, now, this was to death, everything that mattered in his life coming down to this moment, to the next few heartbeats. Without conscious thought he released the pit-hound in his soul.

He half stood, realising he had lost his axe but still held the cleaver. He looked at the red-eyed man, seeing him with too-sharp clarity, all around them faded to blurred shapes that fought and screamed and bled. The red-eyed man fixed Varg with his glare that turned to a look of surprise.

His helm had been knocked loose by Varg. He was old, his grey beard braided, his head shaved. Blood flowed down one side of his face from a gash along the side of his head, skin flapping. He had lost a grip on the bone sword, red eyes searching for it, then he found it and lunged, sweeping it up as Varg scrambled to his feet and threw himself at the old man again, his cleaver raised high in a downwards slash, his teeth bared in a rictus snarl. Dimly, he thought he heard a wolf growling.

The red-eyed man swung his sword in a horizontal slash.

Varg's cleaver crunched into the red-eyed man's head, deep, wedged, blood and bone spraying, his body jerking and spasming, his strength vanishing in a heartbeat, but the momentum of his sword swing kept the bone sword moving. It connected with Varg's waist.

A searing pain, white light and Varg howled. Then darkness.

CHAPTER FORTY-FOUR

ELVAR

Elvar walked through a land of mist-shrouded vales and rolling hills freckled with woodland. Ash, elm, oak and linden grew in swathes and copses. Streams gurgled, crows squawked in branches and at night wolves howled and foxes screeched.

And these are the Dark-of-Moon Hills, sung of by skálds throughout the land for three hundred years.

They are no different from the land south of the Boneback Mountains.

Except that humanity does not exist, here. They had passed a pile of troll dung once, a bull marking the boundaries of his territory, but other than that they had seen little evidence of vaesen, either.

Elvar felt a little disappointed.

"What's wrong?" Grend grunted beside her.

He had woken almost two days ago, and now it seemed that he had never been injured, if not for the hint of a bandage visible beneath his iron helm and the scrapes and scratches all over his body. All of the Battle-Grim wore their full battle gear, even for marching, the lesson of the tennúr hill at the bridge still vivid in all of their minds. Elvar's iron helm was buckled at her belt, a weight on her hip.

"I thought there would be more . . . danger," she said.

"Be careful what you wish for, Elvar Fire-Fist," Biórr said with a smile, who was walking close to her. He was never far from her, now.

"I know, you're right," Elvar said, smiling at the young warrior.

Grend gave Biórr a dour look.

Elvar had taken Biórr to her bed each night since the willow tree and made no secret of it. Grend had refrained from commenting, but the fact that he could have uttered the words Biórr had just spoken, and yet only scowled at the young warrior, showed that he did not approve of Elvar's choice.

Their column halted, Agnar hidden from view as he led them, somewhere up ahead, with Uspa, Sighvat and the *Hundur*-thrall. They were following a winding track up a ridge, slow going with their carts. Elvar looked around and frowned. It was not an obvious place to make camp, and they had not been marching long enough to stop now, anyway.

"I'm going to see what is wrong," Elvar said with a frown. Grend followed her, which was no surprise.

They strode along the column, past wagons and horses and the Battle-Grim, warriors staring into the woods around them, other shadowed figures scattered among the trees, scouts of the Battle-Grim. An air of excitement and anticipation hovered over them all, sharpening their senses. Elvar could almost feel it tingling in the air and prickling her skin, like before a thunderstorm.

The prospect of Oskutreð. It feels so close, I can almost smell it, taste it, hear its whispered call in the wind.

The front of the column came into view, Agnar standing upon the driving bench of a wagon. He was staring back along the column, over Elvar's head.

"What is it?" Elvar asked as she drew near.

Sighvat shrugged. "Chief thought he saw something," he said. The *Hundur*-thrall was sitting with his back against a tree, Uspa stood beside him. Her expression was drawn and stark compared to the warriors around her. Her hand absently patted the *Hundur*-thrall's shoulder, like a faithful hound.

Elvar put a foot on the cart's wheel and climbed up beside Agnar. He was staring back over the hills and woodland, a hand over his eyes against the glare of the sun in a cloudless sky. Elvar followed his line of sight. Back along the path they had taken, a patchwork of woodland, streams glistening among them like silver wire. In the distance were black specks of crows in the sky, silhouetted by Eldrafell's red-veined glow, far to the west.

"What is it, chief?" Elvar breathed. She could feel his tension.

Agnar was silent a while longer.

"Nothing," he eventually breathed, dropping the hand from his eyes and looking at her. "Just a feeling." He sighed, turned and looked at Uspa.

"How much longer?" he asked her.

"Soon," she shrugged.

"You have been saying that for two days," Agnar growled.

"That is all I can say," Uspa said. "The *Graskinna* was a Galdrabok, not a map."

"Fine," Agnar grunted. He patted the shoulder of the man in the driving seat of the cart, then leaped down to the ground.

"Onwards," he shouted.

Elvar traced a finger across Biórr's shoulder as she lay beside him, following the curl of a blue-twisting tattoo, moving on to his striated chest, his sweat glistening on the dense curl of his dark hairs. White lines ran diagonally, from right to left, a lattice of silvered scars.

"What did these to you?" Elvar said, still a little breathless from their lovemaking.

Biórr shifted on to his side and looked into her eyes.

"That was a whip," he said. "There were knots in the leather." He opened his mouth to say more, but paused, shifted, looked away, uncomfortable. There was a tenseness to him, Elvar thought, that she had noticed growing in him throughout the day.

"When?" Elvar said, frowning at the change in him.

A long silence stretched.

"Too long ago to remember clearly," Biórr said.

Elvar knew he was lying. *You were young, then*, she thought. *Most likely a bairn*. She felt a wave of pity for Biórr, and a flush of anger at whoever could have done this to him. "When we have the wealth of Oskutreð I will pay a warband a chest of silver to hunt down whoever it was who did this to you. I will make them pay."

"No need," Biórr said, a finality in his words that made Elvar feel like that deed was already done.

"How old are you, Biórr?" she asked him.

"I have twenty-two winters weighted across my back," he said, and tapped her forehead. "What is happening in your thought-cage, to besiege me with these questions?" He smiled at her.

"I want to know you."

"I think you already do," he said, smiling again, his hand stroking her sweat-cooling belly. She shivered.

"More than that," she said. "In other ways. Where are you from? What food is your favourite?" She paused, looking intently at him. "Who are your kin?"

He stiffened, then rolled away, on to his back. "My kin are all dead." He sat up, reached for his breeches and pulled them back on, then searched for his tunic. "I'm hungry," he said as he stood and looked down at her. He offered her his hand.

We all have our scars, and not all of them are etched in our skin. It was a long time before I would speak to anyone of my father, and I still do not like to talk of my mother, though she deserves to be spoken of far more than my father ever does. Elvar rolled from the ground and found her clothes, dressed quickly. Finally she slithered into her *brynja* and buckled on her weapons belt.

They stepped out from the cover of the carts they had been hiding within, walked through the hobbled horses and into the camp. It was night, Elvar thought, judging by the mist-like twilight that was settled about them. Wind hissed in the boughs above, bringing a chill from the north, though the fires of Eldrafell still warmed the ground, keeping it free of frost.

Biórr strode to the fire pit and spooned out two bowls of food, passing one to Elvar. She looked in the bowl and sniffed it.

There was a pad of footfalls and Grend approached.

"Hungry," he said.

Biórr smiled at the old warrior and handed him a bowl.

"Nettle and garlic," Biórr said, then snatched up a handful of cold oatcakes that sat at the edge of cooling stones and strode away.

Elvar nodded a greeting at Grend, then followed Biórr. She heard Grend sigh behind her, followed by the pad of his footfalls as he strode after her. For a big man he could walk lightly.

Elvar walked through the camp, men and women gathered in small groups, eating and drinking, some singing quietly, others telling tales. Sharpening weapons, stitching kit. She followed Biórr and saw that he had found Uspa. Elvar thought he always sought her out because of his guilt over her son, how he had been their guard the night Bjarn was taken. Uspa was sitting with Kráka and the *Hundur*-thrall, as was her way. Biórr offered them all oatcakes as he sat with his back to the trunk of a fallen tree and they took them happily. The *Hundur*-thrall sniffed the air.

"Soup smells good," he said.

"It is nettle and garlic," Biórr said, "and it *is* good." He offered his bowl to the thrall, who waved a hand, declining, looking alarmed.

"You should be able to tell what kind of soup it is," Elvar said as she joined them. "What kind of *Hundur*-thrall are you if you cannot smell nettle and garlic?"

"His name is Ilmur," Biórr said, a note in his voice that made Elvar feel ashamed. She sat down, wondering why she had never thought to find that out.

Grend joined them, sat and silently slurped on his soup.

"What is wrong, Uspa?" Elvar asked the Seiðr-witch. Her face was drawn, eyes pinched, as if she were in pain.

She sucked in a long breath. Held it, then blew it out.

"I think we shall see Oskutreð on the morrow," she said.

Elvar almost leaped to her feet, a thrill jolting in her belly and tingling through her limbs.

"Why did you not tell Agnar this earlier?" she asked.

"Because I am not sure. It is just a feeling," Uspa said. "Like a song in my blood. A throbbing in my skull." She shook her head. "I may be wrong."

"Ha," Elvar said, looking at Grend and grinning. He regarded her over his soup spoon, then slurped some more. "You should look a little happier," Elvar said to Grend, "and you, too, Uspa. This will be the greatest moment of our lives. To look on the great tree, on the place the gods fought hardest. Their bones . . . " She shook her head. "It will be a wonder."

"It will be a curse," Uspa said bitterly.

"How can you say such a thing?" Elvar said. "What we find at Oskutreð, it will bring us fame and wealth beyond all imagining."

"You think so?" Uspa asked. "Perhaps, but I only see blood and death and misery coming from this. The gods are dead and forgotten here, and this is where they should stay. The gods were spoiled, selfish, violent siblings. To drag their bones, their weapons and treasures south to the land of men . . . " She made a sound deep in her throat, like a serpent hissing. "They will be a poison, infecting human hearts. It will start the whole bloody saga spinning again. Rivers of blood."

"It does not have to be that way," Elvar said. "It will be in our hands. Our choice."

"Exactly," Uspa spat. "Look around you. Petty men and women, dreaming of battle-fame, as if that were the greatest thing in life."

"Well, it is," Elvar said fiercely. "Men die, women die, all creatures of flesh and blood die, but battle-fame survives. To become a song, a saga-tale told from generation to generation. That way we will live *for ever.* That is what I want, what all of us want."

"I know," Uspa said, "which is why I pity you, Elvar Störrsdottir."

Grend shifted and growled in his throat.

"Easy, Elvar's Hound," Uspa said. "It was a sharp word, not a sharp blade." She looked at Elvar, earnest and sad. "Battle-fame is nothing; it is chaff on the wind. Bonds of love, of kinship, of passion, of friendship: that is what we should all be yearning for. What you and Biórr are doing behind the wagons each night, now that is real. If you longed for that above battle-fame. If you loved and honoured your kin more than you wished for glory and saga-tales." She shrugged. "The world would be a better place."

"Not *my* kin," Elvar said, glowering at Uspa, thoughts of her father's disdainful face in her thought-cage, of her brother Thorun's sneer. "My kin are not so easy to love, and would sell you as quick as look at you. And if you feel so strongly, then why are you guiding us to Oskutreð?"

"For my son," Uspa said, her shoulders slumping. "I am prepared to give up all I hold dear and important, all my fine principles, every great thing I have ever believed in, for my son." Her lips twisted with self-loathing. "I am a hypocrite, you see. Because a mother's love is a powerful thing. An instinct like no other. I would let the world drown in blood if it would mean my Bjarn was safe and back in my arms again." She looked away.

"You are wrong," Elvar said. "It is kin who are a curse. You cannot choose them; they are inflicted upon you. They are the poison." She waved a hand. "Grend is closer to me than my father or brothers, and he is faithful, loyal. Good. He chose to walk that path, chose me, as I chose him. And those choices are paid back ten-fold with faithfulness and loyalty. But Grend is not my kin; the same blood does not flow in our veins. It is our *choices* that count. Look about you, at Agnar, Biórr, Sólín, the Battle-Grim: *they* are closer kin. Better. I *choose* them, not because of the shared blood in our veins, but because we have chosen each other. Because we have sworn our oaths. We stand shoulder to shoulder in the shield wall, live or die together." She realised her heart was thumping and her knuckles were white, fists clenched. A deep-drawn breath, slowly exhaled.

"Our choices decide the future. Who we trust, who we love. And our choices will determine what comes of the treasures we find at Oskutreð. Kin are not the answer. Blood is not the answer."

Uspa looked at her with pity and sympathy in her eyes. She shook her head.

"To be young and naive," she said. "Blood is *always* the answer."

CHAPTER FORTY-FIVE

VARG

Sounds filtered into Varg's thought-cage, gently, like dawn seeping into the world. The crackle of torches burning, echoing, the murmur of voices, indistinct. The dripping of water, rhythmic.

He realised he was cold. And that he hurt.

He opened his eyes.

A roof of stone, slick with moisture, shadows shifting on it. He saw figures moving, stooping, heard the rustle of hushed conversation.

"He's awake." A face filled Varg's vision: Torvik, who grinned at him.

"I knew you'd live. I told them," he said. "I *told* them. You're a fighter, brother."

"Live," Varg croaked. Memories swirled in his thought-cage, of a red-eyed man, Glornir on his knees, bloodied, Vol screeching and flames in the air. A pale sword.

Pain thumped rhythmically inside his head, and his left side felt numb.

Where the bone sword hit me.

More faces over him: Svik, Røkia, Einar.

"Where . . . " Varg mumbled. He shifted, felt straw stabbing into his back.

"We are underground, in a catacomb," Torvik said. "This place is a marvel. It is filled with treasures. Relics, silver. The bones of a *god*!"

Varg turned his head, which was a mistake, a flare of pain shooting through him. He saw he was lying on a stone floor, straw beneath him, a figure beside him: Jökul, unconscious, a blood-soaked bandage wrapped around his head. Beyond Jökul were other figures laid out on the floor, two of them wrapped from head to boots in linen. Halja kneeled beside one of them. Tears streaked channels through the blood and grime on her cheeks.

Varg looked away, her grief etched so raw that he felt wrong to watch her.

Røkia appeared over him.

"You managed to take the cover from your spear, and buckle your helm on," she said. "I am very proud of you." Varg was not sure if he was really awake or just dreaming, because she smiled at him.

Svik pushed Røkia out of the way.

"Back with us, then, scrapper," Svik said with a grin and twirled one of his moustaches. He did not look like he'd just fought in the shield wall, against skraelings and a troll the size of a barn. Einar's big head loomed behind him, grinning more broadly than he had done to Svik's fireside tales.

He heard the sound of a door opening, a voice behind Svik and the others, commanding.

"You did good," Svik whispered, smiled at Varg and patted his cheek. Then Svik was being yanked out of the way, a new face appearing. It was Vol, looking down at him. Her face was grey and drawn, black pools around her eyes.

"How do you feel?" she asked him.

"I hurt," Varg grunted. He moved and realised that most of the pain came from his left side, focused around his ribs.

"You are fortunate to feel at all. Orna's talon has left its mark upon you." She smiled at him, a cool hand resting on his forehead. "You have a courageous heart, Varg No-Sense."

He did not feel courageous. He had just been trying to stay alive. Until the red mist had swept him up in its violent currents.

He tried to speak but she shook her head.

"Sleep is your healer. Rest, now, and ask your questions when you wake."

He shook his head, wanting to ask his questions now. There were so many of them.

"*Sofaðu græðandi svefninn*," Vol whispered as she stroked his forehead and his eyes fluttered, his thought-cage sinking into a soft and swirling river.

Varg jerked awake. Blinked. He had been dreaming. Of blood and combat, of trolls and other creatures, of wild, ferocious bears and pale-eyed serpents. Of wolves.

"It's all right, brother," a voice said, a hand patting his shoulder, and he looked to see Torvik sitting beside him, his back leaning against the rough-carved rock of the chamber they were in. Varg sucked in a deep breath and realised that he could feel his left side now. The pain made him grimace. He tried to sit up.

"Don't rush it," Torvik said to him. "You have been struck with the bone of a dead god; it is going to hurt for a while." He grinned and shook his head. "You fought a dragon-born wielding the talon of dead Orna, the eagle-god, and you slew him." He whistled. "That is a saga-tale, and no denying. Better than Svik's troll-tales for sure. One to rival even the tales about old Skullsplitter."

"Where are we?" Varg croaked.

"A catacomb," Torvik said. "Full of ancient wonders. They have been digging here a long while, have unearthed an ancient place. Vol thinks it is Rotta's chamber."

The name was familiar to Varg from fireside saga-tales. Rotta was one of the dead gods, the rat, who had played his siblings Orna and Lik-Rifa off against each other, fanning the hatred between the eagle and dragon that had exploded on the day of the gods-fall. In the end Rotta had betrayed Orna too many times and fled from her wrath. She had hunted him down and found him, confined him to eternal punishment in the chambers beneath Frang's Falls, where he was chained to a rock and bewitched serpents were made to crawl across him for eternity, their poison dripping upon him, burning and searing his flesh.

"And you know what else the saga-tales say was supposed to be kept in these chambers?" Torvik whispered, leaning closer.

"What?" Varg breathed.

"The *Raudskinna*, Rotta's Galdrabok, rune-carved on the bloodied skin of Orna's daughter."

Varg sucked in a long breath. The *Raudskinna*, said to contain the knowledge of life and death. Orna used Rotta's own rune-spells to keep him alive during his torment, always living, pain without ending.

"Just a saga-tale, surely," Varg said.

"Aye, that's what I thought about Rotta's chamber, and dragon-born, until yesterday."

Varg couldn't argue with that.

"It is a strange place," Torvik said, "and far more beneath the ground than you would ever imagine. Chambers and scores of tunnels. Barrack rooms and kitchens. They even have horses stabled down here. And there is a chamber full of hundreds of straw mattresses, but only big enough for bairns." He shook his head.

Varg realised his throat was dry, and painful. It hurt to swallow his own spit. He lifted a hand and touched his neck.

"Ah, yes, that most likely hurts as well," Torvik said. "The troll tried to squeeze the life from you, remember?"

It came flooding back.

"But you stabbed him a dozen times in his hand, like a furious wasp," Torvik smiled.

"Water," Varg wheezed.

Torvik unstoppered his water bottle and helped Varg to sit up, leaning him against the cold rock wall. Varg realised his tunic was gone, his torso wrapped in a linen bandage. The pain in his left side surged and spasmed with each movement, but the water in his throat was worth it, soothing as liquid silver. Varg looked around the chamber: a room maybe twenty paces across, with thick wooden doors at either end. Water dripped from the roof, glistening in the torchlight. Jökul still lay close by on a bed of straw. His bandage had been changed, his chest rising and falling rhythmically. Beyond him the two dead Bloodsworn lay wrapped in their shrouds. One was Vali. Varg remembered fighting shoulder to shoulder with him in the shield wall.

"You have won your battle-fame, brother," Torvik said. "Glornir must surely invite you to make your oath. I just hope he asks me too."

Through the pain, Varg noticed that he was growing accustomed to Torvik calling him brother. More than that, he was liking it.

"He will. You fought well, and bravely," Varg croaked. "I saw you."

"Aye," Torvik looked away. "Truth be told, I was scared to death and cannot remember the half of it. But I am alive, and there was blood on my spear when the fighting stopped." He looked at Varg. "But you have outshone me with your battle-fame, Varg No-Sense, like a sun outshines the stars." He looked at Varg, his smile gone. "I think many would be jealous of your battle-fame." He shrugged. "But not I. I am proud to call you brother."

"You saved my life," Varg said, remembering the skraeling as it had stood over him. "That is battle-fame enough, in my thought-cage."

Torvik's grin returned, warm and genuine. "And I will save your life again, if need calls, and I have breath in my body."

"And I you," Varg breathed.

Torvik laughed. "Listen to us," he said, "like two grey-beards of battle."

Varg could not help but laugh, and regretted it, pain pulsing in his ribs.

One of the doors opened and Vol walked in, a plate of bread and a bowl in her hand. She smiled to see Varg awake and pulled up a stool, sitting down beside him.

"Fish stew and some bread," she said, offering the plate and bowl to Varg. She looked him up and down. "I did not expect to see you looking so well. To be struck by the talon of a dead god is no small thing."

Varg realised he was starving hungry and spooned the fish stew into his mouth, huffed and blew at its heat. He dipped the chunk of bread into the bowl, soaking up the stew and sucked on that instead.

"Where is it?" Varg asked her as he blew on the stew.

"In there," Vol said, nodding at the door on the far side of the chamber. Varg realised he could sense it, a pulsing through his body, like a dull headache. Vol undid the knot of his linen bandage and unwound it, nodded and clicked his tongue as she looked at Varg's wound. He looked down and saw that his whole left side was mottled purple and black, a line of blisters across his rib where the bone sword had connected with him.

No wonder it hurts.

Vol laid her hand upon the wound, palm open.

"*Sár gömlu guðanna, sára galdrabeins, lækna, laga, ná sér,*" Vol breathed, and Varg felt a relief from the pain, like when he had scraped the skin from his knee as a bairn and Frøya had blown upon it.

Vol looked into Varg's eyes.

"You saved me. You saved Glornir, and we are grateful." She smiled at him. "This *akáll* you want. Tell me of it."

Varg stared at Vol.

He sucked in a deep breath. It was a responsibility he had guarded like treasure. As if speaking of it would release it, like a captive bird. He swallowed.

"I do not know all that happened. Some of it is . . . blurred," he said.

"Tell me what you know, then," Vol asked him.

"It is for my sister, Frøya. She was murdered."

"Yes," Vol nodded, "this we know." A look came over her face, a pain shared with Varg.

"I understand love for a sister," Vol whispered, squeezing Varg's hand. "My own sister is . . . missing. I worry for her."

"I am sorry to hear that," Varg said.

Vol shook her head. "It is probably just my thought-cage, making things seem worse than they are. Uspa is strong. I imagine I will see her soon." She looked at Varg. "So, you were telling me . . . "

"All right then," he said, summoning the strength to tell his tale. "Frøya and I were sold to a farmer, Kolskegg, when we were young. Five, six winters." He shrugged. "Kolskegg was not a kind man. All Frøya and I had were each other. We were close." A smile twitched the corners of his mouth at the memory of his sister. "So close that we came to know how the other felt, without having to say it. Just a look. And as we grew, even when apart I could . . . " He looked up at Vol. "I could feel her, in here," he touched his chest. "It sounds like I am moon-touched, saying it out loud, but it was real." He paused as he dealt with the surge of memories. "One day I was out clearing a new field of rocks for a winter pasture, and I felt her scream. I felt it in my bones. I knew something was wrong." Another pause, then he continued. "When I got back to the farm I was told that Kolskegg had sold her. This was a year ago, I do not know to whom. Kolskegg told me that if I continued to fight for him in the pugil-ring, earned him enough coin and won the pugil-purse of our district, that I would buy my freedom, and maybe even enough to buy Frøya back. He said if I won this last fight that he would give me a sack of coin and the name of those who bought her."

"Did you win, brother?" Torvik asked.

"Aye," Varg muttered. "I won. Though I was beaten and battered. Afterwards I was carried back to Kolskegg's barn and flung on a pile of rotting hay, could hear Kolskegg and his freedmen celebrating their win in his hall. As I lay on the ground, I . . . " He choked on the words. "All the time we were apart, I knew she was there. That Frøya was well." He shrugged. "I just knew. But as I lay there, tasting my own blood in my mouth, I felt her scream. And then I felt her die." Muscles in his face twitched and his fists clenched, knuckles white. A tear rolled down his cheek. Torvik reached out and squeezed his arm.

"I got up," Varg continued, wanting to get it all out now that he had begun. "I went to Kolskegg and asked him for my coin, asked him to remove the thrall-collar around my throat. He laughed, said he would be a fool to ever allow such a gold-bringer to just walk away from him. I . . . " Varg looked down at his hands, shook his head. "The next thing I remember, my hands were around the throat of one of his freedmen, crushing the life from him. They were dead: Kolskegg, all of them, the walls of the hall covered in their blood, pools of it glistening on the ground, and I was stood there among them, chest heaving, blood-drenched. I found the key to my collar, took it, and a purse of coin, and ran."

A silence settled among them.

"And that is why Leif Kolskegg hunted you, for the murder of his father," Vol said. It wasn't a question.

"It wasn't murder," Varg snarled.

Vol just looked at him, held his gaze and Varg returned it, fierce, raw.

"And you have something of your sister?" Vol asked as she looked away. "If I were to attempt this *akáll* I will need a link to her."

"Aye. I have a lock of her hair from a comb she left behind."

"Good," Vol nodded. She looked up at Varg, sympathy in her eyes. "You are aware, an *akáll* will show you the last moments of her life? That could be hard for you. They will not bring you joy."

"I understand," Varg said, "but I must know what happened to her. I have sworn vengeance on her murderer. I will see who did the deed, in an *akáll*."

Vol squeezed his hand.

"Will you do it?" Varg asked her.

"I will speak to Glornir," Vol said. "He is chief; it is his decision."

"But, have I not earned it?" Varg said, with surprise, a flicker of fear and anger.

"That is not for me to say," Vol said, wrapping the bandage back around him. A draught blew through the chamber, making the torches flicker. The door creaked and Skalk walked in, Olvir and Yrsa behind him. He was smiling, limping and leaning on his knotted oaken staff.

"Here you are," he said to Vol. "I have been looking for you. I have injured my leg and hoped you would be able to help."

"Injured?" Vol said.

"How can you be injured when you did not fight?" Torvik muttered under his breath.

"Yes, here," Skalk said, stopping and pointing down at his leg.

"Where?" Vol said, shifting her weight to turn and look at Skalk.

He swung his staff into Vol's head, a short, hard blow, a crack and she collapsed, her eyes rolling back into her head.

Torvik grunted and rose, reaching for his seax.

Yrsa stepped forward and punched her spear into his throat,

ripped it free, arterial blood jetting. Torvik clutched at the wound, blood spurting through his fingers, gurgled and flopped back against the wall, slid down to sit beside Varg, who was staring, frozen. He moved, grunted with pain, and then Olvir's sword was hovering over his chest. He stared wildly at Torvik, who looked back at him. His friend's hand grasped for him, and Varg held it, looking into Torvik's eyes.

"Brother," Torvik choked through his own blood.

"He needs a weapon in his fist, to walk the soul road," Varg cried.

"I am not putting a weapon anywhere near you," Skalk said. "I saw you fight a dragon-born."

"I will do nothing, I swear it," Varg pleaded. "Please," he said, his eyes still locked with Torvik. He could see the life draining from him. Then there was a gurgled hiss and Torvik was gone.

"Can you walk?" Skalk asked him as Yrsa strode to the door on the far side of the chamber, opened it and went in.

"You are a *murderer*," Varg breathed, shock, fear, anger swirling through him.

"Enough of that," Skalk said with a wave of his hand. "We do what we have to do."

Varg glowered up at Skalk. "Why am I still alive?"

"You have a choice, Varg. I watched you slay one of the Tainted. A dragon-born."

"I attacked him from behind," Varg muttered. "Took him by surprise."

"The dragon-born have been widely thought to be a saga-story," Skalk continued, ignoring Varg. "Extinct, if they ever existed, until I saw that one walk out into broad daylight with a talon of dead Orna in his hands. And you slew him. That is a rare deed. Glornir with all of his battle-fame could not do that. So . . ." He sucked in a deep breath, staring at Varg intently. "I know that you wish an *akáll* performed, which I can do for you, and I would like you at my side, as one of my oathsworn. That is my offer: come with me, swear your oath to me, and I will give you what you want."

Varg just stared back at Skalk. The pain in his side, the murder of Torvik, the stink of blood and voided bowels filling the room: it was like some fevered nightmare.

Yrsa emerged from the far room carrying a chest. She placed it at Skalk's feet, and he squatted, slid the bolt and opened the lid. Waves of power leaked from the chest like heat from an opened oven. Varg saw the pale gleam of the bone sword, a sheaf of rolled parchments, and other things as well. He grimaced and looked away.

"What is wrong?" Skalk asked him. Frowned. "Can you feel this?"

"You cannot?" Varg muttered.

"Hhmmm," Skalk murmured, a glitter in his eyes. He closed the lid with a snap and the throbbing power receded. The Galdurman stood and hefted the chest.

Varg looked at Torvik's hand in his, already growing cold.

Torvik is dead. He was my . . . friend. It felt strange to think that, when Varg had been friendless his whole life. He felt the surprise and fear becoming overwhelmed by the anger rising in his belly. Looked to Vol, who lay unconscious on the rock floor.

"Take her," Skalk said to Yrsa, who squatted and pulled Vol up over her shoulder, stood and walked to the chamber's exit. She looked out.

"Clear," she said to Skalk.

"Take her to the horses," Skalk said and Yrsa disappeared from view, her footsteps echoing, fading. He was watching Varg and saw his eyes following Vol.

"She is coming with me," Skalk said, "I have never seen a Seiðr-witch so powerful. She is wasted on the Bloodsworn, will make a fine thrall to me." He smiled. "So, back to my offer. Swear your oath to me, and you will have your *akáll*. Yes?"

My oath. Varg's hand went instinctively to the pouch at his belt, but it was gone: must have been taken off with his tunic. A rush of panic. *Frøya.* Only moments ago, he had been talking of her with Vol. His hopes were like ashes in the fire now. And Skalk offered him a chance of fulfilling his oath to Frøya. *My oath*, he thought. *My whole life, everything I am is bound up within that oath.* He looked at Torvik, at his dead eyes.

"I can walk," he said. He shifted his weight, grimaced, pushed himself up with one hand, then stopped when Olvir's sword tip touched his chest.

Skalk smiled and nodded. "Help him," the Galdurman said to Olvir, who lowered his blade and offered Varg his arm.

Varg gripped it, and heaved Olvir forwards, the warrior stumbling and falling on to Varg, trying to raise his sword.

He felt a burst of pain as Olvir fell on him, the man's mail coat scraping on Varg's bare skin, an elbow in Varg's ribs. Olvir's feet scrabbled on the rock floor and Varg locked the warrior's sword arm and punched him in the face with his other hand, Olvir grunting, spitting blood. He twisted, breaking free, and Varg dug his heels into the wall at his back, propelled himself forwards and the two men fell across the room. Bright bursts of pain but Varg ignored them, spat and snarled at Olvir, bit into skin as Olvir was crushed close to him. He felt the spurt of blood in his mouth, hot and metallic, bit down harder, wrenching his neck. Olvir screamed, Varg feeling the change in the warrior, from fight to fear, writhing and bucking, now, terror-filled, just trying to get away. Blood was in Varg's throat, on his face, in his eyes, blinding. Olvir's body was jerking, slowing, twitching. Varg rolled away, gasping, spitting up globs of blood. Wiped his eyes. Saw Skalk's snarling face, his boot hurtling towards Varg, connecting with his wounded ribs.

An explosion of pain: he heard himself scream, but that was sucked away into darkness.

CHAPTER FORTY-SIX

ORKA

Orka pulled on Trúr's reins, the horse slowing and coming to a halt, stamping his feet and blowing bouts of hot breath. His coat was steaming and sweat-soaked. Orka's breath blew clouds, too, the temperature dropping as they climbed steadily into higher ground.

She stared at the sight before her.

They were in the highlands: sweeping hills that shifted into the slopes of the Boneback Mountains, sombre forests of pine spreading before her, frost glittering on the bark. Orka leaned and spat, then twisted in her saddle and looked back over her shoulder.

Mord and Lif were not far behind, cantering across an open meadow before they reached the treeline. Behind the two brothers the world sloped away, down to the river valleys that twisted through the land. Orka followed the line of the River Drammur, tracing it as it grew ever fainter and eventually disappeared, knowing it led to Darl, and along that line their pursuit would most likely come. Guðvarr was tracking them by land, as evidenced by the columns of smoke that rose from his pit fires each evening.

Idiot that he is. Orka snorted. But she also suspected that boats were following them via the River Drammur, as well. Sleek-hulled *snekkes*, rather than dragon-prowed *drakkar*, because of the stretches of rapids and shallows. To the east, the slopes they were climbing dropped away to the Drammur, the river narrowing and becoming fiercer as they approached its headwaters in the Boneback Mountains. The curl of smoke gave away a village upon the river's banks, one of many that Orka and the two brothers had avoided on their journey towards the Grimholt, though being forced to take less-travelled paths had cost them in time. Orka feared the gap between her and Drekr was slowly widening.

But if he is heading where Skefil told me, then he may stop there, rest awhile. That is where I will catch him.

At the Grimholt. Orka stared north, eyes creasing as she saw the gap between the peaks of the Bonebacks that marked where the Grimholt Tower lay, a fortress built to guard one of the few passes through the mountains. To the north vaesen roamed in greater numbers, the Grimholt barring their entrance into the southlands of Vigrið.

The drum of hooves and Mord and Lif reached her, slowing as the horses left the soft meadow and entered the needle-soaked ground beneath the trees. Sunlight dappled the ground as branches swayed.

"Why have we stopped?" Lif asked her.

Orka nodded ahead.

They were a little way into the pinewoods, Orka following what she had thought was a fox trail. Ahead of them a small glade opened up, at its centre the shattered remains of an oath stone, much like the one on the Oath Rock in the fjord, back at Fellur village.

A slab of rock jutted from the ground, splintered and broken, lumps of granite scattered around the glade, overgrown with grass and moss. Upon what was left of the central slab a fresh carving stood out, a twisted, sinuous knot-carving with gaping, fanged jaws. It was coated in something dark and cracked, almost oil-black.

But that was not what drew Orka's eyes.

Above the shattered oath stone a dead eagle hung, tied by one talon with rope to a bough above it. The eagle was huge, twice the length of Orka, its great, rust-feathered wings hanging down into the glade, blood dried in a slick from a wound on its white-feathered throat that had dripped from its curved beak. The rope creaked, the dead eagle twisting ponderously as the breeze soughed through branches.

Orka clicked her tongue and Trúr walked into the glade, let out a whinny to show his discontent. Dismounting, Orka padded across the glade, ducked beneath the eagle and kneeled before the oath stone. She touched the new carving, saw it had been coated in the eagle's blood, now dried to black and cracked like a scab. She looked back at the two brothers, who sat on their horses looking uneasily at Orka.

"I saw something like that carving back in Liga," Orka said as she stood and walked back to her horse.

"Worshippers of Snaka in Helka's realm," Mord said, incredulous. He hawked and spat.

"Not Snaka," Orka said as she climbed back into the saddle. "Look closer."

Mord and Lif urged their mounts into the glade and they both leaned in their saddles. Lif saw it first. He hissed.

"It has wings," Lif said.

"Aye. Whoever did this, they worship Lik-Rifa, the caged dragon."

Orka set her feet and waited.

Mord and Lif spread around her, left and right, seaxes in their hands, wrapped in wool. Mord moved first, darting in, and Orka stepped left, slapped his stabbing seax away, turned as Lif slashed at her side, twisted, felt it graze her waist. Another stab from Mord, Orka moving in to meet him, grabbing his wrist and heaving him forwards, a flicker of pain in his eyes from the wound in his shoulder. Orka ignored that, twisting to spin Mord into Lif's path, who was already moving, committed to another attack, and he stabbed Mord in the belly. Or would have, if his seax were not wrapped in wool.

"Better," Orka said. "You are both using your thought-cages, and beginning to react better. When you have done this enough times, you will not have to think. Your body will do it for you."

"No hesitation," Lif said.

"Yes," Orka said with a curt nod. "Now, again."

They fought on, Orka silent as they attacked, defeating them every time, though both Lif and Mord were getting closer to touching her with their blades, Lif especially. He was calmer, more thoughtful, and listened more openly, without any of the hubris that entwined Mord. He wanted to be skilled and dangerous, but without admitting that he was not good enough, yet. Mord's patience would not last, and he would often try to rush Orka, which inevitably ended up with him on his arse.

"Hold," Orka said, raising a hand. She tugged her nålbinding cap off her head, Thorkel's cap, and wiped sweat from her brow. It was cold this high in the hills, their sweat steaming. Orka had seen the tell-tale gleam of a frost-spider's web that afternoon in the pinewoods. "Enough for tonight."

Mord and Lif did not look disappointed with that decision.

Although it was still light, even in the shelter of this pinewood, Orka knew that it was late in the day, and she knew rest was vital if they were going to avoid capture by Guðvarr and Sigrún's *drengrs*.

"Tend to your weapons," Orka said, walking to a bag and rummaging inside for the bread and cheese they had bought yesterday. They had crossed paths with an old farmer on the road, leading a mule and cart and heading to a nearby village to sell his goods at market. After they had convinced him they were not lawless men about to rob him, they had given him some coin in return for bread and cheese, a jar of milk, a dozen oatcakes and a joint of salted pork. She took it out and sliced them all a portion, handed it out and sat with her back to a tree. The wound in her back that Drekr had given her pulled as she stretched, the skin tight. Lif had cut the stitches and drawn them out, and it felt good to Orka. Just a little stiff, a tightness during some movements. She pulled her cloak about her, cold seeping in now that she had stopped moving, and there would be no fire to warm her bones.

Twilight lay heavy upon them, the long days and lack of darkness confusing Orka's body. There was a stinging behind her eyes that spoke of exhaustion. She felt a weariness deep in her bones, and the weight of Breca's absence gnawed at her.

You must rest, a voice whispered in her thought-cage, sounding like Thorkel's rough voice.

I will rest when Breca is safe at my side, and when you are avenged, my beloved, she answered. Her thought-cage felt full to overflowing and sluggish. Fractured images of the glade with the dead eagle and rune-carved oath stone would not leave her.

Carvings of Lik-Rifa. Worship of the dragon-god. And at the same time a dragon-born whom all think are just saga-tales appears, slaying my husband and stealing my son. What does it mean? It ate away at her, like saltwater dripping upon a fine sword, rusting and corrupting. Her nerves felt frayed. The thought of finding Drekr and putting a blade in his belly, twisting it just to hear him scream, played through her head, over and over.

Answers before vengeance, she told herself, *though I will settle for Breca back safe and Drekr in the ground*. She unbuckled her weapons belt and took a whetstone from the small pouch built into the scabbard of a seax, and began the rhythmic *scrape* as she ran it across the blade.

Lif was checking on their horses, the three animals nearby, hobbled by a stream, and Mord sat close to Orka. He lay his spear, seax and hand-axe on the pine needles and began to check them, cleaning with scouring sand and a linen rag, then sharpening their blades. Lif joined then and the three of them sat in silence, eating and sharpening.

"What is the plan, then?" Mord asked over the hiss and rasp of whetstones.

Orka did not answer for a while. She was still thinking it through.

After fleeing Guðvarr she had thought to travel north after Drekr, towards the Grimholt, hoping to either catch up with him or find a place suitable to ambush Guðvarr. Thus far neither of those hopes had borne fruit.

"We will continue to the Grimholt, and see," Orka muttered. "It is maybe a day's travel away, no more than two."

"What is the Grimholt?" Lif asked her.

"A fortress, built to guard a gap through the Bonebacks against the vaesen of the north," Orka said. "A hall, walls north and south."

"Have you seen it, then?" Mord asked her.

"Aye," Orka nodded. "A long time ago."

In another life, or so it feels.

Mord and Lif glanced at one another.

"We may end up caught between hammer and anvil," Mord said. "Enemies before and behind us."

A precipice in front and wolves behind. Orka did not like that thought, either.

"You have seen the campfires on our trail," Orka said. "Guðvarr not even having the clever to hide his fires. We have opened up the gap between us and him. Maybe a day and a half." She shrugged. "If we get to the Grimholt, then we shall make a decision. Move on, or stand and fight Guðvarr." She looked at them both. "Blood will be shed, and soon."

Lif nodded, and Mord smiled.

"Fighting me is one thing," Orka said, "and you are doing well."

"Less bruises," Lif smiled.

"Aye," Orka nodded. "But for you to fulfil your oaths of vengeance you must fight Guðvarr."

"That is what we want," Lif said. "And I don't think he will be as hard to kill as you are."

"He is a troll-shite *niðing*," Mord grunted, and shrugged, as if dispatching Guðvarr would be a simple task.

"True," Orka said, "he *is* a troll-shite *niðing*, but he will be a troll-shite *niðing* who wears a coat of mail and carries a shield and sword. A *drengr*'s kit. And there will likely be other *drengrs* with him, such as Arild, and Helka's warriors who were with him at the farm. So, you must be ready to fight a *drengr*, and more importantly, know how to defeat one. Their strengths and weaknesses. You will be in wool, most likely with a seax or axe in your fist."

"Aye," Lif grunted attentively.

"So, are you ready? How do you defeat a warrior in mail, with sword and shield? They are better protected than you, and skilled in weapons craft."

The two brothers were silent a while.

"Speed," Lif eventually said.

Orka nodded. "Good. You must use what you have to counter what they have. So, you will be light, not carrying a coat of mail on your back. A *brynja* chafes the shoulders and slows your movement.

Move in quick, never a straight rush, though. Small steps, sway, and get in close, inside their guard; make it harder for them to swing a sword or stab with a spear. Their shields will be a problem. Again, move to the sides, not straight on. If you are using your axe, hook the shield rim, pull them off balance. And once you are in close, their mail will be another problem." She stopped scraping the whetstone along her seax. "Strike here," she touched her throat. "Or here," and put her hand to the inside of her thigh, high, close to her groin. "Open those veins and your opponent is dead. And a *brynja* does not cover those spots perfectly." She shrugged. "Of course, while you are trying to do that to them, they will be trying just as hard to stab you anywhere, as you will be wearing wool that parts like butter."

"That's encouraging," Mord said, frowning.

"Realistic," Orka said. She shrugged. "Speed will win you your vengeance. And remember. Do not—"

"Hesitate," they both said.

Orka smiled.

"And how about you?" Mord said. "You were on your knees with Drekr's hands around your throat the last time you saw him. How do you plan on killing him?"

Orka looked at Mord.

"Slowly," she said, then went back to the rasp and scrape of whetstone on steel.

CHAPTER FORTY-SEVEN

VARG

Varg woke to screaming: dull, distant, growing louder as his consciousness returned, like being buried alive and clawing out from the soil. He gasped, twisted, felt hands holding him down.

"Easy, No-Sense," a voice said.

He didn't listen; saw blurred figures around him and fought and twisted, until other hands were grabbing him, holding him. He fell back, gasping, his vision focusing, tasted iron and spat blood. The first person he saw was Røkia. She was holding him, her face twisted with worry.

"You're with friends," she said to him, and he blew out a long breath and sagged in her arms, and Svik's, he realised.

He was still in the same chamber, the smell of blood thick and cloying. Olvir's corpse lay close by, limbs twisted, his throat a ragged, open wound. And then he saw Torvik and felt the weight of grief fall upon his shoulders.

Torvik is dead. Vol is gone.

Someone was still bellowing. There was a crashing and pounding sound and he saw Einar standing by the door to the bone-sword chamber.

Before Skalk stole it.

Einar was leaning against the door, bracing it with his shoulder, a few other Bloodsworn with him, Sulich and Halja, all holding the door shut. As Varg stared he saw the door tremble and buck, Einar straining to keep it shut. Muffled sounds leaked out: pounding, a growling, grief-filled roar.

"What is in there?" Varg muttered, thinking they had caught another troll.

"Glornir," Svik said to him.

Varg blinked at that.

"He is a little angry," Svik said. "Best that he is not around others right now."

Another crash against the door. A splintering sound.

"What is happening?" Varg breathed, then lifted his hands and knuckled his eyes.

"Vol is gone," Røkia said, as if that explained everything.

"I know," Varg muttered, "but . . ."

"Vol is not a thrall," Svik said. "She is Glornir's woman."

It took a few moments for that to sink into Varg's thought-cage.

"Skalk took her," he said. "Yrsa stabbed Torvik." Varg felt a fist clench in his belly: anger, grief. "I . . ." He stopped, remembering Skalk's offer to him, how he had thought about accepting, just for a moment, felt a wave of shame, and loss. If Vol was gone, then the chance of fulfilling his oath to Frøya was gone, too.

"We have to get Vol back," Varg said, stumbling to his feet. Pain in his side, pulsing from his ribs, stealing his breath, but he pushed through it. Swayed, fought the urge to vomit.

"That's the spirit," Svik said, smiling at Varg, "but perhaps you should put some clothes on first."

Varg looked down and saw that he was still in his boots and breeches, but he had no tunic on, his belt gone.

Svik held up a linen tunic for Varg, helped him thread it over his arms. Then a woollen one. Varg hissed and gasped, gritted his teeth to the pain. Røkia held up his belt. His seax, cleaver and axe were hanging upon it, and his pouch. He felt a weight lift from his shoulders at the sight of it and took it from Røkia.

The door crashed again and Einar was thrown back into the room, scrambling back to brace the door.

Varg stared. "Glornir is strong, but he cannot do that to a door," he said. "Not with Einar on the other side of it."

"He can," Svik said.

"How?"

Svik looked at Røkia and she nodded.

"It is time," she said.

"I think so, too," Svik shrugged. He looked at Varg. "Glornir is *Berserkir*," Svik said to him.

Varg just stared at him, feeling the beginning of a laugh sputter and die in his throat. "Glornir is Tainted?" he breathed.

"Aye. He is god-touched, has the blood of Berser the bear flowing in his veins."

Varg stared at the door, incredulous.

"I am Tainted, too," Svik said to him. "Refur the fox lives on in my blood."

Varg stared at him. A silence fell over the chamber. Even Glornir's pounding and roaring stopped for a few moments.

"This is one of your twisted jests," Varg said.

"No jest," Svik shook his head. He stepped closer to Varg and tugged on his red beard, an abrupt intensity in his gaze. A change came over his face, a subtle shifting of features, the angles sharpening. His eyes, always so blue, swirled and clouded, shifting to a greenish yellow, and the teeth in his mouth changed, suddenly small and sharp-edged.

"You see," Svik smiled. A toothy grin.

Varg stumbled back and collided with the wall.

"There will come a time when you can control the beast in your blood, summon it when it is needed. But you are a long way from that," Svik said. He cracked his neck and his eyes shifted back to blue; his teeth reverted to normal.

"This can't be true," Varg said, shaking his head. "You and Glornir, Tainted . . . "

"It *is* true," Svik said, "but not just Glornir and me. All of the Bloodsworn. We are all god-touched."

Varg looked from Svik to Røkia to Einar. Røkia nodded, and Einar looked back over his shoulder and grinned at Varg.

"Welcome, brother," Einar said.

"Brother?" Varg whispered.

"Aye," a voice from the far door said. It was Edel, standing in the entrance with her two wolfhounds. "You are Tainted, Varg No-Sense." She reached into a pouch at her belt and pulled out a linen rag, black with dried, crusted blood. She held it up. "This was used to tend your cuts after you fought Einar, in Liga. Hundur the hound lives in my veins, and I could smell the wolf in you the moment your blood was spilled."

"Wolf," Varg mumbled.

"Aye, Ulfrir lives in your veins," Røkia said. "You are *Úlfhéðnar*, like me." A shy smile touched her lips.

"No," Varg said.

"Search yourself," Røkia said. "All your life you have hidden it, suppressed it, no? But it has always been there. A whisper in your thought-cage. A howling in your blood. A fierceness, a red mist that gives you strength and speed when you need it most." She looked pointedly down at Olvir's corpse, his throat open, and Varg remembered waking up on Kolskegg's farm, seeing Kolskegg and a handful of his freedmen dead, blood everywhere. Kolskegg's throat had been torn out.

"You know it to be true," Røkia said.

Varg stared at them all, felt the world spinning in his thought-cage, his gut twisting, found it hard to breath, as if the walls were pressing in upon him, squeezing him, crushing the air from his lungs. He bent over and vomited, wiped his mouth and stumbled away, pushing past Edel and out through the door.

A tunnel split two ways, but he just followed the path in front of him, stumbling. He spilled into a larger chamber, his footfalls taking wing and echoing like a swarm of bats. In the hall's centre was a huge slab of rock, roughly chiselled. Great chain links had been hammered into it, four iron collars for wrists and ankles. The rock was pitted and scarred like a blacksmith's apron. Close to the rock Varg saw a handful of Bloodsworn around a hearth fire. They raised hands to him in greeting.

"Air," he grunted.

They pointed to a tunnel and Varg ran through it, the path climbing, and then he saw light and burst out into the bright day, fell to his knees and gasped in fresh, clean air. He still had his belt clutched in one fist, weapons hanging from it, and his pouch.

I am Tainted. He knew it was true, the thought a dark, malignant cloud in his thought-cage. He did not want to believe it, felt ashamed, sickened, repulsed. *Tainted. Lower than a thrall, only good to be hunted, enslaved, used.* But he knew it was true, his whole life fitting together, making sense, like a key fitting into a lock.

He looked up and saw the muddy glade was busy with Bloodsworn. A hearth fire burned, a pot hanging over it, and elsewhere warriors were saddling and harnessing a line of horses. The body of the troll lay close to Varg, where it had fallen, but the other dead had been carried to one side of the glade and laid out side by side: skraelings, warriors, thralls. The warriors had been stripped of their war gear.

A line of thralls stood close to the hearth fire, at their head a man using hammer and a chisel to free them of their iron collars. He looked up and Varg saw it was Jökul. He saw Varg and handed the hammer and chisel to another Bloodsworn, then strode to the hearth fire, where he spooned porridge into a bowl and walked towards Varg. A bandage was still around Jökul's head.

"They have told you, then," the smith said as he squatted beside Varg.

Varg grunted, nodded.

"Here, you look like you need a good meal."

Varg ran his tongue around his mouth, could still taste blood. Not his own.

Jökul took a water bottle from his belt and handed it to him.

Varg swilled it around his mouth and spat it out, then drank some. He handed the bottle back to Jökul, who pushed the bowl of porridge at him.

"Eat. It will help."

Varg sniffed the porridge and his belly growled. He began to eat.

"It is a shock, and no denying," Jökul said. "I remember when I discovered the truth: descended from Gröfu the badger." He shook his head and was quiet a while, then sighed. "But you must deal with this, and quickly. We have Vol to find and Torvik to avenge."

Varg looked at him and felt those words light a spark in his soul.

Svik walked out of the tunnel entrance, Edel and Røkia with him. They saw Varg and Jökul and made straight for them. Sat around him.

"Cheer up," Svik said, smiling. "I know you are probably jealous and wish that you were descended from Refur the Handsome as I am, but you cannot have everything." He shrugged.

Varg glared at them. "You have all deceived me, kept it hidden for so long."

"You have been watched with a close eye," Edel said. She shrugged. "We have to be careful. If word spread of what we are, we would become the hunted, not the hunters. We had to know that you could be trusted. If we had told you and you had left," she shrugged. "Vigrið is not a safe place for the Tainted."

"Being Tainted does not mean you are Bloodsworn," Svik said, his smile gone. "We are not the only Tainted in the land, or the only warband of Tainted. And not all of them are as . . . agreeable, as us." He leaned forward and held Varg's eye. "It was not enough for us to know that you are Tainted. We had to know what kind of man you are, in here." He poked Varg in the chest. "An oath-keeper, or an oath-breaker?"

Varg bowed his head, feeling a rush of shame, remembering how close he came to accepting Skalk's offer.

But I did not go. I am here.

"And now we know," Røkia said. She smiled again, which Varg found disconcerting. He was not used to seeing that expression on her face, except when she had put his arse on the ground or given him a new bruise.

"You will have many questions," Svik said, staring intensely at Varg, "and we shall try to answer them all. But before all of that, you must hear this. We are the Bloodsworn, closer than kin. A brotherhood, a sisterhood: we live and die together. You have not sworn the oath, yet, but you are one of us. Of that I am sure."

That was not a thought that Varg could fully comprehend. All of his life he had been alone, apart from Frøya. They had kept the flicker of life burning in each other's hearts. Their only kin, their only home was each other.

"But before your questions, we need to know what happened with Skalk. Tell us everything that happened," Edel asked him.

Varg took a deep breath, pushing away the questions that were buzzing in his thought-cage like bees after pollen, and he began to speak.

"That is all I remember," Varg said and blew out a long breath.

Svik, Røkia, Edel and Jökul sat there in silence.

"Good that you slew that snivelling arseling, Olvir," Jökul said.

Røkia stood up and walked away, across the muddy glade.

Einar emerged from the tunnel entrance. He saw Varg and the others and approached them, walking around the troll's corpse.

"Not one of your kin, I hope," Svik called out to the big man.

Einar just shook his head. "Svik is only joking. I am not really a half-troll," he said to Varg. "I am just big-boned."

"Glornir?" Edel asked Einar.

"He is in his right mind," Einar said. "He is coming."

Svik got up and strode into the tunnel.

Einar looked at Varg. "So, Biter, are you all right?"

Varg looked up at him, not even knowing how to answer that.

Røkia walked back to them. She carried a bundle of mail tied with rope, and a helm. When she reached them, she dropped the mail and helm at Varg's feet.

"This is yours, earned in the battle-fray with your blood and valour."

It was the red-eyed man's *brynja*, and his helm.

"You have won yourself quite the collection, since you have walked with the Bloodsworn," Edel said. She tugged on the ear of one of her wolfhounds and it licked her arm.

"You have," Einar said. "I think we are bringing you good luck."

Varg put a hand to his ribs, where the red-eyed man had struck him.

"If this is good luck, I would hate to see what bad luck looks like," he muttered.

"That," Røkia said, pointing at the stripped corpses that lay along one side of the glade, their bodies pale, eyes sightless.

Glornir strode from the tunnel, his long-axe and shield both slung across his back. Svik walked at his right shoulder, talking to him, and Sulich at his left. The rest of the Bloodsworn that were not already in the glade walked at Glornir's back. They were dressed in their battle-mail, bristling with weapons, shields upon their backs.

Glornir walked up to Varg and stopped, looked down at him. His eyes were red-rimmed, black pools around them, a vein pulsing at his temple.

"So, you know what we are," Glornir said. "And what you are."

"I do," Varg breathed out.

"I, Glornir Shield-Breaker, lord of the Bloodsworn, invite you to join us, Varg No-Sense. To bend your back with us on the oar-bench, to stand with us in the shield wall, in the battle-storm, to drink with us in the mead hall. Will you take our oath?"

Varg stood and looked around at the Bloodsworn, Svik, Røkia, all of them, staring at him.

"I will," Varg said.

A cheer rang out in the glade.

Glornir drew the sword at his hip, looked at the sharp-glint of steel, then took an arm ring from his bicep, twisted silver with bear's heads at its terminals. He threaded the ring on to his sword blade and held it out to Varg.

"Take this and know that I am indebted to you. And that you are one of us."

Varg stared at the sword and arm ring, then held his hand out. Glornir tilted his blade and the ring slid down it, into Varg's palm. He threaded it around his left bicep and squeezed it closed.

Svik grinned his approval.

"The oath-words shall be spoken soon," Glornir said, "but now there is no time. Now, we must go and get my wife back."

There was another roar from the Bloodsworn, but this one filled with malice and threat. Varg joined his voice to theirs.

Skalk, the Bloodsworn are coming for you.

CHAPTER FORTY-EIGHT

ELVAR

Elvar looked up at the trees about her, an endless sea of elm and oak, the clouded sky beyond them a grey and sombre mantle, heavy with snow and flickering with the muted colours of the *guðljós*. The dark trees stood like sentinels, the woodland silent, no birdsong, no buzz or rasp of insects. Just a cold wind that hissed through branches, making them sway and creak.

Bodies hung from their boughs. Ancient, desiccated corpses with thick-knotted, half-frayed ropes around their necks. Each one had the ribs at their back hacked and torn outwards, looking like a bloody parody of wings.

"The blood-eagle," Elvar whispered, staring. Hundreds of them hung all around, disappearing into the forest's gloom, the creaking of their ropes sounding like a thousand skeletal corpses whispering and groaning.

"This is the Gallows Wood," Uspa said.

"I had guessed that myself," Sighvat muttered, looking up and turning in a slow circle, a hand going to the frost-spider's claw hung about his neck, as if it were some good-luck talisman.

The Battle-Grim stood tight around their column, four carts with their harnessed ponies, forty warriors in mail. Instinctively they had drawn closer together as they'd passed through these new woods, spears held ready, eyes scouring the shadowed woodlands. That had been before they had even seen the first hanging corpse.

"The skálds call it the traitor-sea," Kráka said. "Where Orna answered the betrayal of her sister, Lik-Rifa."

Elvar knew the tale well. The skálds had sung of it in her father's hall, and if the saga-tale was true then these corpses were dragon-born, children of Lik-Rifa, gathered and slain by Orna, their backs hacked and chopped open in answer to Lik-Rifa's slaying of Orna and Ulfrir's winged daughter, Valkyrie. Elvar's mind flashed back to the oath stone where they had camped during the journey from Iskalt to Snakavik. She had seen an image of this carved into the stone and scoffed at it.

We are walking through the saga-tales, now, Elvar thought.

Agnar strode to the head of the column. He was dressed in his war gear, his iron and bronze-etched helm buckled upon his head. Again, no word had been said when they had risen and broken camp, but all had checked their weapons, donned their coats of mail if they had one, and buckled their helms on their heads.

"Onwards," Agnar called out, his voice loud and harsh, but falling dead in the woods, hardly carrying. He hefted his spear and gestured to Uspa, who stood a little ahead of them.

They walked on, horses neighing and cartwheels creaking.

Elvar was in the vanguard today, Agnar shifting the marching position of all of his crew daily, and so she walked with Agnar and Sighvat, Grend at her left shoulder. Biórr was close as well, walking with Ilmur the *Hundur*-thrall.

They moved on in silence, following a path that ran north-east through the woods, Elvar's eyes constantly flicking left and right, the movement of swaying corpses in the branches snagging and snaring the eye. It was unsettling. She picked up her pace until she was walking beside Agnar.

"Can you feel it?" she said to him.

Agnar glanced at her. His eyes were bright with excitement, but she could see a tiredness deeper within him, almost exhaustion, with dark pools around his eyes, his skin pale and red-veined, a hunch beneath his bearskin cloak to his shoulders and frame.

"I can feel something," he said, "though I do not know what it is."

"The presence of the gods?" Elvar wondered out loud.

"But they are all dead," Agnar said. He looked around. "At least, I hope they are."

"Aye, but we are close to where they died. Their blood spilled on this land, soaked into the ground we are treading. Perhaps something of them still lingers."

"I hope so. Their bones and their power, that we can harness or sell." He flashed a grin at her. "We will be rich beyond all imagining, our fair-fame known throughout all Vigrið and the world beyond."

"Yes," Elvar said, Agnar's smile and excitement infectious, banishing the sense of dread and unease that had been building within her.

His eyes lingered on her. "You are . . . happy?" he asked her, hesitantly. "With him?" His eyes flickered to Biórr.

"I am," Elvar said, her own grin spreading.

"You *sound* happy enough," Agnar said. "Your humping behind the carts each night has been keeping me awake."

Elvar flushed.

"I am glad that you are happy," Agnar shrugged. "And I am glad you are here, part of the Battle-Grim. You are a fighter, no question of that, but you are an oath-keeper, too. Someone to be trusted. That is a rare thing in this world." He looked at her, no smile, eyes serious. Elvar did not know what to say. Agnar just nodded to himself and they strode together in silence.

They were walking up a slow, gentle incline, the trees around them thinning. Elvar felt the gentle flicker of something on her cheek, looked up and saw it was starting to snow. Uspa walked ahead of them, leading their column. She reached the top of the incline they were climbing and stopped. Agnar broke into a run to reach her and stopped, staring at something over the ridge.

"Behold, Oskutreð," Uspa said.

Elvar felt her heart quicken in her chest and broke into a run. She stumbled to a halt as she reached the crown of the slope, and stared.

A wide, treeless valley opened up before her, rolling in all directions as far as her eyes could see. The undulating ground was covered with snow, here and there tugged by the swirling wind. Great mounds lay scattered across the plain, covered in earth and moss and snow. Elvar saw the gleam of rusted steel, the glint of yellowed bone. Other shapes, the twisted and blackened branches of a tree, but longer and thicker than a *drakkar*, lay strewn across the plain.

Straight ahead and set deep into the plain like the iron boss of a huge shield stood the stump of an ancient tree, blackened as if lightning-struck, wider than the fjord of Snakavik.

Snow fell from the sky, gentle and cold as winter's first kiss, the lights of the *guðljós* flickering behind the clouds, and behind or beneath it all there was a sound, a dull thud, more a feeling than a sound, vibrating through Elvar's bones.

There were gasps as other Battle-Grim reached the ridge and stopped, staring. The creak of carts and whinnies of horses.

"It is a saga-tale made real," Sighvat sighed.

Grend stood silent at Elvar's shoulder.

Ilmur and Biórr ran on a few steps, both grinning like bairns on their name-day.

Uspa's eyes swept the plain, a frown etched deep into her brow.

"Not much of a tree," Sighvat huffed as he reached them.

"It was burned and broken in the last battle," Uspa said.

That makes sense, Elvar thought, though in her mind she had expected to see the Ash Tree rearing impossibly tall and wide.

"On," Agnar said, his eyes alight, back straightening, exhaustion falling from his frame like a discarded cloak.

They moved on, a fast march now, down a gentle slope and on to level ground. Elvar looked down and saw that it was not snow that coated the ground, but ash. Grey flakes stirred and swirled as they moved through them, sticking to Elvar's boots and leaving footsteps where no one had trod for three hundred years. Elvar passed by a hundred ash-covered shapes, her urge to run and uncover what lay beneath each one overwhelming, but the broken stump of the tree seemed to call to all of them, drawing them across the plain like a rope-hauled *drakkar*.

And then Elvar saw a mound to her right, large as a mead hall, lying stretched upon the ground. Moss and ash lay thick upon it, but a gleam drew Elvar's eye, like a hook in fish's mouth. She veered away from the column, Grend calling her name and then following. Elvar stopped before the mound, staring up at it, and stabbed her spear into the ground. It towered over her, larger than her father's hall at Snakavik, and as wide. A looming entrance curved and draped with vine stood before her. She took a step inside and peered into the darkness. A smell wafted out, of decay, and with it a sense of unbridled malice, of blood and savagery so strong that it snatched Elvar's breath away. A wave of fear rippled through her, thick and palpable and she stumbled back, out into the daylight. She breathed deeply, and let the gently falling snow cleanse her.

"Can you feel it?" Elvar asked Grend, who was stood beside her, scowling into the dark maw before them.

"Aye. Violence deep as the marrow," he muttered. "It is putting a trembling in my bones, making me want to kill something."

Elvar drew her seax and scratched at a small section of the moss and lichen-covered entrance, a curved beam, like a giant whalebone and long as two spears. Slowly the accumulation of detritus fell away, the decades of ash and moss and growth scraped clear by her blade, revealing the glint of something old and yellow.

Elvar stepped back.

"It is a tooth," Grend said. "A wolf's, or a bear, I think."

"It is Ulfrir," Elvar breathed, stumbling away, looking again at the mound. And she could see it now, as she put some distance between her and the mound: the outline of a huge wolf's skeleton, lying upon its side, limbs sprawled, jaws wide in one last defiant howl or snarl. Moss and grass and ash covered it like a new pelt. Close by something glinted in the ground and Elvar nudged it with her toe, saw that it was a lump of iron jutting from the earth. A curve in it showing forge-craft before a sharp break.

"A link from Ulfrir's chain?" Grend said, frowning.

"Aye," Elvar said, remembering again the oath stone they had camped beneath, and the image of the wolf snared and bound by a chain, jaws wide as it howled while warriors swarmed it, stabbing with sharp steel.

"Come away from it," Grend said, and took Elvar's arm, guiding her back to the column of the Battle-Grim. Elvar tripped and stumbled over something, saw the glint of rusted steel, an ancient sword held in a skeleton's grip, but Grend steadied her and led her on, back to the column.

"We have found Ulfrir's bones," Elvar blurted, her voice a rush, words tripping in her excitement and awe.

"The Ravener," Uspa nodded, glancing back at the wolf-shaped mound. She did not stop, though, leading them on across the plain, winding through the mounds and hillocks, until they were close to the blasted stump of Oskutreð, the great tree. Agnar held a fist up and the column drew to a halt. He strode on, Uspa and Sighvat at his side, Kráka, Ilmur and Biórr behind them. Elvar did not hesitate, but followed after, Grend padding beside her.

Elvar stared at the blasted stump of the ancient ash tree, wide as a lake, stretching jagged and sharp across the ground. The remains stood high as a mead hall's wall, perhaps two men high. Something green against the blackened wood caught Elvar's eye and she stared at it.

It was a sapling, the trunk as wide as a normal ash tree, boughs with green leaves sprouting upon it. New life, among the ash-grey wasteland. And into the tree's trunk the likeness of a woman was carved, with flowing hair, a sharp jaw and wide, somehow-knowing eyes, a wooden staff in her hand.

Beside the new tree there was a flattened area of the ancient, fire-blasted trunk, that Elvar could have stepped on to. Filling much of the base and as wide as her father's feasting hall was the outline of a great trapdoor, bolted a hundred times. As Elvar looked at it she could see a faint, rhythmic tremor running through the door like a pulse, as if the tree had a heart that was beating, deep within the ground.

They threaded closer, their path taking them towards the living tree, winding around what looked like huge, shattered branches until Uspa stopped before the last one that separated them from the stump. Elvar joined them as Agnar and his small band stared at it.

Elvar blinked, suddenly realising what it was.

A giant's head, bigger by far than Hrung's head in her father's hall. And it looked to be carved from wood. Dry and dark as charcoal. Ashes lay thick in the carving's eyes and mouth, which was open and stretched in a rictus scream. What Elvar had taken for branches nearby were in fact its body and limbs, broken and blasted, twisted, hands and fingers grasping.

"That is my mother, Aska, the Froa of Oskutreð," a voice said, like the creaking of branches and rustle of leaves. Elvar and the others started, looking around and reaching for weapons.

Uspa saw her first.

The woman carved into the tree was moving. There was a cracking of bark, a splintering sound and she was stepping out from the trunk. She stood there a moment, stretching, a series of crackles through her limbs; she tilted her neck and there was another crack.

"I have been waiting for you a very long time," she muttered. Then she was walking towards them. Her hair swirled about her shoulders like roots as she took careful steps through the ash. Elvar and the others just stared, wide-eyed. Sighvat hefted his bearded axe.

"And who are you?" Uspa asked.

"I am Vörn Askasdottir, Froa-spirit and newborn guardian of Oskutreð," the woman said. Now that she was closer to them Elvar saw that she was tall, taller even than Sighvat. Her skin was grey as an ash tree, dark grain running through her like veins. Bark rippled across her arms and legs; her torso was yellowed with lichen.

"And who are you, that has come to disturb my sleep?" she asked, pausing a dozen paces away and looking intently at them, head to one side, her gaze piercing. Her eyes touched Elvar and she took a step back; it felt like leaves and branches were brushing across her skin.

"The blood of the gods has faded in so short a time," she said, taking a long, deep-shuddering breath. Her bare feet twisted in the earth, toes digging deep, like roots. "Though they live on, still, faint as a whisper in some of your veins. Hundur the hound, Snaka and Orna, and Rotta, too."

Rotta? thought Elvar.

Vörn took another step closer to them, her face proud and strong. "Why are you here?" she said. There was a threat in her voice.

Agnar stepped forwards. "To gaze on Oskutreð and the Battle-Plain," he said. "In the new world the remnants of the gods are valued. Prized. We would take some of them."

Vörn snorted, a twisted curl of her bark-covered lips.

"You are carrion-crows, then, come to pick the dead clean." She nodded to herself, then waved her staff. "Disappointing. I had hoped for something . . . more. Never mind, just take what you will, but you cannot approach the dead tree. No hand may touch it, or foot tread upon it."

Sighvat grunted and stepped forwards.

"We have crossed the Isbrún Bridge, fought a swarm of vaesen," he said. "And now that we are here, I'll not have some talking branch tell me what I can and cannot do."

"Not another step," Vörn said to him, raising a hand, one long, twig-like finger waving at him, like a mother scolding her bairn.

Sighvat raised his axe and swung at her. He was tall, broad-shouldered and fat-bellied, but he moved faster than any would think by looking at him. His axe was a blur, hissing towards Vörn's head.

A whispered word, a blurred movement and Sighvat's axe was crunching into her staff. It sank in a way, wedged, Vörn holding it two-handed, eyes flashing with green fire.

Sighvat yanked on the axe but it stuck fast.

A twist of her wrists and Vörn ripped the axe from Sighvat's grip, struck him in the head with her staff and he fell like a pole-axed bull. He lay on the ground, groaning and bleeding. He shifted and tried to roll over.

"*Rætur, sinum jarðarinnar, vaxa og binda þennan feita mann*," Vörn breathed and the ground around Sighvat moved, rippling and twisting, as if a hundred serpents writhed and burrowed beneath him. Vines burst from the ash-covered soil, wrapping around Sighvat's body, drawing tight like fetters until he was held firm.

"I do *not* like axes," Vörn said. She glared down at Sighvat. "Or the fat men who wield them."

The vines constricted and Sighvat groaned.

Vörn looked at Agnar and the others.

"Who else wishes to touch Oskutreð's sacred ground?" she whispered.

No one moved.

"Will you release him," Agnar said, crouching beside Sighvat and resting a hand on his chest, "if I swear we shall not set foot on that tree?"

Sighvat groaned and looked wild-eyed at Agnar.

"I don't like this, chief," he grunted.

Agnar patted his vine-wrapped belly.

"When you are ready to leave, and you have kept your word," Vörn said. "Then, I shall let this fat maggot go free."

"Heya," Agnar agreed, standing and stepping away. "We want nothing from the tree, anyway. What would we do with the remains of a dead tree?" He paused, looking back at Vörn. "Why do you still guard it? What is there left to guard except ash and cinder?"

Vörn did not answer him.

The distant tremor rumbled louder, the bolts on the carven door rattling, puffs of ash rising in small clouds.

"What is down there, in Oskutreð's bowels?" Agnar asked.

Kráka stepped forwards.

"It is Lik-Rifa," she breathed. "The saga-tales are true. The dragon is still caged deep within the roots of Oskutreð."

"Of course it is true," Vörn said. She scowled at them. "And I vow to you, the only way for you to touch Oskutreð is over my dead and splintered trunk. That will not be easy. And even if you managed to see me defeated and broken, you would have to face the three sisters. They would not take kindly to the door being opened."

"The three sisters?" Elvar said, feeling her skin prickle, fear dancing down her spine at the thought of Lik-Rifa, the dragon-god, corpse-tearer, prowling in her prison chamber somewhere beneath their feet.

"Aye. Urd, Verdani and Skuld, Orna's and Ulfrir's daughters, gaolers of the dragon."

"That doesn't sound good," Sighvat mumbled from his prison of vines.

"You have my word," Agnar said, "none of my company shall set foot near your dead tree. Come," he called to those around him, turning away and raising his voice. "Let us do what we came for, and search this ground for the relics that will turn us into a saga-song of our own."

The Battle-Grim let out a cheer and emptied out the carts, taking spades and axes, sheets of stitched linen and poles, and began to search through the mounds scattered all around them. Exclamations and cheers rang out as relics were unearthed, bones and weapons, armour and jewels, all of it being collected and piled together, wrapped in the linen sheets and carried to the carts.

Elvar and Grend set to work, digging at a mound close to the head of Aska, the dead Froa. They uncovered the skeletons of two people, twisted together in death. Elvar saw the teeth of one were unnaturally long and sharp. Seaxes of steel were in their fists, gold and silver glinting on the hilts. Elvar tapped Grend to show him, and saw that he had dropped his spade and was staring into the distance, back the way they had come. She stood and stared.

Through the snow she saw figures were emerging from wooded slopes: people on horseback, and wagons, many, many wagons.

"What is this?" Vörn said as she stood over Sighvat's form. "I wait three hundred years and see no one, and then you humans all come at once."

Elvar dropped her spade. The figures spilling down the slope towards them bore grey shields with the black wings of ravens upon them.

Ilska the Cruel had come.

CHAPTER FORTY-NINE

ORKA

Orka rode along a narrow path, a sharp slope falling away to her right. Far below the white-foaming headwaters of the River Drammur roared through a narrow spit of rock. In the distance she could see the vale of Grimholt Pass, passing between the steep slopes of the Boneback Mountains that seemed to reach high as the sky. Orka could make out the line of a wall built across the vale, just a dark smudge from this distance, and behind it a hall and tower rising from an outcrop of rock. Smoke rose in thin columns from the fortress into a blue summer sky. Behind her stones shifted and spilled down the slope, Lif's horse neighing as the mare lost its footing. Lif called out as the horse slid, but then righted itself.

The path veered away from the river, up a sharp slope of loose scree, and then the ground levelled and Orka was dipping her head to avoid branches, riding back into more pinewoods. There was a sound of shingle sliding as Lif and Mord urged their horses up the path and then they were all in the woodland.

"Was that the Grimholt?" Lif asked as he urged his horse up alongside Orka.

"Aye," she said.

He nodded and swallowed.

She felt it too. The time of reckoning was drawing in upon them. Frost glittered on the ground, and Orka spied a long, thick thread of ice-reamed web in the boughs above them, shimmering as it caught a shaft of sunlight.

"Be alert," Orka said, scanning the boughs.

"What for?" Mord asked, riding up on Orka's other side.

"Frost-spiders," Orka said.

"Berser's hairy arse," Mord muttered under his breath, his head twisting in a dozen different directions as he tried to look everywhere at once.

"Mord doesn't like spiders," Lif leaned and whispered.

Orka stifled a smile as they rode on through the mountains.

Orka squatted behind a rock and peered out at the Grimholt.

She was sat on a cliff edge, a steep slope draped in pine trees falling away to the River Drammur about fifty or sixty paces below her. To the north lay the Grimholt, set within a timber wall that ran across the river valley, taller than three men, anchored to the cliffs at both ends of the valley. A gate stood closed, armed men and women visible on the walkway upon the stockade wall. Mail and helms glinted in the sunlight. Behind the wall was an open space like a courtyard, ringed with outbuildings: stables, barns, a smithy, barracks and coops and pens. At the top of a gentle slope reared a thick-timbered hall with a green-turfed roof, smoke rising from a smoke hole, and at its rear a squat tower that hugged the cliff face, tall enough to command a view of the valley, both north and south.

Beyond the hall, to the north, another wall stretched across the valley, looking to be identical to the southern wall. More figures walked upon it. A fire smoked and flickered in a brazier inside the gates, figures standing around it and warming themselves.

The river frothed and foamed through the valley, but a new route had been carved into the land, a horseshoe-shape curling away from the natural river course, clearly built for vessels to row close to the hall, a pier jutting out into the river from the courtyard. Two *snekkes* were moored there now, and a wide, flat-bottomed trader.

"What now, then?" Mord whispered beside Orka.

Orka was muttering under her breath.

"What?" Mord said.

"I count sixteen warriors," Orka said. "On the walls and in the courtyard. Probably more in the hall, or off-duty. Then there will be thralls and craftsmen. Their families. And Drekr, with his crew."

If he is still here, she thought. *He could be five or six days ahead of us, with the longer route we've been forced to take.*

"Forty people in there, at least," Orka whispered to herself.

Too many for me to kill.

"Well?" Mord said. "What now?"

"Too many for my first plan, which was to walk in and kill them all, except one."

"I am starting to think that this is always your first plan," Mord said, shaking his head. "It is what you did in Fellur, when you broke into Jarl Sigrún's chamber, and back at the inn in Darl."

Orka shrugged. "It is a plan I like," she said.

"Not overflowing with deep-cunning, though," Mord pointed out.

"No," Orka admitted. "And deep-cunning is what we will need here. We watch a while, see if there is any sign of Drekr. Any bairns. We wait," Orka said. "Perhaps we will go in when they sleep."

"How?" Lif whispered, staring down at the fortress.

"Over the wall, or swim up the river," Orka shrugged. "Either that or we will need to lure some of them out, into these woods, and thin their ranks a little."

"How would we do that?" Lif asked.

"Some kind of distraction," Orka muttered. Then she frowned and cocked her head.

"What is it?" Mord asked her.

"Listen," Orka grunted.

In the distance, behind them, a sound filtered out from the trees.

"What *is* that?" Lif said.

It was a raucous, grating sound, like a disturbed murder of crows flapping and squawking as they rose into the sky, but Orka thought she could pick out words in the sound.

Ignore it. You have other things to worry about. The Grimholt. Drekr.

The sound grew louder.

Orka looked to the gatehouse of the Grimholt. If they heard it, they would send people to investigate.

"Perhaps we have our lure," she said.

The sound grew louder, filling the pinewoods.

Orka ground her teeth and snarled. Then she was creeping away from the cliff edge and striding into the cover of the trees. She took her spear from where it leaned against a tree beside Trúr. The gelding whinnied at her and she patted his neck. Then she strode into the pinewoods towards the sound.

"Where are you going?" Mord called after her.

"To kill anyone who comes out of the Grimholt to investigate," she said.

Lif and Mord followed, Mord swearing under his breath.

Orka ducked under boughs as the trees grew thicker and felt something brush her face, a sharp tingling sensation across her cheek and she looked up to see a hanging strand of frost-web. Twisting, she looking up, but the boughs above her were empty. She shifted her grip on her spear and walked on.

The ground sloped downwards, Orka moving north through the woodland, a voice in her thought-cage telling her that she was moving steadily closer to the Grimholt and west-running track she had spied from the cliff. There were more strands of frost-web in the trees, thicker, criss-crossing, making sunlight dance in fractured beams. The noise was deafening, now, the sound of boughs shaking and cracking, and as Orka walked deeper into the woods a word amid the clamour became clearly discernible.

"*HELP!*" Terror-filled: over and over.

"Orka," Mord hissed. She glanced at him, saw fear in his eyes. "It sounds . . . dangerous."

"This is Vigrið," she answered. "Living is dangerous." And she marched on.

She heard Mord and Lif's voices behind her. It sounded like they were arguing, but she ignored them. After a few moments their footsteps followed her.

The sound was close: branches splitting, a voice screeching, a noise like a storm raging through the woods. And other sounds: a scuttling, scraping noise that echoed in the branches above her. It was darker here, the boughs above dense with frost-webs as thick as Orka's wrist. She pointed at trees and bushes for Mord and Lif to hide behind, then stepped around a tree and froze, taking a moment for her eyes to adjust and fully understand what she was seeing.

She was looking into a glade, with dappled sunlight falling in beams through a thin canopy. On the ground was a dead elk, flies buzzing, its belly opened, entrails glistening.

And in the boughs above it was a black-feathered bird, huge as a horse. It was struggling and squawking, strands of frost-web stuck to its wings and body, wrapping around it. The more it struggled, the more enmeshed it became in the web, dragging on branches, bending them close to snapping, pine needles cascading like rain, black feathers fluttering down like autumn leaves.

Frost-spiders lurked in the trees, many of them, each one as big as a boar, eyes sparkling, venom glinting on icicle-like fangs. They waited, none brave enough to risk the thrashing talons and beak of the raven, yet.

And then one of them moved, a fat bodied, hoar-crusted creature with long spindle-legs, bright, glittering eyes and dripping fangs. It scuttled along a single strand of web that was curled around one of the raven's talons.

"*HELP!*" the ensnared raven croaked, loud enough to make branches tremble and Orka's chest vibrate.

Another sound: branches cracking, a shower of pine needles, and then a black shadow was crashing through the canopy. Another raven, huge as Trúr. It was squawking as it beat its wings and flew at the frost-spider on the thread. One claw reached out and it was snatching up the spider, talons puncturing and shredding the bloated abdomen. White, mucus-like fluid exploded and rained out over the forest floor.

The raven dropped the eviscerated strands of spider-flesh and set to pecking and clawing at the web that ensnared its mate, who flapped and shrieked.

"*STOP FLAPPING, YOU FOOL,*" the new raven rasped at the trapped one.

"*BUT I'M STUCK, I'M STUCK, I'M STUCK*," the bird in the web yelled.

"*I KNOW, I KNOW, I KNOW*," the newcomer yelled back.

Spiders moved in the boughs, as if the trees had come to life. One ran across a branch above the free raven, who was beating its wings, half airborne, half clinging to branches with one taloned claw as it tore and ripped at the web around its partner. The spider dropped towards the bird from the branch on a strand of ice-web.

Orka's muscles twitched with the urge to move, to help.

This is Vigrið, she thought, *a world of tooth and claw, where life is battle. Let nature take its course.*

A memory slipped into her thought-cage, her last night with Breca, when she had seen him saving the moth from the spider. She had said something similar to him.

"But that is not a good death, Mama," he had said in answer to her, as the spider had scurried towards the moth. He had looked at her with pleading eyes.

Without thinking Orka stepped forwards, set her feet and hurled her spear. It flew straight and hard, punched into the spider's head and burst out the other side. There was a spray of fluids and the spider dropped like a stone, legs curling.

The spiders in the trees all stopped moving, many glistening eyes snapping to focus on Orka.

Mord stepped out of the shadows and stood at her shoulder, his spear raised. Lif strode out and set himself at Orka's right side.

Even the new raven paused in its web-ripping to look at them with one shiny, too-intelligent eye.

The spiders hissed. Then they began to move, a seething mass of shadowed, many-jointed limbs.

"What have you got us into?" Mord said, fear a tremor in his voice. "I thought we were waiting to ambush the Grimholt warriors?"

"All plans go wrong," Orka grunted. "Do this quick, and we can still hunt the Grimholters." She looked at the frost-spiders. "Just don't let one of them bite you," she added.

"That's unnecessary advice," Mord said.

"What will happen if they do?" Lif gulped.

"Your blood will chill and slow in your veins," Orka said, "until you cannot move, and then they will puncture you and suck it from you, as if your body were a horn full of crushed ice and mead."

Lif shivered.

"So, their venom will not kill us?" Mord hissed.

"Not usually," Orka said, her eyes fixed on the closest spider. "Unless they pump too much of it into you. I saw a man's hand snap off at the wrist, once, because the blood in his veins had turned to ice."

"This is not encouraging," Mord breathed.

"Use your spears to keep them from closing," Orka muttered. "Don't be an idiot and throw yours away."

Like I did mine.

She drew a seax and axe, set her feet.

A hissing from above and she looked up to see a spider speeding at her, dropping on a single thread from its spinneret.

Mord's spear stabbed into its open mouth, Lif's piercing its head. A gush of fluid as they ripped their blades free and the spider crashed to the ground, twitching.

The ravens went back to their web-ripping, the trapped one freeing a wing. A spider dropped upon its head, but the free raven skewered the spider with its beak and threw it through the air to splatter against a trunk.

There was a *thud* of spiders dropping to the ground around Orka and the brothers, three or four of them, forelegs raised, fangs twitching. Lif leaped in front of Mord and stabbed, but two more jumped at Lif, forelegs lashing out, throwing him to the ground. Mord screamed and lunged with his spear, and Orka stepped in close, sliced through a leg with her seax and buried her axe into a cluster of eyes. It collapsed, jerking and hissing.

A scream came from Lif, on one knee trying to stand, a spider on his back, fangs sunk into his shoulder. Mord bellowed, rising in pitch, but he was slicing and stabbing his spear at two spiders as they spread about him, hissing. Lif's eyes bulged, his limbs turning blue and stiffening, and he toppled to the ground, shivering violently. Frothed ice dribbled from his chattering jaws. Orka darted in, chopping into the abdomen of the spider on Lif's back, the creature's legs jerking, and it fell away, hissing and frothing, liquid pouring from the rent Orka had made in its body, thick like soup.

Then something slammed into Orka's back, throwing her to the ground. She kept hold of her weapons and tried to roll, but a great weight pinned her down. A foul stench swept around her, of death and decay and putrescence. She twisted, thrashed with her blades and felt the seax bite, a malevolent hissing in her ear, something wet and ice-cold dropping on to her cheek. A glimpse of a huge, curved fang, green-white poison beading its tip, and many, many eyes.

And then the spider was gone, the weight lifted, and Orka spun over and scrambled to her feet.

One of the ravens was flapping above her, the spider grasped in its talons, its many legs thrashing. As Orka watched, the raven's talons constricted and the spider burst apart, an explosion of skin and cartilage and fluid. The other raven was free, and it was flying at the spiders around Lif, claws raking their backs, thick slime erupting in the talons' wake.

"*MUCH THANKS, MUCH THANKS*," the raven squawked at Orka and then the two giant birds were beating their wings and rising, crashing through the boughs in a burst of pine needles and sunlight.

A handful of spiders were still moving in the boughs, two more on the ground. Mord stood over Lif, his eyes wild, movements stuttered and jolting as he thrust his spear at any spider that moved.

Orka heard shouts in the woodland and saw the flicker of figures through the trees.

"Bollocks," she muttered. "We need to get away from here," she snapped at Mord.

"That's the best idea I've heard from you in a long while," he snapped, a tremor in his voice, stabbing his spear at a spider scuttling in. He looked at Lif, still shivering and convulsing on the ground. "My brother, will he live?"

"Not if we stay here," Orka said.

There was a hissing, spraying sound and Orka looked up to see a spider hanging from a bough above her, spinning and turning a web between its legs. Orka shouted a warning as she leaped away, the spider casting the web into the air, floating down to drape over them.

It grazed her leg, sticking like pine tar to a ship's hull, and Orka fell, hacked and sliced at it, cutting it free, though some still clung to her calf, burning and numbing even through her wool *winnigas* and breeches. Mord was stumbling, web clinging to one arm and leg, waving his spear over his brother's twitching form. He was screaming. Spiders ran at him.

Orka heard the sound of hooves drumming on the pine-needle litter, growing louder, and two riders burst into the glade: a tall, blond-haired man with an ash-knotted staff in his hand and a woman in mail behind him. She was leading a third horse with a bound form unconscious and draped over the saddle, and a large chest strapped to it.

Orka felt a thumping in her head, like an extra heartbeat.

The woman raised a horn to her lips and blew on it, ringing out through the trees.

The blond man took one look around the glade. He drew a small seax and sliced it across the top of his hand that gripped the staff, blood trickling between his fingers on to the wood, then he raised his staff and shouted.

"*Starfsfólk valds, forn aska, brenna þessa frostkönguler, þessar fölsku álfar.*"

Flames erupted on the tip of the staff, as if it were a torch, and the blond man spurred his mount at the spiders, stabbing his staff into them like a spear. The first spider trembled and shook as the flames touched it, the blue veins that ran across its abdomen turning orange and then red. The skin on its back began to bubble and melt away, flames bursting and erupting. The spider screeched and hissed as it died.

Orka ran to Mord, limping with one leg numb and ice-touched. Mord spun around, waving his spear at her.

"Come on," Orka said, sheathing her seax and trying to get close to Lif so that she could throw him over her shoulder. Mord stared at her a moment, eyes manic. "Mord, we need to leave now," Orka said to him, trying to keep her voice calm, as if it would drive out the fear and panic in his veins.

He is terrified, and yet has fought: has stood over his brother.

Mord sucked in a deep, quivering breath and lowered his spear.

Orka stooped and swept Lif up into her arms, hoisted him over her shoulder and turned to run.

Figures loomed out of the trees: a woman in wool and leather following a hound, and warriors behind her, some in mail. Mord raised his spear and stabbed at a mailed warrior, his blade grating up their chest and plunging into their throat. The warrior stumbled, gurgled and fell away. Mord stood there, staring as other warriors ran into the glade and circled him.

Orka hefted her axe and snarled, moving to cut a gap in the warriors around Mord.

There were hooves behind her and she turned and saw the blond man, his staff swinging at her. A crunch to the side of her head and she was spinning, Lif falling from her grasp, the ground rushing up to greet her.

CHAPTER FIFTY

ELVAR

Elvar shrugged her shield from her back and hefted it. All about her the Battle-Grim were doing the same as Ilska's Raven-Feeders spilled over the ridge.

"To me," Agnar called, warriors moving, checking weapons, buckling helms. Elvar saw Agnar appraising the land. He shouted orders and warriors were jumping on to the driving benches of the carts, cracking whips and reins, the carts rolling into a new position.

"HERE, ON ME!" Agnar yelled, standing between the carts and the huge mound that Elvar thought was Ulfrir-wolf. The Battle-Grim drew up behind Agnar, roughly two rows of twenty warriors, Agnar in the centre of the front row. Elvar pushed through to stand at his left, Grend taking his place at Elvar's side, his shield hanging loose. She saw Huld and Sólín in the front row, sword and long seax in their fists, and felt Biórr's hand on her shoulder behind her. She glanced back and smiled at him, though he looked grim, the flutter of coming battle in his eyes, fear and anger mixed. There was a tremor in his spear. Warriors with long-axes and spears stood in the second row, with more room for stabbing or hacking over the heads of those in the front.

"What's happening?" Sighvat called out, struggling in his bonds, trying to twist his head.

Agnar unbuckled the brooch of his bearskin cloak, folded it over his arm and walked to the nearest wagon, carefully draped it over the cart's bench, then walked back to the centre of their line.

Behind them Elvar heard Vörn moving, the unsettling rustle and creak of branches. The Froa-spirit was climbing up on to the head of her dead mother.

"A battle? Excellent," Vörn said as she sat and made herself comfortable from her vantage point. "You have no idea how *boring* the last three hundred years have been."

"A battle!" Sighvat cried. "Let me up." He struggled, twisting and writhing.

"Be silent, fat man," Vörn called down to him. A muttered word from her and a vine snaked over his mouth and pulled tight.

Ilska and her warriors were closer, now, and the Battle-Grim stood in silence as they approached through the snow, across the plain of ash and bones. Fifteen riders rode at their head, all in oiled *brynjas*, all with raven-black hair. Maybe three-score warriors marched after them, and behind them rolled a dozen carts, warriors sitting on their benches, linen covers stretched upon the cart-bed's frames, hiding what was held within.

Ilska rode at their head, black hair wind-whipped behind her, like her raven-winged banner. She wore a fine *brynja* and held a spear in her fist, her sword and helm hanging at her belt, a dark cloak across her shoulders and a round shield slung across her back. Either side of her rode two men, both in coats of mail, both dark haired, like Ilska, the look of kin about them.

Brothers to Ilska? Elvar wondered. One of them Elvar had seen before, standing in the stern of the Raven-Feeders' *drakkar* as it had rowed out of Snakavik's harbour: a warrior, tall and hulking, with the sides of his head shaved like Agnar's and a long-axe in his fist. That axe was slung over his back now. The other warrior was black-haired and hunched with muscle, clothed in mail with a hand-axe hanging at his belt. His face had four livid scars running through it, as if he had been clawed by a bear.

Ilska raised a hand and the riders reined their mounts in, the warband and carts behind them rippling to a halt. The warriors spread behind her, forming a loose line, wider and deeper than the

Battle-Grim. Ilska dismounted, handing her reins to a warrior in the line behind her and walked forwards, the two men either side of her dismounting and following after her.

Agnar stepped forwards to meet them.

Elvar scowled. She was used to seeing Sighvat at Agnar's shoulder, and seeing him walk out alone seemed wrong. Without thinking she stepped out of the line and strode after him. There was a moment's gap, and then she heard the pad of Grend's footfalls behind her. And then another pair of feet. She glanced back and saw Biórr following after her, concern on his face. Elvar liked it.

Ilska stopped and waited.

Close up, she was older than Elvar had realised. She had deep lines around her eyes.

"Surrender to me and I shall allow you and your warriors to live," Agnar said as he reached her, a grin on his face.

Ilska looked at him, hard and cruel. She snorted a laugh, but there was little humour in it.

"Your days are done, Agnar Broksson, chief of the Battle-Grim," she said, her face flat, her voice emotionless. "Step aside or die." She shrugged.

"I was here first," he replied, still smiling, as if he were just chatting over a game of tafl. "Besides, I am glad that you are here. I have sworn a blood oath to find you, so you have made my task easy." He raised his hand, looking at the white scar that wound around it, then looked over his shoulder at his warband. "My oath will be fulfilled to you this day," he said to Uspa.

The Seiðr-witch dipped her head to him, then stepped around the warband and walked to them.

"Ilska," she said, a familiarity in her voice, and a hatred. "My son?"

"He lives, Uspa," Ilska said.

"Give him back."

"No. He will change the world. As you could have done."

"It is not the way," Uspa said, a deep sorrow in her voice. "Please, do *not* do this."

"Enough," Agnar barked at Uspa. "There will be no pleading, no bargaining. We will take your boy back from these *niðing* child-stealers," he said, his smile gone, iron and steel in his voice. He looked over Ilska's shoulder to her warband and sniffed. "My Battle-Grim will make a fine song of this. Of you and your Raven-Feeders."

"A song that they will not hear sung," one of the men at Ilska's shoulder growled, the one with the long-axe. "You and your Battle-Grim will be food for ravens soon enough."

Agnar shifted his gaze to him, and took his time to look the huge warrior up and down. "Best be silent when your betters are talking," Agnar said to him.

The man took a step forwards, his hand reaching for his axe. Ilska held a hand up, slapped his chest and he stopped.

"We have work to do and little time to waste," she said, her eyes flickering to Vörn the Froa-spirit, perched upon her mother's head, then back to Agnar. "A *holmganga* to resolve this, Agnar Broksson," she said.

"You would risk all on a duel, when you outnumber us?" Agnar said, raising an eyebrow.

Elvar was surprised, too. Despite Agnar's words, it was clear that they were in the weaker position: the Raven-Feeders outnumbered them, and their reputation was formidable, so to suggest a duel that would level the odds to one on one, that seemed foolish.

"I value my people, as no doubt you value yours," Ilska said. "My Raven-Feeders will win, there is no doubt of that. But this way, the only death on this field will be yours." She shrugged.

"So, you would fight me?" Agnar said.

"Not I," Ilska said. "My brother, Skrið, has begged for that pleasure."

The warrior with the long-axe smiled.

"Him?" Agnar said with a twist of his lips, then he laughed. "I accept."

"Good," Ilska said, turning on her heel. "Skrið, make it quick. Drekr, with me," she snapped at the scarred man. He stood there a moment, looked from Agnar to Elvar, from Grend to Biórr, then gripped his brother's arm and squeezed it before striding away after Ilska.

Elvar hesitated a moment, then leaned in to Agnar.

"Kill this arseling," she whispered. "We have a saga-tale to make."

"I'll see you after," Agnar said, not looking at her, his eyes fixed on the bulk of Skrið, and then Elvar was walking away, Grend and Biórr following her.

She settled into Agnar's position in the front row of the Battle-Grim and looked back. Skrið shrugged his axe from his back, gripped it two-handed and swung it around his head, loosening his shoulders. It hissed through the air, snatching snow into its swirling wake. His dark *brynja* rippled and gleamed.

Elvar looked along the line of the Battle-Grim and saw the tension and excitement she felt in her own bones mirrored in those about her. Huld held the bear-claw around her neck; Sólín's white-knuckled hand gripped her sword hilt; Biórr tugged on his neat beard; others were restless, shifting.

Behind them Vörn the Froa-spirit frowned, was sniffing the air.

Agnar had his shield held loosely in his hand. He drew his sword with hardly a sound, the blade shining with the oil and grease from the scabbard's sheepskin liner. He looked back at the Battle-Grim, saw Elvar and winked at her, then he fixed his gaze on Skrið, set his feet, hefted his shield and gave his sword a lazy turn with his wrist.

"Come on then, big man," Agnar said. "See if you can earn your battle-fame this day, and stand against Agnar Battle-Grim."

Skrið's lips moved into a twisted snarl, and Agnar laughed at whatever the hulking warrior had said. Elvar felt a flush of pride for her chief, for his boldness and wit, even as he must surely feel death's raven-wings flapping above him. Agnar was not a small man – rather, he was tall and broad – but Skrið towered over him, like a bear over a wolf.

Elvar whispered a prayer, though there were no gods left to pray to.

Except for the dragon beneath her feet.

Let Agnar win. Let Agnar win. Let Agnar win.

The muted pounding beneath the ground beat on, like a war drum keeping time, faster now, as if it sensed the imminence of violence, the proximity of blood and death.

Skrið stepped forwards and swung his long-axe in a great, looping arc.

Agnar stepped away, letting it slice harmlessly through air. He smiled at his opponent.

Skrið did not pause. He strode in after Agnar, quickly for a big man, closing the gap between them, his axe whirling above his head, slicing again, lower. Agnar jumped away this time, stumbled on an ash-covered skeleton and Skrið rushed in, shifting his axe to a two-handed grip. There was a grunt as Agnar raised his shield, fighting for his balance. The axe's butt cracked into his shield, hard enough to smash a door from its hinges, sending Agnar stumbling back another few paces. Skrið followed, his hooked axe head darting forwards, catching the shield rim and tugging Agnar towards him. Agnar stumbled forwards and swayed to his left, the axe blade slicing across his cheek, blood leaking, and he chopped with his sword into Skrið's chest.

Brynja rings sprayed and blood welled, but Skrið just grunted and slammed his axe butt into Agnar's shield again, sending him staggering back a few paces again, the sound of wood cracking. The axe whirled around Skrið's head and whistled down at Agnar, who side-stepped to the right, raising his shield. The clang of iron as the axe blade grated off Agnar's shield boss and deflected, sending the blade chopping into the ground.

Elvar grinned to see it, a move she had seen Agnar perform on the training field countless times. It was perfectly executed. She knew what Agnar would do next, even as the axe blade hacked into the ground with a burst of ash and earth.

Agnar pivoted on a heel and stepped in close, slamming his shield into the big man's face and slicing his sword across Skrið's thigh as he stepped away, out of range again.

Skrið stumbled back, spitting blood from his bloodied mouth.

A gasp erupted from the Raven-Feeders, a cheer from the Battle-Grim.

"I can almost hear the skálds singing," Agnar said, a smile on his face as he followed Skrið, who retreated a few steps, limping, blood sheeting down his breeches from the cut in his thigh, just below the links of his mail coat. "Of the death of Skrið the Witless, the giant who thought he could kill Agnar Fire-Fist."

He moved in on Skrið with small steps, left and right, always closing in, and Skrið shuffled back a few paces.

Elvar grasped Grend's arm, the scent of Agnar's victory so close. She glanced beyond Agnar and Skrið and saw Ilska and her brother, Drekr, watching. Ilska looked almost disinterested.

Skrið stopped retreating and straightened. Smiled with bloodied teeth. Elvar frowned. Something . . . changed about him. He looked at Agnar and hefted his axe. A glint of red flashed from his eyes.

Agnar hesitated.

"He is *Tainted*," Elvar hissed.

Skrið moved, surging forwards more quickly than Elvar could follow, his axe swinging, too fast for Agnar to side-step, too powerful to defend against. Agnar raised his shield and took the brunt of the blow, the axe bursting through the linden-wood in an explosion of splinters, slicing into his arm. Skrið ripped the blade free in a spray of wood and blood, dragging Agnar with it. Agnar's shield was rent, half-shattered in his fist. He stabbed with his sword, a short, powerful blow, but Skrið was already twisting away, Agnar's blade grating sparks across Skrið's mail. A short chop from Skrið, two-handed with his axe and the blade bit into Agnar's shoulder, ripped down his chest, mail links shattered, a spurt of blood and a scream as Agnar dropped to his knees, sword falling from his grip, shield arm hanging limp. He stared up at the man towering over him, axe raised.

"Food for ravens," Skrið snarled and swung his axe.

Agnar dragged his seax from its scabbard and stabbed down into Skrið's foot. The big man bellowed, stumbled, his axe swinging wide, whistling past Agnar's shoulder. At the same time Agnar rammed his shattered shield up, long splinters stabbing into Skrið's throat, bursting out of the back of his neck.

Skrið slumped and gurgled, blood jetting, and with a bellow Agnar heaved him away, Skrið toppling to the side, ash exploding around him, settling back upon him as he lay gasping and twitching beside Agnar.

A silence settled over the plain, snow falling, ash swirling.

Elvar screamed and punched the air with her spear, the Battle-Grim letting out a triumphant roar, banging weapons on shields.

"AGNAR," they yelled. "AGNAR!"

Agnar moved, half-rose, then slumped back down to his knees, gasping.

Ilska stared, face pale and twitching. Her brother beside her stood with his mouth open, stunned. Ilska took a step towards Agnar.

Elvar stepped out of the line and started to walk to him, then to run.

Behind her Vörn shouted something.

She heard the sound of feet behind her, Grend following, and Biórr.

"DRAGON-BORN!" Vörn shouted, and Elvar's footsteps faltered. She stopped, turned and looked at Vörn.

The Froa-spirit was standing upon her mother's head, pointing at the corpse of Skrið, her hair rippling like branches in the wind.

"DRAGON-BORN," she yelled. "I SMELL YOUR BLOOD. CHILDREN OF LIK-RIFA, YOU SHALL COME NO CLOSER!"

Elvar stared, uncomprehending for a moment, then she remembered Skrið's eyes glinting red, his unnatural speed and strength.

He was Tainted: dragon-born. But . . . they do not exist.

Grend reached her and slowed to stand with her, Biórr running on to Agnar.

Elvar turned, stared at Skrið's dead body lying in the ash beside Agnar, then at Ilska and Drekr, both striding towards Agnar.

They are kin, she thought: *Ilska, Skrið, Drekr.* She looked at the others who had ridden in behind Ilska, another score of warriors, all with crow-black hair. *All of them are dragon-born.*

Ilska stopped, staring at Vörn. She turned, waved a hand in the air and the carts at the back of their warband began to move, their drivers guiding them wide, around the warband, towards Vörn and the blasted remnants of the great tree. As they moved the linen sheets covering their cargo were ripped away, revealing scores of people sitting on benches in the cart's beds. Children. Iron collars glinted around their necks.

"Bjarn!" Uspa cried out.

Biórr reached Agnar and stood over him, the Battle-Grim's chief raising an arm to the young warrior, his mouth moving as he said something.

Biórr raised his spear and stabbed it down, into Agnar's open mouth, down into his throat, and ripped it out. Blood sprayed, Agnar swaying, falling backwards.

Elvar screamed.

CHAPTER FIFTY-ONE

ORKA

Orka woke to a rhythmic shaking, blinked and stared, trying to make sense of the world. The sound of water, fast-flowing, a timber wall, voices. A stabbing, thumping pain in her head, one side of her face wet. The iron scent of blood. She tried to move, but found that her hands and feet were bound. Then she realised she was slung across her horse Trúr's back like a trussed deer.

She twisted her head and caught a glimpse of the blond-haired man who had struck her with his staff.

A Galdurman, she thought. *He spoke words of power and his staff burst into flame.* She could smell burned hair, and thought it was probably hers, where he had struck her.

Other shapes moved around her: warriors on horseback, and others walking. Hounds loped alongside them. Shouts and the creak of gates, then they were turning, hooves on hard-packed earth, and they passed through an open gateway and into a wide courtyard.

The Grimholt, Orka thought. *This is not the most deep-cunning way of gaining entry within its walls.*

They walked up a gentle slope, following the curve of a channel carved from the river. Two sleek *snekkes* were moored to a jetty, their hulls freshly painted in yellow and black, Queen Helka's colours. Around the courtyard were a tangle of buildings. Barns, a forge, the clang of hammer on iron echoing. Stables, chicken coops, pigpens. Goats bleated and chickens ran clucking as the party rode through the courtyard. Then Trúr was stopping and Orka was being dragged from his back and slung on to the floor. She saw Mord, unconscious and bound, and Lif, still shivering and blue-veined from the frost-spider's venom, though his eyes were open and aware.

"If I cut your bonds about your ankles, will you be a good prisoner and walk?" a voice said behind her. "You're a big lump and I'm not getting any younger." She twisted and saw an older man looking down at her, his thinning hair close-cropped, and a white beard, a scar running through a large, lumpy nose.

Orka nodded. She heard the rasp of a seax being drawn and the rope binding her feet was sawed. Arms pulled her upright.

She stretched, clicked her neck and looked around.

The Galdurman was dismounting, the warrior with him. A blonde-haired woman took the reins and rode on towards stables, leading another horse with an unconscious woman slung over its back and a chest tied to its saddle. Orka winced as she looked at them, the pain in her head throbbing harder.

"No time for sight-seeing," the white-haired man said as he dragged on the rope about her wrists. Orka stumbled on, blood returning to her feet in a prickling, stabbing flood now the rope-binding was gone. Other warriors fell in about them as she was steered towards the wooden hall and tower, Mord and Lif carried between them. The hall had a roof of birch-bark and turf; the tower had wooden tiles pegged to the lathe-beams.

Men and women paused in their work, thralls and craftsmen, all staring at Orka and the two brothers. A sound rang out from a barn close to the river.

A child's voice, a cry.

Orka stopped, staring at the barn.

"Breca," she croaked, discovering that her throat was dry and cracked.

The white-haired man pulled her on; another warrior prodded her back.

"Breca?" Orka said, louder.

"Move on, you big bitch," the warrior behind her snapped, and prodded her again.

There was the sound of a slap and a child's voice rang out again.

Orka ripped her hands from white-hair's grip and turned, head-butted the warrior behind her, his nose bursting with a *crack*. He dropped to the ground, a long-axe falling from his fingers. She kicked a woman in the knee as she stared at the fallen warrior, the woman doubling over with a yelp. Orka raised her bound hands and slammed them down on to the woman's head, sending her sprawling.

A blow to Orka's shoulder spun her, the white-haired man glaring at her, slamming his spear butt into her belly. She felt another blow across the back of her legs, dropping her to her knees, and heard thuds and grunts as warriors closed about her, beating her with spear butts, punching and kicking. A boot connected with her chin and white light exploded in her head.

Orka snapped awake, gasping, ice-cold water dripping from her face. She was hanging suspended: pain in her wrists that were tied tight and raised over her head, bound to an iron ring in a wall; her feet dragging on the floor. She took her weight and slowly stood, relieving the pressure on her wrists. Blinked and shook her head, water spraying.

She was in a room of the tower, judging by the view from a window through stretched and scraped animal skin. She glimpsed turfed roofs below, and the ice-glitter of the river. Mord and Lif were similarly restrained, tied to iron rings bolted into the wall. A fire burned in an iron brazier, and a long table was sat against a wall, all manner of sharp and unpleasant looking tools spread upon it. A pair of tongs was heating in the fire. White-hair was there, along with broken-nose. He was leaning against a wall and had his long-axe back in his hands, and the woman whose knee Orka had kicked was stood in front of her. She turned away and limped across the room with an empty bucket. Others were spread around the room: a bald man wearing a pitted leather apron with rolled up sleeves standing by the fire, and the blond-haired Galdurman sitting on a chair by a door.

"What were you doing lurking in the woods about the Grimholt?" the white-haired man asked Orka.

"Just . . . travelling through," Orka muttered.

"Travelling through the Boneback Mountains, half a league from any road, in the middle of a frost-spider nest," he said.

"Got . . . lost," Orka grunted. She rolled her tongue around the inside of her mouth and felt a loose tooth. Spat a glob of blood. "I'm a trader."

"A trader," white-hair said, smiling. "Dressed in a fine *brynja*, carrying a spear, axe and two seaxes, and that's just you." He held up her weapons belt and dangled it. "What is your trade? War?"

"Vigrið is a dangerous place," Orka said. "Best to be prepared."

White-hair laughed and looked her up and down. "I've seen your sort before, but never in a trader's market. More often across the rim of my shield, in the battle-fray."

Orka shrugged. "My father was a big man."

"You killed one of my men," white-hair said. "Well, not you. Him." He pointed at Mord. "Haga, wake him up."

"Aye, chief," the woman said, refilling her bucket from a barrel in the corner and walking to Mord. She threw it in his face and he woke spluttering and gasping. He shook his head, looked around and saw Lif, who was barely conscious, heaped in the corner on trembling limbs. Lif coughed and spat up ice-rimed phlegm.

"Brother," Mord said to him, worry in his eyes.

"He'll live," white-hair said. "Those pale spiders like their meat alive, just not kicking. Now," he said, taking the tongs that had been heating in the fire and walking towards Lif. "I can burn the ice from your veins, if you like." He held the tongs close to Lif, heat rippling in waves, then looked at Mord.

"So, who are you?" he asked Mord.

"Fishermen," Mord said, still groggy.

"A-ha," white-hair laughed, "so, the same question asked twice, with two different answers. Which is it? Fishermen, or traders?" He looked from Mord to Orka. "I think I'll take this one's eye, just to convince you I'm serious. And then I'll ask you again: Who are you and why are you here?"

He moved the tongs towards Lif's face, who pressed himself into the wall, whimpering through his chattering teeth.

Mord yelled and thrashed in his bonds.

"Drekr," Orka said.

White-hair stopped and stared at Orka. Frowned.

"I'm hunting a man named Drekr," Orka said. "He stole my son, and I want him back. I was told Drekr was coming here."

A look passed between white-hair and the other guards.

The Galdurman sat up straighter.

"Never heard of no Drekr," the white-haired man said.

"I heard a child cry out in the courtyard," Orka said.

"Just one of Rog's brats," broken-nose blurted, too quickly, Orka thought and she saw his eyes flicker to the Galdurman.

"Drekr," Orka repeated. "I tracked him to Darl, and then from Darl to here. My informer told me he trades in Tainted children, and that they pass through the Grimholt."

"Shut up," white hair snarled at her. "Shut her up," he said, and the man with the rolled-up sleeves lifted a hammer from the table and walked towards Orka.

"I saw Drekr in an inn in Darl," Orka continued, staring only at the Galdurman, now. "*The Dead Drengr*. He was meeting with Hakon Helkasson."

The bald man raised his hammer.

"Hold," the Galdurman said, and the hammer hovered in the air. "Skapti?" the Galdurman said, standing and frowning at the white-haired man.

"Don't know what she's talking about, Lord Skalk," Skapti said, though he could not hold the Galdurman's gaze.

"You fought at Svelgarth, did you not?" Skalk said to Skapti.

"Aye, lord. With distinction. Was awarded this for my bravery," he said, gesturing to a silver arm ring around his wrist.

"Who gave it to you? Who led your warband?"

Skapti looked away, at the other guards in the room.

"Prince Hakon," he said.

A silence fell in the room: heavy. Broken-nose shifted, taking the weight of his long-axe.

Skalk saw. "Try anything foolish, and I will burn the flesh from your bones," he growled at broken-nose. The warrior held his gaze a moment, shuffled his feet, then looked away. "Now," Skalk said to Skapti, "tell me: What is Hakon up to behind his mother's back?"

Another silence, then Skapti sucked in a deep breath.

"We just let Drekr bring his . . . goods here. Sometimes he . . . stores them here awhile, sometimes they go west, sometimes north. Orders from the prince were that we are supposed to let Drekr do as he pleases."

"Hhmmm." Skalk tugged on his blond beard, frowning.

"Is my son here?" Orka growled. She felt the need for him deep in her bones, the possibility that he was close stirring her blood like heat boils water.

"Shut *up*," Skapti snarled at Orka.

The sound of shouts came from outside, the drum of hooves passing through the gates. Voices in the courtyard. Haga limped to the window and peered out.

"Riders," she said. "*Drengrs*, some with Helka's eagle."

"Bring them up," Skalk said, and a warrior close to the door left.

Orka knew who it was in the courtyard, or guessed who it was. She tested her bonds, the rope thick and tight about her wrists. If she stood on her toes, she could reach the knot with her teeth.

"Be still, bitch," broken-nose said to her.

Footsteps sounded in the hall below, thudding up the stairs, and the door opened, the warrior who had left leading them. Behind him strode a *drengr*, a young man in mail with a sword at his hip, dark-haired with a pointed, dripping nose.

Mord made a sound in his throat: a growling snarl.

"Guðvarr," Orka muttered. Arild stood in the doorway behind him, more *drengrs* behind her.

In the distance Orka heard a child scream.

"Is that my son?" she snarled. Her blood was bubbling in her veins, a red mist beginning to filter through her thought-cage.

Guðvarr stood and stared, taking all in the room in. His eyes settled on Mord and Lif and he smiled as he strode towards them, drawing his sword.

"Wait!" Skalk shouted, but Guðvarr was already in motion, drawing his arm back and stabbing his sword into Mord's belly: deep, punching out of Mord's back in a spray of blood. He twisted the blade. Mord screamed and writhed.

Lif screamed in horror, spraying chips of ice.

Guðvarr grabbed a fistful of Mord's hair and lifted his head to stare into his eyes.

"A weasel-turd *niðing*, am I?" he said as he twisted his sword again, Mord's screaming rising in pitch.

Lif yelled and thrashed in his bonds as Guðvarr ripped his sword from Mord, releasing a tide of blood, Mord slumping, whimpering and mewling.

Another child's wail drifted up from the courtyard.

Something shifted, deep inside Orka, her consciousness and clarity sharpening between one heartbeat and the next. She felt her blood storming through her veins, the heat of anger changing, abruptly cold, primal, sweeping her body, fire and ice mingled. A flush of strength flooded her muscles, her vision sharper, senses keener. She lunged up and bit into the knotted rope that bound her wrists, her teeth suddenly sharp, ripping and tearing. The rope fell away.

All were staring at Guðvarr and Mord. Orka moved towards her weapons belt on the table.

Haga with the limp saw her first, dropped her bucket, reached for her spear propped against a wall and opened her mouth to shout a warning.

Orka let out a howl as she swept up her weapons belt and drew her seax and axe, leaped at Haga, kicked the spear shaft and stabbed her seax up into the woman's belly, blood sluicing over Orka's fist, then shoved her away and rose in a storm of iron, bellowing, a rush of rage and power consuming her.

All around her warriors were yelling, drawing weapons. Guðvarr was shouting, stumbling away from Mord and Lif, towards the open doorway where more warriors crowded. Orka buried her axe in the skull of the bald man and wrenched it free as he fell back into the brazier, flaming embers scattering, fire erupting. Warriors came at Orka and she ploughed into them, laughing and howling as they screamed and died, then she found herself close to Lif and sliced the rope binding his wrists.

He reached for a fallen weapon.

"No," Orka growled. "Stay behind me," she snarled at him, a warning, and then she was moving again, throwing herself into the warriors that crowded the room, though they hesitated now.

"*Eldur logar björt*," a voice cried out. It was the Galdurman, Skalk, and flames crackled into life on his staff. Orka hurled her axe at him, the blade spinning and slamming into his shoulder, sending him falling back into the warriors in the doorway, losing his grip on his staff.

Warriors lined up against Orka, sword, axe, spears, all pointing at her. Seven, eight men and women in the room, more in the doorway and corridor beyond. She paused, set her feet, even the wolf in her blood knowing that there was no defeating these odds.

She smiled at them, a blood-flecked leer.

A sound came from above: a ripping, tearing, cracking sound. Shouts and yells erupted from the warriors in the room, looking up.

Daylight flooded in as a portion of the roof disappeared, ripped away in the talons of a huge raven, wings beating, a storm of wind in the room, fanning the scattered flames. Beams erupted in fire, crackling, smoke billowing.

"FAVOUR FOR A FAVOUR," the raven squawked, and then a second raven swooped down, ripped more of the roof free and grabbed a warrior running at Orka in its talons, lifted him high and threw him, spinning and screaming, from the tower.

"FOUND YOUR FRIENDS LOOKING FOR YOU," the first raven cawed as it rose higher on beating wings, and two small shapes swept close, buzzing into the room in a blur of wings.

One landed upon a woman's shoulder, a chitinous, segmented body and a too-human face, bulbous eyes under grey-sagging skin, and a mouth full of too many sharp-spiked teeth. A tail curled up over its back, tapering to a needle-thin sting, which whipped forwards and stabbed the woman in the cheek.

"*Finally, Spert found you, mistress*," Spert said as the woman staggered and choked and dropped her sword, hands grasping for her face. Her veins were turning black, spreading from the sting in her cheek across her face like a diseased spiderweb, down her neck. She tried to speak, to scream, but her tongue was already black and swelling. She collapsed and Spert's wings buzzed, hovering and darting after his next victim.

Another small figure sped around the room on parchment-thin wings: sharp-clawed Vesli, with Breca's spear in her fist, stabbing it into faces as she flew.

Orka smiled and growled, looking for new people to kill.

Broken-nose came at her, shrugging his shoulders, hefting his long-axe, warriors parting to give him room. He swung a great looping blow at Orka, but she ducked beneath it and leaped close, stabbed her seax up under his chin and thrust with savage strength until the blade scraped on the bowl of his skull. He collapsed, twitching, dropping his long-axe. Orka left her seax lodged in his skull and caught the long-axe in both hands as it fell, felt its familiar and long-missed presence shudder through her body, like the touch of an old lover.

She kicked broken-nose's body away and stood before the warriors crowded in the doorway, Spert and Vesli hovering over her.

A silence fell. All that could be heard was the crackle of flame, groans of the dying, heavy breaths of the living as a dozen warriors stared at her.

They turned and ran.

Orka swept after them, swinging the long-axe, chopping, explosions of blood. Bodies fell tumbling down the tower's stairs, Orka still hacking at them, her axe rising and falling in a torrent of blows as she carved into them. When she blinked and looked up, shaking her head to clear the blood from her eyes, she found she was on the feast hall's steps, staring out into the courtyard, not knowing how she got there, and she was standing over corpses, gore-drenched, panting, snarling, wanting only to kill.

More people were here: warriors, some running at her, more running from her, others leaping into the boats on the jetty, cutting frantically at mooring ropes. She glimpsed Skalk and Guðvarr there.

A fresh pulse of rage and strength swept her as she glowered at them all, both the dead and the living. At these people who would keep her from her child.

Cut them, tear them, rend them, she thought.

She broke into a run, snarling, slavering, her long-axe rising.

CHAPTER FIFTY-TWO

ELVAR

Elvar stood and stared. She distantly heard herself screaming; could not believe what she was seeing.

Biórr stood over Agnar's body as he bled out into the ash and snow of Oskutreð's plain. Agnar's feet twitched, a last spasm rippling through him, and then he was still.

Biórr stooped down beside Agnar, ripped the pouch from his belt and delved inside it, then stood and raised jangling keys.

"Ilmur, Kráka," Biórr cried out, "you need be thralls no longer. Join us. Take your freedom."

Elvar looked back and saw Ilmur burst from behind the ranks of the Battle-Grim, bounding forwards across the ash-plain. Behind him came Kráka. She was running too. Ilmur sped past Elvar and Grend, and reached Biórr, who placed the key in the lock of Ilmur's thrall-collar and turned it, the collar opening with a click. Biórr took it from the *Hundur*-thrall, then held it out to Ilmur. He looked at it, grabbed it and hurled it away. Kráka reached them and Biórr did the same for her.

Elvar heard the clank of the collar hitting the ground.

"BETRAYER!" Elvar screamed.

Biórr looked at her.

"Join us," he said, holding a hand out to her.

"Agnar," Elvar cried.

"He got what he deserved," Biórr snarled. "A slaver, dealing in others' misery."

"Why?" Elvar said.

Biórr spread his arms wide.

"Because I am Tainted, too," he said. "Ilska protects us, gives us a home." His face bubbled with rage and anguish, tears in his eyes. "We Tainted are human, too, are people of flesh and blood, can feel joy and happiness, pain and heartbreak. We are not animals to be hunted and sold."

The blood of Rotta that Vörn sensed among us, Elvar thought. *Rotta the rat. Rotta the betrayer, deceiver, trickster.*

"You killed Thrud," Elvar said, remembering Thrud's wound in the back, Biórr lying unconscious on the tavern floor.

Biórr's face twisted with shame and guilt. "I did not want to do that," he said.

Elvar took a step towards him, hefted her spear and hurled it at him. It flew straight and fast. Biórr raised his shield and stepped to the side, unnaturally fast, the spear slicing through the space where he had just stood.

Elvar drew her sword and strode towards him.

Grend grabbed her arm and pulled her back.

"Look," he said, pointing with his axe.

The Raven-Feeders behind Biórr were marching forwards, drawing into lines, their shields raised.

"Let them come to us," Grend said.

She pulled against him, rage bubbling through her, at what Biórr had done, to Thrud, to Agnar, how he had made a fool of her. She snarled and spat, the thought of his blood spilling on the ash-covered ground raging through her.

"Stay here and you'll not avenge Agnar," Grend shouted at her, his knuckles white around her wrist. "Stay here and you'll die." He pulled on her again. "Face him in the shield wall, with the Battle-Grim about you."

Elvar stared at him, snarled and nodded, then they were running back to the Battle-Grim, slotting into the front row and turning to face the Raven-Feeders.

Ilska was leading her surviving brother and the others who had ridden with her off the field, towards the carts and Vörn, who had leaped down from her mother's head, silently waiting. Elvar saw that Uspa had gone to stand close to Vörn.

The Raven-Feeders who had marched behind Ilska, over sixty warriors, were striding towards the Battle-Grim.

Elvar sheathed her sword and drew her seax, the blade almost as long as her forearm.

This will be shoulder to shoulder, shield to shield, knifework, seax work, a time of heave and stab, no room for sword skill. She was breathing heavily, could hear her heart pounding in her head, not from exertion but from shock.

Agnar is dead. He had always been so full of life, of courage and energy. And he had won, slain Skrið the dragon-born in single combat, a deed worthy of a saga-song. It was too much for her thought-cage to comprehend: rage and grief raw and surging through her. She ground her teeth and hefted her seax, one side razor sharp, the broken back that tapered to the tip sharpened too.

"BATTLE-GRIM!" a voice cried out: Grend, beside her. "Be ready for the shield-storm, the battle-fray. These gutless worms are betrayers, carrion-feeders come to steal our gold and our glory. They have slain our chief like the *niðing* cowards they are. Time to show them what true courage and battle-fame is."

The Battle-Grim roared a cold-hearted cheer.

"SHIELD WALL!" Grend bellowed, and as one the Battle-Grim shuffled tight in their lines, raised their shields and pulled them in, a crack of linden boards as they set the wall, hide-covered rim pressed tight to iron boss, like the rippling scales of a snake. Elvar pounded the iron cap of her seax against her shield, Grend doing the same with his axe, all about them warriors following suit, beating a death march for the Raven-Feeders as they approached.

Thirty paces away, twenty, ten, and the Raven-Feeders halted. Elvar searched for Biórr in their ranks but could not see him among the faces before her, growling and spitting and hurling insults from behind the shield rims as they sought to summon their courage. In their eyes she saw pride, anger, and fear too. It is a hard thing to fight in the shield wall, where death is closer than a lover and the world condenses to the steel-fisted warrior before you: a place of snarling fury and gut-churning fear, of blood and shite and pain.

Shouts came from Elvar's right. She recognised Vörn's voice, and Uspa's joined to it. There was a flicker of flames, a flash of incandescent light, a tremor in the ground, and there was more screaming. A horse neighing and the sound of wood splintering.

A cart? Elvar had no time to look. The Raven-Feeders roared and surged forwards.

"READY!" Grend bellowed. Elvar saw the brightness of his eyes and the trembling in his limbs that took him when the battle-rage swept him. She set her feet, shoulder into her shield, Seax drawn back.

There was a concussive crack as the Raven-Feeders slammed into them, Elvar's shield battered, Grend beside her snarling. She felt the line wavering, a tremor through her shield arm, her feet scraping and sliding in the ash-thick ground as she fought to keep her place, heaving back against the immense pressure bearing down upon them. She knew that the Raven-Feeders outnumbered them, their wall at least three lines deep, all of that weight pushing and grunting and heaving against her. A gap opened between her shield and Huld's next to her. Elvar thrust her seax through it, felt the blade bite, and then hot blood slicked her hand. She shoved harder, twisted the blade and heard a scream, pulled her seax back and rammed the gap closed.

To her right Grend grunted and growled, chopping his axe over the top of his shield rim. She heard the clang of iron, saw a body slump to the ground, then shifted her weight and stabbed down into a glimpsed body, flesh bared above the neckline of a *brynja*, white, panicked eyes in a bearded face. Another scream cut short; the grate of bone and she dragged her blade free.

Behind her a shield held her upright, one of the Battle-Grim stabbing over her head with a spear, and the weight against her shield slackened. Elvar pressed hard, set her feet and looked over the top of her shield. There was a gap as a warrior fell away, hands clasping at blood gushing from a hole in their throat. They sank to the floor, dragged away by someone in the second row, and another figure loomed, stepping into the gap before Elvar could press into it. It was a woman, a pitted iron helm on her head, a hand-axe in her fist, screaming death and murder. Elvar swayed away from the bearded blade as it chopped at her face, ducked and pushed, stabbed under the rim of her shield and sawed through *winnigas* and flesh, felt the blade grind on shinbone, sawed the seax back and then stabbed over the top as the axe-wielding woman hissed with pain and lurched on her injured leg. Elvar's seax stabbed into her open mouth. A gush of blood and a gurgled scream.

"AGNAR!" Elvar screeched. "BATTLE-GRIM!" She heard the cry swept up around her and the battle-joy filled her, a wild strength in her limbs, a hot rage in her thought-cage, driving her on. More faces loomed before her: men, women, they appeared snarling and fell away screaming, her seax and Grend's axe reaping bloody ruin. The battle-storm raged around her, sounds merging, a deafening, roaring, muted din that echoed inside her helm as steel clashed, shields splintered and warriors screamed. All was blood and death. Slowly the strength leeched from her, pain pulsing from a score of cuts and bruises, her limbs heavy, shield arm numb, battered, muscles burning. She gasped ragged breaths, continued to stab and shove and stand. Beside her Grend was roaring, eyes bulging, spittle spraying from his mouth as he hacked and chopped and killed.

Something slammed into Elvar's shoulder: it felt like a punch, making her stagger. She saw a man diagonally across from her spitting curses, an ash-spear in his fist. She tried to stab back at him, but her seax would not rise, her arm not obeying. Looked down and saw his spear blade had torn through her *brynja* and stabbed into the meat of her shoulder. She shoved hard with her shield, pushed the warrior in front of her back a half-pace and the spearman pulled his weapon back for the killing thrust.

Elvar spat at him, knowing there was nothing she could do.

Then Grend's axe smashed into his face, carving through nose and mouth. He ripped it free in a spray of blood and cartilage and teeth, the spearman falling away, a gurgled scream through his ruined mouth.

Elvar swayed and took a step back, her legs buckling, and then an arm was wrapping around her, dragging her back, the line behind her parting, a warrior stepping forward to take her place in the wall.

"Let go," Elvar grunted at Grend, who was pulling her free of the shield wall, half-carrying her back into the open ground behind. She tried to lift her seax, saw she still gripped it in her blood-slick fist, but her arm wasn't doing what her thought-cage was telling it to do.

Grend pushed her down so that she fell on her backside and sat in the ash and mud, looking up at him. It was strangely quiet here, a dozen paces behind the wall, where battle was still raging. Elvar saw the Battle-Grim were holding. Here and there was a prone body, boots poking through, or a corpse lying still, dragged out of the way by the second row, but she could see the Battle-Grim were gaining ground. Step by battered half-step they were pushing the Raven-Feeders back. Agnar had chosen his battleground well, the Ulfrir-wolf mound protecting the left flank, the carts arrayed to protect the right.

Grend kneeled beside her and gave her his water bottle.

"Drink," he grunted and she realised her mouth was dry and sticky with ash and blood. She drank, swilled her mouth out and spat, then drank some more. Grend took a swig from the water bottle, then poured the rest over Elvar's wound, leaning close.

"Cut the muscle," he muttered. "You'll have to fight with your left hand."

Elvar nodded. Grend had trained her since she was a bairn, drilled her in the weapon court at Snakavik until she could use both left and right with little difference. But she could not hold a shield as well.

"Find a spear and kill them from the second row," Grend said.

A high-pitched screeching erupted behind them and Elvar twisted, looking back.

Vörn stood beside Uspa, both of them side by side, barring the approach to the remains of Oskutreð. Uspa stood with her hands raised, a rune of fire glowing in the air before her, and a handful of warriors lay on the ground before Uspa and Vörn, some blackened and charred with flame, others looking like they had been torn to pieces, their wrists, ankles and necks wrapped with thick vine. Others stood impaled and slumped on branches that appeared to have just sprouted from the earth. Ilska and the surviving warriors were stood with her in a line facing them, all with bloodied fists. They were chanting, and runes of flame were igniting in the air before them, melding and glowing, flames leaping to the ground and spreading, speeding in a crackling line towards Vörn. They swept past Sighvat, who was still bound by vines to the ground, the fat warrior squirming and shouting.

"*Greinar vernda mig*," Vörn cried out, the ground before her shifting and bubbling, and vines punched free of the earth, knitted together like a wattle-fence in the fire's path, but the flames crackled and hissed and engulfed them, a wave of flame surging through the vines and on, snatching at Vörn's legs like hungry beggars.

There was a hiss and crackle and Vörn screamed as her feet ignited. Flames rippled up her legs, gouts of black smoke billowing, the stench drifting across the plain. Vörn batted at the flames, but they only spread, catching in her fingers and hair, her screams rising in pitch, and she gasped for air, mouth contorted. She swayed and fell, crashed to the ground, flames devouring her.

Ilska walked forwards, her dark cloak billowing behind her.

"*Farðu frá*," she said, as she squatted down and punched the ground. There was an explosion of ash and the ground bucked, a rippling line rushing away from her like a serpent hidden just beneath the waves. It slammed into Uspa, exploded beneath her and sent her hurtling through the air. She crashed to the ground and rolled, then came to a stop, unmoving.

Ilska stood and moved on, the surviving warriors behind her following, maybe seven or eight of them left standing, including Drekr. Other warriors were jumping from the carts' driving benches and dragging the children from the backs of the carts, hauling them towards the dead tree by ropes and chains. Seventy, eighty, ninety children, all with collars of iron about their necks. Elvar thought she saw Bjarn among them.

Ilska reached the blackened stump of Oskutreð and set her foot upon it, climbing up on to the open space where the huge, bolted door lay. Puffs of ash filled the air, the pounding beneath the earth rocking and rattling the door.

Those that followed Ilska climbed up on to the blasted tree, the children behind them. Some cried and wailed; others walked silently, like warriors who have accepted their fate.

"Bjarn," Elvar croaked, her voice hoarse.

She saw him clamber up on to the tree, a collar around his neck, and join the others upon the giant trapdoor.

Ilska and the warriors with her shouted at the children, dragged them, commanded them until they stood in a circle, feet edging the line of the great door. The warriors from the carts joined Ilska's band, swelling their ranks. Ilska reached inside her cloak and pulled out a book. It was thick, wrapped in some kind of red hide. She opened it, then began to read.

"*Réttu upp hendurnar, þú verður að hlýða. Spillað blóð í saklausu barni, sameinast og vaxa af krafti. Brotið rúnir og innsigli töfra.*" Ilska called out, and there was a flare of red within each thrall-collar about each child's throat, a ripple of fire. The children cried out, and their eyes glazed over. Each child raised their right arm, palm open.

Ilska drew a small seax from a scabbard across her back and sliced her hand that held the book, then slashed the palm of the child in front of her, and the ones to either side. They said nothing, made no move, did not cry out.

All of Ilska's companions did the same, cutting their own palms, then the hands of the children about them, until all of them stood there, bleeding, blood dripping on to the wooden door beneath their feet.

"*Blóð drekans, lík rífa, voldugur, sameina og binda, brenna þessa hindrun, opna leið fyrir herra okkar,*" Ilska cried out, shaking her hand, droplets of blood spraying around her.

"*Blóð drekans, lík rífa, voldugur, sameina og binda, brenna þessa hindrun, opna leið fyrir herra okkar,*" all those on the great tree cried out, echoing Ilska, shaking their hands, and blood rained down upon the ancient door, pooling, trickling through the cracks into the darkness beneath.

Elvar and Grend just stared, entranced, even as the battle still raged behind them.

The constant pounding beneath the earth stopped abruptly, as if a giant had sucked in a deep breath and held it.

And then there was a crash, the huge door on the tree jolting. Ilska staggered, some of the children falling.

A huge, muted roar leaked out from the cracks around the door, vibrating in the soil, deeper than an ocean storm, other voices joining it, higher in pitch but fierce and proud. Screams. Roaring. A growing, rumbling thunder.

"RUN!" Ilska shouted, finding her balance and breaking into movement, sprinting and leaping from the tree's stump. All those around her were doing the same: Ilska's followers, children, a flood of people.

Something crashed into the trapdoor and there was a great splintering, cracking sound, a cloud of dust and ash rising up, engulfing all still on the tree as they were hurled into the air. Ilska was thrown from her feet, the red-skinned book spinning from her grip. A silence. Elvar holding her breath, staring, and then there was another crash beneath the door, huge splinters of wood erupting, the ground shaking like a ship in a storm-wracked sea.

Elvar and Grend were thrown into the air, a tremor passing beneath them like the ripples of a boulder hurled into water, throwing the fighting shield walls into chaos, men and women falling, staggering.

Another silence, like a held breath, and then the door exploded, splintered wood and bodies tossed skyward, disappearing in an expanding shroud of dust and ash and debris. Elvar was heaved from her feet, weightless, the rolling cloud engulfing her. She crashed to the ground, tumbling, came up against something solid, knocking the wind from her, then just lay there, coughing and wheezing as the dust settled around her, searching for Grend. He was nowhere to be seen, bodies everywhere, scattered like chaff on the wind.

From the centre of the dust storm, deep within the earth, screams echoed. A roar of pain. The earth shaking. Voices shouting.

A figure burst from the smashed-open doorway, spinning through the air, rising high and then falling, crashing to the ground a hundred paces away from Elvar and rolling, coming to a standstill. A winged woman. She was red-haired, rust-feathered wings draped around her; her body was wrapped in a coat of mail that glittered like fish-scales, a scabbarded sword at her hip. She groaned. Elvar just stared at her, open-mouthed.

A roar burst out from the shattered door, rolling across the plain, filling it until Elvar put her hands over her ears, a fresh cloud of dust roiling out. The hint of something huge moved within that dust cloud, and a darker shadow emerged from the earth.

And then Lik-Rifa, corpse-tearer, dragon, last of the dead gods, burst into the air.

Elvar lay on the ground, slowly took her hands from her ears and sat up, staring.

A stench rolled across the plain, of something long dead, of death and destruction and age-old corruption. Lik-Rifa beat her tattered wings, the turbulence of their motion buffeting Elvar and all those around her back to the ground. The dragon's body was thin and emaciated, ribs stark through pallid scales, almost white and translucent with dark patches of rot and weeping yellow pus. Her jaws were wide and razored with teeth longer than spears, pale horns rowed and curling upon her head. Maniacal eyes blazed red with feverish intensity, like a forge-lit fire.

It was hard to tell how big she was, up there in the sky, but when she spread her wings she blotted out the wan sun that gleamed behind the clouds. Small shapes dangled from her wings and body, snagged and snared upon her scales. Elvar realised they were corpses, flesh-rotted and putrefying.

Two smaller figures burst from the ruin of the broken door, both winged, like the woman who had crashed to the ground close to Elvar. One had golden wings and blonde-flowing hair, a spear in her fist; the other had white-feathered wings and silver-bound braids in her hair, a nocked bow in her hand and a sword at her hip. They beat their wings and spiralled up after the soaring dragon, the white-winged woman loosing arrow after arrow. They speckled the dragon's side, small eruptions of white flame where they pierced her, and the dragon roared her pain, tucking a wing and looping in the sky. Her huge, razored tail lashed out but the winged figures soared around it, continued to stab and pierce the dragon's hide with spear and arrows.

The golden-winged woman screeched like an eagle and flew at the dragon, raked her spear along Lik-Rifa's belly, scales and blood raining down. The dragon let out an agonised roar and twisted in the air, head snaking out on a serpentine neck, jaws snapping at the woman, who veered. There was a spray of feathers as dragon teeth snagged a wing and the woman crashed into the dragon, her spear plunging deep into the beast's neck, blood sluicing. Lik-Rifa let out a scream that sent Elvar huddling back to the ground with her hands over her ears. The dragon twisted and spun in the air, one tattered wing slapping into the bow-wielding woman, sending the bow flying and the woman hurtling away. The warrior with the injured wing clung to the spear in Lik-Rifa's neck and drew a long knife from her belt, then started stabbing into the dragon's throat. Another screech and Lik-Rifa was spiralling and diving, speeding towards the ground. There was an explosion of earth and ash as she crashed to the surface, skidding and ploughing through a wagon, timber smashed to kindling, the horse bound to the cart thrown on its side, neighing wildly, legs broken. A great dust cloud rose up about the dragon and woman.

The white-winged warrior appeared in the air again and circled the cloud, drawing her sword.

Dust settled, the dragon rising from the ashes, the golden-winged woman standing before Lik-Rifa, long-knife in her hand.

The woman above tucked her wing and dived like a well-cast spear, slamming into Lik-Rifa's back, her sword stabbing deep. Lik-Rifa's head reared high with an ear-splitting scream. The woman on foot ran at the dragon, one golden wing hanging limp, long-knife glinting, and she leaped, her knife punching deep into the dragon's chest, blood spurting. Another agonised scream from Lik-Rifa.

They are going to kill her, Elvar thought.

Figures moving, a blur and Ilska appeared, running into the fray, the hulking Drekr behind her. They both leaped at the golden-winged woman, sword and axe stabbing and chopping. Feathers erupted and the woman screeched and twisted, ripping her knife free of the dragon, who was bucking, throwing the white-winged woman from her back.

Drekr slammed into the golden-winged woman and the two of them crashed to the ground, rolled together and came to a halt. Ilska ran after them, hovering as the woman grabbed Drekr's axe-fist and pinned him, raising her long-knife. Ilska hacked down, her sword chopping into the woman's neck. There was a scream and a spurt of blood, Ilska's sword rising and chopping again, the winged woman collapsing, blood spraying.

Lik-Rifa was roaring as the white-winged woman spun through the air, wings beating, trying to pull herself out of her fall, but she was too low. She smashed into the ground, skidded and stopped, rose to her knees and then the dragon slammed a long-clawed foot down upon her. Jaws lunged, crunching down on to the woman's head. A savage wrench of Lik-Rifa's neck and a screech was cut short.

The dragon lifted her neck and gulped, swallowing the head, then let out a ground-shaking roar and stamped on the headless woman, again and again, ripping and rending with her taloned feet: blood, bone, feathers torn and pulped and mashed to a fine mist.

Ilska and Drekr stood silently, staring.

Lik-Rifa slowed, then stopped, looked around and saw the horse from the cart, still laying on its side, eyes wide and white, sweat-streaked with fear and pain. The dragon's wings beat and Lik-Rifa lurched into the air, came down hard upon the horse, claws pinning it, jaws biting, tearing. Flesh ripped, blood spurting, bones cracking as the long-caged dragon feasted.

Elvar stared in silent awe and horror.

Then the dragon was raising her head, the scales of her jaws dripping red with gore. She licked her lips and shivered, huge and proud and dreadful, her razored tail lashing, gazing about with red-glowing eyes. She took a long, shuddering breath, her eyes focusing upon Ilska and Drekr standing before her, small and insignificant against her hulking form.

"Ahhh," the dragon sighed with a rumble that shook Elvar to her bones and reverberated in her chest. She heard a scraping sound behind her and saw Grend, ash-covered and bleeding, crawling towards her. She moved to him, dragging herself across the ground with her one good arm, and they collapsed upon each other, lay there staring at Lik-Rifa.

A silence settled, punctuated by the groans and screams of the wounded or dying, the wailing of children scattered by the dragon's arrival.

Figures appeared from the ash: more of Ilska's dragon-born and Raven-Feeders, rising from around the battlefield where they had been tossed like the wooden figures on some giant tafl board.

Ilska approached Lik-Rifa, twice the size of Snakavik's mead hall, and fell to her knees before her, Drekr and the others doing the same.

The dragon regarded them, dipped her sinuous head and breathed deeply, stirring hair and clothes and ash.

"My children," Lik-Rifa growled, her voice like a mountain slide, like a summer storm fractured with lightning, rumbling into the distance. A tremor passed through her, from snout to tail, and then her shape was shimmering, twisting and coiling like mist, shifting and changing, contracting, shrinking, until a woman stood before Ilska and her kin. She was tall, taller than any man, at least as big as the bull troll Elvar had slain on Iskalt Island. Her body was lean and striated, skin pale and raw and scabbed, weeping pus. Blood oozed from wounds. She was clothed in a tunic of grey, red-woven at the neck and hem, a belt studded with gold about her waist and a dark cloak billowing about her like wings. Her hair, black as jet, streaked with silver, was pulled back tightly, braids woven into it. She had a sharply beautiful face. Red coals glowed in her eyes.

"What has become of my world, my children, my warbands?" she said, her voice hard as the north wind, a tremor shivering through it. She looked around at the battle-plain, the shapes of the long-dead become part of the landscape. Her red eyes flickered to Ilska.

"What has Orna done?" she snarled, lips twisting, wringing her hands. "I heard them screaming, my children, my faithful, but I could not help them, because of that winged BITCH. ORNA DECEIVED ME AND I WAS CAGED." She roared those last words, the sound of it seeming too loud for her lungs to create, but Elvar felt it in her bones, felt the ground quake beneath her.

"The world has changed, my lady," Ilska said. "But we are your faithful, the pure. We have laboured the long years to set you free. We are few, but more will come, now that you are released from your cage."

"Hhmmm," Lik-Rifa rumbled, then reached a hand out and stroked Ilska's cheek. It was big enough to crush her head, if she wished. She looked around again, her eyes coming to rest upon the shattered stump of Oskutreð, and shivered. "I hate this place," she snarled, the muscles twitching in her face. "I must get away from here. I would see my hall of Nastrandir." She shook, a tremor passing through her, and suddenly she was shifting and changing, growing, expanding, wings sprouting and arching from her back, until she was a dragon again, bigger than two mead halls. Her wings snapped out, pale and tattered, with a blast of foul air, and then they were beating, lifting her from the ground. "I have languished in a hole and devoured nothing but corpses for three hundred years," she said with a disgusted twist of her lips. "I would feel the wind in my face and hunt again," she rumbled as she rose into the air, wings lashing and rising higher and higher, spiralling up.

Ilska and the others burst into motion, gathering up the carts that were still in one piece, turning them back on to their wheels, rounding up horses that had bolted in a flurry of motion. Other warriors searched the plain, gathering up the thrall-collared children and loading them upon the wagons. Elvar and Grend just lay there, numb and staring, as if the end of the world had come and there was nothing else they could do except observe its destruction.

Raven-Feeders passed close to them, but ignored them, just hurried on with their search for the children or rounding up horses. Here and there Elvar saw others of the Battle-Grim, lying in the ash, stunned, staring, pale-faced.

And then Ilska was shouting out commands and whips were cracking, the carts pulling away, warriors riding or marching around them.

And above them Lik-Rifa spiralled in the air. She opened her jaws and roared, shaking the sky, and then she beat her wings, flying south into the soft-glowing sky. Corpses hung from her wings.

Elvar watched the dragon shrink into the distance, Ilska and her Tainted warband following after her like a serpent slithering across the ground. She looked at Grend.

"Only blood and death and misery will come of this." She remembered Uspa's words to her, only a few nights ago. She had not believed the Seiðr-witch then, had thought her mad. She believed her now.

"What have we done?" she whispered.

CHAPTER FIFTY-THREE

VARG

Varg ran through the pinewoods, his spear in his fist, the scent of needles and sap sharp in the air. Cold crackled in his chest as his breath misted in billowing clouds. Pain rippled down his ribs with each indrawn breath, a reminder of the dragon-born's blow, but it was dull and manageable now, blending with the other hundred pains from the bruises and cuts he had acquired during the fight at Rotta's chamber. Varg ran ahead of the Bloodsworn, some riding, others on foot. He could hear them behind him: Einar's pounding feet, the drum of hooves. Ahead of him he saw the outline of Edel and her hounds as she flitted through dappled woods, running light-footed and soundless across the thick, spongy pine-needle litter.

I am Tainted. The thought spiralled through his thought-cage, the first thing there when he awoke each day, staying close throughout the course of the day until he lay his head upon his cloak and slept at night. *I am Tainted.* It was so clear to him, now. How he had been able to run faster and longer than anyone else on Kolskegg's farm, the speed and savagery that had gripped him in the pugil-ring, but always controlled. He had been alone, set apart. A stranger in a hostile land.

Except for Frøya. My sister. She was Tainted too. Is that why I could feel her deep in my bones, in my veins, hear her death-scream in my head? He blinked and shook his head.

I am Tainted. When Svik and Røkia had first told him, he had felt cursed, and ashamed. Now, he no longer felt like that. He knew how the world viewed him: as less than human, as a commodity to be harnessed, enslaved and used. He was familiar with how that felt, had been a thrall all his life, so he understood why the Bloodsworn had not told him, had watched and waited until they trusted him.

Trust me. That felt . . . strange to him, gave him a lightness in his belly. To be trusted, to be called kin. Called brother. And as strange and shocking as it felt, it also made him feel . . . content. Like a smile locked away tight in his chest.

Edel slowed ahead of him and whistled, then stopped and waited, her two wolfhounds sitting beside her, their tongues lolling. Varg drew close to her and slowed, stopped and leaned on his spear. Other figures flitted through the woodland, to the left and right, Edel's scouts moving towards them.

"Torvik told me you would make a fine scout," Edel said to him as he rested a hand on his knee and breathed deeply. "He said you noticed other Bloodsworn scouts in the woods around Rotta's chamber, before we attacked."

The thought of Torvik was a knife in the gut, a sharp pain. Grief, anger. He missed his friend; had only realised Torvik *was* his friend now that he was gone.

Varg nodded.

"You have the makings of a fine scout, then, within the Bloodsworn," she said. "Each of us finds our place."

Røkia emerged from the trees, breathing heavily, sweat glistening and clouding in the cold. She had a spear in her fist, was running in her mail coat with her shield slung across her back, like Varg. She nodded a greeting when she saw him.

"You look fine in your new mail," she said as she drew near.

He shrugged his shoulders, still getting used to the weight of his new-won *brynja* and his shield across his back. The belt around his waist helped to take some of the weight of mail from his shoulders, and once he had wriggled into it, which was easier said than done, it did not feel as heavy as it had in a rolled-up bundle. Even so, the mail, weapons and shield were all extra weight that he was unused to carrying.

"Why have we stopped?" he asked Edel.

"Can you smell anything?" she asked Varg, Røkia and the other scouts who were filtering out of the trees to join them.

Røkia caught the scent first, Varg a few heartbeats behind.

"Smoke," Røkia said.

"And blood," Varg muttered.

Behind them the drum of hooves and feet grew louder, closer, and Varg looked back to see Glornir riding out of the woodland, Svik and Sulich riding either side of him, Einar running alongside them, the rest of the Bloodsworn following. Glornir was glowering, danger leaking from him. He reined in and Edel told him of the scents ahead, of smoke and blood.

"Kit check: make yourselves ready," Glornir called out.

Varg pulled a nålbinding cap from his belt and pulled it over his head, despite his sweat, then unbuckled his helm from his belt, the helm he had taken from the dragon-born at Rotta's chamber, and pulled that over his woollen cap and buckled it under his chin. Sound changed, muted and dull, but he could still hear well enough. He checked the curtain of mail was spread across his neck and shoulders, then gripped his spear and waited. He saw Jökul crouch and scoop up a handful of pine needles and dirt, rub it between his palms and let it fall back to the ground. The smith stood and took his hammer from his belt, rolled his shoulders and clicked his neck.

"Onwards," Glornir said, then kicked his horse on.

Edel moved ahead, Varg, Røkia and the scouts behind her like a flock of geese, spreading wide, Glornir behind them, the Bloodsworn all about him. Varg felt the first rush of danger, a tingling in his blood. They travelled in silence apart from the drum of hooves and feet, the clink and jangle of harness and mail, and the rhythmic breaths of the runners. Two days they had been on Skalk's trail now, and all sensed that they were closing in.

They were travelling along a wide track through the trees, the mountains of the Bonebacks rearing tall as the sky on the left. Varg heard the sound of water ahead, fast-flowing, and the scent of smoke and blood grew stronger. A scream drifted on the wind, faint but clear, sending chills running across Varg's neck. It was terror-filled.

The path opened up, a tree-shrouded hill sloping up to the right, and then they were moving into a valley, the cliffs ending on the left, and a timber wall appeared, built tight to the cliff face and running parallel to the path. A black cloud of smoke billowed across them. Varg held his breath, and then he was out the other side. Beyond the timber wall he saw a hall and tower on a slope, pressed to the cliff face. The tower burned like a rushlight, flames crackling and hungry, smoke wafting. The smell of blood and death was thick in the air, now. Behind the crackle and hiss of flames there was no other sound.

"Shields!" Glornir shouted and Varg shrugged his shield from his back, hefted it and ran on, all about him the Bloodsworn doing the same.

Edel held her fist up ahead of him and they slowed, moving from a run to a jog, then a walk as a gateway in the timber wall appeared, a river beyond it. The gates were open. Edel slowed, her hounds loping ahead. The wolfhounds reached the gateway first and stopped, crouched and snarling, hackles raised.

Glornir rode up, reining his horse in, letting her walk through the open gates of the fortress. Edel, Røkia and Varg entered beside him, spreading out into a sloping courtyard, the Bloodsworn following behind.

The ground was littered with the dead, first in their ones and twos, then more of them the further into the yard Varg walked. Ahead of him the slope climbed to a hall and tower. There was a splintering sound as part of the tower gave way and collapsed, smashing through the turf roof of the hall. An explosion of sparks and ash.

There were more dead in the courtyard, piled deeper around the steps to the hall, bodies twisted together, hacked and mutilated. And on the steps in the midst of it all sat a woman. She was gore-drenched, red with blood from her head to her boots, a long-axe lying across her lap. An ugly creature was perched upon her shoulder, with a nasty-looking sting on its tail, and another vaesen sat on the steps before the woman. It was small, with sharp claws and a half-spear in its tiny, slim-fingered hand. A tennúr. It had a mound of what looked like blood-covered nuts piled at its feet and was crunching on one of them as it looked at Varg. A shiver of revulsion passed through Varg as he realised they weren't nuts: they were human teeth. And he didn't like the way the tennúr's gaze fixed for a long moment upon his own mouth. The two vaesen regarded Glornir and the Bloodsworn with suspicious, violent eyes.

Sitting around the woman's legs were children, maybe twelve or fifteen of them. They were the only things in the area not spattered in blood. They didn't seem to be scared of the woman, which Varg found strange, as his blood was tingling, and he felt the ripples of fear and danger pulsing off her. If he had hackles like Edel's wolf-hounds, they would have been standing stiff and straight.

Ahead of him Varg heard Glornir gasp a breath.

The woman looked up at them as they approached, her eyes fixing on Glornir. Varg saw recognition dawn in them.

"He's not here," the woman said, shaking her head, "he's not *here*." The pain in her voice was palpable. Tears had streaked clean lines through the blood and gore and fragments of bone that were thick on her cheeks.

Glornir reined in his horse and slipped from his saddle, then walked a few steps towards her and stopped.

"Orka Skullsplitter," he whispered.

The woman stood.

"My brother?" Glornir asked.

"They killed him and took my son," she said, fresh tears rolling down her cheeks.

Glornir walked up to her and spread his arms wide, pulling her into an embrace.

The story continues in…

Book Two of The Bloodsworn Trilogy

GLOSSARY

Pronunciation Guide

ð: "th" in "they"; Guðvarr is pronounced "Guthvarr"
j: "y" in "yellow"; Jord is pronounced "Yord"

Norse titles/terms/items

akáll – an invocation, a magic ceremony to reveal the last moments of the dead
Althing – meeting, an assembly of freepeople
Berserkir – person descended from Berser, the Bear god. Capable of great strength and savagery
blóð svarið – blood oath
brynja – a coat of mail
byrding – coastal boat
drakkar – a longship
drengr – an oathsworn warrior, trained to a high level
druzhina – elite horse-mounted warrior
Galdrabok – book of magic
Galdurman – magician, specifically rune-magic
Graskinna – grey-skin, a book of magic scribed on flayed skin
Guðfalla – the gods-fall
guðljós – god-lights
hangerock – a type of dress
hird – warriors belonging to a lord's household
heya – agreed

holmganga – a duel recognised by law, a way of settling disputes
jarl – lord or earl
knarr – a merchant/trade ship
Maður-boy – a human child
niðing – "nothing", "nobody", an insult, meaning without honour
nålbinding – to bind or weave. An early form of knitting used to make clothing
Raudskinna – red-skin, a book of magic, made from the flayed of a dead god
seax – single-edged knife, often with a broken back, of varying sizes. A multi-purpose tool, from cooking/shaving to combat
Seiðr – a type of magical power, inherited from Snaka, the father of gods
Seiðr-witch – a woman who wields magical power
skáld – a poet, teller of tales, often employed by a jarl or chief to sing of their heroic deeds
skál – good health
snekke – a smaller version of a longship
tafl – a game of strategy played upon a board with carved figures
thrall – a slave
Úlfhéðnar – person descended from Ulfrir, the wolf-god
vaesen – creatures created by Lik-Rifa, the dragon god
weregild – a blood-debt
winnigas – cloth covering for the legs, from ankle to just below the knee
whale-road – the open sea

ACKNOWLEDGEMENTS

Writing this first book in the Bloodsworn Saga has been a lot of fun. Norse mythology and history has fascinated me for as far back as I can remember, and this series is my love-song to that. Since I opened the pages on a retelling of *Beowulf* when I must have been nine or ten years old, I have been captivated with that unique sense of Norseness, with its mystery, its tragedy, its darkly comic view of both the gods and humanity, and, of course, its brutally pragmatic epic battles. That might go some way to explaining why I am now a Viking reenactor, who enjoys standing in the shield wall with my sons around me. This book in essence is inspired by both *Beowulf* and Ragnarök, that end-of-days battle where the gods fell, and the world was made anew.

As always, a virtual warband has helped in making this book happen.

Firstly, I must thank my wife, Caroline, for the myriad ways she supports me, not least of which is putting up with my vacant look when my head is off in other worlds. She is the engine room of my family and the reason I rise each day.

My sons, James, Ed and Will are always so involved in my imaginary worlds and they make writing them a joy.

And of course, my daughter, Harriett, who brings the sunshine every day with her smile and her laughing eyes.

A huge thank you to my agent Julie Crisp, legendary for her

bloodthirsty suggestions. It may say something about this book that upon reading it she did not suggest that I kill a single extra character. This is a first. I am deeply grateful for her belief and hard work in bringing this world to life. She is a consummate professional and a dear friend.

James Long, my editor at Orbit UK, who has been a pleasure to work with on this, our first venture together. His passion and enthusiasm for this tale has been a great encouragement and I am looking forward to journeying across the Battle-Plain with him.

A thanks also to Priyanka Krishnan, my editor at Orbit US, for her constant hard work on my behalf, and a massive thank you to the Orbit team, both in the UK and the US.

My thanks must also go to those people who have read my first draft and helped shape it into the book you are holding. My sons Ed and Will for reading this book from when it was just one chapter long, and for their passion for the world and characters of the Bloodsworn. I think they already see themselves as standing in the shield wall alongside the likes of Glornir Grey-Beard and Einar Half-Troll.

Kareem Mahfouz, a great friend and always bursting with enthusiasm and a keen eye, thank you for your indomitable spirit. Our telephone conversations are becoming a well-loved tradition.

Mark Roberson, whose support, historical knowledge and enjoyment of my made-up worlds is always so helpful. I will never tire of our chats over a good breakfast.

And of course, I thank you, the reader, because without you there would be no more journeys into fantastical worlds.

I hope you enjoy this book, and that you will join me on this new adventure as I follow the Bloodsworn while they carve a bloody path across Vigrið, the Battle-Plain.

extras

meet the author

Photo Credit: Caroline Gwynne

John Gwynne studied and lectured at Brighton University. He has played double bass in a rock 'n' roll band and traveled the United States and Canada. He is married with four children and lives in Eastbourne, where he is part of a Viking reenactment group. When not writing, he can often be found standing in a shield wall with his three sons about him. His dogs think he is their slave.

Find out more about John Gwynne and other Orbit authors by registering for the free monthly newsletter at orbitbooks.net.

interview

Your love of Norse mythology and Viking culture was a strong influence on this story and your world of Vigrið; were there any saga tales in particular that inspired your creative process?

You're absolutely right, the Bloodsworn Saga is really my love song to Norse mythology, and I have drawn deeply on Viking-era history and Scandinavian folklore for this series. That has involved diving deep into research, but if I had to choose a book or tale that was the most inspirational, I would have to say *Beowulf*, that epic poem about a monster-hunting hero and his mercenary band of warriors. In my tale, they are not quite so heroic and more self-serving, but Beowulf's search for battle-fame and his desire to hunt the monsters that roam the dark places was definitely an inspirational starting point for this series.

You're already a paid-up history buff and historical re-enactor, but how much more research did you have to do in preparation?

I am a Viking re-enactor and enthusiast, and I love standing in the shield wall, shoulder to shoulder with my three sons and snarling at our enemies over the rims of our shields, being a Viking re-enactor has, I hope, added some layers of detail and authenticity to my writing. Things that I just wouldn't think of, for example, just how hard it is to hold a shield and spear up in combat for any prolonged period of time, or how difficult it is to get into a coat of ring mail. It is not as easy as you'd think, and I must confess to getting stuck in a coat of mail the first time I tried one on. Embarrassing moment.

Doing Viking re-enactment has helped me to understand the combat, the weapons and the clothing, but there's a lot more to writing a Norse-inspired fantasy novel than the combat. Since my childhood, I've been enamoured with stories of berserkers, of dragons, of shape-shifting gods, but to really try and capture a sense of Norseness for this series I read *a lot* of books in the year or so before I began writing book one.

I can give a few examples of the types of books I read, but if I were to list them all we'd end up with a very long bibliography here. At the heart of the research, I went back to the source material – the *Poetic Edda* and the *Prose Edda* – which are essentially old compilations of the Norse mythological tales, and also to the Icelandic sagas, which are a wonderful collection of tales from Iceland during the Viking period. I read many more sagas, such as *Njal's Saga*, *Egil's Saga* and the *Tale of Ragnar Lodbrok*. I've also read a lot of historical texts about the Viking period. Some excellent reads that stand out in my memory are *The Children of Ash and Elm* by Neil Price, *Vikings at War* by Kim Hjardar and Vegard Vike, and *Valkyrie* by Jóhanna Katrín Friðriksdóttir. I would also recommend *Vaesen* by Johan Egerkrans.

These books are just a snapshot of the reading that I've been through in an attempt to soak up those historically authentic details, as well as the tone and sense of Norse mythology and sagas. And I have loved every single minute of it. I love 'doing the research.'

The Shadow of the Gods *is set in a brand-new world, unrelated to your previous novels. Was it daunting to create this new world from scratch? What was your starting point?*

There was definitely a sense of nervousness when I began this new project. I was excited as well to be able to step into another world with a blank page and just play around in that creative sandbox, but my entire writing career – seven books over eight years – has been centred on the Banished Lands, so to begin another series in an entirely new world did at first feel a little daunting, and I felt nervous right up until I started writing the first chapter.

But as soon as I started writing Orka's first chapter I felt at home, like I'd known this character and this world for a long time. I think the characters, world and tale had been brewing in my mind for so long that it was just a joy to start exploring them and put the tale down onto the page.

Going back a little, my starting point in terms of inspiration for this new series was *Beowulf.* Equally inspiring, though, was the tale of Ragnarök, that end-of-days epic battle from Norse mythology, where all the gods fought and mostly died. I remember clearly reading through the *Voluspa*, which is a book within the *Poetic Edda*. It's also called the *Seeress' Prophecy*, and it recounts how Odin questions a seeress about the build-up to Ragnarök, and then the details of the last battle. There is a passage right at the very end, after the gods have fought and died:

> There comes the shadow-dark dragon flying,
> The gleaming serpent, up from Dark-of-Moon Hills;
> He flies over the plain, and in his pinions
> He carries corpses.

This is talking about the dragon Nidhoggr, who had been chained in the halls beneath Yggdrasil, the great ash tree, but the destruction and ruin of Ragnarök had set him free. So, I read this passage and just leaned back in my chair, thinking 'wow, that's cool.' Then I thought, 'I wonder what happened next…' And that was the spark that became the Bloodsworn Saga.

Readers have responded very positively to the roles that women play in* The Shadow of the Gods, *with Orka proving an instant favourite. Was it a deliberate move on your part to show that women in Vigrið are just as capable and deadly with an axe as the men?

That response has been wonderful to see. Depicting women as strong, capable warriors was a definite choice, and I did that for several reasons.

Writing in a Viking world is a good fit for writing strong female warriors, because female warriors are mentioned throughout Norse mythology – Valkyries and shieldmaidens are a regular feature – and even in Viking-era history there is a heated debate going on about the level of female involvement in the warrior ranks. This has been spurred by the recent discovery at Birka – a Viking-era trading town where many graves have been examined – that a grave always presumed to belong to a male warrior (a skeleton buried with the accoutrements of an elite warrior: sword, spear, axe, seax, shield, bow, horse) is in fact the skeleton of a female. So, there is evidence of at least one elite-level female warrior. How far-reaching this is – a one-off or just the tip of the iceberg – we don't know yet, but looking at the Icelandic Sagas we can see that Scandinavian culture, while still patriarchal and misogynistic, was significantly more progressive than the European cultures around it in terms of gender. For example, women could legally get divorced and own their own property, which was unheard of in other cultures of the time.

So, it wasn't as big a leap to write strong female warriors into this story as it would have been if I was writing a series inspired by, say, fourteenth-century France.

But to be honest, even if this wasn't the case, I still would have written the female characters in *The Shadow of the Gods* in the same way. I write to entertain, not to use my writing as a platform to preach my own personal values. But in saying that, I think something of who you are cannot help but leak into your work. Academically, I come from a sociological background, and am deeply aware of issues revolving around class, race and gender, and the issues of inequality, so themes around these issues will always tend to seep into what I write.

Also, I have to say that in my re-enactment group there are many women in the shield wall who are all extremely capable warriors, with excellent weapons-craft. One of our captains is an expert with the Dane-axe, which is considered an elite-level weapon and extremely difficult to master. I certainly would not want to go up against her in a scrap.

Talking specifically about Orka, she came about during a conversation with my wonderful agent, Julie Crisp.

I like to play around with tropes from the fantasy genre, sometimes to try and subvert them, and other times to write them with a more contemporary twist. Orka came out of a conversation with Julie back when the Bloodsworn Saga was just a few ideas in my head. I told Julie that I wanted to do something with the trope of the 'retired person of violence,' similar to Clint Eastwood's William Munny character in the film *Unforgiven*. I can't remember who suggested it first, but out of the conversation came the idea to write this character as female, because traditionally that trope is usually written as male. So, that is how Orka was born.

What is your favourite scene in* The Shadow of the Gods *and why?

Haha, I don't think that's fair to ask. ☺ If I were pushed, I would probably say the scene where Orka walks into a bar. That sounds like the opening line to a joke, but I can assure you it was no joke to those who were sitting in the bar.

When I wrote that scene, I felt that it came out as not just an action scene, although that part was fun, but also as a turning point for the plot and a statement of Orka's character. I try to write character into action scenes, and also plot twists and turns, so that they are never just action/combat for combat's sake. In this particular scene I hoped that the reader would come out of it understanding Orka's character on a new level, while also laying plot seeds that become more apparent in the last few chapters of this book and then more so in book two.

What's one thing about* The Shadow of the Gods, *either about the world or the characters, that you loved but couldn't fit into the story?

Probably more monsters. I came across so many wonderful, interesting and creepy creatures during my research into Scandinavian folklore and mythology, but the book only allowed for so many to be featured. I wanted to give each creature its moment to shine, rather than just throwing a scrunched up 'monster-bomb' at the book. In an act of will I saved some for book two. ☺

The Shadow of the Gods has an amazing cast of characters. If you had to pick one, who is your favourite? Who was the most difficult to write?

I'm honoured that you think that, thank you. I really enjoyed writing the cast of characters in *The Shadow of the Gods*, both the point-of-view characters and the side characters. One of my favourite characters to write was Svik.

One of the things that I wanted to inject into the tale was a specifically Norse sense of humour, and I used the character of Svik to try and do that. I noticed while doing my research and reading that, while Viking-era history can feel extremely grim, with the environment being cold, harsh and deadly, there is still a wonderfully dark, pragmatic sense of humour running through Nordic tales, and I wanted to try and capture that. The tale that Svik tells about the troll, the cheese and the porridge is my adaptation of a Scandinavian folktale, just tweaked a little to fit into my fantasy world, and it's a wonderful example of the sense of humour and pragmatic attitude to life that I found in the Norse literature.

My most difficult character to write? I'd say the dragon Lik-Rifa was a challenge. I loved writing her, but the combination of dragon to human shapeshifter presented its challenges: finding the right personality, and carrying it on between her two incarnations, of dragon and human, making her feel real, but also believable on both levels. I've given it my best shot and I hope that she comes across as interesting, sympathetic and terrifying all at the same time.

Without spoilers, can you give us a hint of what's in store for the Bloodsworn in The Hunger of the Gods?

Ha, okay. So, in *The Hunger of the Gods* the world has changed a little. The arrival of a dragon-god will do that. But Varg and the

Bloodsworn are caught up in their own private quest, chasing after the galdurman Skalk, who has abducted Vol, seiðr-witch of the Bloodsworn and wife of Glornir, their chief. Varg is one of the Bloodsworn now, but the quest for his sister's killer is still heavy in his mind.

Elvar is left with the shocking realisation that she has played a part in loosing Lik-Rifa the dragon-god upon the world, but she is also bound by the blóð svarið, the blood oath, to rescue a child abducted by Ilska the Cruel and her band of Raven-Feeders. So Elvar has to come to terms with the horror that her quest for battle-fame has inflicted upon the world, plus she has to try and figure out a way of rescuing a child who is surround by tainted warriors and a dragon-god.

And Orka just wants her son back. Nothing else matters to her but that.

These three characters will continue along their personal quests, but echoes of war are stirring in Vigrið and all three characters are slowly but surely drawn into a larger conflict.

You'll also find two new point-of-view characters in book two. Biórr, a member of Ilska's Raven-Feeders who had infiltrated the Battle-Grim and become Elvar's lover. And Guðvarr, nephew of Jarl Sigrún. I hope that these two additions will help to give a fully rounded view of the events happening in Vigrið.

Lastly, we have to ask: if you were Tainted, which godlike powers would you prefer to inherit?

Oh, that's easy. Ulfrir the wolf-god. I'd like to be *Úlfhéðnar.* What can I say, I've always loved wolves.

if you enjoyed
THE SHADOW OF THE GODS
look out for
SON OF THE STORM
Book One of The Nameless Republic
by
Suyi Davies Okungbowa

From one of the most exciting new storytellers in epic fantasy, the first book in the Nameless Republic trilogy is a sweeping tale of violent conquest and forbidden magic set in a world inspired by the pre-colonial empires of West Africa.

In the thriving city of Bassa, Danso is a clever but disillusioned scholar who longs for a life beyond the rigid family and political obligations expected of the city's elite. A way out presents itself when Lilong, a skinchanging warrior, shows up wounded in his barn. She comes from the Nameless Islands—which, according to Bassa lore, don't exist. And neither should the mythical magic of ibor she wields.

Now swept into a conspiracy far beyond his understanding, Danso will set out on a journey with Lilong that reveals histories violently suppressed and magics found only in lore.

Chapter One

Danso

The rumours broke slowly but spread fast, like bushfire from a rain-cloud. Bassa's central market sparked and sizzled, as word jumped from lip to ear, lip to ear, speculating. The people responded minimally at first: a shift of the shoulders, a retying of wrappers. Then murmurs rose, until they matured into a buzzing that swept through the city, swinging from stranger to stranger and stall to stall, everyone opening conversation with whispers of *Is it true? Has the Soke Pass really been shut down?*

Danso waded through the clumps of gossipers, sweating, cursing his decision to go through the central market rather than the mainway. He darted between throngs of oblivious citizens huddled around vendors and spilling into the pathway.

"Leave way, leave way," he called, irritated, as he shouldered through bodies. He crouched, wriggling his lean frame underneath a large table that reeked of pepper seeds and fowl shit. The ground, paved with baked earth, was not supposed to be wet, since harmattan season was soon to begin. But some fool had dumped water in the wrong place, and red mud eventually found a way into Danso's sandals. Someone else had abandoned a huge stack of yam sacks right in the middle of the pathway and gone off to do moons knew what, so that Danso was forced to clamber over yet another obstacle. He found a large brown stain on his wrappers thereafter. He wiped at the spot with his elbow, but the stain only spread.

Great. Now not only was he going to be the late jali novitiate, he was going to be the dirty one, too.

If only he could've ridden a kwaga through the market, Danso thought. But markets were foot traffic only, so even though jalis or their novitiates rarely moved on foot, he had to in this instance. On this day, when he needed to get to the centre of town as quickly as possible while raising zero eyebrows, he needed to brave the shortest path from home to city square, which meant going through Bassa's most motley crowd. This was the price he had to pay for missing the city crier's call three whole times, therefore setting himself up for yet another late arrival at a mandatory event—in this case, a Great Dome announcement.

Missing this impromptu meeting would be his third infraction, which could mean expulsion from the university. He'd already been given two strikes: first, for repeatedly arguing with Elder Jalis and trying to prove his superior intelligence; then more recently, for being caught poring over a restricted manuscript that was supposed to be for only two sets of eyes: emperors, back when Bassa still had them, and the archivist scholars who didn't even get to read them except while scribing. At this rate, all they needed was a reason to send him away. Expulsion would definitely lose him favour with Esheme, and if anything happened to their intendedship as a result, he could consider his life in this city officially over. He would end up exactly like his daa—a disgraced outcast—and Habba would die first before that happened.

The end of the market pathway came within sight. Danso burst out into mainway one, the smack middle of Bassa's thirty mainways that crisscrossed one another and split the city perpendicular to the Soke mountains. The midday sun shone brighter here. Though shoddy, the market's thatch roofing had saved him from some of the tropical sun, and now out of it, the humid heat came down on him unbearably. He shaded his eyes.

In the distance, the capital square stood at the end of the mainway. The Great Dome nestled prettily in its centre, against a backdrop of Bassai rounded-corner mudbrick architecture, like a god surrounded by its worshippers. Behind it, the Soke mountains stuck their raggedy heads so high into the clouds that they could be seen from every spot in Bassa, hunching protectively over the mainland's shining crown.

What took his attention, though, was the crowd in the mainway, leading up to the Great Dome. The wide street was packed full of mainlanders, from where Danso stood to the gates of the courtyard in the distance. The only times he'd seen this much of a gathering were when, every once in a while, troublemakers who called themselves the Coalition for New Bassa staged protests that mostly ended in pockets of riots and skirmishes with Bassai civic guards. This, however, seemed quite nonviolent, but that did nothing for the air of tension that permeated the crowd.

The civic guards at the gates weren't letting anyone in, obviously—only the ruling councils; government officials and ward leaders; members of select guilds, like the jali guild he belonged to; and civic guards themselves were allowed into the city centre. It was these select people who then took whatever news was disseminated back to their various wards. Only during a mooncrossing festival were regular citizens allowed into the courtyard.

Danso watched the crowd for a while to make a quick decision. The thrumming vibe was clearly one of anger, perplexity, and anxiety. He spotted a few people wailing and rolling in the dusty red earth, calling the names of their loved ones—those stuck outside the Pass, he surmised from their cries. Since First Ward was the largest commercial ward in Bassa, businesses at the sides of the mainway were hubbubs of hissed conversation, questions circulating under breaths. Danso caught some of the whispers, squeaky with tension: *The drawbridges over the moats? Rolled up. The border gates? Sealed, iron barriers driven into the earth. Only a ten-person team of earthworkers and ironworkers can open it.* The pace of their speech was frantic, fast, faster, everyone wondering what was true and what wasn't.

Danso cut back into a side street that opened up from the walls along the mainway, then cut into the corridors between private yards. Up here in First Ward, the corridors were clean, the ground was of polished earth, and beggars and rats did not populate here as they did in the outer wards. Yet they were still dark and largely unlit, so that Danso had to squint and sometimes reach out to feel before him. Navigation, however, wasn't a problem. This wasn't his first dance in the mazy corridors of Bassa, and this wasn't the first time he was taking a shortcut to the Great Dome.

Some househands passed by him on their way to errands, blending into the poor light, their red immigrant anklets clacking as they went. These narrow walkways built into the spaces between courtyards were natural terrain for their caste—Yelekuté, the lower of Bassa's two indentured immigrant castes. The nation didn't really fancy anything undesirable showing up in all the important places, including the low-brown complexion that, among other things, easily signified desertlanders. The more desired high-brown Potokin were the chosen desertlanders allowed on the mainways, but only in company of their employers.

Ordinarily, they wouldn't pay him much attention. It wasn't a rare sight to spot people of other castes dallying in one backyard escapade or another. But today, hurrying past and dripping sweat, they glanced at Danso as he went, taking in his yellow-and-maroon tie-and-dye wrappers and the fat, single plait of hair in the middle of his head, the two signs that indicated he was a jali novitiate at the university. They considered his complexion—not dark enough to be wearing that dress in the first place; hair not curled tightly enough to be pure mainlander—and concluded, *decided*, that he was not Bassai enough.

This assessment they carried out in a heartbeat, but Danso was so used to seeing the whole process happen on people's faces that he knew what they were doing even before they did. And as always, then came the next part, where they tried to put two and two together to decide what caste he belonged to. Their confused faces told the story of his life. His clothes and hair plait said *jali novitiate*, that he was a scholar-historian enrolled at the University of Bassa, and therefore had to be an Idu, the only caste allowed to attend said university. But his too-light complexion said *Shashi caste*, said he was of a poisoned union between a mainlander and an outlander and that even if the moons intervened, he would always be a disgrace to the mainland, an outcast who didn't even deserve to stand there and exist.

Perhaps it was this confusion that led the househands to go past him without offering the requisite greeting for Idu caste members. Danso snickered to himself. If belonging to both the highest and lowest castes in the land at the same time taught one anything, it was that when people had to choose where to place a person, they would always choose a spot beneath them.

He went past more househands who offered the same response, but he paid little heed, spatially mapping out where he could emerge closest to the city square. He finally found the exit he was looking for. Glad to be away from the darkness, he veered into the nearest street and followed the crowd back to the mainway.

The city square had five iron pedestrian gates, all guarded. To his luck, Danso emerged just close to one, manned by four typical civic guards: tall, snarling, and bloodshot-eyed. He made for it gleefully and pushed to go in.

The nearest civic guard held the gate firmly and frowned down at Danso.

"Where you think you're going?" he asked.

"The announcement," Danso said. "Obviously."

The civic guard looked Danso over, his chest rising and falling, his low-black skin shiny with sweat in the afternoon heat. Civic guards were Emuru, the lower of the pure mainlander caste, but they still wielded a lot of power. As the caste directly below the Idu, they could be brutal if given the space, especially if one belonged to any of the castes below them.

"And you're going as what?"

Danso lifted an eyebrow. "Excuse me?"

The guard looked at him again, then shoved Danso hard, so hard that he almost fell back into the group of people standing there.

"Ah!" Danso said. "Are you okay?"

"Get away. This resemble place for ruffians?" His Mainland Common was so poor he might have been better off speaking Mainland Pidgin, but that was the curse of working within proximity of so many Idu: Speaking Mainland Pidgin around them was almost as good as a crime. Here in the inner wards, High Bassai was accepted, Mainland Common was tolerated, and Mainland Pidgin was punished.

"Look," Danso said. "Can you not see I'm a jali novi—"

"I cannot see anything," the guard said, waving him away. "How can you be novitiate? I mean, look at you."

Danso looked over himself and suddenly realised what the man meant. His tie-and-dye wrappers didn't, in fact, look like they belonged to any respectable jali novitiate. Not only had he forgotten to give them to Zaq to wash after his last guild class, the market run had only made them worse. His feet were dusty and unwashed; his arms, and probably face, were crackled, dry, and smeared with harmattan dust. One of his sandal straps had pulled off. He ran a hand over his head and sighed. Experience should have taught him by now that his sparser hair, much of it inherited from his maternal Ajabo-islander side, never stayed long in the Bassai plait, which was designed for hair that curled tighter naturally. Running around without a firm new plait had produced unintended results: Half of it had come undone, which made him look unprepared, disrespectful, and not at all like any jali anyone knew.

And of course, there had been no time to take a bath, and he had not put on any sort of decent facepaint either. He'd also arrived without a kwaga. What manner of jali novitiate *walked* to an impromptu announcement such as this, and without a Second in tow for that matter?

He should really have listened for the city crier's ring.

"Okay, wait, listen," Danso said, desperate. "I was late. So I took the corridors. But I'm really a jali novitiate."

"I will close my eye," the civic guard said. "Before I open it, I no want to see you here."

"But I'm supposed to be here." Danso's voice was suddenly squeaky, guilty. "I *have* to go in there."

"Rubbish," the man spat. "You even steal that cloth or what?"

Danso's words got stuck in his throat, panic suddenly gripping him. Not because this civic guard was an idiot—oh, no, just wait until Danso reported him—but because so many things were going to go wrong if he didn't get in there immediately.

First, there was Esheme, waiting for him in there. He could already imagine her fuming, her lips set, frown stuck in place. It was unheard of for intendeds to attend any capital square gathering alone, and it was worse that they were both novitiates—he of the scholar-historians, she of the counsel guild of mainland law. His absence would be easily noticed. She had probably already sat through most of the meeting craning her neck to glance at the entrance, hoping he would come in and ensure that she didn't have to suffer that embarrassment. He imagined Nem, her maa, and how she would cast him the same dissatisfied look as when she sometimes told Esheme, *You're really too good for that boy.* If there was anything his daa hated, it was disappointing someone as influential as Nem in any way. He might be of guild age, but his daa would readily come for him with a guava stick just for that, and his triplet uncles would be like a choir behind him going *Ehen, ehen, yes, teach him well, Habba.*

His DaaHabba name wouldn't save him this time. He could be prevented from taking guild finals, and his whole life—and that of his family—could be ruined.

"I will tell you one last time," the civic guard said, taking a step toward Danso so that he could almost smell the dirt of the man's loincloth. "If you no leave here now, I will arrest you for trying to be novitiate."

He was so tall that his chest armour was right in Danso's face, the branded official emblem of the Nation of Great Bassa—the five ragged peaks of the Soke mountains with a warrior atop each, holding a spear and runku—staring back at him.

He really couldn't leave. He'd be over, done. So instead, Danso did the first thing that came to mind. He tried to slip past the civic guard.

It was almost as if the civic guard had expected it, as if it was behaviour he'd seen often. He didn't even move his body. He just stretched out a massive arm and caught Danso's clothes. He swung him around, and Danso crumpled into a heap at the man's feet.

The other guards laughed, as did the small group of people by the gate, but the civic guard wasn't done. He feinted, like he was about to lunge and hit Danso. Danso flinched, anticipating, protecting his head. Everyone laughed even louder, boisterous.

"Ei Shashi," another civic guard said, "you miss yo way? Is over there." He pointed west, toward Whudasha, toward the coast and the bight and the seas beyond them, and everyone laughed at the joke.

Every peal was another sting in Danso's chest as the word pricked him all over his body. *Shashi. Shashi. Shashi.*

It shouldn't have gotten to him. Not on this day, at least. Danso had been Shashi all his life, one of an almost nonexistent pinch in Bassa. He was the first Shashi to make it into a top guild since the Second Great War. Unlike every other Shashi sequestered away in Whudasha, he was allowed to sit side by side with other Idu, walk the nation's roads, go to its university, have a Second for himself, and even be joined to one of its citizens. But every day he was always reminded, in case he had forgotten, of what he really was—never enough. Almost there, but never complete. That lump should have been easy to get past his throat by now.

And yet, something hot and prideful rose in his chest at this laughter, and he picked himself up, slowly.

As the leader turned away, Danso aimed his words at the man, like arrows.

"Calling me Shashi," Danso said, "yet you *want* to be me. But you will always be less than bastards in this city. You can never be better than me."

What happened next was difficult for Danso to explain. First, the civic guard turned. Then he moved his hand to his waist where his runku, the large wooden club with a blob at one end, hung. He unclipped its buckle with a click, then moved so fast that Danso had no time to react.

There was a shout. Something hit Danso in the head. There was light, and then there was darkness.

if you enjoyed
THE SHADOW OF THE GODS
look out for
LEGACY OF ASH
Book One of The Legacy Trilogy
by
Matthew Ward

An epic tale of intrigue and revolution, soldiers and assassins, ancient magic and the eternal clash of empires,* Legacy of Ash *is the first in an unmissable debut fantasy trilogy from a major new talent.

A shadow has fallen over the Tressian Republic.

But as Tressia falls, heroes rise.

***Viktor Akadra** is the Republic's champion. A warrior without equal, he hides a secret that would see him burned as a heretic.*

***Josiri Trelan** is Viktor's sworn enemy. A political prisoner, he dreams of reigniting his mother's failed rebellion.*

***Calenne Trelan**, Josiri's sister, seeks only to break free of their tarnished legacy, to escape the expectations and prejudice that haunt the family name.*

As war spreads across the Republic, these three must set aside their differences in order to save their home. Yet decades of bad blood are not easily set aside. And victory—if it comes at all—will demand a darker price than any of them could have imagined.

Fifteen Years Ago

Wind howled along the marcher road. Icy rain swirled behind.

Katya hung low over her horse's neck. Galloping strides jolted weary bones and set the fire in her side blazing anew. Sodden reins sawed at her palms. She blotted out the pain. Closed her ears to the harsh raven-song and ominous thunder. There was only the road, the dark silhouette of Eskavord's rampart, and the anger. Anger at the Council, for forcing her hand. At herself for thinking there'd ever been a chance.

Lightning split grey skies. Katya glanced behind. Josiri was a dark shape, his steed straining to keep pace with hers. That eased the burden. She'd lost so much when the phoenix banner had fallen. But she'd not lose her son.

Nor her daughter.

Eskavord's gate guard scattered without challenge. Had they recognised her, or simply fled the naked steel in her hand? Katya didn't care. The way was open.

In the shadow of jettied houses, sodden men and women loaded sparse possessions onto cart and dray. Children wailed in confusion.

Dogs fought for scraps in the gutter. Of course word had reached Eskavord. Grim tidings ever outpaced the good.

You did this.

Katya stifled her conscience and spurred on through the tangled streets of Highgate.

Her horse forced a path through the crowds. The threat of her sword held the desperate at bay. Yesterday, she'd have felt safe within Eskavord's walls. Today she was a commodity to be traded for survival, if any had the wit to realise the prize within their grasp.

Thankfully, such wits were absent in Eskavord. That, or else no one recognised Katya as the dowager duchess Trelan. The Phoenix of prophecy.

No, not that. Katya was free of that delusion. It had cost too many lives, but she was free of it. She was not the Phoenix whose fires would cleanse the Southshires. She'd believed – Lumestra, *how* she'd believed – but belief alone did not change the world. Only deeds did that, and hers had fallen short.

The cottage came into view. Firestone lanterns shone upon its gable. Elda had kept the faith. Even at the end of the world, friends remained true.

Katya slid from the saddle and landed heavily on cobbles. Chainmail's broken links gouged her bloodied flesh.

"Mother?"

Josiri brought his steed to a halt in a spray of water. His hood was back, his blond hair plastered to his scalp.

She shook her head, hand warding away scrutiny. "It's nothing. Stay here. I'll not be long."

He nodded. Concern remained, but he knew better than to question. He'd grown into a dependable young man. Obedient. Loyal. Katya wished his father could have seen him thus. The two were so much alike. Josiri would make a fine duke, if he lived to see his seventeenth year.

She sheathed her sword and marched for the front door. Timbers shuddered under her gauntleted fist. "Elda? Elda! It's me."

A key turned. The door opened. Elda Savka stood on the threshold, her face sagging with relief. "My lady. When the rider came from Zanya, I feared the worst."

"The army is gone."

Elda paled. "Lumestra preserve us."

"The Council emptied the chapterhouses against us."

"I thought the masters of the orders had sworn to take no side."

"A knight's promise is not what it was, and the Council nothing if not persuasive." Katya closed her eyes, lost in the shuddering ground and brash clarions of recent memory. And the screams, most of all. "One charge, and we were lost."

"What of Josiri? Taymor?"

"Josiri is with me. My brother is taken. He may already be dead." Either way, he was beyond help. "Is Calenne here?"

"Yes, and ready to travel. I knew you'd come."

"I have no choice. The Council . . . "

She fell silent as a girl appeared at the head of the staircase, her sapphire eyes alive with suspicion. Barely six years old, and she had the wit to know something was amiss. "Elda, what's happening?"

"Your mother is here, Calenne," said Elda. "You must go with her."

"Are you coming?"

The first sorrow touched Elda's brow. "No."

Calenne descended the stairs, expression still heavy with distrust. Katya stooped to embrace her daughter. She hoped Calenne's thin body stiffened at the cold and wet, and not revulsion for a woman she barely knew. From the first, Katya had thought it necessary to send Calenne away, to live shielded from the Council's sight. So many years lost. All for nothing.

Katya released Calenne from her embrace and turned wearily to Elda. "Thank you. For everything."

The other woman forced a wintery smile. "Take care of her."

Katya caught a glint of something darker beneath the smile. It lingered in Elda's eyes. A hardness. Another friendship soured by folly? Perhaps. It no longer mattered. "Until my last breath. Calenne?"

The girl flung her arms around Elda. She said nothing, but the tears on her cheeks told a tale all their own.

Elda pushed her gently away. "You must go, dear heart."

A clarion sounded, its brash notes cleaving through the clamour of the storm. An icy hand closed around Katya's heart. She'd run out of time.

Elda met her gaze. Urgency replaced sorrow. "Go! While you still can!"

Katya stooped and gathered Calenne. The girl's chest shook with thin sobs, but she offered no resistance. With a last glance at Elda, Katya set out into the rain once more. The clarion sounded again as she reached Josiri. His eyes were more watchful than ever, his sword ready in his hands.

"They're here," he said.

Katya heaved Calenne up to sit in front of her brother. She looked like a doll beside him, every day of the decade that separated them on full display.

"Look after your sister. If we're separated, ride hard for the border."

His brow furrowed. "To the Hadari? Mother..."

"The Hadari will treat you better than the Council." He still had so much to learn, and she no more time in which to teach him. "When enemies are your only recourse, choose the one with the least to gain. Promise me."

She received a reluctant nod in reply.

Satisfied, Katya clambered into her saddle and spurred west along the broad cobbles of Highgate. They'd expect her to take refuge in Branghall Manor, or at least strip it of anything valuable ahead of the inevitable looting. But the western gateway might still be clear.

The first cry rang out as they rejoined the road. "She's here!"

A blue-garbed wayfarer cantered through the crowd, rain scattering from leather pauldrons. Behind, another set a buccina to his lips. A brash rising triad hammered out through the rain and found answer in the streets beyond. The pursuit's vanguard had reached Eskavord. Lightly armoured riders to harry and delay while heavy knights closed the distance. Katya drew her sword and wheeled her horse about. "Make for the west gate!"

Josiri hesitated, then lashed his horse to motion. "Yah!"

Katya caught one last glimpse of Calenne's pale, dispassionate face. Then they were gone, and the horseman upon her.

The wayfarer was half her age, little more than a boy and eager for the glory that might earn a knight's crest. Townsfolk scattered from his path. He goaded his horse to the gallop, sword held high in anticipation of the killing blow to come. He'd not yet learned that the first blow seldom mattered as much as the last.

Katya's parry sent a shiver down her arm. The wayfarer's blade scraped clear, the momentum of his charge already carrying him past. Then he was behind, hauling on the reins. The sword came about, the killing stroke aimed at Katya's neck.

Her thrust took the younger man in the chest. Desperate strength drove the blade between his ribs. The hawk of the Tressian Council turned dark as the first blood stained the rider's woollen tabard. Then he slipped from his saddle, sword clanging against cobbles. With one last, defiant glare at the buccinator, Katya turned her steed about, and galloped through the narrow streets after her children.

She caught them at the bridge, where the waters of the Grelyt River fell away into the boiling millrace. They were not alone.

One wayfarer held the narrow bridge, blocking Josiri's path. A second closed from behind him, sword drawn. A third lay dead on the cobbles, horse already vanished into the rain.

Josiri turned his steed in a circle. He had one arm tight about his sister. The other hand held a bloody sword. The point trembled as it swept back and forth between his foes, daring them to approach.

Katya thrust back her heels. Her steed sprang forward.

Her sword bit into the nearest wayfarer's spine. Heels jerked as he fell back. His steed sprang away into the streets. The corpse, one booted foot tangled in its stirrups, dragged along behind.

Katya rode on past Josiri. Steel clashed, once, twice, and then the last wayfarer was gone. His body tipped over the low stone parapet and into the rushing waters below.

Josiri trotted close, his face studiously calm. Katya knew better. He'd not taken a life before today.

"You're hurt."

Pain stemmed Katya's denial. A glance revealed rainwater running red across her left hand. She also felt a wound high on her shoulder. The last wayfarer's parting gift, lost in the desperation of the moment.

The clarion came yet again. A dozen wayfarers spurred down the street. A plate-clad knight rode at their head, his destrier caparisoned in silver-flecked black. Not the heraldry of a knightly chapterhouse, but a family of the first rank. His sword – a heavy, fennlander's claymore – rested in its scabbard. A circular shield sat slung across his back.

The greys of the rain-sodden town lost their focus. Katya tightened her grip on the reins. She flexed the fingers of her left hand. They felt distant, as if belonging to someone else. Her shoulder ached, fit company for the dull roar in her side – a memento of the sword-thrust she'd taken on the ridge at Zanya. Weariness crowded in, the faces of the dead close behind.

The world lurched. Katya grasped at the bridle with her good hand. Focus returned at the cost of her sword, which fell onto the narrow roadway.

So that was how the matter lay?

So be it.

"Go," she breathed. "See to your sister's safety. I'll hold them."

Josiri spurred closer, the false calm giving way to horror. "Mother, no!"

Calenne looked on with impassive eyes.

"I can't ride." Katya dropped awkwardly from her saddle and stooped to reclaim her sword. The feel of the grips beneath her fingers awoke new determination. "Leave me."

"No. We're getting out of here. All of us." He reached out. "You can ride with me."

The tremor beneath his tone revealed the truth. His horse was already weary. What stamina remained would not long serve two riders, let alone three.

Katya glanced down the street. There'd soon be nothing left to argue over. She understood Josiri's reluctance, for it mirrored her own. To face a parting now, with so much unsaid…? But a lifetime would not be enough to express her pride, nor to warn against repeating her mistakes. He'd have to find his own way now.

"Do you love me so little that you'd make me beg?" She forced herself to meet his gaze. "Accept this last gift and remember me well. Go."

Josiri gave a sharp nod, his lips a pale sliver. His throat bobbed. Then he turned his horse.

Katya dared not watch as her children galloped away, fearful that Josiri would read the gesture as a change of heart.

"Lumestra's light shine for you, my son," she whispered.

A slap to her horse's haunch sent it whinnying into the oncoming wayfarers. They scattered, fighting for control over startled steeds.

Katya took up position at the bridge's narrow crest, her sword point-down at her feet in challenge. She'd no illusions about holding the wayfarers. It would cost them little effort to ride straight over her, had they the stomach for it. But the tightness of the approach offered a slim chance.

The knight raised a mailed fist. The pursuers halted a dozen yards from the bridge's mouth. Two more padded out from the surrounding alleys. Not horsemen, but the Council's simarka – bronze constructs forged in the likeness of lions and given life by a spark of magic. Prowling statues that hunted the Council's enemies. Katya swore under her breath. Her sword was useless against such creatures. A blacksmith's hammer would have served her better. She'd lost too many friends to those claws to believe otherwise.

"Lady Trelan." The knight's greeting boomed like thunder. "The Council demands your surrender."

"Viktor Akadra." Katya made no attempt to hide her bitterness. "Did your father not tell you? I do not recognise the Council's authority."

The knight dismounted, the hem of his jet-black surcoat trailing in the rain. He removed his helm. Swarthy, chiselled features stared out from beneath a thatch of black hair. A young face, though one already confident far beyond its years.

He'd every reason to be so. Even without the armour, without the entourage of weary wayfarers – without her wounds – Akadra would have been more than her match. He stood a full head taller than she – half a head taller than any man she'd known.

"There has been enough suffering today." His tone matched his expression perfectly. Calm. Confident. Unyielding. He gestured, and the simarka sat, one to either side. Motionless. Watchful. "Let's not add to the tally."

"Then turn around, Lord Akadra. Leave me be."

Lips parted in something not entirely a smile. "You will stand before the Council and submit to judgement."

Katya knew what that meant. The humiliation of a show trial, arraigned as warning to any who'd follow in her footsteps and dare seek freedom for the Southshires. Then they'd parade her through the streets, her last dignity stripped away long before the gallows took her final breath. She'd lost a husband to that form of justice. She'd not suffer it herself.

"I'll die first."

"Incorrect."

Again, that damnable confidence. But her duty was clear.

Katya let the anger rise, as she had on the road. Its fire drove back the weariness, the pain, the fear for her children. Those problems belonged to the future, not the moment at hand. She was a daughter of the Southshires, the dowager duchess Trelan. She would not yield. The wound in Katya's side blazed as she surged forward. The alchemy of rage transmuted agony to strength and lent killing weight to the two-handed blow.

Akadra's sword scraped free of its scabbard. Blades clashed with a banshee screech. Lips parted in a snarl of surprise, he gave ground through the hissing rain.

Katya kept pace, right hand clamped over the failing left to give it purpose and guide it true. She hammered at Akadra's guard, summoning forth the lessons of girlhood to the bleak present. The forms of the sword her father had drilled into her until they flowed with the grace of a thrush's song and the power of a mountain river. Those lessons had kept her alive on the ridge at Zanya. They would not fail her now.

The wayfarers made no move to interfere.

But Akadra was done retreating.

Boots planted on the cobbles like the roots of some venerable, weather-worn oak, he checked each strike with grace that betrayed tutelage no less exacting than Katya's own. The claymore blurred across grey skies and battered her longsword aside.

The fire in Katya's veins turned sluggish. Cold and failing flesh sapped her purpose. Too late, she recognised the game Akadra had played. She'd wearied herself on his defences, and all the while her body had betrayed her.

Summoning her last strength, Katya hurled herself forward. A cry born of pain and desperation ripped free of her lips.

Again the claymore blurred to parry. The longsword's tip scraped past the larger blade, ripping into Akadra's cheek. He twisted away with a roar of pain.

Hooves sounded on cobbles. The leading wayfarers spurred forward, swords drawn to avenge their master's humiliation. The simarka, given no leave to advance, simply watched unfolding events with feline curiosity.

Katya's hands tightened on her sword. She'd held longer than she'd believed possible. She hoped Josiri had used the time well.

"Leave her!"

Akadra checked the wayfarers' advance with a single bellow. The left side of his face masked in blood, he turned his attention on Katya once more. He clasped a closed fist to his chest. Darkness gathered about his fingers like living shadow.

Katya's world blurred, its colours swirling away into an unseen void.

Her knee cracked against the cobbles. A hand slipped from her sword, fingers splayed to arrest her fall. Wisps of blood curled through pooling rainwater. She knelt there, gasping for breath, one ineluctable truth screaming for attention.

The rumours about Akadra were true.

The shadow dispersed as Akadra strode closer. The wayfarers had seen none of it, Katya realised – or had at least missed the significance. Otherwise, Akadra would have been as doomed as she. The Council would tolerate much from its loyal sons, but not witchcraft.

Colour flooded back. Akadra's sword dipped to the cobbles. His bloodied face held no triumph. Somehow that was worse.

"It's over." For the first time, his expression softened. "This is not the way, Katya. It never was. Surrender. Your wounds will be tended. You'll be treated with honour."

"Honour?" The word was ash on Katya's tongue. "Your father knows nothing of honour."

"It is not my father who makes the offer." He knelt, one gauntleted hand extended. "Please. Give me your sword."

Katya stared down at the cobbles, at her life's blood swirling away into the gutter. Could she trust him? A lifetime of emissaries and missives from the north had bled her people dry to feed a pointless war. Viktor's family was part of that, and so he was part of it. If his promise *was* genuine, he'd no power to keep it. The Council would never let it stand. The shame of the gallows path beckoned.

"You want my sword?" she growled.

Katya rose from her knees, her last effort channelled into one final blow.

Akadra's hand, so lately extended in conciliation, wrenched the sluggish blade from her grasp. He let his own fall alongside. Tugged off balance, Katya fell to her hands and knees. Defenceless. Helpless.

No. Not helpless. Never that.

She forced herself upright. There was no pain. No weariness. Just calm. Was this how Kevor had felt at the end? Before the creak of the deadman's drop had set her husband swinging? Trembling fingers closed around a dagger's hilt.

"My son will finish what I started."

The dagger rasped free, Katya's right hand again closing over her left.

"No!" Akadra dived forward. His hands reached for hers, his sudden alarm lending weight to his promises.

Katya rammed the dagger home. Chain links parted. She felt no pain as the blade slipped between her ribs. There was only a sudden giddiness as the last of her burdens fell away into mist.